D0008039

Fragile Heritage

By the same author

My Sister Clare
Tomorrow's Rainbow
The Hills Are Eternal
The Whispering Glade
The Talisman of Set
The Crimson Falcon
Jacintha
Caprice

FRAGILE HERITAGE

by

Sara Hylton

St. Martin's Press
New York

 For information, address St. Martin's Press, 175 Fifth Avenue, New York, N.Y. 10010.

Library of Congress Cataloging-in-Publication Data

Hylton, Sara.
Fragile heritage / Sara Hylton.
p. cm.
ISBN 0-312-04849-1
I. Title.
PR6058.Y63F73 1990
823'.914—dc20 90-37394
CIP

First published in Great Britain by Century Hutchinson Ltd.

First U.S. Edition: December 1990
10 9 8 7 6 5 4 3 2 1

'Tis all a Chequer-Board of Nights and Days
Where Destiny with Men for Pieces plays;
Hither and thither moves, and mates, and slays,
And one by one back in the Closet lays.

from the *Rubaiyat* of Omar Khayyám

BOOK 1

CHAPTER 1

Rain lay soft on the wind like a caress, soft summer rain that clung to the beech leaves as though reluctant to fall to the grass, so gentle that it turned the village into an ethereal place, a fairytale mirage obscuring the harsh lines of the housetops and the squat tower of the church.

I sat on a stile by the side of the lane with my eyes glued on the village school waiting for Kitty McGuire, and I began to grow anxious. I had been the first to emerge from the school and couldn't have missed Kitty, I felt sure. Indeed she usually dawdled or was so engrossed in conversation that she was the last to leave, but the single chime of the bell in the church tower told me it was already half past four and I would have to go soon or I would not be home before my father.

Through the mist I could see that the churchyard was empty apart from old Ned loping towards the church gates accompanied by his son, both of them armed with the shovels they had used to fill in the grave of Mrs Morrison who had died over the weekend. They had only just come through the gates when I saw the vicar hurrying after them, his face bent against the rain, his gown flapping round his ankles.

My father, the sexton, would be the next to leave after locking up the church and seeing that everything was tidy, and anxiously I looked up the road towards the school. It was time to go, something had detained Kitty and I didn't want to encounter Father in the lane. Over the last three years, ever since the McGuires had come to live in the village, he had made it abundantly clear that he didn't approve of Kitty or her folks, and even less of my friendship with her.

Sadly I scrambled down from the stile and after a swift glance towards the school I turned to walk towards the village. Coming through the mist was a small figure – Michael, Kitty's young brother. He walked slowly with his hands thrust deep into the pockets of his thin inadequate jacket, a shrimp of a boy with his shock of ginger hair and a gamin face liberally sprinkled with freckles. He looked a lot like Kitty and when I smiled at him brightly he said, ''Ave ye seen our Kitty? Mi mother's sent mi up 'ere to look for 'er.'

'I've been waiting for 'er, Michael, she's still at the schoolhouse.'

'Well I've got ter go up ter the Masons' 'ouse ter tell'er mi mother won't be there in't mornin'. If ye see our Kitty will ye tell 'er mi father's gone?'

'Gone!' I echoed stupidly.

'Ay, gone. 'E died just 'afore a got 'ome. Will ye be after tellin' 'er, Ellen?'

Before I could gather my scattered wits he was away, trotting up the road and quickly becoming hidden by the floating mist.

Paddy McGuire had been coughing his life away ever since he came to the village. In the summer he had done labouring work of one sort or another to help support his wife and eleven children but in the winter he had taken to his bed while Ann McGuire, his long-suffering wife, scrubbed her fingers to the bone at Mrs Mason's big house.

I was more than reluctant to break the news to Kitty, but all the same I turned back towards the schoolhouse.

The stout wooden door leading into the main hall was still open but inside there was silence and I stood in the doorway listening until I heard footsteps in one of the classrooms beyond. Gingerly I opened the door a fraction, wide enough to see Kitty standing alone before the dais, her head lowered in wrapt contemplation, and with such a look of innocent appeal it was hard to imagine that she had been guilty of a sin horrendous enough to have been detained after all the other children had gone home. I was about to call to her when Mrs Grundy's voice came from behind me, harsh enough to make me almost jump out of my skin.

'What are you doing here Ellen Adair? It's half an hour since you left to go home.'

I spun round to find the teacher staring down at me with an annoyed expression.

'Please, Mrs Grundy, I've got to see Kitty. Can she come home now?'

'Indeed she can't. She's to stay there an hour or until I lock up the school for the night. Now get off home at once, I don't want your parents thinking I'm responsible for sending you home at this time.'

When I didn't immediately dash off into the mist her frown deepened.

'Well Ellen, what are you waiting for?'

'Please, Miss, I must tell Kitty 'er father's gone, she's wanted at 'ome.'

'What do you mean her father's gone?'

'He's dead, Miss, just this afternoon.'

She opened the door wider and I could see that Kitty was looking at us with wide anxious eyes. Mrs Grundy said firmly, 'Did you hear that, Kitty McGuire, were you listening?'

She nodded mutely and in a kinder voice Mrs Grundy said, 'Come here, child.'

Kitty advanced and now I could see the tears on her cheeks and her trembling lips.

'You should have said your father was ill, Kitty, I wouldn't have kept you in even though there are times when I don't know what to do with you. Get your things and run off home. And you too, Ellen Adair.'

In silence I waited while Kitty shrugged her arms into her coat, then we set off down the lane. We had almost reached the village street when she said, 'Did our Micky say anythin' else about mi father, Ellen?'

'No.'

'Nor mi mam?'

'No, Kitty.'

'Will ye come as far as our house with mi? I'll not be askin' you to come inside.'

It was late, my father would be home and I was desperately afraid of his anger. He did not rage like Kitty's father had done after one of his drinking bouts, rages that were sudden and frequent and quickly over. My father was not a drinker, but he could sit white-faced and tight-lipped for hours behind a wall of silence that encompassed us all, including my mother. I had never known her to answer him back even when he was being most unjust and horrible.

I stole a look at Kitty's face as we trudged through the rain. It was pale and anxious and I hadn't the heart to leave her to go home alone.

She took hold of my hand in a grateful gesture and we turned up the narrow lane towards the McGuires' house.

It was a farm labourer's cottage, two up and two down, and I had often wondered how they managed in the two tiny bedrooms and the one parlour and kitchen. Kitty had once told me that the older children slept head to toe in two double beds, with another for the younger children placed in their parents' bedroom, and I felt how lucky I was to be living in the sexton's house belonging to the church where we had three bedrooms and an attic.

We stopped outside the gate looking at the cottage with its drawn blinds and I shuddered thinking about Paddy McGuire lying dead in that front bedroom.

'I wish I didn't 'ave to go in,' Kitty said quietly, 'it'll be days to the funeral.'

Just then the door opened and Mrs Peel came out. She was the village midwife, who also laid out the dead. Catching sight of us standing at the gate, she said, 'Do ye know about yer father then, Kitty McGuire?'

'Yes, Mrs Peel.'

'Well yer'd best get in there an' comfort yer mother, he's lyin' there right peaceful now. He's gone to 'is rest after much sufferin'.'

I'd heard these were the words she used to all those recently bereaved. We stood aside as she bustled down the path, then in a brisk voice she said to me, 'You'd best get off 'ome, Ellen, there's nothin' ye can do 'ere.'

At that I took to my heels and ran, never slowing until I reached the vicarage and the path leading up to the church.

I could see our house now, a square ugly building surrounded by a large garden. My father didn't like gardening so it was left to my brothers and me to weed and tend it. Dismay and trepidation filled my heart when I saw him standing at the door. He was holding his big silver watch, and on his face was the look I had come to dread.

As I reached his side he stared down at me in tight-lipped anger, then flinging open the front door he said, 'Hang your wet clothes in the lobby and wait at the dining room door.'

I waited there while he hung his coat on the stand behind the door, then with long strides he came towards me. I followed him into the dining room where the rest of the family sat at the table, and Mother looked at me anxiously and started to ask, 'Where have you been . . .'

She was cut short abruptly by him saying, 'Get on with your meal, Mary. I shall question her later.' Then he told me, 'Stand there behind Luke until we've finished our meal, then you shall tell me why ye were kept in at school.'

'Father, I wasn't . . .'

'Not another word, girl. Like I said I'll speak to ye later.'

I didn't dare to say I was hungry, that every morsel I saw the rest of them place in their mouths gave me an actual pain, I simply had to stand behind my brother's chair in silence. Once I caught Peter's sympathetic glance across the table, and watched Naomi put out her tongue at me before asking Father for a second helping of gooseberry pudding.

When the last crumb had been eaten Father said, 'You may all leave the table now.'

We were on a strict rota to help with clearing the table and washing the dishes, not one of us was spared; but it was not my turn and I remained standing while Sarah and Mark went about their task and Mother disappeared with the rest of them into the living room.

When the door closed behind them my father took his seat at the table with the Holy Bible in front of him, motioning me to stand before him.

'Well,' he said sternly, 'why did your teacher find it necessary to keep you in school?'

'She didn't, Father, I was out before anybody else this afternoon.'

'Then is it too much to ask you to tell me where you've been and who you've been with?'

So I told him about my meeting with Michael McGuire, about the death of his father and my promise to walk all the way home with Kitty, but there was no softening of his stern features, no compassion for the deceased Paddy McGuire or his grieving family. If anything the frown became more pronounced.

'I don't like your association with that family, Ellen, I've made it quite plain in the past. Shanty Irish they are and Roman Catholics into the bargain. No doubt the Bull's Head's lost its best customer now that McGuire's gone but you'll have no more truck with 'em if I 'ave to keep ye locked up for the rest o' the week. Am I makin' miself plain, Miss Ellen?'

'Kitty's mi best friend, Father, and her mother's a real nice lady. Wouldn't it be more Christian to ask them into the house and let 'em see how sorry we are?'

'Hold your tongue, girl. There'll be no McGuires in this house and if I hear of you being in their company again I'll pack you off to your Aunt Liza. She'll know what to do with ye.'

Aunt Liza was Father's half-sister and during the time she had spent with us waiting for her shop in the Dales to be decorated, she terrified me. She was tall and thin and angular, a female version of my father but with a tongue even more caustic, and she had thought nothing of grabbing my hair and pulling it to emphasize her point.

'Now go up to your room and stay there until breakfast,' he said. 'I want your lamp out in five minutes and there's to be no readin' in bed. I'll send one o' the girls up to see that mi orders are carried out. Now be off with you.'

'But I'm hungry, Father, I've had nothing to eat.'

'And yer not gettin' anything to eat. This is yer punishment for being disobedient. In future I want you straight home from school at four o'clock and on yer own. No more Kitty McGuire, do you hear me?'

'Yes, Father.'

I passed in front of him when he opened the door, and fled. With shaking fingers I lit the lamp in the bedroom I shared with two of my sisters and after undressing crept between the chill sheets. For a long time I lay staring up into the darkness wishing something dire would happen to my father – or to me, I didn't much care which.

Once before I had been sent to bed without supper, and when the house was still and I thought the family were in bed, I had crept downstairs hoping to find food in the larder. My father had found me perched on the kitchen table eating bread and butter and then had followed two long days of near starvation and the lashing of his tongue. Only once my mother remonstrated with him over his harsh treatment, and she too earned his displeasure by long sulky silences. Then I began to see why she allowed him to have his own way because those silences punished us all.

This time I would not attempt to creep downstairs when the rest of them retired, I would lie hungry and sleepless until breakfast. Tomorrow was Saturday when Kitty and I would normally walk up on to the fells or linger around the stalls at the market held in the main street of Marsdale, spending our pocket money. Kitty received twopence a week from Mrs Mason for helping her mother carry the shopping basket up the hill, and I received twopence from the vicar's wife for collecting her groceries. Kitty got nothing from her parents because they had none to spare, and Father said we were fed and clothed and that should be enough.

We spent our twopences on sweets, coconut ice and brightly coloured turnovers. I liked these best because they contained bits of cheap jewellery, a silver-coloured ring with a glass stone, or a tiny gold-coloured chain, which needless to say I was never able to wear in the presence of Father.

He had forbidden me to see Kitty ever again, but somehow I would. Not perhaps while her father lay dead in the house, but afterwards, even if I had to lie and cheat so that Father wouldn't know.

There was a soft tap on the bedroom door and I sat up, watching it open with hope-filled eyes. It was my brother

Peter, a year younger than me and my favourite amongst the lot of them.

He held a cautioning finger up to his lips and carefully closed the door before coming to sit on my bed.

'I've brought ye two slices of bread and an apple, Ellen. I've quartered the apple and taken the core out so ye can eat it without leavin' anythin' ter show yer've 'ad it. Mi mother buttered the bread for ye.'

'Did mi father see her do it?'

'No, 'e's in the dinin' room wi' some o' the women fro' the church. I reckon 'e'll be there for a while.'

'What time is it?'

'Nigh on eight o'clock.'

I wolfed the bread and the apple. I would have given anything for a glass of milk or a mug of tea but I couldn't ask Peter for that, so instead I gasped angrily, 'What am I goin' to do about Kitty, Peter? She's mi friend, I can't not see her any more.'

He stared at me solemnly. He was a nice-looking boy with blond hair and honest straight eyes, and my question troubled him, I could tell.

'I don't know, Ellen. Ye know what mi father's like, 'e hates the McGuires.'

'But why, what have they ever done to 'im?'

'Nothin, but 'e's like that. Look 'ow 'e hated old Mr Pierce coz he went to the pub every Saturday, and the Philbys coz they were Chapel instead o' Church.'

'I thought religion was supposed to draw us together not pull us apart.'

'But it does, doesn't it, Ellen? He'd like mi to be a parson when I grow up, I've heard 'im talkin' to the vicar about it. But where would we ever get the money to send mi to college? The vicar said as much.'

I stared at him in astonishment.

'Do ye want to be a vicar, Peter?'

'I don't know.'

Suddenly a smile spread over his face and his eyes twinkled merrily. 'I wouldn't mind livin' in a house like the vicarage wi' a nice garden. Sides 'e really only works on Sunday or when there's weddins, funerals and christenins.'

'He's allus writin' his sermons, mi father says, an' folk are allus goin' up to the vicarage to ask his advice about someat or other. Could you like doin' all that?'

'Well o' course not, but I'll never be a vicar, Ellen, we 'aven't got the money. The vicar went to a good school then 'e went to the university. He knows Greek and Latin; where would I ever learn things like that?'

'What will ye do, Peter? Another year an' you'll be leavin' school.'

'What'll you be doin? Yer'll be leavin' school 'afore me.'

'I know what I'd like ter do. I'd like to get away fro' this place and mi father. I'd like ter go to a big city and work in a big shop sellin' furs and things.'

'What sort o' things?'

'The sort o' things rich women wear. Kitty showed mi some pictures out of a book Mrs Mason's daughter sent her fro' York, lace an' georgette, lovely frocks that sweep the floor, ermine coats, and emeralds round their throats and in their ears. I'll never 'ave 'em for miself but it'd be lovely to 'andle 'em and sell 'em to others.'

'Yer've about as much chance o' doin that, our Ellen, as I 'ave of bein' a parson. Besides, mi father'd never let ye leave the village.'

'When I'm old enough 'e'll not be able to stop mi.'

'Ye do talk a lot o' rubbish, Ellen, but yer fun, I'll say that for ye. I'd better be goin', I don't want 'im findin' me here. I'm sorry I couldn't bring somethin' a bit more appetizing.'

'Thanks Peter, yer've saved mi life.'

I watched him letting himself gingerly out of the room, then I lay down amongst my pillows and gave myself up to the imagination which helped me to survive. I had my dreams of beautiful clothes and handsome men, of some distant future in a home where I was loved, but my childhood was never obsessed with Kitty's longing for jewels and furs, in those days it was sufficient for me to grow up quickly in order to get away from my father and his restrictive influence.

CHAPTER 2

The events of that night were with me all over the weekend. I did not see Kitty round the village and when I accompanied Mother to the market much of the talk was of Paddy McGuire's death.

There was no Catholic church in Marsden and the funeral would have to be held in a neighbouring village, which had the only one for miles around. We heard that it was to take place the following Tuesday so I didn't think Kitty would be at the school until Wednesday at least.

'Good job Mrs McGuire's got that place up at the Masons',' Mrs Jones confided to Mother. 'Mrs Mason doesn't pay much but I reckon she gets plenty butter an' eggs, vegetables too no doubt.'

'Poor woman,' Mother said, 'she doesn't look as though she gets much in the way o' food, she's that thin.'

'Oh ay, scrawny she is, but wouldn't you be with a baby every year and every one o' them wantin' feedin'? Pulled down she was, wi' 'er 'usband allus in the Bull's Head an' no doubt spendin' all 'is money on booze.'

'When did Paddy McGuire ever earn anythin' proper? Labourin' 'e was, an' ailin' most o' the time in the winter. I'm surprised the farmer ever took 'im back. What were they doin' over 'ere anyway, why didn't they stay in Ireland where they belonged?'

'They said there was little or no work in Ireland.'

'Well there's barely enough 'ere for our men let alone shanty Irish.'

On and on it went while I stood patiently beside my mother clutching a basket filled with vegetables and wishing with all my heart they would leave the McGuires alone.

On the way home I was so quiet that Mother asked softly, 'You're all right aren't you, Ellen? There's influenza about.'

'I'm all right, Mother.'

'Don't take it hard about last night, love, your father's only talkin' to ye for yer own good. He only wants what's best for all of ye.'

'I don't see that sendin' mi to bed without supper and stoppin' mi seein' Kitty's doin' mi much good, Mother.'

'He thinks she's a bad influence on ye, Ellen. She's a little madam wi' that red hair and that sharp tongue of 'ers, and I've 'eard her mother say she's a hard one ter manage.'

'She's allus been nice ter me. She's such fun, Mother. I can laugh at all the things she says and she's never mean or catty like some o' the girls.'

Mother sighed. 'I don't like trouble in the 'ouse, Ellen. I don't like ter see yer father sittin' starin' at his food wi' never a word ter say to the cat an' all of us feelin' that miserable. 'E's not a bad man, Ellen, 'e's just tryin' te do 'is best wi' what we've got.'

I said nothing, but I didn't agree with her. I thought my father was a horrid little man, all religion and no Christianity, parsimonious, mouthing prayers and platitudes that were as restrictive as they were cruel, and I felt sure the good Lord could see right through him for the mean-spirited person he was.

'When ye sees yer father at supper you'll be respectful, Ellen, for my sake,' she said, eyeing me anxiously.

'Yes, Mother. I'm allus respectful, I never mean ter make 'im angry. I reckon he picks on me and I never know why.'

'Oh Ellen, o' course he doesn't pick on ye, he just wants yer to grow up decent, wi' the right set o' values.'

I had values even if they weren't my father's. I believed they were more honest than his – but I kept my opinion to myself.

I didn't see Kitty until Wednesday morning, after her father's funeral. Father had walked with us to the school that morning – largely, I felt sure, so that he could see me going in to school with my sisters instead of waiting for Kitty as I usually did.

I heard some of the other children talking about the funeral.

'Only one coach after the hearse,' Martha Longstaffe

said, 'and only Mrs McGuire and three o' the older children in it. Mi mother said the rest o' the McGuires ran wild in the street all afternoon.'

'There weren't many flowers,' her friend said, 'only a bunch on top o' the coffin an' two wreaths. I wonder who sent them.'

'Like as not Mrs Mason an' their next-door neighbour, out o' Christian charity I expect.'

I ground my teeth in anger. There wasn't much of Christian charity in any of them, and I entered the classroom and went to sit at my desk with deep anger in my heart. Kitty wasn't there, and Mrs Grundy had begun the first lesson before she appeared.

I could tell that she had been hurrying from her rosy cheeks and the riot of red curls that had escaped her hair ribbon. There was a tear on the sleeve of her blouse and mud on her skirt, and Mrs Grundy looked at her with some distaste.

'You're late, Kitty McGuire. What have you to say for yourself?' she demanded.

'I'm sorry, Mrs Grundy, I ran all the way here, I did.'

'Have you been fighting with somebody?'

Kitty stood without speaking while a dull flush coloured her cheeks.

'Well, have you?' Mrs Grundy said sternly.

'I hit Jimmy O'Reilly.'

'Why?'

'For sayin' mi father owed 'is father some money an' mi mother shouldn't be let ter keep the cottage. I wish oi'd hit 'im a whole lot harder. Sure and didn't mi father 'elp 'im 'ome drunk every Saturday noight?'

Mrs Grundy's expression didn't relax. 'I suppose Jimmy O'Reilly tore your blouse? Your mother isn't going to be too pleased about that.'

Angry tears filled Kitty's eyes. 'Oi'll 'ave ter mend it. It's a new blouse, foive and sixpence it cost mi mother fro' the market an' now that rotten boy's ruined it.'

'It might teach you a lesson not to hit out at anybody who says something you don't like, Kitty. There should be dignity and restraint in your behaviour, it can be far more cutting than a taste of the fisticuffs.'

'Oi gave 'im a black eye oi did, an' he deserved it.'

'Go to your desk and attend to your lessons. Thanks to you we've lost half an hour.'

Meeting Kitty's eyes I grinned and received a grin in return, and Mrs Grundy snapped, 'That'll do, Ellen Adair. Now settle down, all of you.'

I was with Kitty in the playground when Naomi came up to us and said, 'I'll tell Father I've seen you with Kitty McGuire.'

I was so enraged I grabbed hold of her pigtail and hissed, 'You do and I'll not give you mi pink frock with the blue flowers on it.'

She yelped, then with round eyes said, 'I didn't know you were goin' to give it to me.'

'Well I won't if you tell him, I'll give it our Mary instead.'

She ran out of reach and tossing her dark head said, 'I'll think about it,' before running away to join her classmates.

'What did she mean, Ellen, she'd tell yer father she saw you talkin' to me?' Kitty demanded. 'Is it that he's told ye not to talk to me?'

'Oh Kitty, I wasn't going to take any notice of 'im, 'onest, but 'e was cross that night I was late home from school. He sent mi to bed without any supper.'

'Didn't ye explain ye'd bin waitin' fer me?'

'Yes, an' that made 'im a whole lot crosser.'

'Then ye shouldn't be talkin' to me, Ellen Adair, ye should be doin' what yer father asked.'

'I don't agree with him, Kitty. Sometimes I think I hates him fer the things he says. I wish I could go away, somewhere where I wouldn't have to see 'im every day of mi life and listen to 'im goin' on an' on about people an' everything.'

'Where would ye go if ye left 'ere? Be sensible, Ellen, yer whole loife's 'ere, it's me who should be goin' away. We've never belonged 'ere, never since we came.'

We were both close to tears. In my heart I felt I had betrayed her, and more so when she tossed her red head and ran across the yard, leaving me staring after her. That night she was the first out of school and ran off without waiting for me. I waited for Peter to catch me up so that we could walk down the lane together.

'She ran and left ye then?' he said philosophically.

So I told him about Naomi and our words during playtime, and he said seriously, 'P'rhaps it's for the best 'til the storm wi Father blows over. At least if he's waitin' for us 'e'll see yer doin' what he asked.'

'It's Kitty 'erself who's makin' me, Peter.'

'Ye should be glad, Ellen. 'Ere's Father comin' to meet us.'

Sure enough he came striding down the street with set purpose, and Naomi ran to meet him, taking his hand and laughing up into his face.

'If she tells 'im I was with Kitty I'll kill 'er,' I said angrily. But Naomi knew which side of her bread was buttered, and she had her eye on my pink dress. I hadn't intended to part with it, it was my prettiest dress even if it was a little tight for me and a bit too short. Now however I would have to keep my promise even when I had little faith that she wouldn't tell him once the dress was in her hands.

If the truth was known I didn't much like Naomi, she was the one sister I had little in common with, pert and cheeky, and very much my father's daughter. She was his favourite and could bring the smiles to his face when none of the rest of us could, and that night as I met her eyes across the dining table she smiled and her eyes grew sly and secretive.

In some glee she said, 'I got an A from Mrs Pilkington for mi readin', Father. She says I'm the best reader in the class.'

'Yer arithmetic's not up ter much,' Peter said to my utmost joy.

'Don't deflate the child,' Father snapped. 'I'm pleased about your readin', Naomi. There's no reason why you shouldn't 'elp Naomi with 'er sums, Peter.'

'I've got mi own homework te do,' Peter said.

'You'll help 'er when you've done it then,' Father snapped.

In the days that followed it was Kitty who avoided me but I knew why – she didn't want me to get into trouble with Father on her account.

Sunday was his busiest day with church in the morning, Sunday school in the afternoon and then church in the evening. More often than not it was quite late when he had finished tidying up and putting the church to rights before locking up, and it was Sunday I looked forward to most.

I sat with Mother and the family in church where Father pompously performed his duties with more verve than the vicar himself, but after Sunday school the rest of the afternoon was free. I knew that Kitty invariably took some of her younger brothers and sisters to the park and I couldn't wait to get out of the cold draughty schoolroom fast enough to join her.

'You shouldn't be comin' to see me, Ellen,' she admonished. 'Yer father's not goin' to loike it.'

'He's not goin' to know, is he? Who's ter tell 'im?'

'Well, yer sister Naomi fer one.'

'Well then we won't stay 'ere, we'll go up on to the fells. It's nicer up there.'

We made our escape before my sister and her cronies arrived, and up on the windswept moor Kitty opened her heart to me while her brothers and sisters scampered over the short thick grass.

'We're goin' to 'ave to split up, Ellen, mi mother can't afford te keep us all with what little she gets fro' the Masons. Our Mary and Joe's goin' to mi aunt in Merton and she's puttin' up the baby an' young Terry for adoption. It's breakin' 'er heart, Ellen, but there's no way she can keep 'em and go out te work.'

'What about you, Kitty?'

'Mi aunt sez when I leave school she can get mi a job workin' in a seamen's hostel near the docks in Liverpool.'

'What sort of a job will that be?'

'Servin' food and makin' the beds, I expect. I'll be livin'

in so whatever they pay mi'll be mine, some te keep and some te send 'ome.'

'It sound horrible.'

Her eyes filled with tears. 'It's a long way from ermine an' emeralds, to be sure. Do ye remember 'ow we used to say that one day we'd 'ave 'em? Well sure an' I don't think it'll ever happen. We were clutchin' at moonbeams, Ellen, an' I for one 'ave got to learn some sense. Mi father's gone, not that 'e ever tipped much up at 'ome, but at least 'e took some o' the weight off mi mother's shoulders.'

'Your mother must be very sad, Kitty, 'avin' to part with the little ones. Do they know?'

'Oh, there'll be a lot o' wailin' an' anguish but there's no way we can avoid it. 'Ave ye thought what you're goin' to do when ye've left school?'

'No. Mi father'll be thinkin' o' something respectable but there's not much work in the village. I only ope 'e doesn't send me off to Aunt Liza's.'

'Where's she, then?'

'Up in the Dales somewhere. She 'as a little shop, draper's it is. I've allus thought I'd like te work in a shop, but not 'ers. I couldn't work in 'ers.'

'Do ye think he moight be sendin' you there?'

''E might, Kitty. Wi' mi father, anythin's possible.'

CHAPTER 3

For weeks my luck held. We exchanged greetings only at school and we seldom let others see us together, but at the weekends we were together roaming the countryside and giving the market a wide berth.

My father believed he had won, and one evening after supper he said, 'I don't suppose you know that your friends the McGuires are splitting up. If Patrick McGuire had been a better provider they'd 'ave had a bit o' money put by for a time such as this, but I do 'ear the two youngest children are to be put up for adoption or in some 'ome or other and Miss Kitty's bein' sent off to Liverpool to work as soon as she's left the school. I might add I'm mighty glad about that, she was a bad influence on you, Ellen. Since you stopped seein' her you've been a better girl, more obedient and nowhere near as flighty.'

I sat with bowed head and Mother said anxiously, 'I'm sorry for the McGuires, Thomas, it must be heartbreakin' for the poor woman to 'ave ter part with the children.'

'Well in another couple of months Ellen 'ere can say goodbye to Kitty McGuire, and good riddance.'

My hands were clenched tightly together under cover of the tablecloth and I very near choked on a crust of bread so great was my desire to call my father a humbug. Reading his Bible and saying his prayers and about as much Christian charity in his heart as the cat sleeping on the hearth rug.

Christmas came around and as usual on the last day of school there was a party when we all wore our Sunday-best clothes and took fruit and mince pies and anything else our families could spare to eat in the big hall where we were expected to sing carols and recite poetry. The girls in my family took mince pies and the three boys took pasties.

On our way to the school Naomi whispered, 'I wonder

what the McGuire girls'll take, and them as poor as church mice?'

Needless to say I ignored her but I remember that all that day I was happy, singing my head off with the other children, and sampling the different foods we had taken. I loved singing although I had no great voice, not like Kitty who had a hauntingly sweet voice, low and melodious.

I was so enchanted with the proceedings I had little thought of danger as we walked home that afternoon in the bitter cold wind that swept straight off the moors.

Kitty pulled her thin coat round her and shivered because under it she was wearing her best dress which unfortunately was a summer cotton and quite unsuitable for a winter's day.

'It's early, Ellen, yer father'll still be seein' to his duties at the church. Would you like to come 'ome with mi and 'ave a word with mi mother? She'll be that glad.'

So with only a brief glance I walked on past the lane where our house stood. Mrs McGuire was just letting herself into the house when we arrived, and smiling a welcome she held the door open for us.

In the grate a few pathetic cinders burned dully and from the look of the dark little room it was evident there would be no Christmas decorations. When Kitty saw me looking round she said, 'We 'ave a Christmas tree but I 'aven't 'ad a chance to put it up yet. I don't know if I'll bother.'

'Oh but ye should, Kitty, it'll make the place look more cheerful.'

'It's a mangy little imitation tree, Ellen, mi father found it on a rubbish heap two years since an' 'e brought it 'ome. I've done a bit at it to make it look a bit more presentable but we've nothin' to hang on it this year and it'll only look worse standin' in the winder on its own.'

We'd been given small packets of sweets at the school, and an apple and orange each. Now eagerly I profferred mine. 'Take these, Kitty, we'll 'ave others. The vicar's wife allus sends us sweets and nuts and raisins. Honestly, Kitty, I don't really want these.'

'Well of course ye do, and didn't yer eyes light up like stars when they were given to us at the party?'

'Please, Kitty, I want you to 'ave them. I'll be upset if you don't take 'em, they're mi Christmas present to you.'

She took them gratefully and then hurried upstairs to look for the tree.

It was indeed a sad little tree with its branches flattened, and it was none too steady on the table. We both sat back to look at it and Kitty said, 'Ye see what I mean, Ellen, it's not worth decoratin'.'

'Oh but it is,' I cried enthusiastically. 'If ye can find a bit o' ribbon we'll hang up the sweets and if ye can find a bit o' coloured paper we can have some o' them lanterns Mrs Grundy showed us how to make.'

So, oblivious of the time we set about decorating the tree until Mrs McGuire came out of the kitchen with two steaming mugs of soup, saying, 'Yer'd best be gettin' 'ome luv, it's gone five o'clock.'

Startled, I jumped to my feet, my heart sinking. Kitty and the children stood at the door watching me flying down the lane with my coat wide open and my heart fluttering wildly in my breast. I prayed anxiously that my father had been delayed at the hall and my heart sank in my boots when I saw that every light in the hall had been put out. Arriving home breathless, I turned the knob gingerly on the front door, but it was closed fast. With my fists I pounded on the door but it remained closed and so I walked round to the back of the house and pounded on the kitchen door, which was also locked. I climbed up a tree outside the kitchen window and rapped on that. After ten minutes or more I realized that I was locked out and nobody was inclined to open the door.

A thin drizzle of icy rain had begun to fall and it trickled down my coat collar so that soon my teeth were chattering and I had to stamp my feet and flap my arms to keep warm. Surely I wouldn't have to spend Christmas Eve in the coalshed, that would be too cruel. But how long could they expect me to stand on the doorstep freezing to death? Finally in exasperation I lifted the letter flap and called out, 'If ye don't open the door I'll go down to the vicarage, I will.'

Then I heard my father's heavy footsteps. The door was flung open and he stood silhouetted in the doorway like some avenging angel. He grabbed my arm in a grip of iron and dragged me into the house, all the way to the kitchen. My mother sat white-faced at the table surrounded by the rest of them, speechless and afraid.

'Ye've bin at the McGuires', 'aven't ye? In spite of all I said to ye, in spite of what I said I'd do to ye if ever ye went off wi' that Kitty McGuire again.'

'It was early, Father,' I whispered in a small voice, 'I only went for a few minutes to wish 'em a Merry Christmas.'

'A few minutes is it? Look at the clock, girl, what time is it?'

'I know, Father, I'm sorry but we were decoratin' the tree, I lost all track o' the time.'

'This grieves me more than it grieves you, Ellen Adair, but I will be master in mi own 'ome. I'll make ye sorry ye disobeyed me, I'll make you so sorry yer'll never disobey me again. Now come upstairs.'

I looked round at my mother with large appealing eyes but she sat trembling, looking down at the head of Tommy on her knee. In sudden appeal I ran to kneel at her side. 'Please, Mother, don't let him punish me. Please, Mother, I haven't done anything wrong, an' I'll never go to the McGuires' again, never as long as I live.'

I was babbling now like a demented thing and my mother looked at me sorrowfully, biting her lip with anxiety, and only Peter spoke up for me.

'Don't hit her, Father, it's Christmas Eve, we shouldn't be miserable on Christmas Eve.'

'Be silent, boy, or you'll be sent to bed as well as this one. She's got to learn. Don't think I enjoy what I'm doing, it's for the girl's own good if she's to grow up chaste and decent. Now get up off the floor, girl, and come with me.'

So I followed his tall gaunt figure along the passageway and up the dark stairs towards my own room at the back of the house. I was shivering with fear, sobbing in my throat, but he paid no heed. When we reached the room he put a match to the oil lamp and pulled down the blind.

'Now take off yer shirt and blouse and everythin' else except yer shift, and lean over this chair.'

My fingers trembled so much I could barely cope with the fasteners, and it was so cold. He stood in silence watching me undress, then I watched him take off his belt. There was a look in his eyes which seemed to say he was enjoying my terror and I shrank away from him, trembling in my thin underskirt, but he pulled me forward with hard unyielding hands and thrust my body across the chair.

I prayed that I would faint, that blessed oblivion would shield me from the blows to come, but I did not faint. Instead I gritted my teeth and clenched my hands until the nails dug into my palms, waiting for the blows to fall. I have no memory of how many there were, I only know that after the first one the pain went on and on until I heard the blissful slamming of the bedroom door and his footsteps dying away.

For what seemed an eternity I stayed where I was, then painfully I dragged myself to my feet and stood swaying with my fingers curled round the back of the chair to prevent me falling down.

My skirt was sticking to my body and I felt the warm blood trickling down my back and legs. After a few minutes I found the strength to climb on to the chair so that I could see my back in the dingy mirror above the chest of drawers. Across it were dark red scores that were bleeding profusely so that my shift was saturated. I had no strength to bathe my wounds or go in search of ointment. In any case I didn't want anybody to see what my father had done to me, so I took off the shift and hid it under the chest until I could get rid of it in the morning.

Although I was freezing with cold I daren't get into bed where the blood would soil the bedclothes and I was afraid of my nightdress sticking to the wounds, so I lay on top of the bed on my stomach.

From downstairs came the sound of laughter and I guessed they were decorating the tree which the vicar always provided at Christmas. I dimly heard the front door knocker and laughter from father's friends who had come in for a tot of whisky before the evening's festivities started at the village hall. Soon after I heard the closing of the front door and laughter outside the house.

My parents had gone with their friends, and downstairs my brothers and sisters would be gathered round the tree playing games after listening to Father's instructions to be in bed by eight.

All knowledge of time eluded me and the next thing I knew Peter was standing by my side carrying a basin of warm water and a flannel. His face was set and white as he looked at my tattered back, and then gently he started to wipe the blood away. When he was satisfied that it had stopped bleeding he smoothed on some ointment with hands as gentle as a woman's.

'Ye can put yer nightie on now, Ellen, the bleedin's stopped.'

'I'll never be able to lie on it, Peter,' I murmured, 'and I'm so tired.'

'What made ye stay at the McGuires' so late, Ellen, didn't ye realize what e'd do?'

'I didn't see the time, Peter. We were fixin' up that awful little tree with sweets and coloured paper, right pretty it looked too when we'd finished. Please, Peter, don't tell anybody what happened tonight, but if ye see Kitty tell 'er nothin's changed.'

I shall never forget the fierce resentment and hatred that stayed with me after that night. There was no joy throughout the days of Christmas, the pain of my wounds was a constant reminder of his cruelty and the look of sadistic pleasure on his face before he started to beat me.

I had lost all respect for my mother also – poor downtrodden woman who had allowed him to torture me in that manner. But perhaps she was more to be pitied than blamed, and I got to thinking that she never had had a personality outside of his.

The food I ate at his table stuck in my throat and there

were times when I was sick, and even that made me glad that I had been saved from swallowing it.

I was determined that he would never touch me again, if I had to kill him first, and with that in mind I stole a carving knife out of the kitchen drawer and hid it among my underclothes. I even congratulated myself that I didn't flinch when it was missed and we all came under suspicion.

I stared straight into his face, saying, 'What would I want with a carving knife, Father? Like as not it's bin thrown out wi' the peelings.'

I was admonished by Mrs Grundy to sit straight at my desk instead of slouching but I couldn't tell her that the seat hurt my back, and on the day I slipped in the snow and fell on it I howled like a baby.

I lost weight, I could tell by my skirt which twisted round my waist so that I had to put a safety pin in it. One day when I took in the vicar's groceries the vicar's wife said to me, 'Is anything wrong, Ellen? You don't look well.'

'I'm all right, Ma'am, I slipped in the schoolyard and hurt mi back.'

'I hope you haven't cracked a bone, it's easily done.'

'I don't think so, Ma'am, it'll go right in a day or two.'

At those times when my mother looked at me appealingly, as though asking for my forgiveness, I merely tried to be cheerful so that she wouldn't feel so bad about it but it was hard living in a house where I hated my father, felt pity for my mother and truly loved only my brother Peter.

I'm not sure when the idea was born in me, perhaps it was on the morning I heard Father shouting at Peter because his shoes weren't cleaned properly, or the evening before when Naomi said slyly, 'Kitty McGuire's goin' ter work i' Liverpool, I 'eard 'er tellin' Mary Jordan.'

There was a moment of silence at the table, then Father said, 'She'll not be missed in the village, right little madam she is walkin' along the street with 'er nose in the air and the entire family of 'em little more than tinkers.'

I went on with my meal even when the silence seemed filled with anticipation that I would leap to Kitty's defence.

That night I wrote a brief note and slipped it into my

school atlas. The following morning I handed it to Mary Jordan with the whispered command that she give it to Kitty McGuire at playtime.

The note asked Kitty to meet me on the moor, wet or fine, the following Saturday afternoon. I knew Father would be in attendance at the wedding of the blacksmith's daughter Polly and that he and my mother had been invited to the reception after the service. Most of the village would be watching the wedding, including my sister Naomi.

As we walked back into the classroom Mary nudged me to say she had delivered my note.

It was a fine day for Polly Seddon's wedding and Father set out early wearing the sombre black garb in which he performed his official duties.

Mother wore her navy-blue skirt and white silk blouse. I had spent about half an hour crimping her hair with curling tongs and she looked very nice even though her grey coat was years old and didn't look much like a wedding to me.

When I had said it was a pity she hadn't bought herself a new one she merely said, 'Yer father needed new shoes an' it's more important fer 'im te look decent than me who doesn't go out much. With 'is job at the church 'e 'as te look respectable. I like 'im to look the part.'

I hoped I never became so besotted with a man that I allowed him to swallow me up alive, and when I didn't speak she said, 'I'm glad yer not bearin' 'im any malice about that night, Ellen, 'e only wants what's best for ye all. If yer does what 'e asks 'e's a reasonable man.'

'There now,' I said, 'take a look in the mirror and tell me what ye thinks about yer hair.'

She peered into the mirror and a smile spread over her face.

'It's nice, Ellen, real nice. I'll tell folk you did it for me. Now I'll probably spoil it wi' puttin' mi hat on.'

'Here, let me put it on for ye. You probably won't be takin' your hat off, but take off that awful coat as soon as ye can.'

Sure enough all the village seemed to have gathered around the church. They lined the path and perched on the walls, some of them even sat on the gravestones, and my father stood importantly at the door waiting for the guests to arrive. Mother went in alone leaving us to watch the proceedings, and Mary whispered, 'Why is Father standing outside?'

''E's got to escort everybody down the aisle and into the pews, like as not 'e doesn't trust the ushers to do it right.'

My sarcasm was lost on Mary but Naomi said, 'They don't know the church like mi father does.'

'You two stay 'ere,' I hissed, 'I'm goin round the other side to see what's 'appening.'

It was only half the truth, from the place I had in mind I only had to cross the churchyard, climb over the wall and I was almost on the moor.

I watched Polly arriving, swathed in white lace, on the arm of big Jim Seddon the blacksmith. Polly was a big girl with a jolly smiling face and she looked very beautiful in her bridal attire, but there was no time to stand and stare. Once I had satisfied myself that Father was inside the church I made good my escape up to the moor.

I saw Kitty sitting on an old dead tree stump and as I climbed the hill she waved and came to meet me. Her hair blew about her face in a riot of colour against the blue sky, and she was wearing some sort of coloured skirt which seemed to turn her into a gypsy before my eyes. As I drew nearer I could see that she was wearing earrings like bright green pears, and seeing my incredulous look she said, 'I picked 'em up at the jumble sale. I 'ave to put 'em on when there's nobody about, sure and mi mother'd kill me if she caught mi wearin' 'em at 'ome.'

As we settled companionably on the tree stump she said, 'I didn't wait te see the weddin' although I've nothin' agin' Polly Seddon or any o' the Seddons. Many's the chicken John Seddon's given mi father on Christmas mornin' an' even last Christmas didn't they send up enough turkey to feed all of us. An' John Seddon doesn't reckon on bein' a church goer.'

I didn't respond to the sly gibe at my father, and with a

little smile she said, 'I don't suppose yer dad knows yer up 'ere, Ellen?'

'No. Kitty, are you really goin' to Liverpool to work?'

'That I am, as soon as mi schooldays are over.'

'I want to come with ye.'

She stared at me aghast.

'Ye can't, Ellen, fer one thing yer father wouldn't let ye and for another it costs money to go to Liverpool and where are ye goin' to get that from?'

'I'll get it if I have to steal it.'

'Yer talkin' rubbish, Ellen, where would ye steal it from? Yer father doesn't leave the church collection 'angin' about and I reckon yer mother needs all she can get. There's bin a job promised me at the Seamen's Mission and a bed and board. I'm not sure there'd be anythin' fer you, Ellen.'

'Then I'll find somethin', in all that big city surely there must be somethin' I can do.'

'And then yer father'd come lookin' for ye and 'e'd nigh on kill ye, and me too if 'e thought I 'ad a hand in it.'

'He'll never find me, I'd run and I'd run 'til there was nowhere left to go an if 'e got mi cornered I'd kill 'im afore I'd come back 'ere.'

She stared at me startled, then shaking her head dubiously she said, 'I've never 'eard ye talk like this about 'im afore. Why are ye suddenly hatin' 'im like this?'

Springing to my feet I tore off my coat and flung it on the grass, then hitching up my skirt and underwear I bared my scored back to her shocked gaze.

'Did 'e do that to ye, Ellen?' she gasped.

'Yes, on Christmas Eve just because I was late 'ome, after we'd decorated that little tree. I'll never forget it, Kitty, an' I'll never forgive 'im or the pleasure 'e took in doin' it. Kitty, I'm frightened of 'im. I've seen 'im lookin' at mi, like 'e used te look at mi mother afore they disappeared upstairs to their bedroom, like 'e'd look at mi if I were a woman. Do ye know what I mean?'

Kitty shook her head slowly, her face shocked, then in a tight voice she said, 'Yer father thought nowt o' mi dad but *'e'd* never 'a done that to any of us. P'rhaps yer wrong,

Ellen, p'rhaps it's all in yer mind, p'rhaps if ye never make 'im angry again it'll all blow over.'

I shook my head in exasperation. 'I stole one o' the carvin' knives an' I've got it 'idden in my underwear. If 'e comes near mi again I'll use it, Kitty, either on 'im or on me.'

'Ye must tell the vicar, Ellen, either 'im or Mrs Grundy. Between 'em somethin'll be done.'

'If I tell the vicar it'll be my word against mi father's and 'e could lose 'is job. Mi mother and the others'll suffer if I does that. No, Kitty, it's better for mi to get right away, I'll get the money somehow. Only please tell me when yer goin' so that I can come with ye.'

I was struggling into my coat, pulling down my skirt so that it covered the tops of my boots, and Kitty was helping me with a sad and troubled face.

When she didn't speak I urged, 'Please, Kitty, if ye've ever bin mi friend help mi now. Yer the only one I could ever ask, the only one I could ever tell about mi father, nobody else'd believe mi. You believe me, don't ye?'

She nodded, then with something of her old humour she said, 'Mi father said 'e was a sanctimonious old humbug struttin' off to church an' 'im with an eye for Phoebe Patterson. There was the vicar prayin' for 'er soul an' yer father 'elpin' to damn it.'

I stared at her in disbelief. 'Mi father and Phoebe Patterson!' I echoed. 'Nay, I can't 'ardly believe that, why often's the time 'e's said she were little more than a Jezebel, the village 'arlot.'

'I shouldn't 'ave bin tellin' ye, Ellen, 'e's yer father after all.'

'Tell me about 'im, Kitty, nothin' ye could tell me would make mi 'ate 'im more than I do now. Tell me 'ow true it is, Kitty, tell me so that I'll know for certain I'm right in wantin' te get right away from 'ere.'

'Oh it's only that mi father saw 'em together at the back o' the village 'all one night when 'e was reelin' 'ome in 'is cups. My mother said 'e'd imagined it but I believed 'im. When mi father was drunk 'e allus spoke the truth, 'e didn't know 'ow to lie, 'e saved 'is lies fer when 'e was sober as a judge and could remember what 'e'd said.'

For a long time we stared at each other, then Kitty said, 'Better get off 'omc now, Ellcn, the mist is comin' down an' I don't want ye gettin' another beatin'.'

'They'll not miss mi, Kitty, they'll be at the weddin' feast.'

'They may be, but that young sister o' yours could be tellin' 'im.'

'I'm comin' with ye, Kitty, whenever ye go. I mean it,' I said sternly.

'All right, Ellen Adair, when I'm ready for goin' I'll tell ye, but I've no money to be 'elpin' ye and I'm makin no promises I might not be able to keep.'

'I know. I'm not expectin' anythin', Kitty, only I'd feel 'appier if I 'ad somebody te travel with.'

We threw our arms round each other and stood for a few minutes in the keen wind that blew off the moor. Without another word I ran leaping down the short coarse grass until I reached the stilc in thc wall, thcn with more decorum I strolled nonchalantly down the village street. The lamps had been lit and the mist swirled around my feet. From inside the church hall came the sound of music and laughter which told me Polly's wedding feast was in full swing. As I reached our front gate I saw that the door was opcn and Naomi stood peering out into the gloom. She said sharply, 'Where've ye bin, our Ellen? I waited for ye at the church.'

'Why did ye, then? Ye said you were goin' to the park.'

'Mi father said I was to wait for you.'

'I went to the back o' the church an' saw some o' the other girls from school. After the weddin' we went walkin' on the moor.'

'Wi' Kitty McGuire do ye mean?'

'No I don't, you little sneak. I 'aven't seen Kitty McGuire fer weeks, if she's any sense she doesn't want te see me, or anybody else who thinks she's nowt a pound.'

She stared out of her thin sharp little face with suspicious eyes but I met her gaze unflinching. Lying was coming easy. I hoped stealing would be just as easy, or killing if that's what it came to.

CHAPTER 4

As the weeks wore on I grew more and more excited. Beyond a brief smile and a wave of her hand I had had no more contact with Kitty. That she would keep her promise I had no doubt, and news of her plans came to me from the other girls.

'Kitty McGuire's leavin' the school at Easter, goin' ter work i' Liverpool,' Mary Jordan informed me. 'Yer'll not catch me goin' ter work i' Liverpool, mi mother sez it's full o' foreign sailors and shanty Irish.'

'When exactly is she goin'?'

'Easter Saturday mi mother sez, and that came from Kitty's mother so I reckon it's right.'

Now that it was almost upon me I was beginning to realize the enormity of my decision. I would be leaving the village where I had spent all my young life and I began to see it with a new warmth and affection. The straggling village street with its stalls on market day, a street that ran upwards until it met the fell and the rolling moor of the lower Pennines. Somehow the clear bubbling stream that trickled along the side of the street where I lived and the narrow bridges which crossed it became suddenly important. Like the snowy ducks on the pond near the stone Saxon church and the village pub with its window boxes filled with early daffodils.

My resolution began to waver until the night I saw my father send Peter skidding across the kitchen floor with a fierce blow from the back of his hand. He staggered to his feet with the blood pouring from his forehead which had caught the edge of the table, and I ran to help him. But my father clutched my shoulder with a heavy hand.

'Keep out of this, girl, or I'll deal wi' you in a similar fashion,' he growled.

'Now,' he said, standing scowling over my stricken

brother, 'ye'll clean them shoes like I asked ye to do an' leave yer books be.'

'I was goin' to clean them, Father, 'onest I was, but I 'ad to write this down while it was still in mi mind,' Peter cried.

'I told ye I had an important meetin' tonight, now get on wi' them shoes while I change into mi suit, and make a good job of 'em,' was Father's parting shot.

At that moment my mother came in and I was shocked at the greyness of her face and the dark hollows under her eyes. Piteously she looked at Peter, then at my father who snapped, 'What ails ye, woman, goin' about the house like a shadow? I've more than 'ad mi fill o' disobedient children and a wife who looks ready fer death.'

Trembling, Mother sank down on to a chair and Peter reached for the box which contained the blacking for Father's boots. As for myself, I ran to the tap and saturated a cloth with clean water in an attempt to stem the blood from his forehead. It was still bleeding profusely and I could only imagine that it was throbbing painfully.

After I had attended to Peter I made Mother a cup of hot sweet tea and advised her to go to bed.

'There's the little ones to see to, Ellen, and yer father's supper for when 'e comes 'ome.'

'I'll do that, Mother, please go to bed,' I urged.

I watched miserably while she sipped her tea, then Father was back in the kitchen wearing his best suit, scrutinizing the boots Peter handed to him and saying not a word of thanks.

'I'll not be wantin' any supper,' he said, 'so if ye wants ter go to bed yer can.'

Looking at him in surprise my mother said, 'Will ye be getting somethin' to eat at the meetin', then?'

'I've bin asked te the Skidmores' after the meetin's over,' he answered tersely, then left the house.

'Please, Mother, go to bed,' I urged her. 'I'll see to the children and I'll bring you something warm up to bed later.'

Wearily she dragged herself to her feet and shuffled out of the room.

After she had gone was the moment I told Peter what I planned to do, but he was quick to urge against it.

'Ye can't go, Ellen, think about mi mother and the children, think about me. I can't stay on 'ere without you, Ellen, we're the oldest, together one day we'll beat mi father.'

It had been a mistake to tell him, and as I coped with the evening meal and the washing up afterwards my resolution to leave with Kitty was faltering. In three weeks it would be Easter and I had very little money saved and now my mind was weighed down with doubts about the sanity of my decision.

I sat in the kitchen mending Mary's pinafore while Peter sat at the table poring over his books. At eight o'clock I got the children ready for bed and when Naomi protested I snapped, 'Mother said you had to go to bed with the others, ye don't want to lend a hand wi' the 'ousework and I don't want ye under mi feet. I've made cocoa and when ye've drunk it I want ye in bed, all of ye.'

'Mother didn't mean me,' she stormed. 'Yer only three years older than me anyway.'

'All right then, it's either bed or ye 'elp to clean the sittin' room and the kitchen.'

She glared at me furiously, then taking up her cocoa she marched out of the kitchen and up the stairs.

Peter's pale face broke into a smile. 'Ye can be somethin' of a martinet yerself, our Ellen, when ye wants ter be,' he said.

'She gets on mi nerves, sometimes I can't stand 'er at any price and it's awful that I should be feelin' this way about mi own sister.'

At nine o'clock I went upstairs with a cup of hot milk for Mother. Her face looked grey and pinched against the white pillows, and I was shocked at the cold clammy feeling of her nightdress as I helped her to sit up.

'I should send for the doctor, Mother. Please let me,' I begged.

'No, Ellen, I'll be better in the mornin' but I don't think I'm goin' te be able to get to the Nelsons' and I promised

Mary Nelson faithfully I'd be there to help 'er with 'er simnels.'

'I'll go as soon as I've tidied up the kitchen, Mother. I'll be up later to tell you what she's said.'

'Yer a good girl, Ellen, I wish ye'd try to get on wi' yer father a bit better. It upsets me when yer forever at logger'e-ads with 'im.'

I went about shaking up her pillows and settling her into bed without answering, and she caught my hand in hers anxiously. 'Promise me ye'll try, Ellen, it worries me so.'

'I'll try, Mother.'

'I sometimes wonders what'll 'appen to this family when I've gone, who'll look after the little uns and ye and yer father 'ardly speakin' a word to each other.'

'What do ye mean, Mother, when ye've gone?'

'I mean if I should die 'afore' 'e does. I've never bin the strongest an' when I feels real badly I can't 'elp worryin'.'

My throat felt tight with unshed tears but I bent down and kissed her cheek. 'Try to sleep, Mother, I'll look in on you later.'

I finished tidying the kitchen, then told Peter I was going up to the Nelsons' house.

'Do ye want me to come with ye, Ellen? I can finish me 'omework later.'

'I'm all right on mi own, Peter, I shan't be long,' I answ-ered him before letting myself out.

It was a dark murky night. Mist hung low over the fields and the solitary gas lamp burning in the street shone eerily through the gloom. Even the lights from the pub failed to dispel the damp floating vapour, and I hurried along with my head covered by a warm woollen scarf and my hands thrust deep inside my coat pockets.

I was not usually afraid of the dark or of walking the country lanes alone, but this was a night of floating shadows and weird figures conjured up by the mist and I was glad when the Nelsons' house loomed in front of me.

As soon as I touched the latch on the side gate a dog started to bark and then there were two of them leaping at the gate with teeth bared and hackles bristling so that I backed off, afraid. I was unused to dogs. We had never had them as pets, indeed there had only ever been the tabby cat Matilda, and Jet the black cat who was still with us. Matilda had left home one day after one of Father's blustery rows, never to return. Weeks after I saw her sunning herself on the window sill of Miss York's cottage and although she came to greet me she refused to return home with me so that I always credited Matilda with a lot of common sense.

I stood outside the gate shivering and wondering what I should do next. How was I to reach the kitchen door with those massive dogs barring my path?

Suddenly a light streamed out into the darkness and a voice called out, 'What ails ye, kickin' up such a fuss at this time o' night? Who's there?'

A man's shape came lumbering through the gloom and then he was at the gate looking down at me with amazement.

''Ello, lass,' he said. 'There's no cause to be affeared, they'll not touch ye. Come into the light, I can't see ye properly standin' there.'

Gingerly I moved towards him and then he laughed. 'Why it's young Ellen Adair. Ye'd best come into the kitchen an' I'll tell Mother ye're 'ere.'

After a sharp word the dogs retreated to their kennel at the back of the yard, and smiling down at me he said, 'I can see yer not used ter dogs, lass, but we 'as to 'ave 'em livin' out 'ere away fro' the village. Come on in, now sit down i' that chair an' I'll sent mi wife in te see ye.'

I had never been inside the Nelson house before and I was amazed at the size of the kitchen – we could have got ours into it three times over. A half-carved fowl sat in the middle of the table and beside it a bowl of rosy-red apples. On a side table stood a huge bowl covered with a snowy cloth which I suspected contained dough for bread making and on the floor stood churns of milk and buttermilk.

Mrs Nelson was a wonderful cook, taking all the prizes for her preserves and fruit simnels at the country shows, and occasionally samples of her cooking found their way into our pantry.

I was still staring around when I heard footsteps and then

Mrs Nelson was there, large and bustling behind her snowy-white overall and with her grey hair pushed under a white mob-cap.

'Why it's Ellen,' she said, smiling. 'Now what brings you up here on such a dark night?'

'I've come te say mi mother won't be able to come in the mornin', she's real sick. I wanted to send for the doctor but she won't 'ave it.'

'Oh dear, I'm sorry to 'ear that, Ellen, I was 'opin' she could give me a hand wi the simnels but I reckon it can't be 'elped. Now you tell your mother to stay in bed 'til she feels 'erself again, and see that she gets plenty of nourishment. Lots 'o fresh milk, eggs and butter.'

'Yes, Mrs Nelson, I will. And if I can run any errands for ye I will.'

She beamed affably. 'Thank you, Ellen, that's very willin' of ye. I hope you're gettin' on a bit better with yer father, it worries your mother somethin' awful.'

When I didn't speak she shook her head a little, then packed a box with fruit cake, half a dozen eggs and a piece of fresh country butter. By this time Mr Nelson had returned to the kitchen and sat regarding me with a smile.

'Take these to yer mother, Ellen, and see that she gets them for herself. She hasn't to give them to the children, she's the one that's ailin'.'

'Thank ye, Mrs Nelson, ye're very kind. Mi mother'll be that grateful.'

'That's all right, Ellen, but remember what I said, try to get along with yer father for yer mother's sake.'

'I do try, Mrs Nelson, honestly.'

'Well p'rhaps ye don't try hard enough. He's a fine church-goin' man, Ellen, I'm sure there's no cause to be quarrellin' with him.'

'No, Mrs Nelson,' I murmured, wishing with all my heart that I could show her my scarred back, but just then I caught Mr Nelson winking at me with cynical humour.

'Goin' to church doesn't make 'im a saint, eh Ellen?' he said smoothly.

‘Stop that, George,’ his wife admonished him. ‘Ellen knows what I mean.’

He grinned, quite uncontrite. ‘She knows what I mean too, don’t ye, lass? Now get off ’ome with yer parcel an’ I’ll come to the gate to see ye through the yard. Would ye like mi to walk ’ome with ye?’

‘No, thank you, Mr Nelson, just to the gate so that the dogs won’t get me.’

He threw back his head and laughed uproariously. ‘Nay, them two lazy ’ounds’ll not touch ye, their bark’s worse than their bite.’

I was not anxious to find out, and after thanking Mrs Nelson for the parcel I stayed very close to her husband until the gate had slammed between me and the dogs. Docile now, they came and stood looking solemnly through the gate while their master spoke.

‘Get off ’ome, luv, I’ll stand ’ere at the gate ’til I watches ye down the road.’

People were coming out of the church hall where Father’s meeting had taken place, and I hung back not wishing to encounter him on the way home. I watched him leave the hall, locking the door carefully behind him, then he started off down the road. I followed more slowly, surprised when he passed the entry to our lane. Instead he took the opposite direction, down Holly Lane. Curious, I crept noiselessly after him.

I stood in the shadow of a wall watching him open a gate and walk quickly up the path of a cottage garden halfway up the lane. After a few moments the door opened and he went inside.

By this time my curiosity was so great I didn’t care whether I was seen or not. I walked down Holly Lane until I stood in front of the house he had entered – Phoebe Patterson’s. I saw the play of candlelight in an upstairs room and then I shrank into the shadows as a lamp was lit in the front bedroom and the curtains were drawn close.

For several minutes I stood staring up at the closed curtains, then the light was turned off and the room was in darkness like the rest of the house. My heart was hammering painfully as I took to my heels and ran without pausing until I threw myself exhausted into the kitchen.

Peter leapt up with alarm after taking one look at my burning face.

'What is it, Ellen,' he cried, 'was somebody chasin' ye?'

I wanted to tell him what I had seen but something indefinable held me back. I don't know even now if it was loyalty or shame, only that I gathered my scattered wits and after handing my parcel to Peter sank down with trembling knees into Father's big horsehair chair.

'I was frightened by the shadows, the mist is thick out there.'

'Ye should 'ave let mi go with ye, Ellen.'

'I'm all right now, Peter. Did ye look in on mi mother?'

'Yes, she was asleep. We'd best get to bed, Ellen, mi father'll be back soon.'

'Not yet awhile he won't,' I said stonily.

'Why not? The meetin'll be over by this time.'

'Didn't he say he was goin to the Skidmores'?'

'O' course, I'd forgotten.'

After Peter had gone to bed I busied myself putting away Mrs Nelson's offerings, then set the table for breakfast, made cocoa and took it upstairs to Mother's room, but she was fast asleep. I decided not to wake her but took it back to the kitchen and drank it myself.

I went through the downstairs rooms to assure myself that they were as tidy as a new pin and on returning to the kitchen was surprised to find that it was just after midnight. Still I dawdled until I heard the garden gate closing behind my father and his footsteps under the window, then there was his key turning the lock and we were staring at each other across the kitchen floor.

His face flushed with anger. 'What are ye doin' up at this time, why aren't ye in bed?'

'I cleaned the house, Father, and laid the breakfast table, I saw the children in bed and took care of mi mother.'

'That didn't take all night, did it?'

'No, Father. I went up to the Nelsons' house to tell Mrs Nelson mi mother wouldn't be fit to go there in the mornin'.'

His eyes narrowed and I was gratified to see the uncertainty creeping into his face.

'Did ye go up there on yer own then?'

'Yes, Father.'

'It's not a fit night for a lass to be wanderin' the streets.'

'No, Father, I was glad to get back.'

'And what time was that then?'

'Oh about ten thirty or thereabouts. I saw 'em comin' out of the church hall so it must 'ave been about ten thirty.'

'That's right, my meetin' went on a fair bit after that.'

'Goodnight, Father,' I said calmly, and without undue haste left the room and climbed up the stairs to bed.

CHAPTER 5

I didn't know whether I hated my father more when he was brutal or when he was ingratiating. During the days which followed he praised me constantly for my work around the house and for the way I cared for Mother. Naomi sulked because I was getting the praise and she was being largely ignored, and Peter stared at him solemnly out of curious, bewildered eyes.

Only Mother was pleased by this new-found peace between us. As for myself I cringed whenever his hand fell benevolently on my head, or when he addressed me in companionable terms. I knew very well that it was because he didn't know how much I had seen or knew about his association with Phoebe Patterson.

I didn't think for one moment that he cared about Mother or the rest of us, but he did care about his position as sexton and his standing in the community.

It was on Sunday morning after church when we sat down to dinner that he raised the subject of Phoebe to the family at large. 'I see Phoebe Patterson was in the church this morning, that little talk I had with her must have done some good.'

I sat with my head bowed while Mother said, 'You talked to her? Nay, surely it was the vicar 'imself who should 'ave done that!'

'He reckoned she'd take it better comin' fro' me, less like preachin' if ye understands.'

'And 'ow did she take it then?'

'Well she came to the church, didn't she? The first time for months so she must 'ave 'ad thoughts on what I said to 'er. She's not really a bad lass, Mary, she's never bin shown anythin' proper if gossip's to be believed.'

'I knew 'er mother, there was nothin' wrong wi' Mrs

Patterson, worked 'er fingers to the bone she did and got precious little thanks from Phoebe.'

'Well, I've 'eard different. 'Er father was a wastrel just like Kitty McGuire's father, that's why I don't want our Ellen 'avin too much to do with 'er. Like as not she'll end up like Phoebe Patterson.'

The food stuck in my throat so that I choked while the tears rolled down my face. How I hated him at that moment, and even more so when he came to pat my back. I couldn't bear for him to touch me and it was only when he'd left the table to sit with his newspaper in the one big easy chair in the kitchen that I made up my mind irrevocably that I was going with Kitty come what may.

I waylaid her in the school playground, making sure that none of my sisters were in the vicinity, but Kitty greeted my urgency with doubtful eyes and anxious persuasions to think more carefully.

'I've thought about it, Kitty. As a matter of fact I've not thought about anything else for days. You were right about mi father, he is friendly with Phoebe Patterson and I can't bear to see mi mother treatin' 'im like God. 'Ow much money shall I need and when are we goin'?'

'Ye'll need at least five shillings for the fare and any food we moight be needin', and somethin' to spare. I'm catchin' the seven o'clock train from the station on Saturday mornin' and I 'ave to change at Leeds and get the Liverpool train. I'm goin' early cause I don't want to be arrivin' in Liverpool when it's dark.'

I nodded wordlessly. I was thinking about Leeds and Liverpool, two big cities I had only heard of, and to a girl born and bred in that remote Pennine village as alien as Vancouver and Brisbane.

'I'll be at the station, Kitty, I swear it,' I said fiercely. 'What do I need to bring in the way of luggage?'

'Nightwear and a change o' clean clothin', Ellen. Whatever ye think ye'll need. Are ye sure ye'll be able to get out of the 'ouse without anybody seein' ye?'

I nodded. 'They don't get up very early on Saturdays unless there's a weddin' or a funeral. I'll keep out o' sight of anybody lookin' through their windows, and I'll be there, Kitty, ye can bank on it.'

'Well if ye're not I can't wait for ye, Ellen, I 'ave to be on that train.'

'Will yer mother be seein' ye off, Kitty?'

'I'd rather she didn't, I'd rather leave 'em all in the house, and it's better she doesn't if yer that intent on comin' with mi. Yer father'd worm it out of 'er sure as mi name's Kitty McGuire if 'e thought yer'd left wi' me. If mi mother knows nothin' she can't tell 'im anythin'.'

At that moment the younger classes were coming into the schoolyard so with a quick smile and a whispered 'See ye Saturday, Kitty,' I left her.

The next couple of days passed in what seemed like an instant. I collected the things I would need and made a neat parcel of them which I hid behind some books in the bedroom cupboard and I smuggled my Sunday coat downstairs and hid that too at the back of the hall cupboard.

It was inevitable that I should take stock of my life and all I would be leaving behind. In those days somehow the village took on an enchanted air and I looked with nostalgia at the tiny Saxon church and the giant yews that surrounded the churchyard, at the snowy ducks that squabbled and splashed in the pond and the friends of my childhood I would be leaving behind.

My throat ached with unshed tears as I watched my mother's head bent over her sewing and Peter poring over his books. Even Naomi took on an attraction I had never felt before and instead of feeling impatient at her pertness, now I was seeing the humour in her thin gamin face.

In those days I began to doubt my courage. Would it fail me on the morning I had promised to meet Kitty? And then I would find my father's hand fondling my bare arm, have his eyes burning into mine with the unspoken question forever there: How much did I know?

There was a thin drizzle of rain that Saturday morning and mist hung low across the fields. All night long I had tossed and turned in my bed until I heard Ben Johnson's rooster crowing before first light.

Gingerly I slipped out of bed, gathered my clothes together and crept silently downstairs. There was one tread that creaked ominously and I paused anxiously to listen, but all I could hear was Father's snoring and the loud ticking of the grandfather clock.

I washed and dressed hurriedly in the kitchen, shivering from the cold water. I took my coat out of the cupboard and felt in the pocket for the note I had composed days before, addressed to my mother. In it I said I was sorry for causing her pain and hoped she would forgive me, I swore I would pay back the money I was taking, as soon as I was earning enough. And I promised never to forget her and to love her always.

My next act was to reach up to the mantelpiece and take down the tin where she kept the money for the coalman and the milkman. There were ten shillings in it and I took three; the rest of my money had been saved out of what I had received from running errands for Mrs Nelson and the vicar's wife.

I shrugged my arms into my coat and my feet into my best Sunday shoes. Then I heard footsteps in the passage and I stood petrified. Next moment I was staring into Peter's horrified eyes as he beheld me dressed and ready to leave, carrying my paper parcel, my hand on the latch of the yard door.

'Shsss,' I cautioned, and hurried to close the door behind him.

'Please, Peter, don't say a word. I'm leavin' and nothin' ye can say or do is goin' to make mi change mi mind,' I said firmly.

'But where are ye goin', Ellen? Ye can't just go like that.'

'I've a job to go to and I want ye to go back upstairs and not say a word that ye've seen mi this mornin'. That way my father can't blame ye for not stoppin' mi or tellin' 'im.'

'Ye can't go, Ellen. If you go I'll go too. I can't live 'ere when ye've gone, I 'ates 'im just as much as you do.'

'I'm older than you, Peter, and ye've got yer way to make. One day I'll see that ye knows where I am but for now I wants ye to keep quiet. Please go back to bed and let me go. Nothin' ye can say'll make me change mi mind.'

'It's mi father, isn't it?'

'Yes it is. I'll never forgive 'im for what he did to me and I'll never forgive 'im for bein such a sanctimonious liar. One day ye'll be a man and I hope ye'll be a match for 'im. But all that's in the future, Peter, for now ye've got to bide yer time.'

'But 'ave ye got any money, Ellen? Ye needs money to leave 'ere.'

'I've got a bit I saved and I've borrowed three shillin' out o' the box there. I'll pay it back when I can, mi mother'll just 'ave to trust mi.'

''E'll come after ye, Ellen, ye'll never get away with it.'

'Oh yes I will, I'll travel to the ends of the earth to get away from 'im, but if 'e does catch mi and want to bring mi back I'll kill miself, I swear it.'

'I've got a bit o' money saved, Ellen, ye can 'ave that.'

'I won't take a penny of yer money, Peter, ye'll need all that for yerself one day. Will ye promise mi one thing?'

'What, Ellen, that I won't tell 'im I've seen ye this mornin'?'

'That you'll get away too if ye can when the time's right. If ye don't ye'll regret it for the rest of your life.'

From upstairs came the sound of Father's coughing and then voices, and urgently I said, 'I'm goin', Peter, get back upstairs 'afore ye're seen.' Then I threw my arms round his neck and left him without another word. I ran down the lane without a backward glance, my eyes swimming with tears so that the village was a blur.

It was too early for the train, and not wanting to be seen loitering near the station I climbed the stile near the church and walked up on to the fell. Dew lay heavy on the grass and the earth smelled of clover. From the fell I could look down on the village which was slowly coming to life. Smoke ascended from cottage chimneys and along the high street I could see Johnty the postman with the sack of letters on his back. Dogs were barking, and wrinkling up my nose I could smell bread baking in the ovens of Cornfield's bakery.

Old Mrs Trainer left her cottage carrying a paper bag of crusts for the ducks she fed every morning, and soon the Saturday traders would be coming to set out their stalls.

I saw Kitty hurrying down the path of their cottage, with her mother standing at the door holding one of the younger children, while another clung to her skirts. Like me Kitty carried her belongings in a brown paper parcel and she was wearing her Sunday-best coat and a bright green woollen tammy. At the end of the lane she turned to wave to her mother, then she ran in the direction of the station. She looked neither right nor left, and anxiously I too started to run down the hill so that I arrived at the station only minutes after she entered the booking hall.

On the platform she turned to me anxiously. 'Ellen, are ye sure?' she breathed.

'I'm sure,' I answered her firmly.

'Did anybody see ye?'

'Not a soul. I waited on the fell 'til I saw ye leavin' the house.'

'I 'opes nobody else's gettin' this early train.'

'Well we don't 'ave to sit together until we're sure.'

We were the only two people to board the country train with its two carriages, but all the same we sat with lowered heads hoping and praying that we might be the only travellers.

The train had been several minutes on its journey before I felt confident enough to look through the window at the passing scenery.

Kitty was the knowledgeable traveller, for they had come to England all the way from County Sligo so that her father could find some sort of work on a farm. It was Kitty now who wasn't afraid to ask the times of trains and whether or not we were on the right platform while I hurried along at her side overwhelmed by the thronged platform and the hustle and bustle of Leeds station.

While we waited for the Liverpool train I murmured, 'Wouldn't it have bin nice to stay a while in the city to look at the shops, Kitty?'

She nodded. 'They'll be just as grand in Liverpool, Ellen.

Will you be lookin' at that woman there, watered silk in the middle o' the mornin' and heels like stilts. I know what I'm goin' to do, I'm goin' to turn miself into a city girl an' wear clothes just like that 'afore I goes back to the village. I'll 'ave 'em all pea green with envy, I will.'

'How do you suppose we're goin' to do that then?'

'I shall, Ellen, just you watch me.'

'Then I suppose I shall too?'

'Well o' course.'

She put her arms round me and gave me a little hug.

'I'm right glad ye've come, Ellen. We're goin' to make somethin' of ourselves just like I allus said we would.'

'Emeralds and ermine?' I prompted with a half smile.

'I'll settle for less for the moment, but we'll keep our sights high. Emeralds and ermine it is. Do ye think we could spend a few pence on a cup o' tea and a bun?'

'Yes please, I'm awfully hungry.'

'Come on then, the train's not due for twenty minutes and the tea room's just over there.'

The tea room was hot and steamy but we found a corner table. I handed over the price of tea and a bun and Kitty went to the counter.

She was chatting animatedly to the woman standing next to her, then she was bringing her over to our table.

'This is Mrs O'Reilly, Ellen, she's goin' to Liverpool. She says we can tag along with 'er and she'll be tellin' us how to find our way about when we gets there.'

I made room for Mrs O'Reilly next to me, and eyeing me curiously she said, 'Yer a bit young, aren't ye, luv, to be goin' to work i' Liverpool? I should 'a thowt yer'd still be goin' to school.'

'I've just left,' I said stoutly, 'Kitty too.'

'Ay well, so she's just towd mi, but you're nobbut a lassy.'

Only a few months separated me from Kitty and I felt unreasonably annoyed that this woman thought me too young to be let out on my own.

'Goin' te relatives, are ye?' she asked next.

'To mi Aunt Mary's,' Kitty replied, 'and we 'ave jobs to go to.'

'Oh well that's different. Work's 'ard to come by. 'Ave either of ye bin ter Liverpool 'afore?'

When we shook our heads she said brightly, 'It's big, ye know, not as big as Manchester to be sure but it's a fair-sized port. A lot o' foreigners live i' Liverpool, particularly near the docks.'

'A lot of Irish too,' Kitty put in quicky.

'Oh ay, it's a great place for the Irish. I married one of 'em so I should know. I 'ated it when we first went te live there but now I likes it. There's someat different about Liverpool, I don't rightly know what it is but there's a sort of adventure about it, romantic like.'

'Why is that?' Kitty asked quickly.

'I reckon it's all them big steamers goin' te romantic places we've only heard of, China and India, South America and Africa. Ye can walk along the river and see 'em sailin' out into the mist, an' ye can take the ferries and sail across to Wallasey and New Brighton on a nice summer's day. That's where the river meets the sea, ye know, and many's the time I've taken mi children to sit on the promenade to watch the big ships disappearin' into the sunset.'

I could have listened to Mrs O'Reilly for much longer, but gathering her parcels together she said briskly, 'Well, we'd best be movin' if we're to get that train. Can ye carry one o' these parcels seein' ye don't 'ave much luggage?'

I took one and Kitty took another, then we hurried along the platform to join the people waiting for the Liverpool train.

My entire being was filled with a strange and new excitement, but as the train eased its way out of the station the spectacle of Leeds seemed depressing with the sea of mill chimneys and warehouses. The sun no longer shone out of a clear blue sky, instead the clouds hung low over the city and the distant line of the Pennines, and a thin drizzle of rain obscured the diminishing city.

I thought about the village I had left. They would have found my note and I could only picture my mother in tears while my father pontificated about my lost innocence, sure that I had taken the first steps towards perdition.

Peter would listen to him with anger in his heart and Naomi would be glad I'd gone. One less in that tiny bedroom had always been much to be desired, and the smaller children were too young to understand that one member of the family had gone for ever.

There would be speculation too in the village. The vicar would pray for me and Mrs Nelson would try to comfort my mother while most of the others would damn me as an ungrateful brat who had not appreciated the good home my decent and upright father had provided.

I thought with a certain grim amusement that my father, when he had had time to reflect, would view my absence with something akin to relief. There was now little danger that I would ever disclose anything about his association with Phoebe Patterson, and I hoped his suspicions that I knew more than I had let on would keep him from trying to find me.

Kitty and Mrs O'Reilly sat opposite and I was left largely to my own thoughts as they chatted. Occasionally my eyes met Kitty's and she smiled encouragment, well aware where my thoughts lay.

Mrs O'Reilly was a chatterbox. Before we reached Lime Street Station in Liverpool the entire carriage was adding anecdotes to match hers, and soon both Kitty and I were laughing at their stories.

Everybody was anxious to give us instructions on how to find our way about the city as well as to Aunt Mary's, and two of the men made it their business to see us on to one of the city's trams, with strict instructions to the conductor to put us off near Aunt Mary's address.

CHAPTER 6

Liverpool on a dismal spring evening with a mist hanging low on the river and the mournful hooting of ships' sirens echoing through the gathering gloom.

Gas lamps shed their weird glow over street corners and as we sat on the wooden seats of the tram it seemed to me that the world was filled with strange sights and sounds. The clanging of the tram and the hooting of the sirens, the cries of the newsboys and the strange accents of the people were all combining to convince me that I was now a part of a strange and alien world, a world in which I would either survive or go under. I prayed with all my heart on that creaking, clanging tramcar that I would survive.

The conductor put us off the tram with smiling good humour and passed us our parcels. We thanked him warmly, and Kitty remarked, 'Well at least the folk we've met so far 'ave bin friendly, I just 'ope the rest of 'em's as nice.'

'How well do ye know yer Aunt Mary, Kitty?'

'Not well at all, I 'aven't seen 'er since we stayed with 'em that first night we crossed from Ireland. I know her husband works on't docks and they've a lot o' children. They're mi cousins, I suppose, but I wouldn't be able to recognize a single one of 'em.'

'She's yer mother's sister, isn't she?'

'That she is, but they're not a bit alike. Mi mother 'ad the loveliest red hair just like mine when she was younger, and mi aunt's dark an' very thin.'

'But she'll be glad to see ye, Kitty?'

'Let's 'ope so. I hope she's as glad to see you, Ellen, she thinks I'm on mi own.'

'Oh Kitty, I promise I won't be any trouble, I'll work hard at the mission and I'll pay mi own way. Yer've bin so good, I don't want to be a burden to ye ever.'

She took hold of my arm and gave it a little squeeze. 'To

be truthful, Ellen, I'm glad of yer company. I wasn't relishin' comin' 'ere on mi own.'

The streets we were walking along were mean and narrow. There were no gardens in front of the tall dismal houses and my spirits sank as we passed the Seamen's Mission at the corner of the street. It was an ugly building with dingy windows through which we could see gas lamps burning dimly. As we passed the door I was aware of a strong smell of carbolic and the single gas lamp above the doorway did nothing to dispel the overall gloom.

Across the road a group of children played noisily outside a Chinese laundry and further down the street other children waited idly outside the dingy doors of a public house.

'Does yer aunt live in this street, Kitty?' I asked unhappily.

'Number twenty-seven. It's worse than I thought it'd be.'

'Well it's an awful night, it'll all look a lot better in the mornin'.'

We stood staring up at number twenty-seven, at a door with dark grey paint which was peeling away to reveal damp and rotten woodwork.

'Goodness knows what it's like inside,' Kitty said doubtfully. 'Mother warned mi that mi aunt 'ad never been 'ouseproud, she was allus the one that liked goin' out and enjoyin' herself while the rest of them cared for the house.'

'With a husband and children she's probably changed, Kitty. We're here, shouldn't you be knocking on the door?'

'I'm just warnin' ye, that's all.'

With that she lifted her hand and brought the knocker down loudly. After a few seconds we heard footsteps behind the door, then gingerly it was opened a few inches and a child looked out at us, her eyes wide with curiosity.

'Is yer mother in?' Kitty asked softly. 'Will ye tell her it's Kitty all the way fro' the West Riding.'

The child didn't move but remained staring at us, then from the back of the house a woman called out, ''Ave ye got the front door open, Jennie? Get it closed, it's cold in 'ere.'

Kitty looked at me helplessly, then giving the door a little push she said, 'We're goin' in, Ellen,' and taking the little girl by the hand she walked into the house while I followed more slowly.

We entered a square living room which seemed too crowded to present any real picture in my mind. A stack of washing was piled on to the square table in the middle of the room and against one wall a sewing machine stood open. There were chairs in the room but they were littered with dressmaking material and items of clean washing, and the woman who faced us across the table looked grey and careworn.

She was small and thin and she wore her faded brown hair taken back from her face and caught by a slide. She wore a grey woollen cardigan over a soiled white blouse and there was a floral apron round her waist.

A little girl played on the floor in front of a low-burning fire, while the child who had opened the door to us went to cling to her mother's skirts, eyeing us suspiciously.

'I'm Kitty, Aunt Mary. Mi mother said ye'd be expectin' mi.'

For a second she continued to stare, then her face relaxed and she smiled. 'Gracious, I'd forgotten it was today ye were comin'.' Then her eyes slid round to me.

'This is Ellen Adair, Aunt Mary, mi friend from the country, she's hopin' to get work alongside of me at the mission.'

Doubtfully Aunt Mary sat down on the edge of a chair. 'Well I don't know, Kitty, yer mother didn't say there'd be two of ye.'

'Can we find out tonight?' Kitty asked.

'Ye can go along tonight to see the Doyles, they're in charge o' the mission. I know there's a room fer ye, Kitty, but I can't vouch fer yer friend.'

She began to scoop up the things off the chairs, then she added a small shovelful of coal to the fire and said to the little girl, ''Elp me clear the table, Jennie. And ye be quiet, our Michael, or I'll send ye out to play. 'Ave ye had anythin' to eat since ye left Yorkshire?'

'Yes thanks, Aunt Mary, we had somethin' at the station in Leeds.'

The fact that that had been almost three hours ago didn't register on Aunt Mary at all, she merely indicated that we should sit down on the now vacant chairs while Michael howled his head off and Jennie continued to stare at us as if we had arrived from outer space.

'Stop starin',' her mother admonished her. 'She's not used to folk comin' that she doesn't know. Go tell the others that their Cousin Kitty's arrived.'

There had been poverty in Kitty's home but it had not been this sort. Kitty's house had shone from Mrs McGuire's polishing. She had cut up old clothes to make rag rugs, and Mrs Mason had been generous in giving her old lace curtains for the windows and the odd item of furniture.

This room was squalid. I doubted if the table and chairs had ever seen polish, the carpet was stained and threadbare, and the huge iron fireplace had never seen black leading. Then I noticed the perambulator in the far corner of the room and the child sitting propped up against a dingy pillow.

In one hand was a pot of raspberry jam and the other hand was spooning jam into its mouth, so that its face and bib were smothered in it. Catching us looking, Aunt Mary said, 'I gave our Susan the jam to keep 'er quiet, she's teethin' and a right mornin' and night I've 'ad with 'er to be sure. Ere,' she said, snatching the jam from the child, 'give it to me, ye'll make yerself sick,' whereupon the child howled with temper and the jam was handed back to keep her quiet.

At that moment we heard what seemed like a regiment dashing along the passage and next moment a dozen children piled into the room and stood staring at us with great solemn eyes.

We stared back and Kitty cried, 'Are all these yours, Aunt Mary?'

'Nay, I didn't tell ye to bring the entire street in, Jennie. Now the rest of ye get off 'ome.'

It was then I noticed that among the childrn were several coloured ones, Negro and Chinese, and they scampered off smartly along with two white children, leaving us to face five more small McLoughlins.

'This is yer Cousin Kitty,' she said, 'and this is 'er friend Ellen. Now come forward one at a time and tell 'em who ye are.'

It seemed so strange to be greeting those children who came forward to announce their names; Jonny, Nancy, Edith, Moya and Cloonie. Introductions over, they went to the far side of the room and sat along the wall on a wooden form, eyeing us curiously.

'Yer dad'll be 'ome soon. Early shift 'e's on but 'e usually calls in the pub fer a drink on 'is way 'ome. Joe works at the docks like most o' the men round 'ere,' she explained.

There was a vague pain in my midriff which I recognized as hunger, and my eyes brightened when I saw Aunt Mary clearing the table. After that she spread a newspaper over it and two of the small girls were dispatched to bring in plates and cups. We watched as she cut thick slices of bread from a large loaf which she placed on a platter, then the jam jar was taken once more from the child in the pram, who had nodded off. Aunt Mary made no effort to clean the jam jar or the spoon.

'Yer welcome to join us, Kitty. We're 'avin' soup and there's bread and potatoes te foller. Pull up yer chairs, if Joe doesn't be comin' soon I'll send one o' the children to tell 'im we're waitin' for 'im.'

Joe it seems was in no hurry, and after a wait of about half an hour Jonny was dispatched to the public house to find his father. Again we waited, then we heard the front door opening and a large dirty man came in, his face flushed and angry.

'What do ye mean, woman, by sendin' our Jonny to the pub for me? Can't a man 'ave a drink in 'is own good time after workin' all day?'

Unperturbed, and evidently well used to his ill humour, she merely said, 'We 'ave visitors, mi sister's daughter Kitty and 'er friend.'

'So, we 'ave visitors, what's it ter me?'

'I thought ye might be after showin' 'em a bit o' welcome.'

'Which is which, then? I didn't know we were 'avin' two of 'em.'

'They'll be wantin' somethin' te eat 'afore they goes to the mission, I thought yer'd like to be 'ere.'

He took his seat at the table without making any effort to wash. Two of the childrn helped their mother serve the soup in the kitchen and carry it into the living room, and I wondered when they were going to join us and where there would be room for them.

'Come on, then,' Joe said, 'make a start 'afore it gets cold.'

The children continued to sit or stand behind us and I realized that they were to wait to see what was left. The soup was thin and watery. I was grateful for its warmth but my appetite seemed to have deserted me when I saw their eyes watching every mouthful, which by this time I was sure we were depriving them of.

Joe ate noisily and I felt sickened by his uncouth manners and the grime on his hands and face. It was my fault, I told myself savagely, if I hadn't come there would have been more for the rest of them, consequently when the potatoes arrived I ate sparingly and adamantly refused the bread and jam to follow. It was only when Joe finally pushed his plate away that the children were allowed to take our places. They ate ravenously, and my heart was filled with pity at their pale pinched faces and the sad hopelessness of their lives.

It was almost seven o'clock when we reported at the mission. The caretaker's wife, Mrs Doyle, looked at me sourly and said, 'Who's this then? I was told there'd be one of ye, Kitty McGuire.'

'That's me,' Kitty said, 'and this is mi friend Ellen Adair. We both left school on the same day and I thought an extra pair of hands might be useful. Mi aunt says you're workin' every hour that God sends.'

Slightly mollified by Kitty's hint of honest toil, the woman said, 'Well I don't know about that, 'ow much are ye thinkin' I might 'ave to pay ye?'

'I'd like to leave that to you, Ma'am, perhaps when you see what I can do you'll make your mind up.'

'That a will, in the meantime I'll be payin' ye two shillings and sixpence a week and for that yer'll wait on the tables and 'elp in the kitchen. You, Missy, will sweep and scrub and see to the bedrooms.'

'All on 'er own?' Kitty asked pertly.

'Nay, she'll get 'elp fro' me and mi 'usband, and there's Mrs Slatterly who comes in every mornin', even if she isn't much good.'

'How many bedrooms are there?' I asked dolefully.

'Well they're not bedrooms as such, they're dormitories. Twelve to a room they sleep and the smell first thing in the mornin'll like as not knock ye over. Ye'll put plenty o' carbolic in the washin' water and mi 'usband sees to it that the men wash as soon as they get 'ere.'

'What sort o' men are they?' Kitty asked curiously.

'They're seamen, most of 'em a long way from 'ome. Rough and ready they are and some of 'em are mighty interested in a pretty face, so I'd advise both o' ye to keep yer distance. On the whole they're decent, all except Black Jake and we're not expectin' 'im for some time seein' as 'e's only just gone to sea agin. Now yer'll find yer bedroom at the top o' the second flight o' stairs, on yer left. There's a double bed there and a chest o' drawers, yer'll find 'ooks fer yer clothes behind a curtain in the alcove and there's a washroom down the corridor. See that yer locks the door when yer in there. Are them all yer things?'

'Yes, Ma'am,' we answered in unison.

'Yer'll call mi Mrs Doyle and mi 'usband Mr Doyle and if 'e starts any of 'is sweet talk just let mi know, I 'aven't lived wi Joe Doyle all these years wi'out knowin what 'e was about. 'Ave ye 'ad anythin' to eat since ye arrived i' Liverpool?'

'Yes thank you, we had somethin' at mi Aunt Mary's,' Kitty said.

'I'm surprised they'd owt te spare wi' all the brood they've got. When yer've unpacked ye can come down to the kitchen and make cocoa. I 'ave to go out but I'll leave everythin' on the kitchen table for ye and ye might be glad o' the fireside.'

'Will any of the men be in the kitchen?' I asked.

'Nay, we keep our quarters locked up at night. Most of 'em'll be in the pub 'til closin' time, yer'll no doubt 'ear 'em singin' their 'eads off all the way down the street. If ye 'ears any shoutin' and quarrellin' don't let it upset ye, they'll 'ave forgot what it's all bin about in the mornin'.'

We climbed the stairs and let ourselves into our room. In it was a small iron fireplace but it was doubtful if a fire had ever burned in the grate since it was stuffed with newspaper, and the chimney too was packed with it so that the wind made rustling noises, like small animals. A solitary gas jet above the fireplace was the only illumination of the tiny dismal room with its threadbare carpet and thin cotton curtains.

Kitty threw back the covers and we both inspected the bed, relieved to find that the sheets were clean and the pillowslips freshly laundered.

'I suppose it could 'ave bin worse, Ellen,' she said miserably, 'but I reckon it's better than stayin' with mi aunt.'

'Well of course it is,' I said stoutly. 'We can make it more cheerful with some of our things.'

'What sort o' things? All I've got are clothes and clean underwear.'

'Well that's all I've got too but when we get a bit o' money we can buy an ornament or two, even some flowers or a plant.'

'I can't think why you're so cheerful, there's nothin' to be cheerful about.'

'There is for me. I don't have to look at my father's face across the table every night or watch him sulkin' at mi mother. I don't have to think about him with that Patterson woman or watch him behave as if he was God's representative on earth.'

'You really do hate 'im, don't ye, Ellen?'

'Yes, I really do. Oh Kitty, it's goin' to be so lovely livin' in this big city with the steamers and the tramcars, then there's the big shops and the museums and art galleries. Can't ye see what fun we're goin' to have?'

'Not without money I can't.'

'But we can. The museums and the art galleries don't cost anythin' and the river's excitin' enough for anybody.'

'I want more in my life than this place and I'm goin' to get it. I don't care much how, but one day I'll get mi emeralds and ermine, just you see if I don't.'

'Well of course you will, Kitty, we both will. In the meantime how about going downstairs and making that cocoa?'

The kitchen wasn't as comfortable as it might have been. There was a white sink in the corner and a white-wood table in the centre, seeming naked without a tablecloth, but there were two large comfortable chairs upholstered in maroon plush and a fire that blazed away in the large grate which had recently been black leaded.

We made the cocoa and curled up in the chairs and somehow life seemed suddenly happier, and even Kitty's dismal face relaxed a little. We made plans for the things we wanted to see in the warm summer days we believed were ahead of us. Then we heard the staccato beating of rain on the windows and the mournful sound of a ship's siren, and Kitty said fretfully, 'I'd hate to think mi life was going to be like mi Aunt Mary's. All them children and a husband who looks like hers.'

'Well of course your life won't be like hers, you wouldn't marry anybody like him for a start.'

'That'll be the sort o' chap we'll be meetin', seamen or dockers.'

'We shan't be workin' 'ere for ever, when we've saved enough we can move on.'

'We shan't save much out o' two shillings and sixpence a week, and what do we move on to without experience?'

'We can go to evening classes and perhaps find work in a shop one day. I'd like that, Kitty, to work in one o' them lovely shops where rich women come to buy beautiful clothes.'

'I'd rather be one o' the rich women than stand behind a counter saying yes Ma'am and no Ma'am.'

It seemed to me that we always came back to the same thing.

I thought Kitty would always keep her dream of ermine

and emeralds. As for me, my ambitions had always been more realistic, a little more adult, perhaps; to survive, away from my father.

The silence was broken by a door slamming outside, then the kitchen door was thrown open and a large man came in, blinking in the light. He had bright red hair and a red face, and wore a woollen muffler over a dark fawn macintosh.

We both jumped to our feet nervously and he grinned. 'I 'eard yer'd arrived fro' yer uncle. Which one of yer's Kitty McGuire?'

'I am,' Kitty said shortly.

'And yer've brought a pal with ye. What did mi missus say about that?'

'She said she could work in the bedrooms for the time bein'.'

'Ay well, that'll make it a bit less for me to do. Ye can make me a cup o' tea while I get out o' these wet things, then off to bed the pair of ye. I likes the kitchen to miself 'til the missus gets 'ome.

We heard him lumbering upstairs and I put the kettle on while Kitty spooned tea into a large brown teapot. I looked at her mutinous face anxiously and suddenly she smiled, then we started laughing, gay uncontrollable laughter which ceased abruptly when Joe Doyle returned to the kitchen.

'It's a couple o' giddy kippers ye are and no mistake,' he said sourly.

'Sorry, Mr Doyle,' Kitty said softly. 'The tea's made, and we'll be sayin' goodnight.'

He didn't answer, and gratefully we made our escape into the hall, now lit by a solitary gas lamp. We took turns to wash in the dark bare washroom then we crept between the chill sheets, shivering with cold.

'First thing I buy with mi wages is a stone 'ot-water bottle,' Kitty complained. 'We were as poor as church mice but mi mother allus saw that the beds were warm, either with oven plates or bottles. That cottage had more cracks lettin' in draughts than there were tiles on the roof.'

'My bedroom wasn't much better but mi father'd never

let us have oven plates in the bed, he said it'd make softies out of us.'

'To think I used to envy ye when first we came to England,' Kitty said softly. 'Livin' in that nice 'ouse with a garden and a father that stayed out of the pub and wi' a decent job. Ye allus seemed to 'ave good clothes for school and a change for Sunday, and ye spoke real nice. For those first few weeks I envied ye and I think I 'ated ye for 'aving the things I didn't.'

'Oh Kitty, I only had nice clothes because the vicar's wife and Mrs Nelson gave mi mother things and she was good with her sewing. I always tried to speak properly. I listened to the vicar's wife and tried to speak like her, and mi mother came from a decent family. They reckoned she'd not done the best for herself when she married mi father but she worshipped him, she did. Never a back answer did she give him, consequently we all suffered for it.'

'I'm goin' to try to talk like you do, Ellen. If I make a mistake will ye promise to put me right?'

'Oh Kitty, I couldn't do that, I'm not good enough for that. Besides I like that Irish lilt in your voice, it's more attractive than my Yorkshire accent.'

'Ye 'aven't got much of an accent, ye copied the vicar's wife and she wasn't Yorkshire. Besides it's yer grammar that I 'aven't got. Promise yer'll 'elp mi, Ellen.'

'I'll do mi best, but you must promise not to get angry when I correct you.'

'I promise, Ellen, and if I breaks that promise don't take any notice, you'll know I don't mean it.'

'What did you think of Mr Doyle, Kitty?'

'Not much. I can handle 'im, Ellen, 'e doesn't frighten me.'

'I wonder what the other men'll be like?'

'Rough like 'im, but I knew 'ow to 'andle mi father when 'e came 'ome worse for drink. Many's the time I've stood between 'im and mi mother and many's the time I've laid into 'im with the broom 'andle and 'e was so drunk 'e couldn't catch me. 'E'd 'ave knocked the livin' daylights out o' me if 'e could.'

'Why didn't you hate him like I hated my father, I wonder?'

'Because when 'e was sober 'e was a darlin' man. 'E could make mi laugh like nobody else and 'e never bore a grudge, not even when I bruised 'is shoulder and mi mother was rubbin' liniment into it for a week. He laughed about it. Oh yes, when he was sober 'e was big enough to laugh about it.'

Into the silence which followed when I found myself comparing my own father with Kitty's came sudden laughter and singing from the street, and instantly we were wide awake.

We jumped out of bed and ran to the window. The pavement shone with rain and lights streamed out of the pub doorway at the corner. The men came towards the mission, about twenty of them, singing lustily, one or two still clutching bottles and occasionally drinking from them, while from the pub doorway the landlord cautioned them to be quiet or the police would be on the scene.

Lamps were lit in upstairs bedrooms and occasionally a window was thrown open and angry oaths were exchanged, then below us the door of the mission was thrown open and Joe Doyle and his wife stood there, arms akimbo, waiting for the men to slink one by one into the building, uncontrite, their raucous voices fading into the stillness of the night.

CHAPTER 7

In the weeks that followed I was too busy to be unhappy, too weary to lie awake thinking about my lot, too afraid of the alternative so that I scrubbed and cleaned until even Mrs Doyle said I was worth all of two shillings and sixpence a week.

I thought I would never get the smell of carbolic out of my system or prevent it from entering the cracks in my hands and hurting agonizingly so that the tears ran down my cheeks with the pain.

'Yer'll get used to it,' was all Mrs Doyle said, 'I 'ave.'

In some anger Kitty said, 'Yer doin' most o' the work up there, Ellen. That Mrs Slatterly's in the kitchen wi' Mrs Doyle smokin' cigarettes and brewin' cups o'tea while your slavin' upstairs. Ye should complain.'

'Oh I couldn't do that, Kitty, she might get rid of me and I couldn't go back home. I've just got to make a go of it here. I honestly don't mind the work.'

One day I was on my hands and knees scrubbing under the beds when I felt a tap on my shoulder and found one of the seamen looking at me with humorous, twinkling eyes.

'Yer scrubbin' all the pattern off that lino, luv,' he said.

'Well there wasn't much pattern on it to begin with, was there?'

'Ye should 'ave 'elp, luv, them two lazy devils downstairs are lettin' ye do all the work.'

'I don't mind.'

'Well ye should, yer a right bonny lass and yer worth someat better ner this. See 'ere, there's a bag o' sweets for ye and don't be lettin' on yer've got 'em. Put 'em in yer pocket, luv.'

'Thank you, thank you very much.'

'That's all right. What's yer name then?'

'Ellen Adair.'

'And a right pretty name it is too. Is the girl downstairs yer sister?'

'No, just my friend.'

'I thowt as much. Different to ye she is, she'll give a good account of 'erself. But this life isn't for ye, luv.'

'Why do you say that?'

'Because yer gentle, luv, gentle and bonny, and if I were ye I'd be lookin' around for someat better ner this. 'Ave the lads bin all right wi' ye?'

'Oh yes they have, they've bin very kind.'

'Well most of 'em are. They're rough lads but they're not bad sorts. Watch out fer Black Jake, though. If yer 'as any trouble from 'im don't ask the Doyles for any 'elp, ye go right to the police, luv. They'll sort 'im out. The Doyles are as feared o' Jake as the rest of 'em.'

'What is he like, this Jake?'

''E's a big bullyin' oaf, 'andsome and loud-mouthed, and 'e fancies 'imself wi the lasses – or 'e's all talk. 'E thinks if 'e crooks 'is little finger they'll all come runnin', and if they don't 'e could be a nasty customer.'

'When is he likely to be back here?'

'Well he signed on a ship goin' to South America so it'll most likely be a good few months 'afore 'e's back 'ere i' Liverpool. Now I must be goin', mi ship's due out tonight.'

'Where are you off to then?'

'Spain's our first call, then through the Med and on to East Africa. It'll be a bit warmer than it is 'ere.'

'Oh how I wish I could travel and see all those wonderful places. I'll never save up enough money to sail on one of those big ships I've seen leaving the harbour.'

'Ye never know, luv, yer just might one day.'

I laughed. 'Never. I've just got to watch them and imagine I'm on board. I'm not as certain as Kitty.'

'Certain, is she?'

'Well, yes. One day she's going to sweep down one of those grand staircases in emeralds and ermine or her name's not Kitty McGuire.'

'And what about you, luv, what do you want?'

'I just want to get away from the smell of carbolic and scrubbing floors.'

He threw back his head and laughed. I heard him laughing all the way down the stairs.

In spite of the carbolic I was not unhappy in those first few months in Liverpool. The money Mrs Doyle paid us was small but we had our food, and large aprons to cover our clothes so that we could keep them decent. The food was filling if not imaginative, and occasionally I saw Kitty slip any leftovers into a basin which she took down to Aunt Mary's.

'Mrs Doyle'll only throw them away,' she said one day when she saw me watching her. 'Mi aunt's so grateful for anythin' I take her, and two of the children are ill with chickenpox.'

In the first few weekends we exhausted the museums and art galleries in the city, and we spent our few coppers riding on the overhead railway from one end of dockland to the other. We took long tramrides out of the city to Seaforth and Waterloo and looked in wide-eyed admiration at the large beautiful houses overlooking the sands and the sea.

'One day,' Kitty said firmly, 'I'm going to live here in a beautiful house set high on a hill overlooking the ocean.'

I didn't continue the conversation – how could I without asking how she was going to achieve such a wish? – and she too remained silent, no doubt asking herself the same question.

My happiest time was when we boarded the ferry which plied between Liverpool and New Brighton. On this tiny chugging vessel it was easy to imagine that we were at one with the big ships which steamed down the Mersey to the open sea, and from the promenade at New Brighton we watched with longing eyes as they disappeared below the horizon.

Only once did we go to the large shops in the city during that first year. The shops fascinated me, I loved the perfumed interiors, the clothes and the jewellery, the furs and the furniture, but Kitty looked at them with haunted longing eyes. Her fierce mercenary little heart resented the expensively dressed women who came to buy things at the glass counters watched over by supercilious assistants, or sat chatting happily over their cups in the luxurious warmth of the tea rooms and coffee lounges.

At one counter she picked up a bracelet which she draped over her wrist. It was not expensive, otherwise it would not have been left on the counter, but all the same the assistant looked at us doubtfully, and catching her eye Kitty hastily put it back on the counter and stalked away.

She didn't stop until she had reached the street and I had to run to keep her in sight. When I finally caught up with her I saw that there were tears of anger in her eyes which she hastily brushed away.

'Kitty, what is it?' I asked helplessly. 'Why are you crying?'

'I'm never coming into Liverpool to walk round the shops again, not until I can afford to show that stuck-up saleswoman that I can afford a better bracelet than that cheap thing she thought I was going to steal.'

'Oh Kitty, she didn't. I suppose they have to be careful.'

'Careful with the likes of us, ye mean?'

'No I don't. They have to be careful with everybody.'

'She wouldn't 'ave given me a second glance if I'd been dolled up in furs wi' rings on mi fingers. No, it's because I'm wearin' this old tweed coat and tam-o-shanter. She knew that I'm a skivvy o' some sort.'

'But it's nice in the shops, Kitty, and it's so lovely and warm on a winter's afternoon.'

'I don't mind if ye comes on yer own, Ellen, I'll find somethin' else to do. I don't mind a bit.'

'But I couldn't come on my own and leave you back at the mission.'

'Well if you want to come to the shops that's 'ow it's got to be, Ellen. I shall never come 'ere again until I 'ave good money in mi pocket and an idea on 'ow I want to spend it.'

Miserably I fell into step at her side, knowing that she meant every word. As we paused to cross the road a long black car, chauffeur driven, pulled in at the kerb. The chauffeur left the car and stood holding the door for his lady passenger. She was fashionably dressed, wearing a large blue hat decorated with feathers and a cape edged with dark fur. Without a look at the chauffeur or us she swept towards the shop door while the commissionaire hurried forward with bows and smiles.

Meeting Kitty's eyes, I found them filled with grim amusement.

'Don't tell me you want to look like her,' I said, smiling.

'Oh but I *do* tell ye, Ellen. One day I want to look just like 'er and arrive like she did in a posh car with a chap i' uniform drivin' mi. What sort o' fur do you think that was?'

'I haven't any idea, but I don't think it was ermine.'

'The only ermine I've ever seen was white, but mi dad said it was only white i' winter. Off a stoat it is and its fur turns white i' winter so it can't be seen agin' the snow. Ye know what I thinks, Ellen? I'll 'ave to settle for emeralds and ermine in the winter an' sapphires and sable in the summer.'

We dissolved into peals of laughter and were frowned upon by both the driver and the commissionaire, then we ran across the road hand in hand like naughty children.

'Little did they know we were laughin' at 'er,' Kitty said impishly.

'What do you suppose I'll be doin' while you're all dolled up in your sable coat shopping for jewels?' I asked her, smiling.

'It's up to you to be climbin' up there with mi, Ellen. I'll do what I can to 'elp ye but if you're not that confident ye can allus come to work for mi. A companion ye can be. Mi mother once worked for an old woman as 'ad a companion. Paid her no more than chicken feed she didn't and the woman was frightened to death of 'er, but I wouldn't be like that with you, Ellen, I'd treat ye like a sister and I'd give ye presents so that ye wouldn't be made to feel inferior.'

I never really knew if Kitty was serious in the things she said, she kept a straight face and spoke with great confidence. I rather think on that Saturday afternoon she would have been surprised if she could have read my thoughts. I was never going to be Kitty's paid companion, she wasn't the only one with a grain of independence. At that time I wanted something more attainable than furs and jewels: the love of a good man and a happy marriage. A nice home in which to bring up our children and enough money so that we didn't have to worry where the next meal was coming from.

Kitty made me smile with her ideas, but I said nothing to her. Dreams were all we had at that time. No words of mine were going to take Kitty's dreams away from her.

It was a night like no other I could ever remember. I had seen wild nights in the country, and deep snow in the early spring when the men had gone up on to the fells to save sheep trapped with their early lambs in the bitter cold, but now the wind moaned like a banshee, from late afternoon throughout the night.

We lay awake listening to the wild weather, and once Kitty got up to stare through the panes and announce that the street was covered with hail, great hailstones the size of marbles. Suddenly there was a great crash from above and we both looked up fearfully to see the ceiling had split from end to end, and a cascade of water gushed down on to the bed. That was the last sleep we had that night, and Mrs Doyle said we must make arrangements with Aunt Mary otherwise we'd have nowhere to stay.

The wind came straight off the sea and the dawn was grey and cold. The windows were covered with salt from the spray swept inland on the wind, and as we walked to Aunt Mary's all we could hear were children crying and chimney pots crashing on to slate roofs.

At Aunt Mary's the children huddled miserably round the breakfast table while smoke puffed back down the chimney, bringing soot that hurt our eyes and filled our throats.

'Is mi uncle still in bed then?' Kitty asked sharply.

'Nay, 'e's out wi' the rest o' the men, called out at three o'clock this mornin' they were and most of 'em needed at 'ome. Mrs Doherty's chimney stack's gone an' the laundry winder's shattered. There'll be no school this mornin' and I reckon yer'd best be seein' what else's 'appened at the mission.'

I had thought she would have objected to our asking for sanctuary with her but she said she would move two of the children out of the attic and we could have that. 'I'll be glad o' the money,' she confided.

The wind when we let ourselves out of the front door almost swept us off our feet but it seemed the mission had escaped other serious damage.

The Doyles were here, there and everywhere issuing orders, and we were told to get on with our work and mind our own business.

'As if we cared whether the roof's leakin' or not,' Kitty snapped, tossing her head.

'Well we do care, don't we?' I replied. 'The mission's our bread and butter.'

'I 'ates the place, it reeks of carbolic and stale cabbage. I 'ates the Doyles too, she's too 'igh and mighty and 'e can't keep 'is 'ands to 'imself.'

I stared at her in surprise. 'He's never once touched me,' I said. 'Has he touched you?'

''E'd very much like to, but just let 'im try it. I'd hit 'im on the 'ead with the frying pan I would.'

I dissolved into laughter and somewhat piqued she snapped, 'You can laugh, Ellen Adair, there'll come a day when ye looks more than fourteen.'

'I look more than fourteen now, I *am* more than fourteen,' I answered stoutly.

'Ye still looks a kid, Ellen. Look at yer figure, it's just straight up and down, there's not a curve into it.'

'Well what's wrong with that? Curves'll come sooner or later.'

She grinned at me and skipped lightly down the passage. It was true my body was maturing slowly, unlike Kitty who had developed a plump rounded bust and hips that curved from a tiny waist. On the landing I looked into a dark film-covered mirror, unhappy with my pale gold hair and dark blue eyes. Kitty was right. I had the face of a child, delicate and somehow fragile, and I wished fervently that I had some of her earthiness, some of her colour and vibrancy.

In the dormitories the windows still rattled in the wind

although it was not nearly as fierce as in the night. The rooms felt cold and there were no curtains to cover the cracks in the window frames and overall was the stench of men's sweat and the carbolic I was using to disguise it.

I worked hard all morning and I worked alone. There was no sign of Mrs Doyle until she came to say I could go down to the kitchen and eat.

'I've 'ad no time ter make a hot meal, yer'll 'ave ter make do wi' corned beef and muffins,' she said sharply. 'A cup o' tea'll warm ye up.'

I ate alone, and was washing the crockery when Kitty came rushing into the kitchen with bright spots of colour flaming in her cheeks. I stared in surprise as she ran to the mirror and started to straighten her hair. Then she spun round and said breathlessly, 'E's 'ere, Ellen. Trust 'im to arrive out o' the storm in a flash o' lightning and a crash o' thunder.'

'Who? Who's here?'

'Black Jake, that's who.'

'What's he like? Is he as bad as they say?'

''E's enormous.' She stretched up her arms to demonstrate his size. 'And 'e's got jet-black hair, a lot of it and a big bushy beard. You'll 'ave to watchout for 'im, Ellen. 'E picked mi up in 'is arms and I 'ad to batter 'im wi' mi fists 'til 'e let mi go. Aw sure but I'll be after 'ittin 'im wi somethin' stronger than mi fists if 'e gets in mi way again.'

Suddenly I found myself laughing uncontrollably and in some annoyance she snapped, 'I don't for the life in mi see what there is to laugh about.'

'Oh Kitty, I love it when the Irish comes into your voice. Why did you ever forsake it for the Yorkshire?'

'What good did the Irish ever do mi in that Yorkshire village? If ye didn't talk like they did they thought yer were foreigners. If I'd bin Chinese or some other heathen they couldn't 'a treated us much worse.'

'Well you're away from the village now, Kitty, ye can let the Irish come back and forget the Yorkshire.'

'I want to forget 'em both, I wants to talk like a lady and so I shall.'

Mrs Doyle marched into the kitchen, in a temper. 'Where's that idlin' 'usband o' mine?' she demanded. 'I've searched the buildin' for 'im but it's my guess 'e's off wi' that Jake down at the pub. It's allus the same when 'e comes back an' what's 'e done wi' all that booze 'e brought in? 'Idden it where I can't get at it, I'll be bound.'

We stared at her without speaking.

With her small black eyes snapping she said, 'Keep out o' Jake's way, you two, I wants no trouble fro' that direction and 'e's a rare one for a pretty face.'

'I don't see why,' Kitty said sharply. ''E's no great shakes te look at even if 'e does fancy 'isself.'

'So, 'e's already 'ad a go at you, 'as 'e? You just watch yer step, Kitty McGuire, it doesn't do to be too cocky wi' the likes o' Jake. An' you keep out of 'is way if ye can,' she ended, addressing me. 'Ye're just the sort o' girl 'e likes.'

She sat down and poured herself a cup of tea, then staring at us balefully she snapped, 'Ye can set about black leadin' the grate, an' there's the tables to set in the dinin' 'all. And mind mi words, keep away fro' Jake.'

We black leaded the kitchen grate and set the dining hall tables, then went in search of Mrs Doyle but met Mr Doyle in the passage. He informed us she'd gone to the shops.

He looked bleary eyed and smelled of beer. He was mighty affable, though, to the point of handing us three-pence each.

''Ere ye are then,' he said. 'Buy yerself someat wi' that, a don't suppose either of ye's got much to play wi'.'

We thanked him gratefully, but brushing our thanks aside he said briskly, 'Get oft 'ome then afore the missus comes back or she'll find ye someat else te do.'

'Won't she be wantin' us to wait on the table and clear away the dishes?' Kitty inquired.

'Nay, Mrs Slatterly's comin' in and bringin' 'er two grand-daughters. There's no way Jake's goin' ter be lookin' at either of 'em. Squints they do, and wi' teeth like a buck rabbit.'

We giggled appreciatively at his attempt at wit even if it

was unkind, and giving me a little push Kitty said, 'Come on then, let's get goin' 'afore she comes back.'

The wind had subsided during the day but it still met us with some force. The corner shop had been boarded up, as was the front window of the Chinese laundry, and a group of children played on the doorstep in spite of the biting cold.

There were ten children living at the laundry, the eldest one, Lo Ying, almost as tall as her diminutive mother. They had shining black straight hair and eyes – strangely slanting to us – like bright black buttons. They were polite, and unlike the English and Irish children in the area seldom got into mischief. Their mother had them well regimented, and to call them in from play she stood outside the laundry with a brass gong which could be heard streets away and which they obeyed implicitly. It amused me to see them drop whatever they were doing to go tearing down the street in answer to the sound of that gong.

'Now what's up?' Kitty said sharply, and I saw that the women in the street were standing in groups or on their doorsteps eyeing a large black car standing at Mrs Wallsingham's front door. Cars in the area were few and far between, which made this one something of a curiosity.

'I'll bet it's Emmie Wallsingham visitin' from the city,' Kitty cried.

'Or somebody's dead,' I echoed.

'It isn't a hearse,' Kitty snapped, 'nobody'd ever 'ave a car for a funeral. It's more likely to be Emmie.'

We had both heard something of the misdoings of Emmie Wallsingham from Aunt Mary.

The black car was rakish and the length of the house. It had a long shiny bonnet and one little boy, more intrepid than the others, had opened the front door and was looking inside. Catching him by the hem of his coat I pulled him out and closed the door.

'Don't you be caught looking in there, Johnny Grimshaw, the owner'll have the police on you.'

He grinned at me cheekily. 'What's it ter yer?' he asked

pertly, and ran round the other side and tried to open the driver's door.

At that moment Mrs Wallsingham appeared at the front door and, arms akimbo, ordered the children away, then turning to the street at large she said, 'I 'opes yer've seen enough, a mother can't 'ave 'er own daughter visit 'er wi'out yer lot gawpin'.'

She went in, slamming the front door, but the women only laughed loudly without moving away.

'Come on in,' Aunt Mary said to us. 'I wants no truck wi' Elsie Wallsingham. She's a wicked tongue in 'er 'ead and a temper to go wi' it. 'Ow is it yer 'ome so soon? Not got the sack, I 'ope.'

'Mr Doyle told us we could get off home and he gave us threepence each,' I said.

When we got in the house Kitty snapped, 'What did yer tell her that for? She'll expect us to treat the kids.'

'I don't mind treating them.'

'Well I do. It's not often we get a bit extra and yer too soft, Ellen, it'll be the downfall of ye.'

Over boiled potatoes and mutton in a weak gravy Aunt Mary elaborated on the shortcomings of Emmie Wallsingham.

'Left 'ome at fifteen she did and never a word 'til she suddenly turned up again when she were nineteen, all done up i' flashy fancy clothes and a face so painted ye could 'a scraped it off. That time she turned up on 'er own, this time she's gotten a fella wi' er.'

'What sort of a fella?' Kitty wanted to know.

'Dark-skinned 'e is, but wi' plenty o' money if the car's owt ter go by.'

'What's she like?' Kitty asked curiously.

'She's pretty, a suppose, and she allus were a pert little madam.'

'Is 'e her 'usband de ye think, Aunt Mary?'

'Not 'im, 'e'll be one of 'er fancy men. I wish a didn't 'ave ter go out, I'd like to 'ave seen 'er when they comes out.'

'Perhaps they're not goin' out.'

'They will be, they'll not be sittin' in there all night. Will one of ye see to the children, put 'em to bed and clean 'em up a bit? I 'ave to go over to Sefton wi' Mrs 'Aslam's dress, I'll want ter see if it fits 'er properly.'

We said we'd see to the children and she left us to clear away the dishes. Actually I was the one who saw to the children because Kitty couldn't keep away from the front door or window and insisted on giving me a commentary on what was happening every five minutes.

It was quite dark now but still front doors were constantly being opened and women were toing and froing as though bent on some errand or other. From the window I saw Kitty talking to a woman from across the street, and felt strangely annoyed. In all my life I had never encountered such a degree of curiosity and there had been enough of it about in the village where Phoebe Patterson had been concerned.

I went back and started to darn the children's clothes. I had always been good with my fingers and my stitches were as neat if not neater than Aunt Mary's. Then Kitty came rushing back. Sinking on to the rug in front of the fire she said excitedly, 'Why didn't ye come out, Ellen? Ye should 'a seen 'er. She looked loverly she did, all i' pink with a feather 'at and a fur tippet. She looked straight at mi and smiled, then she said someat ter 'im and 'e smiled too. Sometimes I just don't understand ye at all, Ellen Adair, fancy sittin' in 'ere when ye could 'a seen Emmie Wallsingham.'

'Why should I want to see her? She isn't famous,' I snapped.

Kitty stared at me because I didn't often snap at her.

'Well she's better and prettier than anythin' else we're likely te see round 'ere. 'E can't be 'er usband, 'e's dark and foreign lookin' wi' a lot o' gold teeth. She wouldn't marry anybody like that, I'm sure.'

I looked at her face, strangely pensive in the glow from the fire. It was an expression I constantly surprised on her face these days, sad and yearning. Next moment however she was heaping coal on to the fire until I remonstrated at her extravagance.

'Your aunt said the coal had to last all night, Kitty, or at least 'til your uncle gets home.'

'I'm sick of sittin' shiverin', mi aunt's out so it's the one chance we 'ave of bein' warm for a change. Where do ye suppose Emmie Wallsingham gets such lovely clothes from, Ellen? After all she were bred and brought up round 'ere, and if she can do it we can.'

'How?'

'I don't know but I'll find out. She's no prettier than we are and she's not as ladylike as you, Ellen, but I reckon she must 'ave some ambition. I've got enough ambition for the pair of us, Ellen. You mark my words, in less than two years it'll be yer and me drivin' up to the front door in a car bigger than that.'

'Oh Kitty, you'd be a lot happier if you didn't always want what you haven't got.'

'I'll never be 'appy 'til I've got what I want. If Emmie Wallsingham's 'ere over the next few days I'm goin' to talk to 'er.

'What are you doin wi' that threepence Joe Doyle gave ye? If ye like I'll nip down to the off-licence and get pop and chocolate, and if yer've got a conscience about it ye can save some for the kids tomorrow.'

I handed over my threepence without a word and the next thing I heard was the slamming of the front door.

CHAPTER 8

I heard a great deal about Black Jake during the next few days but I didn't see him. I heard talk among the men that he had been thrown off his last ship for some misdemeanour and was looking for a new ship in the docks that stretched from one end of Liverpool to the other.

In the mission itself there was a tangible change in the atmosphere. Where once there had been rough camaraderie now there was sullen suspicion and among some of the men seething resentment because they believed Jake was getting better rations.

There was an ugly scene one morning when one of the men hit Mr Doyle, blacking his eye and breaking several front teeth. Kitty said the seaman had accused him of taking bribes from Jake – bottles of rum and gin he'd brought off his last ship – and that the other men were suffering because Jake was getting what they should have. Several days later the seaman's body was found floating in one of the docks and although the police said he'd probably fallen in drunk, nobody among the men believed them for a moment.

I was far from happy at the mission because I was afraid, but I was troubled too about Kitty. I seldom saw her in the evenings. Once we had sat before the fire, tired after our work at the mission, but not too tired to chat happily about the happenings of the day or what we would do on our day off.

Now, as soon as she had swallowed her evening meal she was away to Mrs Wallsingham's, much to Aunt Mary's annoyance as well as mine.

Emmie Wallsingham had become Kitty's idol. We heard nothing but praise of her clothes, her hair and her travels. Once or twice I had seen the man she had arrived with. He was short, slight and swarthy, his clothes were good if flashy, and he wore rings and a thick gold watch chain.

Once when Kitty went on too long about Emmie her aunt flashed, 'I don't know what's come o'er you, Kitty. Can't yer see that nature never made 'er 'air that colour? Out of a bottle it is. Nobody ever 'ad 'air the colour of an orange, Emmie Wallsingham's 'air was mousy, just like the rest of them. Yer own 'air's a lot nicer, lovely shade o' red it is, and look at Ellen's 'ere. Emmie Wallsingham'd give 'er eye teeth for 'air that colour.'

'Well I think she's lovely. She's kind too, she gave me some silk stockings last night. They have a little ladder at the top but I can soon darn that.'

'What else did she give ye?'

'A blouse she's grown tired of. I'm savin' it for summer.'

'Who's the chap she brought 'ome wi' 'er?'

''E's not 'er 'usband, not even 'er boyfriend. She sez 'e's some sort o' boss.'

'Ay and we know what sort o' boss 'e is, don't we?'

'What sort o' boss is 'e then?'

'If ye don't know I'm not up to tellin' ye. Now 'elp Ellen clear away the dishes while I get on wi' mi sewin'. Yer've not bin pullin' yer weight around 'ere, Kitty, it's about time yer did or find fresh lodgings.'

Kitty stared at her balefully but started to remove the dishes, slamming them down on the kitchen table so hard I was afraid they would break. Aunt Mary called out, 'Don't you be takin' yer bad temper out on the dishes, yer little madam, if ye breaks just one of 'em I'll 'ave the money off ye for more.'

I looked cautiously at Kitty's mutinous face but said nothing. This was not the Kitty I had known before we came to Liverpool, the Kitty who had been cheerful in spite of all her troubles, free with her laughter and her ready Irish wit.

On the way to the mission she grumbled constantly about the Doyles, Aunt Mary and her husband, even the children, and more and more I felt frighteningly insecure.

As we donned our aprons Mrs Doyle came out of her kitchen to say, 'We've another load in this mornin' so the place is crowded. Get on with yer work, the pair of ye. The

Slatterlys are comin' in at ten o'clock, we'll need all the 'elp we can get.'

Kitty bustled into the dining hall while I ran upstairs to the dormitories where some of the new men were only just unpacking. Normally they stayed only two or three nights, but if they were changing ships they sometimes had several weeks' wait until they were sent for.

I was glad to see that the seaman who had warned me about Big Jake was back, and catching sight of me he called out, 'Ello there, Little Un. Come over 'ere, I've got someat for ye.'

Shyly I went across to stand uncertainly at his bedside while he rummaged in his pockets.

''Ere's a bar o' chocklit for ye, luv. Don't let old Ma Doyle see it or she'll 'ave it off ye i' no time.'

I thanked him gratefully and pushed the chocolate into my pocket.

'Everthin' bin all right then?' he asked, looking down at me.

'Yes thank you. Big Jake's here but I haven't seen him.'

His face grew sober. 'Keep out of 'is way, luv, don't ye be askin' fer trouble. De ye hear that, lads? Jake's 'ere so mind what yer doin'.'

The Slatterlys duly arrived and I couldn't help thinking that Mr Doyle had spoken nothing but the truth about the two granddaughters. They worked alongside of me when they weren't squabbling, but Mrs Slatterly disappeared into the kitchen where like as not she sat with Mrs Doyle, drinking tea.

They departed immediately after we had eaten and Mrs Doyle said, 'It was 'ardly worth 'em comin' for the work they did.'

'The girls were all right,' I said somewhat resentfully.

'Yer'd get more work out o' the old biddy if yer didn't sit listening to 'er gossipin' in the kitchen,' Mr Doyle said sourly, whereupon his wife immediately snapped back, 'And I'd get more work out o' you if ye didn't go out every night with that Jake. I thought 'e was after findin' a ship, though like as not nobody'll employ 'im since 'e's 'ad trouble on every ship 'e's sailed in. That temper of 'is'll be the end of 'im, mark my words.'

''E'll find one. In the meantime 'e's enough money ter sit back a bit and take a good look around.'

'I don't mind 'im lookin' around, as long as 'e doesn't expect mi 'usband ter look round with 'im. All last Friday yer were supposed ter be lookin' fer a ship and both of yer comin' 'ome long after midnight drunk as lords. I'll be glad when 'e goes and I don't want 'im back 'ere. There's other ports besides Liverpool.'

'Not when yer were born and bred 'ere there isn't. Jake's father and grandfather were dockers right there i' Birkenhead, 'e's a right ter try ter look for a ship leavin' Liverpool.'

'Ay well, the sooner the better.'

Some of the seamen slept until well into the afternoon and without the help of the Slatterly girls I had to change the beds and clean up the dormitory on my own while Kitty was helping to serve dinner. I was bent over one of the narrow beds when I was seized in a grip of iron and lifted clean off my feet, then I heard a man's great booming laughter before he threw me down on to the bed.

He towered over me, this great man with black curly hair and swarthy face, and he was laughing so that his breath sickened me with its overtones of tobacco and beer.

'Well what 'ave we 'ere?' he said. 'I've met the young spitfire downstairs, but they didn't tell me there was another. What's yer name then?'

'Ellen, Ellen Adair.'

'Well, Ellen, I'm Jake, Black Jake they calls me on account of mi black hair among other things. Did they tell ye about me?'

'A little about you, Mr Jake.'

He threw back his head and laughed again. 'Mr Jake, is it? Nay, call mi Jake, I likes all pretty girls to call mi Jake.'

By this time he had settled himself down beside me on the bed and I moved quickly towards the other side. I prayed for somebody to come into the room but all the activity was downstairs. I could even hear Mrs Doyle's voice from the kitchen and the sound of crockery. Something of my hopes must have got through to him because next moment he stroked my hair, saying, 'We're all alone up 'ere, Ellen, jest yer and me, and nobody's goin te come up 'ere 'til the meal's finished. Tell mi about yerself.'

'There's not much to tell.'

'No? What's a girl like yer doin' in a place like this, 'ave yer no folks?'

'Yes, but not in Liverpool.'

'Is that so. Related to the Doyles are ye?'

'No. I came here with Kitty, her aunt lives along the street there.'

''Ave yer got a boyfriend?'

'No.'

'That's good then. 'Ow about me for yer boyfriend?'

I didn't speak, and he laughed. His big hairy hand was on my hair, pulling it and teasing it, then before I could pull away his arms were round me and his mouth was bruising my lips. I felt his hands on my body, lifting my skirts, sliding up my legs, and I fought him with my fists until I felt they would break against the weight of his chest.

I felt nauseated by his breath, his thick lips on mine, the coarseness of his hands and his loud heavvy breathing, and then suddenly, miraculously his arms grew slack and next moment he had sprung to his feet. He was moaning, his hands covering his hair, and there was blood sliding stickily down his face.

Even as he tried to wipe it away with his sleeve Kitty hit him again with the frying pan she held in both hands, and then together we escaped out of the room and down the stairs with Big Jake lumbering behind us, bellowing like a bull so that doors were opening everywhere and fearful faces stared out from the dining hall and the Doyles' kitchen.

Mrs Doyle pushed us both into the kitchen, then stood in the doorway, arms akimbo.

'Stay out o' mi kitchen, Jake. Yer've no doubt asked for what ye've got and yer in enough trouble wi' the police without lookin' fer more.'

'If I gets mi 'ands on that little 'ell cat I'll kill 'er, I will,' he stormed, 'and the other one asked fer all she got.'

'If yer causes any trouble 'ere I'll 'ave ye barred fro' the mission,' she went on stoutly. At that moment she had all my admiration while her husband skulked at the back of the kitchen and the seamen shuffled their feet in embarrassed and cowardly silence in the passage.

'And what will yer do to them two? Look at mi 'ead, pourin' wi' blood it is. Is that little hell cat te get off scot free then?'

'That's my business. Yer'd best get that 'ead stitched. The lasses won't be 'ere when yer gets back.'

'I'll stop right 'ere te see what ye're goin' ter do with 'em.'

'Yer'll go to the 'ospital and mi 'usband'll go with yer. Like I said, the lasses'll be gone when yer gets back.'

'I suppose that means yer won't punish either of 'em.'

'They'll lose their jobs. Is that what yer wants?'

I stared at Kitty in horror. Her face was pale but her hand still clutched the frying pan she had battered Jake with, and if the moment had not been filled with such trauma I might have found her stance amusing.

'Now get off to the 'ospital,' Mrs Doyle insisted. 'Get yer coat on, Joe, and go wi' 'im. And you two get yer things together and I'll give ye what I owes ye. I don't want to see either of ye again. I knew there'd be trouble when I took ye both in.'

Kitty collected her things with her head held high, but I was tearful. It was my fault that we had lost our jobs, my fault for being here. None of it would have happened if I hadn't insisted on coming to Liverpool in the first place, and now Kitty was being made to pay for it.

As Mrs Doyle handed over our money she fixed me with a stern look, asking, 'Did yer ask fer it, Ellen, or was it all 'im?'

'I was making the beds, Mrs Doyle, I didn't even see him come into the dormitory.'

'Well I believes yer but I daren't keep yer on 'ere. Jake's a vindictive devil as any one o' them men can tell ye. Yer'd best get off 'ome now afore 'e comes back.'

We left the kitchen and made our way to the front door.

Some of the men stood in the passage eyeing us sympathetically, and sweets and chocolates were pressed into our hands. One of them gave me a small book, saying, 'I've no chocolate for ye, lass, but ye might like to 'ave this. Do ye like poetry?'

I stared at him stupidly. I had never associated any of these men with a liking for poetry but this man's face was kind, refined and intelligent.

'I liked it at school. Thank you very much, I shall enjoy reading it.'

I stared at the well-worn leather-bound book and saw that it was the *Rubaiyat* of Omar Khayyám. I had never heard of it, but somehow it seemed precious on that terrible day and as we walked dolefully along the street Kitty said, 'What did that seaman give ye? It wasn't chocolate?'

I handed the little book over and she stared at it curiously, then scornfully. 'What's a sailor doin' readin' poetry? A proper man wouldn't be interested in such rubbish.'

'Oh Kitty, it doesn't say because he's a seaman he hasn't got a soul.'

'Well soul or no soul 'ere we are without a job. I don't know what mi Aunt Mary's goin' to say, she can't keep both of us and no money comin' in.'

'But we'll find other work, Kitty. I don't care what I do, I'll start looking first thing in the morning.'

Aunt Mary received our news with dismay. It was a miserable evening. Two of the children were sickly and cried constantly, and on top of that Aunt Mary and her husband were quarrelling most of the night.

Kitty hissed, 'They're quarrelling about us. 'E wants us out of 'ere in the morning, and she's askin' 'im to be patient.'

'But we've nowhere to go, Kitty.'

'Ye could go 'ome, Ellen, ask yer father's forgiveness. 'E'll make yer suffer but 'e'll take ye back.'

'Kitty, I couldn't go back, I'd die before I'd go back.

'What are ye goin' to do then?'

'I'm goin' to find work.'

''Ow about yer Aunt Liza?'

'No, Kitty, I couldn't go to live with her. Besides, she wouldn't have me.'

'Why not?'

'She'll know I've run away from home, she'd send me back there if she knew where to find me.'

'Where does she live then?'

'In Langstone. It's a little village up in the Dales, she keeps a draper's shop in the high street.'

'Did ye say she was yer father's half-sister?'

'Yes.'

'She's called Adair like you then?

'No, she's called Ashington, mi grandmother married twice.'

'If I had anybody to go to I'd get out o' Liverpool, I hates it 'ere, I 'ates the sea and the mournful sound of them 'ooters. I 'ates these mean streets and there's no greenery, it's like livin' in a quarry.'

She turned over crossly without saying another word and the house was silent. Tomorrow would be different, tomorrow was the start of a whole new life. I told myself I was glad to have left the mission and the smell of carbolic and cabbage, and with the optimism of youth I reassured myself that when one door closed another opened. When I said as much to a disgruntled Kitty she merely answered sourly, 'Ye means when one door closes another slams shut.'

CHAPTER 9

The next morning started badly. Two of the children were taken to hospital with scarlet fever and Aunt Mary was distraught, saying, 'I'll never get them two dresses finished now, there's buttonholes to make and buttons to be sewn on. If I don't get 'em finished in time they'll never bring me anythin' else te make.'

'I can do them for you,' I cried quickly. 'Just show me what you want and I'll have them finished when you get back.'

'Are ye sure ye can do 'em, Ellen?'

'She can do 'em as well as you can,' Kitty retorted. 'She allus took the prize for sewin' back at the school.'

Quickly Aunt Mary showed me what was required and I set to with a will, glad to be of some use.

'Ye can try the raincoat factory at the end of the street,' Aunt Mary told Kitty. 'I 'ear they've bin lookin' for machinists.'

'I can't use a machine,' Kitty said.

'Well yer not too daft to learn, Kitty, and ye'll 'ave to find work o' some sort or go back to yer mother.'

'I'd rather go into service than work in a factory,' Kitty retorted.

'I don't care what ye does as long as ye finds work,' Aunt Mary answered wearily.

When she had cleared away and washed the dishes Kitty returned to where I was busy stitching minute buttons down the back of a dress. For a while she stood watching me then she picked up the book of poems the seaman had given me and started to turn the pages.

'I don't understand a word of it,' she said. 'It's not poetry like I've ever read. Who was 'e anyway?'

'I think he was Persian so it's bound to be different.'

'I agree with one thing 'e sez, though, time is slippin'

underneath our feet and we're worse off now than when we came 'ere. I'm going down to the Wallsinghams', perhaps Emmie can suggest somethin' for mi to do.'

Whatever suggestions Emmie Wallsingham had to make, three days later Kitty found work at the raincoat factory packing the finished garments. She hated every moment of it. The concrete floors that were so cold to her feet that she got chilblains, the small draughty windows, her work-mates who were foul-mouthed and vociferous. She hated the men who did the fetching and carrying because they thought she was fair game for their attentions, and she loathed the forewoman who was married to one of them and accused Kitty of encouraging him.

'What would a want with a fella like that?' Kitty stormed. ''E's old enough to be mi father and 'e's no great shakes to look at.'

Perhaps I was fortunate because Aunt Mary was tied down with hospital visiting and caring for the children at home so that I was kept busy with her dressmaking.

More and more I was aware of Kitty's resentment, and one night she said sullenly, 'It's all right for ye, Ellen, ye don't 'ave to turn out on a cold mornin', 'ere ye are with a nice fire doin' the thing ye likes doin!'

'Oh Kitty, sewing buttons on other people's dresses isn't what I came to Liverpool for, but if I don't help Aunt Mary she'll lose the business, and she needs the money.'

She stared at me miserably, then something of the old Kitty reasserted itself.

'I'm sorry, Ellen, none of it's yer fault and I'm a little monster. It's just that I'm not happy workin' at that factory and I don't see any end to it. Mi aunt won't want yer 'elp for ever, so what will ye do then?'

'I don't know. I'll start looking the first opportunity I get. Did Emmie Wallsingham have anything to suggest?'

'No.'

Her reply was short and snappy, and almost immediately she flounced out of the room, saying she was going to buy sweets to take to the children. I was in bed when she returned so I knew she must have called somewhere else besides the shop, and I suspected she had been with Emmie Wallsingham.

The best part of helping Aunt Mary was delivering the dresses. In this way I got to see different parts of Liverpool and how other people lived in the city. Best of all I liked going to Mrs Lister's at Sefton. Her husband was a civil servant and they lived in a nice rather large terraced house with a big garden at the back and a smaller one at the front.

Mrs Lister was a pleasant lady who always invited me in and gave me a cup of tea while she tried on her dress. Once when it didn't fit too well she asked me to stay and alter it, and when she was satisfied with it she said, 'Why don't you take in sewing yourself, Ellen? You sew beautifully and I could find you work.'

'I couldn't do that, Mrs Lister, it would take work away from Aunt Mary and she's been very kind to me.'

'You've had that coat a long time, Ellen, it's getting very worn and it's too short for you. You've grown these last few weeks. I've got one upstairs you can have. I'll bring it down, if it's too big I know you'll be able to alter it.'

The coat was a lovely light navy velour and I only needed to alter the buttons for it to fit me. She also produced a navy skirt and two silk blouses, one in pink, the other white. I was overwhelmed by her kindness and thanked her profusely.

She merely said, 'I'm glad they fit you, Ellen, but don't you be giving them away merely because you're being given a home. These are yours, you must wear them.'

'Oh I will, Mrs Lister, I will really. I'm so glad to have them.'

'Well get off home then before it gets dark.'

I felt troubled about the clothes. Aunt Mary would think it unfair that I should have them when she'd been sewing for Mrs Lister much longer, and Kitty – well, I was never very sure about Kitty these days.

When I walked in with my parcel Aunt Mary said plaintively, 'Don't tell me they don't fit?'

'It's a coat and skirt Mrs Lister's given me, Aunt Mary.'

'They'd a cost a bonny penny in the shops,' she commented when I'd opened the parcel. 'Did she say *ye* 'ad to 'ave em?'

'Yes she did.'

'Oh well, ye 'ave bin a lucky girl, and me sewing for 'er all these years.'

All joy in my new clothes seemed suddenly to evaporate. I felt I had no right to them, and seeing my doleful face Aunt Mary said, 'Yer'd best wear 'em, Ellen, I wouldn't like Mrs Lister to think I'd 'ad any hand in yer not wearing 'em.'

'Perhaps Kitty would like one of the blouses.'

Both the blouses were tight on Kitty, but she said philosophically, 'I'd rather 'ave a shape than 'ave a blouse. 'Ow much is Aunt Mary givin' ye for 'elpin' out with 'er sewin'?'

'I told her I didn't want any money, she's feeding me.'

'She's got a nerve, a few bob a week wouldn't kill 'er.'

I can only assume that Kitty said something to her aunt because at the weekend Aunt Mary placed two shillings in my hand, saying, 'This is a bit towards what yer've done for mi, Ellen. I couldn't 'ave managed without ye.'

CHAPTER 10

Spring came to the city. In the parks snowdrops and crocus carpeted the lawns and daffodils swayed beside the paths. People's footsteps seemed lighter, and faces that had been grey and weary now bore smiles. The shop windows were gayer, with light-coloured clothing and spring millinery.

The children were now on their way to recovery except for the youngest who had a permanent cough and looked destined to be the weakling of the family. Aunt Mary returned to her sewing machine for what she called the heavy work, while she passed less and less work over to me. The week before Easter I got a job as a machinist at the raincoat factory.

My day began at seven and ended at seven. It was slave labour, a veritable sweat shop. Morning and afternoon we stopped the machines for five minutes so that we could have a cup of tea, then it was back to the machines where we were overlooked by an enormous woman called Mrs Edge, and woe betide any of us if we spoke to our neighbour.

I saw nothing of Kitty at the factory, and not very much of her at home. In the evenings we were both weary but it didn't stop her from spending time with Emmie Wallsingham. At the weekends I put on my best coat and went to the shops but I was always alone. Kitty had kept her word, she would not visit the shops until she could buy the best they had to offer, so I pretended to myself that I was in that fortunate position.

I drank coffee in the coffee lounges and smiled at the waitresses. I knew I looked presentable in the coat Mrs Lister had given me, and I had a little money in my pocket. The raincoat factory paid poor wages and after I had given some to Aunt Mary for my keep and treated the children to sweets there wasn't much left – enough to buy the occasional pair of stockings, and put by a little for the bigger things.

Sundays I loved. The ferries were cheap and I sailed upriver or out to New Brighton and Wallasey. I pretended that I was on a great ocean liner and for hours I would sit nostalgically staring out at the great ships sailing to romantic places. I hadn't Kitty's yearning for jewels and furs, but I had a desperate longing to travel, to sail one day on one of those ocean liners.

I didn't want to spend all my young life living at Aunt Mary's. I loved the children but I had no privacy, they were always in my things or leaping on my bed, and at times their squabbles were deafening.

I didn't enjoy seeing Aunt Mary toiling night and day at her sewing machine and cooking meals that were served up cold because her husband was late home from the public house. And I didn't like the way he looked at me.

At long last I was developing a shape. I was taller than Kitty and more slender, and had a sort of grace, Aunt Mary said, that Kitty would never have. But I didn't have her vibrant colouring, my hair was still that fine pale gold it had been in childhood.

I would often find the uncle watching me covertly across the table, and he never lost an opportunity of brushing against me while I was washing the dishes.

Kitty warned, ''E fancies ye, Ellen, yer'd better watch out.'

But it was Kitty herself who troubled me most. All the time now I was feeling her resentment, and the times became fewer when we laughed together with our old comradeship. Her hatred of her job, her home, her workmates and the city itself made her taciturn and rebellious, and only Emmie Wallsingham had the power to bring laughter to her lips and enthusiasm into her heart.

'When is Emmie leaving?' I once asked her.

'Soon,' Kitty replied, 'she's waitin' fer Alex to come back from the city te tell 'er it's all right for 'er to go back there.'

'Why does she have to wait for him, why can't she just go there?'

'I don't know. There was some trouble but what sort o' trouble she didn't say. Ellen, will ye not ask mi anythin' about Emmie when mi aunt's there? She 'asn't a good word to say fer Emmie and a can't see why. Emmie's done nothing to 'er.'

'Perhaps your aunt knows something you don't.'

'Not she. She's jealous because Emmie's well dressed, wi' money in 'er purse.'

'Is Alex the man she came here with, the man with the car?'

'That's right. Any day now 'e'll be back, 'e writes to 'er often.'

Alex appeared several days later, and there were many times I saw Kitty chatting to him on the street, sometimes with Emmie, at others just the two of them. He seemed to be doing most of the talking in a serious persuasive way and Kitty was listening to him, almost as if her life depended on it.

One night as we lay in bed she said, 'What would ye do, Ellen, if I leaves here, would ye stay on 'ere at mi aunt's?'

'I don't know, Kitty. You're not thinking of leaving, are you?'

'Oh well, there's nothin' planned, but ye knows 'ow I 'ates that factory and livin' 'ere.'

'You could get another job you liked better, and one day, Kitty, we might be able to afford a little house of our own.'

'And pigs might fly, Ellen.'

'I don't see why not. We're both earnin' money, all the houses are not expensive.'

'I've had mi fill o' livin' in a rubbish 'eap. Ellen, I just don't want ye to think we'll be spendin' the rest of our lives together.'

'I don't think that either. One of these days I hope we'll both get married and live in nice homes. Isn't that what you want?'

'Right now, Ellen, I'm only concerned with me. If a man turns up fer me and I fancies 'im, well and good, but I'm not sittin' 'ere waitin' for it to 'appen. If I makes mi own life, Ellen, ye won't 'old it against mi, will yer?'

'No, Kitty, I won't.'

'And yer'll be able to look after yerself?'

'Of course. Why don't you tell me what you have in mind instead of asking me questions like that?'

'Because I'm not sure. It all needs thinkin' about.'

'Do Emmie Wallsingham and that man have anything to do with it?'

'Why should they 'ave? And there's no call to be looking down your nose at Emmie, Ellen, she's a good friend with 'er 'ead screwed on right.'

'I wasn't looking down my nose at her, Kitty, honestly.'

'Oh well, I don't want to talk about it any more now and don't be talking about any of this in front of mi aunt. It's time for 'er to know when I've made mi mind up.'

Kitty was asleep long before me. I lay staring up at the ceiling with my thoughts miserably uncertain. Rain pattered on the window and occasionally above the wind came the long mournful hooting of a steamer and the sound of a train speeding through the night.

Two weeks after my conversation with Kitty it seemed my whole life was to change.

I believed that every moment of that Wednesday morning would be implanted in my memory for evermore. The day started as it always did with a rushed breakfast of tea and toast, then the short walk through streets only just coming to life.

I parted from Kitty at the entrance to the machine room, calling out, 'Shall I see you for dinner?' to which she replied, 'I'm not sure, better not wait fer mi in case I shan't be able to get 'ome.'

We sat in rows at our machines and the noise was deafening. Now and again Mrs Edge walked along the aisles picking up a raincoat here and a raincoat there, looking closely at the stitches and the hems, but fortunately she had little to complain about where my sewing was concerned.

I was astonished therefore when she came to my machine about eleven o'clock that morning, indicating that I should stop. Those about me also stopped until she snapped, 'That doesn't go fer the rest of ye, get on wi' yer work.'

'Yer wanted at 'ome Ellen, Mrs McLoughlin's sent one o' the children ter say ye 'ave a visitor. But I wants ye back 'ere as soon as yer've eaten yer dinner. There'll be two 'ours docked off yer wages.'

'Did she say who my visitor was, Mrs Edge?' I stammered unhappily.

'It's none o' my business. Just ye get off now.'

I grabbed my coat off the peg and flew through the packing room. Kitty's eyes met mine briefly but I couldn't talk to her because the forewoman was nearby. Kitty's face was strangely anxious, and before I turned away it had become bright scarlet. That Kitty knew more than I did was very obvious.

I ran all the way home and at the door Jonny, who was off school with whooping cough, said, 'There's somebody ter see ye Ellen, a lady.'

I stared at him in surprise, I had been so sure it would be my father.

'What is she like?'

'Old. She's old.'

All sorts of visions passed before my eyes. It couldn't be my mother, because even if she knew where I was Father wouldn't allow her to come – not unless he was dead, that is.

My heart leapt at that prospect but then the door opened and Aunt Mary said sharply, 'There ye are, Ellen. Here's yer aunt, all the way fro' Yorkshire. Bin travellin' since first light, she 'as.'

I stared at her in amazement, then she shooed me into the living room.

My first thought was that Aunt Liza sat in the rocking chair like a black crow in her long black skirt and coat, with a big black hat on her hair and clutching a large Gladstone bag. Our eyes met and my heart sank for there was no pleasure in the gaze she bestowed upon me, not a glimmer of a smile on her thin lips. Before I could say a word she snapped, 'Well, Ellen, and what 'ave you to say for yerself?'

'How did you know I was here, Aunt Liza?'

'That girl wrote to me, Kitty McGuire. She said if I was interested in your welfare I should get in touch with ye, that there was nothing here in Liverpool for ye.'

Weakly I sat down, not knowing which caused me most anxiety – the arrival of Aunt Liza or Kitty's perfidy.

From the kitchen I could hear Aunty Mary busying herself with crockery, then she came into the room carrying a tea tray.

'I expect yer'd like someat ter eat?' she said. 'I can send Jonny te the shop for barm cakes and cornbeef.'

'No thanks, I want to get back as soon as possible. There's a train to Leeds at two thirty that'll just catch the country train for Langstone. Go upstairs and get yer bags packed, Ellen, I'll settle up wi' Mrs McLoughlin for anythin' ye might owe her.'

'Ye don't owe mi anythin', Ma'am,' Aunty Mary said, 'Ellen's allus bin good both wi' me and the children. I'm sorry she's goin'. Does she 'ave te go?'

'Yer niece wouldn't 'ave written fer nothin', Mrs McLoughlin.'

I remembered all Kitty's questions about Aunt Liza, and felt close to tears when I realized how long she had been planning the events of this morning.

In some anger I said, 'I'm not goin' back to my father's house, Aunt Liza, I'd die before I'd go back there.'

'It's a wicked girl you are, Ellen Adair, to talk about yer father like that.' Then turning to Aunt Mary she said, 'Mi brother's an upright God-fearin' man. Sexton at the church he is and well respected by the vicar and the rest o' the community. He's always bin a good provider, his wife and children have lacked for nothin' and she's bin brought up in a good Christian home. A right nice house it is with a big garden an' every comfort. How any niece o' mine could'ave turned out like Ellen here I'll never know, but for your information, Ellen, yer father doesn't want ye back. He sez yer've made yer bed and ye must lie on it. All the same it's mi Christian duty to take ye in and bring ye up proper if it's the last thing I do.

'But I am brought up, Aunt Liza, I'm sixteen next birthday. I'm no longer a child and I can earn my own living.'

'This good woman's given ye a home because of 'er niece but you're not 'er responsibility. It looks to me as how she's enough to do with her own husband and children, as well as her niece. Why, there's hardly room to swing a cat around and there'll be some sighs of relief when yer've gone, I feels sure.'

'But I don't want to live in Yorkshire, I love Liverpool. I love the sea and boats. What will I ever do back in the Dales?'

'You can 'elp me in the shop, do the shoppin' and help mi to clean the house. By doin' all that one day yer'll make a decent wife for some man, which is more than yer'll ever do if ye stays on 'ere. Now go and pack yer bags, Ellen, you're coming with me. If I have any trouble I'll send for the police. Don't forget you're under age, they'll see that ye does as you're told.'

I packed my bags with the tears streaming down my face and with my heart filled with deep anger and resentment, against my aunt, my father, but most of all against Kitty. Again and again I told myself how much I despised her for what she had done, but by the time I had packed and changed into my best coat I had composed myself. I would rather have died than allow Aunt Liza to think I was desolate.

I kissed Aunty Mary and my aunt shook hands with her formally, then we were walking side by side down the street and lace curtains were being moved aside so that inquisitive eyes might watch us. Then I saw Kitty running across the factory yard with her coat thrown carelessly round her shoulders. She was gasping for breath when she reached me and I could tell that she'd been crying.

'So yer goin', Ellen?' she gasped.

'You've made it so that I have to go, Kitty. Why did you do it?'

'I 'ad to do it Ellen, I'm goin' too. I'm goin' with Emmie Wallsingham at the weekend, I couldn't go and leave ye 'ere.'

'Why couldn't you have told me what you intended to do and left it to me to sort out my own life? Honestly, Kitty, I never thought you'd do this to me, never.'

'In time yer'll thank mi for it, Ellen. This is no city for you to stay in.'

'What will you do with Emmie Wallsingham, where will you live and what sort of work will you do?'

I watched the rich red colour flood into her face and her eyes slid away from mine, confused and embarrassed.

'I wish ye 'adn't asked mi that, Ellen, because at the moment I'm not sure.'

'I know what everybody says about Emmie Wallsingham.'

'Mebbe they're jealous of the way she dresses and the way she looks.'

'No, Kitty, but everybody's pretty sure how she comes by the clothes she wears.'

For the first time there was anger in her face, anger mingled with a strange sort of anguish and at that moment I pitied her because I loved her and understood her anger.

'I won't listen to any more, Ellen, and I don't care what anybody sez about Emmie, she's bin kind to me. I'm not goin' to end up like Emmie, small time and contented with it. One day I'll be somebody and look like somebody and right now I don't much care 'ow I gets there. One day, Ellen, we might see each other again and then yer'll understand why I 'ad to do what I did. Yer aunt's waitin' for ye and she looks none too pleased.'

Aunt Liza was standing near the tram stop, her face registering impatience and displeasure. With another swift look at Kitty's face I turned and ran. The tram came clanging noisily down the road and it was only when I clambered aboard behind Aunt Liza that I turned to look back. Kitty was standing where I had left her and I saw her raise her arm and wave before I went inside.

Hurriedly I brushed away the tears from my cheeks and sat resolutely looking in front of me. A part of my life was irretrievably over and as the tram noisily made its way towards the heart of the city I stared out of the window at the streets I loved.

This city, so vibrant with life, had been my joy. It was not a beautiful city but I had revelled in its sounds and its smells, its romantic obsession with the sea and foreign places, and if Aunt Liza expected me to be sorry for what I had done there was no regret in my heart.

For nearly two years it had been part of my first great adventure. And there would be others – Kitty McGuire was not the only one to have dreams and longings even if we were destined to attain our ends by different means.

CHAPTER 11

It didn't take long to familiarize myself with Langstone because there wasn't a great deal of it: one long straggling high street paved with cobblestones, a square-towered Saxon church standing at one end and the Black Bull inn at the other.

On Wednesdays and Saturdays market stalls were set out along the length of the street and I could see all the activity from the window of my aunt's draper's shop halfway down the street.

Aunt Liza didn't much like market days. 'Sellin' cotton and tape and the like at half the price I sell 'em for,' she complained. 'Like as not they've bin stolen from some mill or other or there's somethin' wrong with 'em.'

Her best crony was Mrs Devlin from the baker's shop across the road and in the evenings they would sit together going over the village gossip, drinking tea and eating the baker's leftovers which Mrs Devlin brought across. On some nights Aunt Liza would trip across there carrying several bottles of stout in her black bag, and when she returned I was amused to see how her temper had improved until she became almost affable.

I enjoyed setting out the shop window and waiting at the counter. Most of the villagers were friendly if curious, and yet I made no close friends so that I wondered how long I would have to reside in Langstone before I became one of them.

Aunt Liza had quarrelled with the vicar and was not going to church, consequently on the first Sunday she said, 'I'm not stoppin' you from goin' to church, Ellen, but I'll want his apology 'afore I sets foot in the place again.'

'What did he do, Aunt Liza, that makes you so angry?'

'I didn't get mi usual stall at the church fete, that's what. I've 'ad that spot for nigh on twenty years and this year if'e didn't go and give it to Molly Weaver for 'er plants and flowers.'

'Didn't you get a stall then?'

'I did, but it was in a draughty corner which did nothin' for mi arthritis. Them that were lookin' for mi in mi usual place had to find mi and I didn't do as well.'

'What did the vicar have to say?'

''E said 'e didn't think I'd mind. 'E's not bin 'ere long, eighteen months that's all. I've stopped the church magazine 'til I get some sort o' satisfaction.'

It all seemed so small-minded and petty, exactly like the village gossip at home, but it did mean that on Sundays I was free to do as I liked, which nearly always meant going for long walks over the fells or along the country lanes.

The sun was warm on my arms as I sat on the hillside contemplating the view below. The sunlight fell on warm red roofs and the rambling high street, on people wearing their Sunday-best clothes on their way to church and on the majestic pile known as Langstone Priory set in its vast parkland and formal gardens.

When I first saw it I thought it might be a boys' school where gentlemen and the aristocracy sent their sons to be educated but Aunt Liza said, 'Of course it isn't a school, it's a family house. Most of us round 'ere call it the Hall, but that isn't its real name.'

'It's awfully big. Who lives there?'

'The de Bellefort family own it. They do say they came over wi' the Normans but there's only old Lady de Bellefort livin' there now. Three sons she had and one daughter. The eldest son lives in a house as big as that one over at Mowbray and the other who was a bit of a tearaway in his younger days lives over in Ireland at County Wicklow. The youngest son was killed in India, and now and again his widow visits and their daughter spends some time 'ere. Yer'd think the young widow'd spend a bit more time with the old lady now she's all alone'.

'What's going to happen to that house when the old lady dies?'

'Who knows? But folks do say one o' the grandsons'll come in for it.'

'I wonder what it's like living in a house like that?' I mused.

I was thinking about Kitty, how her eyes would have grown wide with wonder while her imagination clothed her in the things she longed for.

To give Aunt Liza her due she hadn't asked too many questions about my life in Liverpool, but one evening as we sat over our cocoa she astonished me by asking, 'What made yer leave home, Ellen? I've heard mi brother's version, now I'd like to 'ear yours – particularly if ye intends staying here with me and lookin' after mi little shop.'

She was watching me closely with her lips set tight, her black eyes stern and brooking no prevarication.

'I couldn't get on with mi father, Aunt Liza.'

'Why not! He's a good provider and 'e's bin a good husband and father, hasn't he?'

'I was afraid of him.'

'What nonsense. What 'ad ye to be afraid of him for? I've never seen him take a hand to ye.'

'Well of course not, you were never there when he beat me until mi back ran with blood. You never had to sit through his sulks or watch mi mother's face miserable and unhappy after one of his tirades. I've watched him beat Peter for no reason at all and he was always the first one to sit in judgement on everybody else.'

'Ye must 'ave done somethin' to warrant a beatin'. I know 'e didn't like ye bein friends with that Kitty McGuire and as things 'ave turned out he was probably right about that. Don't ye think he was stern because he wanted ye to grow up proper and decent?'

'You don't know anything about Phoebe Patterson, Aunt.'

'Who's she then?'

'She's the village harlot. Mi father's out to save her soul but he's not averse to visitin' her late at night and comin' home in the early mornin'.

'Nay, I'll not have that, Ellen. I'll not 'ave yer sayin' 'e has a woman friend. Why it's more than his job's worth.'

So I told her what I had seen. Indeed I told her everything except the real fear I had had that my father was beginning to lust after me in a quite unfatherly manner. I could not bring myself to tell her that.

After that night she never referred to my reasons for leaving home again beyond saying that she had written to my father to say I was living with her in Langstone.

It wasn't a particularly busy shop, so I took to embroidering tapestries and tablecloths and one of these I put in the shop window.

'There's no room for it,' Aunt Liza complained. 'Besides, who'll buy it? If they wants embroidered tablecloths they'll do their own.'

'It's worth a try, Aunt.'

'Well if it's still there when the new wools come in it'll 'ave to come out to make room for them.'

Two days later it was sold to a woman visiting one of our neighbours and when I told Aunt Liza how much it had fetched she merely snapped, 'It's not enough, Ellen, yer not paid for yer time and trouble. If ye does another, update yer price.'

I did several others and traycloths also, all of which were sold. Then one day a carriage pulled up at the front door and the coachman stepped down to help an elderly lady out. She was tall and slender and carried herself superbly although she was obviously very old. She was dressed entirely in black, but it was expensive black and there was the rustle of silk as she entered the shop.

I pulled a chair forward for her and she thanked me with a gracious nod. Her voice was low pitched but commanding and almost immediately Aunt Liza appeared from the room behind the shop, almost falling over herself in an effort to please.

'Good afternoon, Lady de Bellefort. What can I do for you?'

'My maid ordered some wool from you, I was passing and thought I would call to see if it had arrived.'

'I'm expecting it any day, Milady. I could send my niece up to the Hall with it.'

'Would that be a lot of trouble?'

'No trouble at all, Milady.'

'Well thank you, that would be very kind. Your window is different, I wondered if you had left the shop.'

'It's mi niece, Milady, she's taken to doin' the window and dressin' it up with some of her embroidery.'

'So I noticed. May I see some of it?'

'Of course, Milady. Ellen, show 'er ladyship what yer've done.'

So I produced cushion covers and tablecloths, babies' bibs and traycloths, all of which the old lady looked at closely.

'Have you done all these?' she asked quietly.

'Yes Milady.'

'You have been trained in fine sewing?'

'Only sewing lessons at school. I like sewing, I was always good with my fingers.'

'Yes indeed. It's nice to see a young girl so skilful. I would like my maid to see some of this work, her own leaves much to be desired. I will take two of the tablecloths and four traycloths, they will do very nicely for presents. I will pay you what you have charged, my dear, but allow me to tell you that they are very much under priced. Don't you agree, Miss Ashington?'

'Well there's not much call for this sort o' stuff in the village, Milady, and if there was they wouldn't want to pay much for it.'

Lady de Bellefort shook her head sadly. 'Yes, it is a pity that more people do not recognize beauty when they see it. You will send the wools then, Miss Ashington?'

'As soon as they arrive, Milady, and thank you for your custom.'

As she passed out of the doorway Lady de Bellefort turned to me with a half smile, saying, 'Do not be discouraged by other people's failings, my dear.'

To say that Aunt Liza was gratified by that visit is an understatement. She retired to her parlour and got out the sherry glasses and one of her iced fruit cakes from which she cut me a generous slice.

'It's a pity the vicar wasn't about when her carriage was outside,' she muttered. 'That would have given 'im somethin' to think about.'

'Does she always drive about in a carriage?'

'Well of course, her ladyship can't be bothered with them smelly motorcars, and those two horses are a picture.'

'She was very kind to buy my embroidery.'

'Yes well, don't you be getting any ideas above yourself, Ellen, yer've a long way to go before ye convinces me that ye've left all that silliness behind ye.'

'Yes, Aunt.'

'I think I'll just slip across to Mrs Devlin's. She's probably seen our visitor but I'd like 'er to know what she's bin buyin'. If I tells Mrs Devlin what's bin happening, in no time at all the whole village'll know, including the vicar.'

I was glad for her to go. I liked having the house and shop to myself so that I could pretend it was all mine. I visualized what I would do with it, the shop window and the shelves above the counter, but when I voiced only half of these imaginings to Aunt Liza she sniffed contemptuously, saying, 'It's good enough for me as it is. Yer seem to have ideas above yer station, Ellen, it's time ye came down to earth. I can understand how ye must 'ave worried yer parents. Ye might as well know yer father's written back saying' they don't want to know anythin' about ye.'

This did not surprise me.

I was neither happy nor unhappy in Langstone. It seemed that I was living in limbo, marking time while waiting for something to happen, but as uneventful day followed uneventful day there seemed little hope that it would ever change.

One day after Aunt Liza had spent a particularly painful night with her arthritis she watched me setting out the window in rather more than her usual close-lipped silence, then said peevishly, 'Ye enjoys doin' the window don't ye, Ellen?'

'Yes, Aunt.'

'Well I wants ye to know now that this shop'll never be yours. I 'ave a bit o' money which I intend to divide between mi brothers and mi niece over at Ripon. If ye gets any, it'll 'ave to come from yer father, and I can't see that happenin'.

I bit my lip to repress the quick retort she was waiting for and which I had no intention of making.

'I know ye likes the shop and the work but that's as far as it goes. I just wanted ye to know that puttin' a roof over yer head is all I'm aimin' to do.'

'I didn't expect anything else, Aunt Liza, why should I?'

'Well I just wanted to be honest with ye, that's all. Now get off to the Hall with Lady de Bellefort's wool. To the back door, mind ye. I don't want ye knockin' on the front door and 'ave that supercilious butler order ye round to the back door thinkin' I 'aven't taught ye anythin' better.'

It was a clear golden morning. A light breeze filled the air with the scent of clover and the hedgerows were white and pink with May blossom. The huge iron gates were open and the drive seemed to go on for ever. Giant oaks stood in the parkland and in the distance I could see deer wandering among the beech trees and swans sailing majestically across the tarn.

I stood in the middle of the path looking back towards the village, which from this point halfway up the hill seemed to be dominated by the sprawling mansion behind me. How Kitty would have loved this house, and I approached it with a strange resentment against all those people who had all the colour of the world while others had nothing at all.

Dutifully I made my way to the servants' quarters where I knocked sharply on the stout wooden door. It was opened to me by a maidservant who reminded me of Kitty with her red hair and pretty pert face.

She stood without speaking, eyeing me over without any sense of urgency, and a voice came from a distance. 'Are ye answerin' the door, Jennie?'

'Yes, Cook, it's a girl from the village.'

'What's she want then?'

Jennie looked at me for an answer.

'I'm Miss Ashington's niece from the wool shop, I've brought her ladyship's wool. She's expecting it.'

'Wait 'ere,' she said, and disappeared with the parcel of wool.

In a few minutes she was back asking, ''As the wool been paid for?'

'I'm not sure, but my aunt didn't mention payment. I'm sure it will be all right if I just leave it.'

'Well ye'd best come in and tell Cook. It's mi half day and I'm late as it is.'

I followed her into the largest kitchen I had ever seen in my life. Cook and a very young girl sat at the table polishing silver and without another word Jennie left me standing in the middle of the floor.

Cook looked up and said sharply, 'Did I 'ear ye say you were Miss Ashington's niece?'

'Yes, that's right.'

'I didn't know she had any kinfolk around these parts.'

'She hasn't. I came from Liverpool but my family live north of Skipton.'

'Yer aunt doesn't come to church much these days, how's that?'

'Her arthritis has been troubling her.'

'I'm sorry to 'ear it. I did 'ear she'd 'ad a bit o' trouble with the vicar. There isn't any truth in it then?'

'I'm sure there isn't.'

'Well a tale never loses anythin' round these parts. Are ye wantin' payin' for this wool then?'

'That's between Lady de Bellefort and my aunt, I don't expect to be paid for it today.'

'Sit down for a minute and 'ave a cup of tea, there's still some in the pot, I think. 'Ave a look, Mary, and get out some o' that simnel. It's nice to 'ave a bit o' company from the village.'

So I sat down at the table with a large piece of simnel and a cup of strong tea.

'There's an awful lot of silver to clean,' I ventured.

'Ay, and this is only a bit of it. We're getting ready for Mrs de Bellefort and 'er daughter, comin' tonight from France they are so the rooms have 'ad to be got ready and the whole house cleaned from top to bottom.'

'It will be nice for her ladyship to have them here.'

'That it will, but the daughter-in-law'll be off almost as soon as she's got here. Never stops long, she doesn't, but Miss Lisanne'll most likely be 'ere for the summer.'

'They don't live round here then?' I asked, anxious to know more about the family who could afford to live at Langstone Priory.

'Well Mrs de Bellefort never lives anywhere for long since 'er 'usband was killed out in India. Cousins they were. The de Belleforts always marry their cousins, that way they keeps the money in the family so to speak, but I don't think it's a good idea at all. If there's anything wrong in the family it's bound to crop up again and again and if the Colonel had lived I 'ave mi doubts that they'd end their days together.'

'Why is that?'

'Well he was always a nice serious sort o' man while 'is wife was pretty and flighty as a butterfly. He liked the country and she liked the shops and the theatre, balls and tea parties. She liked to surround herself wi' all sorts o' young men who danced with her and flattered her, and she spent a small fortune on clothes, and I bet she 'ad a high old time when they were out in India.

'Miss Lisanne's at finishin' school in Switzerland and that's where 'er mother spends most o' the winter, some place they call St Moritz. One o' these days she's goin' to find it awful quiet 'ere at her grandmother's house.'

'She might find it a pleasant change.'

'I doubt it, like mother like daughter. Marriage'll tame 'er.'

'How old is Miss Lisanne?'

'Eighteen or nineteen by this time, I should think. One day she'll marry one of her cousins, but I'm not sure which one. One of 'em'll get the place in Ireland the other'll get this one.'

'Surely she'll have a say in which one she marries?'

'I don't know. There's Miss Geraldine to consider. That's Lady de Bellefort's daughter's daughter, another cousin. She'll get one and Miss Lisanne'll get the other.'

It seemed archaic to me that four young people should

have their entire lives planned for them, who they would marry, even where they would live, but Cook was saying, 'One thing's for sure, none of em'll ever be short of a bob or two.'

'I'd rather be free to plan my own life than be told who I must marry, even if it meant living in the lap of luxury.'

'I'm not so sure, lass. It's very nice to have a bit o' money in your pocket to spend 'ow ye like and be beholden to nobody.'

'Yes of course it is, but it's nice to be able to work for it, not marry for it.'

'Well I'll say this for ye, love, ye knows what ye wants out o' life, but when ye gets a few more years on yer shoulders you might just change yer mind. Would ye like to look over some of the house?'

'Oh yes, I would. But won't anybody mind?'

'I can't take ye over it all but we can see just a bit of it. We can go as far as the long gallery, that way ye can 'ave a look at the portraits of the family.'

For the next hour I was Alice in Wonderland as I wandered along the long gallery decorated with gold leaf and beautifully carved wood. Suits of armour stood the entire length of it, and the windows were stained glass so that their glowing colours were shown on the polished wooden floor where the sunlight fell.

Cook switched on a dozen chandeliers, and the lights placed above the pictures brought the colours to life. It seemed to me that I was looking at portraits of de Belleforts cut from the same mould across innumerable centuries. Women and men in powdered wigs wearing silks and satins and cloaks edged with ermine. Many of the men were in uniform, others wore ceremonial orders across their chests.

The family resemblance was profound. It seemed to me that all the women were flaxen fair with dark-blue eyes, while most of the men were dark with dark blue eyes, and while the women were undeniably beautiful the men were very handsome.

When we reached the end of the gallery cook said 'If we

hurries ye might just be able to take a peep in the library, the more recent potraits are in there.'.

We stood at length below a portrait of a woman sitting on a long low couch. She had a sweet half smile on her lips and behind her stood a tall slender man his right hand resting lightly on her shoulder. With them were two boys, one a little taller than the other, and on the floor beside her sat a younger boy and a little girl.

'Lady de Bellefort,' Cook explained. 'The older boy is Mr Gerald who lives at Mowbray, the other one is Master Steven who lives in County Wicklow and then there's Master Roland who was killed in India and Miss Alice.'

'What a very handsome family they are,' I exclaimed.

'Yes indeed,' she said, moving on, 'and this is Mr Roland and his wife with Miss Lisanne. Ye can see what a pretty woman 'is wife is.'

I looked up with interest at the tall man in army officer's uniform and the beautiful woman by his side. She had soft golden hair framing a perfect oval face and she was wearing a long cream-coloured satin ball gown. There was the gleam of sapphires round her throat and in her tiara.

The little girl was wearing a billowing party dress in what looked like sprigged voille and there was a bright blue ribbon round her waist and another in her pale golden hair.

'They're all very beautiful,' I said wistfully. 'How exciting it must be to wear clothes like that.'

'Ay, the housekeeper says she'd 'eard Mrs de Bellefort tell 'er husband she wanted sapphires and sable for 'er birthday. Do you think you'll ever be askin' for things like that, love?'

'No, I'm sure I shan't, but I once had a friend who yearned for emeralds and ermine.'

She threw back her head and laughed before I followed her down the corridor and back to the kitchen.

I thanked her warmly for having shown me the pictures and she walked with me to the side door. I bade her goodbye on the doorstep where the warm sun fell on my face and lit up my hair, and suddenly she said, 'Ye know, love, ye have a real look of the de Belleforts, it's the pale hair and yer eyes. Has nobody in the village ever mentioned it?'

'No, but then I don't know many people in the village and I haven't been here very long.'

'Well somebody'll mention it for sure. Wait 'til Miss Lisanne gets here, ye could be sisters for sure.'

I thought about that house and the de Bellefort family all the way to the village but one look at Aunt Liza's face soon brought me down to earth.

'Where 'av ye been all this long time?' she complained.

'I'm sorry, Aunt, but Cook would give me a cup of tea and show me the long gallery.'

'The what!'

'The gallery with all the portraits along it. I thought it would seem discourteous not to go with her.'

She sniffed, somewhat mollified. 'And what had Cook to say for 'erself then?'

'She told me a little about the family, as a matter of fact she said I could be Miss Lisanne's sister, we were the same colouring.'

'Rubbish. She'd no call to be puttin' such ideas into yer 'ead, it's filled with high-flung notions as it is. The de Belleforts are gentry and you're just plain Ellen Adair.'

Sufficiently deflated, I watched her set out to the market, clutching the inevitable black bag.

Trade was never good on market days and there was little for me to do except stare through the shop windows at the crowds milling round the stalls. Suddenly I was aware of a young man staring at me through the glass. He was tall and thin, with a white apron over his clothes and a basket over his arm.

The first thing I noticed when he entered the shop was that he had rather protruding eyes under a shock of dark hair. He had a cheeky grin however, and handing me the basket he said, 'I've seen ye walkin' down the street. You're the niece, aren't you?'

'I'm Miss Ashington's niece, who are you?'

'I'm Alec Devlin the baker's son.'

'I didn't know Mrs Devlin had a son.'

‘She ’asn’t, she’s mi father’s second wife. Mi mother died when I was four.’

‘Oh, I’m sorry.’

‘I was asked to bring these over, yer aunt’s at the market.’

‘I know.’

‘There’s a dance at the village hall tonight, would ye like to go?’

‘I’m not sure, I’ll have to ask my aunt.’

‘Starts at seven o’clock. They’re not bad. There’s supper, and a three-piece band’ll be playin’ fro’ Milden. I’ll call round about seven to see if you can come. Mi mother told me to ask ye.’

‘Thank you, that was very kind.’

I didn’t particularly want to go to the dance, nor was Alec Devlin my ideal man, but anything was better than sitting all evening across the hearth from Aunt Liza, listening to the clicking of her knitting needles until it was time for cocoa and bed.

As soon as she returned I told her about my visitor but, contrary to my expectations, she nodded her head, well pleased. ‘Yer can do a lot worse than ’ave Alec Devlin, ’e’s the only lad Devlin’s got so ’e’ll come in for the baker’s shop one o’ these days.’

‘He said Mrs Devlin asked him to invite me?’

‘She wouldn’t have done that if she ’adn’t thought ’e’d take a shine to ye. I’ve seen ’im looking across ’ere somethin’ and often.’

Alec Devlin appeared on the doorstep promptly at seven o’clock, wearing a dark navy-blue suit and with his hair well greased and spruced back, while I wore my navy skirt and pink silk blouse. The colour suited me and I had found a silk ribbon for my hair exactly the same shade as the blouse.

I did not miss the gleam of admiration in Alec’s eyes, but any hopes that I would be the belle of the ball were quickly dashed when I stepped into the village hall and saw what the rest of the girls were wearing.

Most of them were in pretty floral dresses, frilled and flounced, and they looked at my attire in cool disdain. I felt rather better when Alec whispered, 'Ye look's real classy, Ellen, I 'ates them flowered dresses.'

Alec was no expert dancer and I'd always loved dancing. Mrs Grundy had once told me that I had a natural aptitude and grace, and now I found myself being patient with him as I endeavoured to instruct him through the more intricate footwork of the foxtrot, otherwise we merely marched up and down with the precision of a drill sergeant.

At supper we sat in the company of two more couples who Alec knew.

'Where's Alice tonight?' one of the girls demanded of him, and I saw the colour flood his cheeks before he said, 'How should I know?'

'Ye usually bring her,' the girl replied.

Ignoring that remark he helped himself to patties and cakes from the table and I couldn't help noticing that everything came from his father's shop.

'The cakes are nice, Alec,' I volunteered.

He smiled toothily and while he talked to one of the men I found myself weighing up his appearance. I guessed his age to be about nineteen or twenty and he was at the gawky stage. His adam's apple moved up and down as he talked and he had a good appetite from the amount of food he had piled on to his plate. The girl who had asked about Alice turned to me, saying, 'You live at the draper's, don't ye? Where do you come from?'

'From a village north of Skipton.'

'Ye don't sound Yorkshire. Mi mother said she thought ye'd come from Liverpool.'

'I've been living in Liverpool for a few years.'

'Fancy comin' here fro' Liverpool.'

'I'm living with my aunt.'

'Do ye get on with 'er? Right little sourpuss she is. She's not set foot in the church since the vicar gave her stall to somebody else at the village fete.'

When I didn't rise to that one she said, 'Are ye goin' out with Alec then? He used to be Alice Almond's boyfriend.'

'No, I'm not going out with him, he invited me to the dance, that's all.'

I was amused by the knowing looks the two girls exchanged, and then the other girl said in little more than a whisper, 'Alec's parents didn't approve of Alice, poor as church mice her folks are and they've never asked 'er to the house.'

I felt both amused and irritated by their assumption that I was Alec's new interest who would meet with his parents' approval because I was Liza Ashington's niece. I also felt a grim sort of satisfaction in knowing that I was to get nothing from her when she died.

I was glad that it was raining when we left the village hall, which meant that we had to run all the way home. I had not wanted to loiter through the scented dark with Alec, even so he pulled me into the shop doorway and stood with his arms around me asking if I would accompany him to church in the morning, and quite taking it for granted that he only had to ask and I would readily agree.

'I'm sorry, Alec, but I have things to do in the morning and my aunt doesn't go to church these days.'

'*You've* no quarrel wi' the vicar.'

'I don't even know him.'

'When shall I see you then?'

'Well you only live across the way, probably next week.'

'That's no answer.'

'I'm sorry, Alec, I really don't know, I don't know how much free time I shall have.'

He pulled away from me with a sulky expression, and I felt a faint twinge of conscience.

'I've had a lovely time, Alec, thank you for asking me.'

His expression changed somewhat. 'Does that mean you'll come with me again?'

'Yes, of course. Now I must go in, mi aunt'll be waitin' up for me.' With a hurried goodnight and a quick avoidance of his encircling arm I escaped into the darkened shop.

Aunt Liza was waiting for me although it was long past her normal bedtime. Two cups of steaming cocoa lay on the table, and she sat in her favourite chair waiting to be informed about the evening's events.

She watched in silence while I took off my outdoor clothing, then I sat at the table and pulled a mug of cocoa towards me, only too aware that her impatience was mounting.

'Well,' she said at last, 'what 'ave ye got to say for yourself! 'Ave ye enjoyed yourself?'

'Yes, thank you, Aunt. Nobody else wore a blouse and skirt but I reckon I looked as well as they did.'

'Of course ye did, there'd be nothin' at that dance to write home about. 'Ow did ye get on with Alec?'

'Very well. He's no great shakes as a dancer and he eats too much and probably knows how to drink too much but it was kind of him to ask me, and I love dancing.'

She stared at me nonplussed for several seconds before she snapped, 'Are ye tellin' me there was drink at the hall?'

'No, Aunt, but I heard him talking to some other boys about a rare old night they'd had in the Black Bull.'

'It's only high spirits, the lads 'ave to go somewhere to pass their time. Alec's a decent 'ard-workin lad, it'd please me if I thought you were walkin' out with 'im. Like I've said, yer'll not be comin' in for this shop.'

'I wonder if Alec knows that?'

'What does that mean?'

'I wouldn't like to think he was asking me out because he thought I was better off than Alice. Everybody seemed to think it was strange that he was with me instead of her.'

Her face flushed darkly. 'Everybody wants to mind their own business. I don't know anything about any Alice but yer've got a sharp tongue in yer head, Ellen Adair. No doubt it's come from mixing with the likes o' that Kitty McGuire. Has he asked to see you again?'

'Yes, Aunt, but I've made no definite arrangements.'

'Ye don't apparently know which side yer bread's buttered. What I'll say to Mrs Devlin I really don't know.'

She left me abruptly to climb the stairs, calling, 'Put out the lights, Ellen, and don't put any more coal on the fire.'

CHAPTER 12

During the following week I was pestered by Alec. If I went out by the shop door he was either sweeping outside the baker's or cleaning the windows, and if I went to the market he was there too, dogging my footsteps and trying to be clever with the stallholders.

In some strange way I felt trapped. I was sixteen years old with a great many dreams, and even if they seemed impossible I needed to keep them for a little while yet. I was not ready for a steady boyfriend. I had vivid memories of Aunt Mary and her brood of children with a husband who was no good as a provider, and Joe Doyle who had to be nagged and bullied by a despairing wife into pulling his weight at the mission. I had memories of my father and his interminable sulks, and on reflection I couldn't honestly think of a single happy marriage.

I was in the shop one afternoon when in came a large lady wearing a flowered hat and with a fox fur covering her ample bosom, even if it was early September. She swept to the counter like a ship in full sail and seemed very surprised to find me there.

'You must be Miss Ashington's niece then, I've 'eard she had somebody livin' with her.'

'Do you want to see my aunt?'

'Tell her it's Mrs Broadbottom, Alderman Broadbottom.'

Duly impressed I conveyed the message to my aunt who came immediately into the shop. While I dealt with another customer I couldn't help overhearing the conversation from the other side of the shop.

'I 'ear you and the vicar are not friendly,' Alderman Broadbottom began, 'it all seems a storm in a teacup to me. You've missed the bazaar and the fete, it's time ye both made up yer differences.'

'It's nothin' of the kind,' my aunt protested. 'Twenty

years or more I've 'ad that spot in the village hall for the church fete, and last year 'e gave it to Molly Weaver without a by your leave, and Molly Weaver not even a regular church-goer.'

'Ye knew she was cleanin' at the vicarage, though?'

'Well of course I did, but I didn't think 'e'd give 'er preferential treatment because of it.'

'Well I've 'ad a word with the vicar and told 'im what I thought about it. I think 'e's feelin' a bit sorry for what 'e did, after all for a man o' the cloth it wasn't very diplomatic. 'E's promised if ye goes back to 'elpin' wi the fete 'e'll give ye the stall back and put Molly Weaver across the doorway. What do ye say, Liza?'

'Well it's kind of ye to 'ave stood up for me, Janie. Is the vicar goin' to apologize?'

'Nay, Liza, yer wants jam on it. Just forget it ever happened, that's my advice, and the sooner ye gets back to attendin' church the better.'

I watched Aunt Liza's face crumple from resolution to acquiescence. 'Ay well, perhaps I'll go on Sunday. I can't say I 'aven't missed it.'

'See that ye do then, I'll expect to see ye there.'

Alderman Mrs Broadbottom swept from the shop and Aunt Liza stood on the doorstep watching her cross the street. She went straight to the baker's and I couldn't help thinking that what had transpired in Aunt Liza's premises would be duly reported across the way.

After that day it seemed to me that my life no longer belonged exclusively to me. Aunt Liza returned to the fold and became immediately immersed in committees of various descriptions: the vicar's wife's sewing circle and counselling for young women, the Church Bazaar and the Summer Fete, Bible Classes and Sunday school teaching. I was taken along with her and introduced as 'mi niece fro Skipton way'.

I was invited to become a Sunday school teacher but I told the vicar quietly that although I believed fervently in God I didn't know enough about religion to instruct others in it. I came in for some very straight talking when Aunt Liza knew I had turned his request down.

'It's all Kitty McGuire, Ellen. Catholic she was, and no doubt she filled yer head with idolatry.'

'It has nothing to do with Kitty, Aunt Liza, and Kitty wasn't a particularly good Catholic anyway.'

'But she was a Catholic, once a Catholic allus a Catholic. She influenced ye, Ellen, against good Christian faith.'

'Oh Aunt, what bigotry and ignorance you talk. Don't you know that Catholicism was the only Christian religion in England until Henry VIII made it illegal because he wanted to divorce his wife and marry somebody else?'

'I hopes ye never talks to the vicar about such things, Ellen, ye don't know what ye're talkin about.'

I knew it was no use talking to Aunt Liza about religion, or indeed about very little else if she'd made up her mind. It was impossible to shift her on any subject under the sun if she thought she knew best.

Alec Devlin too was becoming a problem, pushed on I have no doubt by his father and stepmother, ably assisted by my aunt.

It gave me perverse pleasure one evening after one of the village dances to bring Alec down to earth. He had been holding forth most of the evening on the money his father was making in the baking business and generally showing off in front of our companions, so much so that one of the boys, catching my eye, raised his own heavenwards in some degree of despair.

On our way home I said, 'Did you have to swank quite so much about your father's shop, Alec? One or two of those boys are out of a job.'

'That has nothin' to do with me, Ellen. Mi father's always said, "If yer've got it, don't be ashamed to say so." One o' these days, Ellen, we're goin' to 'ave a nice little thing goin' for us, me with the baker's and you wi' the draper's.'

I stopped and stared at him. 'What exactly do you mean by that?'

He stammered a little, no doubt thinking he's spoken prematurely. 'Well nothin' really, Ellen, but I'm right fond of ye, and I hopes one o' these days you'll be fond of me.

Mi father has a good business and there's only me for it, just like there's only you for your aunt's.'

'You're wrong there, Alec. I shall get nothing from Aunt Liza.'

His mouth opened in amazement. 'Nothin'! Has she said as much?'

'In no uncertain terms. I'm not in her will. She'll probably leave something to my father, her half-brother, but she'll leave most of it to her full brother Simeon Ashington and his daughter over at Ripon, including the shop. I'll get nothing from my father, I can tell you that now, and when my aunt dies I'll have to get out of the shop and find other work.'

'I can't believe she'd treat ye like that, Ellen, wi' all the work ye puts into that shop. Will her niece even want it?'

'Perhaps not. She could sell it but I have no money to buy it.'

'She's never said nothin' to mi mother about all this.'

'There's no reason why she should, Alec.'

'Well I think there is, particularly when she knows you and me are keepin' company.'

'Alec, we're not keeping company, we're simply good friends. I've been very honest with you about my circumstances and I want to be honest about our friendship. I like you as a friend, that's all. I doubt if it could ever be more than that.'

After that night our relationship cooled and Alec's stepmother too became distant when she met me on the street.

One afternoon Aunt Liza said, 'I 'aven't noticed Alec Devlin comin' round much these days. Have you two quarrelled?'

'Of course not, Aunt.'

'Then why doesn't he call for ye?'

'Alec was counting his chickens, Aunt Liza, he had it all weighed up – his father's prosperous business and your little shop one day. When I told him the shop would never be mine he didn't seem as anxious to continue the friendship.'

'Yer'd no call to be tellin' him how I intended leavin' mi

money. He'll have told 'em at home and like as not the tale'll 'ave been spread round the village.'

'I'm sure you don't mind, Aunt. How you leave your money is your affair and parting with Alec hasn't been painful. I could never have fallen in love with him, never.'

'Love's all very well when ye have someat to back it up, but Alec Devlin would have been a stable influence in yer life, Ellen, and heaven knows ye needs one. There was he with a nice business to look forward to, ye didn't 'ave to tell him yer were getting nothin' from me.'

'Would you rather I'd gone on with our friendship letting him think I was fond of him, perhaps even marrying him? Don't you think he would have held it against me for the rest of my life, seeing this little shop going to somebody else when he'd thought it was coming to me? I'm glad I didn't love him, if I had and he'd turned away from me just like he has now I'd have been desolate. As it is, I really don't care.'

She stared at me but I knew she didn't understand a word of what I'd been saying. I came to the conclusion that I'd never really been understood by anybody.

I went alone to the next village dance and Alec was there with his old love Alice. She was a pretty dark-haired girl, poorly dressed, and obviously out on a limb with the other girls in their party, but I smiled across at her pleasantly and in the cloakroom I managed an odd word with her.

When she had gone back to Alec the girl I had met on the first evening said slyly, 'E'll never marry 'er, his folks wouldn't allow it.'

'Why not? She's pretty and she seems nice.'

'Oh, Alice is all right and she worships Alec but she's the eldest of a big family and they haven't two halfpennies for a penny. Her father has consumption and can't work and 'er mother cleans up and down the village at the big houses. Old Ma Devlin'll never want Alice in the family.'

'That's nothing Alice can help.'

'Course not, but it's life isn't it?'

At that moment I wanted to get out of the village hall and away from these people with their have-and-have-not philosophy. Tomorrow they would all be in church believing themselves good Christians, but between them they hadn't a worthwhile Christian thought. They're all religion and no Christianity, I stormed to myself as I grabbed my coat and made off alone down the village street. I was halfway along it when I heard footsteps running after me and I turned in some fear. It was Alec, without his coat and bare headed, running against the wind.

'Where are ye goin', Ellen,' he cried, 'why are ye leavin' so soon?'

I turned on him savagely. 'I'm leavin' because I can't bear to hear any more about people being unacceptable because they haven't any money and aren't likely to be gettin' any. She's a nice girl, Alec, if ye've any sense at all you'll be hanging on to Alice no matter what anybody says.'

He stared at me stupidly, uncomprehending, and I clutched his arm and shook him. 'I'm talking about Alice, the girl you're at the dance with, Alec. You mustn't let anybody tell you she's a nobody just because she hasn't any money. That's the only reason your folks wanted you to be friends with me. They're not so anxious now they know I won't have any either, but money isn't everything.'

'I don't know what you're talking about, Ellen.'

'I'm talking about Alice. You've been friends with her a long time haven't you, Alec?'

'Since we were at school.'

'And you love her, don't you?'

His face grew rosy red and he stammered a little. Alec was not accustomed to young women asking straight questions.

'I don't know. Mi father sez I'm not old enough to know mi own mind.'

'Your father'll probably make it up for you and it won't include Alice, of that I'm sure.'

He shuffled his feet in an embarrassed fashion. 'Why don't ye come back to the dance, Ellen! It's not like you to rush off like that.'

'You don't know any of the things I'm capable of doing, Alec. I was capable of running away from home when I was fourteen, and living in Liverpool working at a seaman's mission. I ran away from home to be with a girl who had nothing, just like Alice has nothing, but Kitty had all the fire and beauty I ever remember in my early life. I'll probably never see her again but I'll never forget her, never.'

My words didn't make sense to him, they were alien words to this boy brought up in the sheltered world of the village, protected by a father who was making money and a stepmother who had great hopes for the right sort of wife for him. Any words of mine could only fall on stony ground, and realization made me shake my arm free. As I let myself in at the shop door I heard him walking away along the rain-darkened street.

CHAPTER 13

Aunt Liza didn't believe in holidays apart from one week in August she spent with her brother and his family in Ripon, when she closed her shop.

'What will ye do while I'm away?' she demanded of me.

'I'm not sure, Aunt. I've saved a little money, I might spend a few days at the coast somewhere.' Indeed I had managed to save a little by taking in sewing, a thing which Aunt Liza deplored because she didn't want the villagers to think I needed the money.

'Where on the coast?' she snapped.

'Southport, perhaps, or Bridlington.'

'Bridlington's better. They tell me Southport's expensive. Besides, isn't it close to Liverpool?'

'Is it?' I answered innocently. 'I hadn't thought of that.'

'I hope ye're not thinkin' of lookin' that Irish girl up, she'll 'ave forgotten your existence by this time.'

'No, Aunt, I wasn't thinking of it. I haven't really made my mind up yet, I might not even go anywhere.'

'Ye know Alec Devlin's got 'imself engaged, I suppose? If yer'd played yer cards right it could 'ave been you getting married.'

'I didn't want him, Aunt Liza. I hope he'll be very happy.'

'Well, I've been invited to the reception. They didn't invite you, Ellen, because you were one of his old girlfriends and they thought his bride might not like it.'

I laughed without rancour. 'Oh Aunt, I was never one of Alec Devlin's girlfriends, and I don't suppose they've invited Alice.'

'Indeed they 'aven't, they were mighty glad when that finished, I can tell ye.'

'She was a lot prettier than the one he's marrying' on Saturday.'

'What's pretty got to do with it, and her with a father

ownin' two ironmonger's shops in Ottley? Madge Bromley'll bring him plenty o' brass and that'll do him more good than a pretty face. Beauty fades, money appreciates.'

The entire village turned out to watch Alec's wedding the first Saturday in August and most of them followed the bridal party to the Black Bull for the reception.

At midday Aunt Liza closed the shop and began to put on her wedding finery: a new beige skirt and silk blouse, a short brown coat and brown hat with a fair show of veiling and a cream silk rose to top it off. I had hitherto never seen her in anything but black and I had to confess that she looked considerably younger in her latest attire. When I said as much she merely remarked dryly, 'I don't suppose I'll wear this 'til the next weddin', mi niece's at Ripon or maybe yours, although ye're pretty good at letting eligible men slip through yer fingers. Make sure ye opens the shop at two o'clock prompt. Weddin' or no weddin', today's market day, we don't want to miss any customers.'

I walked with her to the Black Bull and stood with a crowd of others watching the bridal party line up for photographs. Alec and his father looked uncomfortable in their formal morning suits, Mrs Devlin was in mauve, a billowing dress with a hat to match and trimmed with bunches of violets. The bride's parents too had evidently spared no expense. Her mother, attired in pale green, was a tall thin woman wearing a severe expression and constantly spoke sharply to her exuberant spouse.

A long white Rolls-Royce stood outside the inn decorated with white satin streamers, and there were a great many pictures of the happy couple taken standing in front of it. The bride was not a pretty girl. She was very much a younger version of her mother, tall and thin, very dark and with an expression of boredom that, I felt convinced, Alec would come to recognize over the years ahead of them.

I noticed with some amusement that Aunt Liza was very much in the forefront of the photo including the guests. Then they all trooped into the inn and I was free to do what I liked for an hour and a half on a glorious warm summer's day. It was then I saw Alice, tearful and miserable half running along the pavement in an endeavour to avoid the stares from unsympathetic eyes.

I chased after her, in and out of the market stalls, and saw that she took the road that climbed towards the fell, where I assumed she would pour out her anguish to the lonely crags and the curlews.

I came upon her sitting dismally on a five-barred gate looking hopelessly down on the village, her mind filled no doubt with the goings-on at the inn. She looked at me without recognition, then shamefaced she jumped down from the gate and started to walk up the road.

'Alice, please wait for me,' I called.

She turned hesitantly and for one moment I thought she was going to ignore me, then her expression changed and she stared at me defiantly, daring me to feel sorry for her or ask why she was unhappy. I knew better than that, I had not been Kitty McGuire's companion all those years for nothing.

'I'm walking on the moor, Alice. I'd like some company if you're going that way,' I said, reaching her side.

'I'm not going far, I've the shopping to do.'

'Well, just to the top of the hill there, then we'll make our way back to the village. I'm eating alone today, would you like to join me?'

For a moment she looked at me uncertainly, then she said, 'I must get back, Ellen, or mi mother'll wonder where I've got to.'

'I'm sure she'll not miss you for a little while, after all it's Saturday. What do you usually do on Saturday?'

I wished I hadn't asked when tears suddenly filled her eyes and she turned her head away sharply.

'Please come back to the shop with me, Alice. I don't know many people in the village. There are times when I think if you've not been born and bred here you'll be a stranger for ever.'

'I suppose yer aunt's at the weddin'.'

'Yes, she went off wreathed in smiles and wearin' her Sunday best.'

'Why didn't they invite you, I wonder?'

Quite suddenly I wanted to bring the smiles back on to Alice's pretty face even if it meant belittling her one-time swain.

'His mother had designs on me when she thought I'd get my aunt's shop and her money. When she found out I wouldn't, they looked around for somebody else for Alec. It was just as well because I couldn't ever have wanted to marry him.'

She stared at me in surprise. 'Ye couldn't, ye mean ye never liked him?'

'Oh he was well enough I suppose, but he wasn't my idea of the man I want to marry. In my mind he was a callow youth with too many spots. Besides he had buck teeth.'

For a moment she seemed angry and I thought she would have leapt to his defence, then suddenly her face crumpled into laughter and there on the hillside we stood laughing until hers turned to hysteria and the merciful tears were suddenly released. I prayed silently that she would never cry over Alec Devlin again.

We ate a hurriedly prepared lunch in the parlour behind the shop, then she left, saying she didn't want to be there when my aunt returned.

Indeed she had only just left when Aunt Liza let herself into the shop well before two o'clock so that she could see we had opened on time. She was in high good humour and as she took off her hat gave me full details of the meal and the bottles of wine the bride's father had ordered from the delighted landlord.

'Money to burn they must 'ave,' she said. 'Young Alec's done very well for 'imself there and the girl seems nice enough.'

'She's not as pretty as Alice and I don't suppose she'll make him a better wife,' I couldn't resist snapping.

Without answering me she stamped into the kitchen to return a moment later asking, 'What are all them dishes doin' in the sink! Who've ye 'ad in, Ellen?'

'I met a friend on the street, Aunt Liza, I didn't think you'd mind if I asked her in to eat with me.'

'Which friend! Ye're allus sayin' ye've no friends in the village.'

'It was Alice if you must know, she was upset at Alec's wedding.'

'Really Ellen, I can't leave ye alone five minutes 'afore ye're pickin' up wi' the wrong companions.'

After that I went into the kitchen and started to do the dishes, and when I returned to the parlour she was sitting in her usual chair staring into the fire.

'They were sayin' at the weddin' that Lady de Bellefort's daughter-in-law and 'er granddaughter 'ave arrived. Yer'll be seein' the girl around the village on that 'orse of 'ers. She's a pleasant sort o' girl, very pretty too. If ye should see 'er yer'll bob a little curtsey and say good mornin', Ellen, let 'er see ye knows yer manners.'

I stared at her in amazement. Life in Liverpool had obscured the need to bob country curtseys to local landowners and their families, and an overpowering feeling of resentment took hold of me.

Once, a long time ago, I would not have been averse to being servile to such people, after all I had been reared in a village similar to this one where we had been taught to bob curtseys to the dignitaries who had attended the school and bestowed half-day holidays on us. But now Aunt Liza was talking about my kow-towing to a girl hardly older than myself, and the deep resentment I felt in my heart frightened me.

Meanwhile, Aunt Liza had changed tack and was issuing more instructions. 'I'll be wantin' ye to 'elp me carry mi bags on Saturday mornin' and while I'm gone I don't want ye lettin' any Tom, Dick or Harry into mi shop. Perhaps ye should go away for a few days.'

'Perhaps I will. I've never been to York or Harrogate.'

'Ay well, either'd be better than goin' off to Liverpool and no doubt looking for that Kitty McGuire.'

I said nothing else, and I was relieved when the subject was not raised again. On Saturday morning I went with her to the bus stop carrying her one piece of luggage while she toted two carrier bags filled with pies and cakes from the baker's as well as knitted jumpers and cardigans for her niece.

I didn't mind, in spite of the fact that not once had she offered to give me one of the things I had seen her knitting. It was very evident that I was not her favourite niece and could expect no softening of her attitude towards me.

On Sunday I tidied up the house and the shop, and first thing on Monday morning I boarded the local train for Leeds and another that would take me to Liverpool.

I had made no plans. I didn't know where I would stay or for how long, but I had a desperate longing to see Liverpool again. At last I stood on Dale Street Station clutching my one piece of luggage, and the sight of a woman with two children both with buckets and spades made my mind up for me. I would take the ferry across the Mersey to New Brighton where surely I could find somewhere to stay.

I had no difficulty. There were small boarding houses in plenty and I found one quite close to the promenade. It was owned by a jolly buxom woman who made me very welcome, carried my case upstairs for me and produced a welcome cup of tea as soon as I'd unpacked.

Across the river I could look at the skyline of Liverpool, the stately towers of the Liver buildings, the lights shining in the water, and I could sit on the promenade watching the boats and the bustling ferries while behind me a band was playing.

That first night I simply absorbed its appeal through a haze of nostalgia. The smell of the river, salty and brackish, the people scurrying off the ferries, the hooting of the tugs and the long mournful farewell sirens from the big steamers. I decided that in the morning I would once more board one of those ferries and go to see Aunt Mary. I slept badly, impatiently waiting for the morning and the meeting with old friends, and hopefully news of Kitty.

CHAPTER 14

I couldn't understand why I had imbued Liverpool with so much nostalgic glamour when I walked along its mean streets on my way to Aunt Mary's. The mission windows were still as dingy with soot and grime and the Chinese children playing outside the laundry seemed a little more numerous than before. They stared at me out of wide coal-black eyes, then recognizing me they waved and bowed their dark heads.

Some of the women were standing at their front doors and they eyed me curiously until one of them recognized me and called out, ''Ave ye come back then?'

'No. Just visiting.'

'Well yer'll not find 'er in, the bairns are on 'oliday so she's taken 'em to the park. Yer'll no doubt find 'er 'usband in the pub.'

'Thank you, I'll walk to the park.'

I had always wondered how flowers ever grew in that little park. The gardener must have had the patience of Job because the borders were immaculate with snapdragons and marigolds. A band was playing in the bandstand while elderly people sat around to listen, and children bowling their hoops along the paths were admonished to keep quiet. I guessed Aunt Mary and the children would be near the paddling pool.

I saw her immediately. On her lap sat Susan, the little girl I had first seen clutching a pound pot of jam while lying in her pram. With one hand Aunt Mary gently rocked a battered perambulator. The other children were playing near the pool and I was almost at her side before recognition dawned in her lack lustre eyes.

'Why Ellen, what are you doin' in Liverpool?' she gasped.

'I'm taking a few day's holiday. I was hoping to see you.'

I looked at the baby in the pram. He was so tiny, like a little wizened old man, then I looked at Aunt Mary.

'He's three weeks old,' she said, 'and 'e's bin a sickly child, allus ailin' somethin' or other since the day 'e were born.'

'What do you call him?'

'Patrick after mi grandfather. He allus got Paddy but I've told the children to call the baby Patrick and not to go shortenin' his name. Ye look well, Ellen, I can see that country life suits ye.'

'It's all that fresh air. I can't say the same for you, Aunt Mary, you look very tired.'

'Well I am tired, I'm up with baby most nights. 'E cries a lot, poor little mite.'

For the first time I saw the poverty in her thin dress and tattered shoes and a wave of pity swept over me. For people like Mary McLoughlin there didn't seem much to look forward to in this bustling city.

'Are you still taking in sewing?' I asked.

'Mi old customers don't come so much now, I kept 'em waitin' ye see when I 'ad the baby and 'e takes up so much of mi time the things were never ready when they came for 'em. No doubt they've found somebody else to do their sewin'.'

'Oh I am sorry. Surely they realized you'd need to look after Patrick?'

'I've no doubt they did, but I couldn't expect 'em to keep 'angin' on, could I?'

'Is the tea shop open? We could walk round there and have a cup of tea.'

'It's probably full up by now. I'm ready for goin' back anyway, we can 'ave a cup of tea back at the 'ouse.'

'I'll collect the children then.'

'They can stop 'ere, Ellen, Mrs Maloney'll look after 'em, she's over there with 'er lot.'

So I pushed the pram and Aunt Mary carried Susan who cried all the way home because she didn't want to leave the park.

There was no sewing lying about the house now but it

was still untidy with shoes left lying on the floor and her husband's betting paper spread out across the table. She plonked Susan into a high chair and parked the pram, then muttering angrily she collected the paper and threw it into a corner.

'If 'e 'as any money to spare it goes on the 'orses,' she complained. ''E's not changed, Ellen, I thought 'e might 'ave done when the new baby came but it was too much to hope for.'

'Was he pleased about the baby?'

'Not he. It's another mouth to feed, but I can't think we'll rear this one, he's too sickly. Sit down, Ellen, and I'll make the tea.'

I had bought sweets for the children and I gave one to Susan, hoping it would dry her tears. The baby was sleeping, his tiny face as grey as his pillow.

She came back to the living room carrying a tray set with cups and saucers and a sponge cake decorated with bright pink icing. I accepted the tea gratefully but refused the cake and she said, 'I'll not 'ave any either, the children like icin', I'll leave it for them. Well, Ellen' what 'ave ye bin doin' up in the country.'

So I told her a little of my life and made her smile at Aunt Liza's narrow-minded views and penny-pinching stinginess.

Then I asked, 'Do you hear from Kitty, Aunt Mary?'

'Not a word since she left. I don't know where she's livin', but it's somewhere with Emmie Wallsingham and we all know what she's up to.'

'What, what is she up to?'

'She's on the streets, that's what. 'Ow else can she afford all them clothes? And that chap she brought with 'er, I do 'ear 'e's got a lot o' young women livin' in the city that 'e finds customers for.'

I stared at her in anguish. 'Surely you can't think that Kitty would be like that Aunt Mary.'

'Of course she could, Ellen. She cried for the moon, that girl, and 'ow could she ever get it on 'onest pay? I tackled Elsie Wallsingham and she more or less admitted that

Emmie got 'er money that way, not that Elsie'll care if Emmie sends some 'ome.'

'I was hoping I might see Kitty.'

'There's not much chance o' that, luv, not round 'ere. She's never coming back to this part o' the city and I'd advise ye not to go lookin' for 'er in the centre, folks might get the idea yer like 'er.'

'Oh Aunt Mary, I can't honestly believe it of Kitty. She was so strong and independent.'

'She's that all right, a girl 'as to be strong to live that sort o' life. Go back to the country, Ellen, and forget Kitty. The likes o' her's are not for you. Now I'd best be getting on wi' mi husband's tea. Yer welcome to join us, Ellen.'

'No thanks, Aunt Mary, I must be getting back, there'll be a meal waiting for me.'

I pressed five shillings into her hand at the front door, and although she seemed reluctant to take it, I did not miss the light that came into her eyes.

'Buy something for yourself,' I urged her, 'don't spend it all on the children.'

She nodded. 'Thanks, Ellen. Ye were allus a thoughtful sort o' girl, and you look after yerself in the country.'

As I walked down the street I knew I would never visit that part of Liverpool again. It belonged to a youth I was not particularly proud of but it had toughened me for whatever the future might hold.

Tomorrow I would go to the shops and mingle with the city girls as if I were one of them. I would take afternoon tea in the cosy warmth of one of the tea rooms and perhaps I would see Kitty and hear from her own lips how she was surviving, for I hadn't believed a word of what Aunt Mary had told me.

I was fascinated by the shops, the perfume counters and the haberdashery, and so ashamed of my cheap cotton gloves that I stuck them in my skirt pocket. I loved the feel of fine leather and crepe de Chine and the delicacy of chiffon flowers. All in all I spent an enchanting morning and was about to enter the coffee lounge when I heard two girls discussing the tea dances held at three every afternoon at the Adelphi Hotel.

Consequently I decided there and then to save the money I would have spent in the coffee lounge and go instead to the Adelphi. I wasn't quite sure if I was properly dressed for such an occasion but my beige skirt fitted well and I had been extravagant with the pure silk of my cream blouse which I had made myself.

I tried not to be overawed by the majestic foyer of the hotel, and the carpet which my feet seemed to sink into. I was intrigued by elegantly dressed women and immaculately suited men, and the waiter who escorted me to my seat in the tea lounge seemed unperturbed that I was alone. My table was set against a wall and reasonably inconspicuous.

I ordered afternoon tea, whereupon he said loftily, 'China or Indian, Madam?'

'Indian, thank you,' I replied, remembering that the vicar's wife had disliked China tea because she considered it too scented.

There were thin cucumber sandwiches and rich cream cakes, all served on fine china, and with the tea came cube sugar to be served with tiny silver tongs. I felt like a queen as I helped myself from the plates set in front of me, and then from the dais the fourpiece band began to play and I gave myself up to the sound of the music.

One or two couples got up to dance and from across the room I noticed that two men were eyeing me curiously. Blushing, I lowered my eyes, wondering what I should do if one of them came across to ask me to dance.

All such thoughts were swept from my mind when a man and two women entered the room. I knew him instantly, he was the man who had accompanied Emmie Wallsingham to her mother's house.

They sauntered to a table at the edge of the dance floor. People were staring at them curiously and the waiters were muttering together in a group near the wall.

For one thing the man was wearing a loud checked jacket, and he stood out like a sore thumb beside the dark-suited men occupying the tables nearby. For the first time I looked at his companions and I gasped with surprise when I recognized Emmie Wallsingham, but a very different Emmie to the one I had seen before.

She had on a large pink hat trimmed with roses and heavy veiling but it was her painted face which caused me the most surprise. Her cheeks were heavily rouged, and her lips were shining with flame-coloured lipstick. Her eyes swept round the room boldly before she sat back and addressed herself to her companion, who sat with her back to me.

The man stood chatting to them for several minutes, then smiling broadly he bowed over Emmie's hand before leaving the room.

Emmie continued to scan the room but I noticed that the waiters did not approach their table. After a few mintues the head waiter went up and said something to the women quietly. I saw Emmie's eyes flash angrily, then with a dramatic flounce she rose to her feet, dragging the other woman after her, they stalked across the room and out of the door.

Quickly I summoned the waiter to ask for the bill, too excited to be stunned by the size of it, then I hurried into the foyer after them. I badly wanted to speak to Emmie to ask if she had any news of Kitty, and was immediately relieved to see the two women standing near the flower shop. They were deep in conversation when I approached them, and when I touched Emmie shyly on her sleeve they both turned to stare at me. I stared back, hardly able to believe my eyes.

This was not Kitty as I had known her, but Kitty it was, wearing a too-tight green dress and incredibly high heels, and with her hair dressed high on her head, redder than I ever remembered it. Her face was painted exactly like Emmie's but not nearly as professionally. The powder was too pale, the carmine lips and rosy cheeks too red, the mascara too thick, yet underneath it was somehow the face of a very young girl.

Her dismay was as profound as my own.

'Why Ellen,' she gasped. 'What are you doin' in Liverpool?'

Quickly I explained, ending with, 'Oh Kitty, I'm so glad to see you, I saw your Aunt Mary but she didn't know where you were living.'

'No, she wouldn't. I 'aven't had much time to see them, 'ow is she?'

'She doesn't look too well, and they have a new baby, a little boy.'

'Ay well, mi uncle's good for somethin' evidently.'

Just then the head waiter came out of the tearoom towards us. Emmie said quickly, 'We'd best be goin', Kitty, we can talk outside.'

They turned away and the man said sharply, 'Please ladies, I asked you to leave, I don't want you loitering in the hotel.'

I stared at him and then at the two girls. Emmie turned away with a toss of her head before stalking towards the door while Kitty and I followed quickly. At the door I turned and found him staring after us. Once on the pavement, Emmie said sharply, 'Stop and talk to yer friend, Kitty, and meet me back at the house. Try not to be late.'

She walked off without giving us a second glance and I stared at Kitty unhappily.

I felt that she would have liked to have gone with Emmie but instead she stood uncertainly on the pavement and I was aware of her hostility in the set of her tight-lipped face and her smouldering green eyes.

'Why did ye 'ave to come to Liverpool again, Ellen, why couldn't ye 'ave settled down in the country and forgotten all about mi?'

'Because you're my friend, Kitty, and I wanted to see you again.'

'Well I didn't want to see you, Ellen, we've nothin' in common any more. It's all over between you and me, Ellen, and I'd rather not be sayin' anything to you.'

'But why, Kitty, what have I done?'

'Nothin' Ellen, you 'aven't done anythin', it's just that we're different you and me, we've gone our separate ways. I suppose mi aunt had a lot to say about me. What exactly did she tell yer?'

'Very little. How could she when you haven't visited her?'

She smiled grimly. 'That wouldn't stop 'er, Ellen, but I can guess what she said.'

'Would it be true, Kitty?'

'Oh Ellen, don't you be gettin' at me. What was there back there for either of us except some chap like mi uncle and a brood o' screamin' kids? It's not fer you and it's certainly not for me. Go back to Yorkshire, Ellen, and forget about mi. I don't suppose we'll ever see each other again but when ye thinks about mi just remember that this is my way of being somebody, my way of gettin' some money together while I'm young enough to enjoy it.'

She stared at me out of hard angry eyes, then suddenly her face relaxed and she smiled. Her face was the old Kitty's, pretty and pert beneath its paint. With a quick gesture she threw her arms around my neck and kissed my cheek, then with a gay wave she was away.

That night I decided I would go home the following morning. I would look my last at the skyline of Liverpool, forget the sound of the sea breaking on the beach, the smells of the river and the long strident noise of the ships' sirens. I would put Liverpool behind me as though she had never existed . . . but even as I was making these vows I knew that my heart would not let me forget.

I was relieved that Aunt Liza showed little interest in how I had occupied my time during her absence. She returned on Saturday afternoon in high good humour, and immediately I was treated to a description of her brother's house, the welcome they had given her, and approval of her niece's young man, George.

She informed me that he was a bank clerk working in Ripon where he lodged with her brother and his wife, and went home each weekend to see his parents in Harrogate taking Jennie, her niece, with him.

Ever since I could remember, the town of Harrogate had been mentioned in hushed tones. People who lived there were considered highly fortunate because it was a spa town where folk went for the cure, a town of broad avenues and green parks, where most of the shops bore the royal arms because the Princess Royal who lived close by at Harewood did her shopping there. All Langstone would soon be made aware that the niece's fiancé lived there, and some of the glamour would most likely rub off.

'Next time I go to see mi brother I'm to be taken to Harrogate to meet George's folks. He's an only child and so's mi niece, so they'll 'ave a nice little bit one o' these days.'

'If she's going to live in Harrogate or even stay in Ripon what will she do with the shop?' I was unwise enough to ask.

'She'll sell it of course, and it'll bring a nice bit o' money, what with the goodwill and it bein' on the main street o' Langstone.'

Her insensitivity amazed me, but it was changing me too. Once I had been a gentle girl, perhaps a little too gullible but always one to look for the good in people, now I was becoming waspish and suspicious.

I was glad when evening came and she set off to see the Devlins. Aunt Liza had just reached the other side when she turned and almost ran back, just in time to greet a girl riding a big chestnut horse down the main street.

The girl raised her whip in greeting, then to my amazement she pulled the horse up outside the shop and jumped down. Aunt Liza, all smiles, stood with me in the doorway and the girl walked towards us smiling a little apologetically.

'I say, I am sorry to come so late. Are you closed?'

'We 'aven't bin open today, Miss Lisanne, not on the local 'oliday you know, but I'll serve ye if ye wants anything.'

We moved inside the shop and I found myself staring at the girl curiously. We were about the same height but that was not the only similarity. She was as flaxen fair as myself, with the same dark blue eyes, and it seemed to me that I had seen her face in the mirror every day of my life.

She too seemed surprised at my appearance, and smiling she said, 'My grandmother said there was a girl in the village who looked like me. I didn't believe her, but now I do.'

'Oh Ellen's not really like you, Miss Lisanne, just her colourin' perhaps. We mustn't 'ave 'er gettin' conceited. Now what can I get ye?'

'I promised Granny I'd call for her tapestry wool and I completely forgot earlier in the day. Did it arrive?'

'Well not 'afore I went away, it didn't. Did it come last week, Ellen?'

'I've been away too, Aunt. Mrs Devlin would know, she said she'd take in any parcels.'

'Yer'd best get over there then and see what's come, I didn't know you weren't 'ere.'

The tapestry wool had not arrived, and when I explained the girl merely smiled and said she'd call again. Turning to me she said, 'Granny says you're good with your fingers. Would you shorten one or two skirts for me? I'm hopeless and Mother's taken her maid back to London with her.'

'Yes of course, will you be bringing them to the shop?'

'I'd rather you came up to the house, that way you can see them on me.'

'When will you want me to come?'

'Monday, if that's convenient.'

I looked at Aunt Liza for confirmation and although she was slightly put out she nodded briskly. 'I can manage without ye, Ellen, if you comes straight back.'

With a swift smile our visitor left us, and we watched her riding away at a brisk canter.

'Don't you be gettin' any ideas that yer workin' for the gentry, Ellen. I couldn't very well say I didn't want ye to go, wi' the girl standin' there, but I wants yer feet on the ground not yer head in the clouds. Now lock up the shop and go inside.'

'Yes, Aunt.'

Before she reached the edge of the pavement she turned again and came back to me. 'Yer said yer'd bin away. Where did ye go?'

'I went to New Brighton for a few days.'

'To see that Kitty McGuire, I'll be bound.'

'I went to see Aunt Mary. Kitty isn't living there now.'

She merely sniffed disdainfully and once more set off across the street.

I felt strangely miserable as the long lonely night stretched out before me. Life held no promise of better things in store but as I sat alone contemplating a wearisome future I was not to know how dramatically it would soon be changed.

CHAPTER 15

On Monday morning I was told to get off to the Hall so I packed a small valise with scissors, cotton and a tape measure, glad of the walk in the warm summer sunshine.

Walking through the park with the pile of Langstone Priory rising up before me I felt I was walking through another world, it was so peaceful. A light breeze stirred the trees over my head, and my appearance startled a young deer grazing on the verge so that she darted away towards the mere where she stood gazing at me cautiously, poised for flight.

Geraniums in tall white urns stood the length of the terrace, and a peacock spread his tail for me while his more humbly attired spouse looked on admiringly.

How Kitty would have loved this, I thought, then more bitterly: Why did I always have to think of Kitty? I doubted if she ever spared me a thought.

A young man wearing a green baize apron let me into the house, and then I was in the presence of Cook and a tall grey-haired woman wearing a long black dress who eyed me from top to bottom before asking who I was and why had I come.

After I had explained she said shortly, 'Wait here and I'll see if Miss Lisanne is available. Does she know you intended to come this morning?'

'She asked me to come today, Ma'am.'

After she had left the room Cook grinned at me. 'Out o'sorts she is this mornin', there's guests arrived and she's only just bin told.'

'Well if it's not convenient I can come another day. Miss Lisanne will let me know when to come.'

'You wait here, love. If Miss Lisanne said today, today she meant.'

She was busy weighing flour and other ingredients before

turning them into a huge mixing bowl, then energetically stirred the mixture with a stout wooden spoon. A kitchen-maid was dispatched to bring a jug of milk while another was busily greasing cake tins.

A huge piece of beef and a leg of lamb stood on a side table and I longed to ask how many people they were expecting when the door opened and two gardeners appeared carrying bunches of roses and copper beech leaves.

'Put 'em down on the side table,' Cook said sharply. 'Miss Lisanne'll do the flowers.'

The men grinned at her, and the younger of the two came up to the table and put his arm round one of the maids.

'I'll 'ave less of that,' Cook snapped, 'they don't need much distraction as it is.'

'Looks as though a regiment's comin',' the lad said with a broad smile.

'There's some buns in the cake tin there, 'elp yerself and then leave us to get on with our work.'

I watched him helping himself to a pile of currant buns out of the tin and handing some to the other gardener. They both departed with cheeky grins and the maid greasing the cake tins simpered and blushed furiously until Cook gave her a hard look that quickly brought her to her senses.

After a few minutes the housekeeper returned with another maid saying that Miss Lisanne would see me in her bedroom and the maid would show me where it was. Dutifully I followed in her wake, and outside the kitchen she turned to say, 'I'm Amelia the under housemaid. Who shall I say you are?'

'Ellen Adair, Miss Ashington's niece from the draper's in the village.'

Without another word she stalked ahead of me and I was left to admire her trim ankles in black stockings and the bouncy curls under the starched frilly cap. Then I forgot the maid in the beauty of marble and pale thick carpets, in the carving of the curved balustrade and the crystal chandeliers. I was not to be blamed if I dawdled a little in such prestigious surroundings but when I looked up the maid was waiting for me with an impatient frown on her pretty face and I hurried to catch up with her.

At one of the rooms along a wide passage she knocked on the door and opened it to announce me. I had never been in such a bedroom, it would quite easily have accommodated all Aunt Liza's shop and living quarters. But the beauty of the room was marred by its untidiness. The wardrobe doors were flung wide open and Lisanne was busy pulling out dresses which she threw across the satin bedspread unceremoniously. Her smile was warm when she greeted me, however, and she said, 'I hope you've come prepared to stay a while, there's more than I thought.'

I stared with dismay at the clothes on the bed, remembering Aunt Liza's terse instruction not to spend all day, that there was work to be done at the shop. When I looked doubtful she said anxiously, 'You have come to stay awhile, I hope?'

'Do all those clothes need altering? Because if they do I'm afraid it will take much longer than one day.'

'Oh dear, will it really? Did your aunt say you had to get back?'

'She did.'

'Well we're having visitors from near Mowbray, they haven't arrived yet so I'll saddle the horse and ride down to the village. I'll explain to your aunt, I'm sure she'll understand.'

She would most certainly take my absence better if the news came from Miss Lisanne, but even so the task in front of me would have been daunting to a more experienced needlewoman than I.

'Some of those are party dresses from the school in Switzerland, and they're far too long. Madame was adament about the length of our clothes and I daresay my grandmother would be too. Mother said they looked antiquated but they're too good to be thrown off. About two inches off all of them please, Ellen. You don't mind if I call you Ellen, do you? It's so much more informal than Miss Adair.'

She was busy picking out the dresses I was to shorten

and I approached the bed and picked up one of them, a beautiful china-blue gown in georgette. Looking at its beautifully draped skirt I couldn't help thinking it would be sacrilege to cut it.

'You're thinking I have too many, Ellen?' she said with a wry smile.

'No, I was just thinking how beautiful they all are. It must be heavenly to wear such a dress.'

'Do be a dear and make a good job of them, then we'll go through them and pick one or two out for you. We're exactly the same colouring, what flatters me will flatter you.'

'Oh Miss Lisanne, I couldn't possibly accept them. Besides, where would I ever wear them? The only function I ever go to is the village dance, I'd stick out like a sore thumb in something like this.'

'Well of course you would. You'd be the belle of the ball and all the other girls would be pea green with envy. We'll find something sophisticated, quite plain but well cut. None of the villagers will ever suspect that it cost the earth. Sometimes the plainer they are, the more expensive. Now you know what to do, don't you? You can work at the window so that you have a lovely view of the mere, and I'll have lunch sent up to you around twelve thirty. I take it you've brought cotton and the like with you?'

'Well I've brought a selection of cottons, I only hope they're the right colours.'

'They will be, Ellen. Now I'm off to beard your frosty old aunt. Don't worry, I'll be all sweetness and light and I'll buy something from the shop just to sweeten her up a bit.'

She was gone like a piece of quicksilver and I gathered up two or three dresses and took them over to the window. There was a beautiful view of the mere and the swans with their brood of cygnets sailing majestically across the water. The parkland looked so green and peaceful that I allowed myself the aesthetic pleasure of absorbing a scene totally alien to every facet of my life until that moment. It was as though I had existed on a different plane and that at any moment the dream would end and I would awake in my narrow bed in Aunt Liza's back room.

I lost myself in the sewing of those lovely dresses and I had no idea of the time. I did not even hear the door open, the first thing I knew was that two cool hands covered my eyes and a teasing voice said, 'Guess who?'

When I struggled the hands left my face but then I was taken hold of by strong hands and lifted bodily from my chair. I found myself looking down into a young man's laughing face, a handsome tall young man with blue eyes in a bronzed face, with the glint of sunlight in his dark wavy hair.

'What are you doing here all alone?' he said, laughing. 'I thought you'd be at the gates to meet me.'

I was staring at him in an astounded way, and gently he lowered me to the ground. 'Well,' he demanded more sternly, 'haven't you a word of greeting for Cousin Lance?'

At that moment there was a peal of laughter from the door and there was Lisanne convulsed with merriment. The young man looked from her to me in a great deal of puzzlement.

'How too romantic for words,' she trilled. 'Cousin Lance and Ellen Adair caught in an ecstatic embrace. You've embarrassed my friend, Lance, but I'm not suprised you thought she was me. We're as alike as sisters.'

He was staring down at me now, his dark eyes contrite and serious. 'I'm so sorry,' he said. 'I really thought you were Lisanne.'

I found my mouth suddenly twitching at the corner, and then the three of us were laughing again and he said, 'It really is remarkable how much alike you are, are you quite sure you're not related?'

'Quite sure, we couldn't possibly be.'

'I ought to introduce you properly, Ellen. This is my cousin Lancelot, but he hates the name and we hate it so we call him Lance. Lance, this is Ellen Adair.'

He took my hand gravely and smiled down into my eyes.

'Well I'll apologize once more, Ellen, although I can't say I regret my action. We'll meet again over lunch, I hope.'

I didn't contradict him, nor did Miss Lisanne, and with a swift smile he was gone. I heard them laughing together as they made their way along the corridor and I picked up my sewing again, though the first enthusiasm had gone.

Lunch was served to me where I was by a maidservant. There was fresh salmon and salad, a concoction of fruit lavishly decorated with cream and a pot filled with delicious coffee. While I ate I was able to look round the room. I felt no envy for the silken drapes at the long windows and the exquisite Chinese carpet, only appreciation. I felt I could never have been untidy in such a room, I would have cherished it and cared for it tenderly, but then if I had been born to such riches I might have felt differently.

After I had eaten I set about putting the room to rights, closing drawers, stacking magazines that had been left lying haphazardly on the floor, straightening lampshades that had been knocked crooked when Lisanne threw her clothes out of the wardrobes.

When the maid came to collect the tray she looked around her appreciatively, then with a smile she said, 'I can see yer've done a bit o'tidyin' up, Miss. It takes us all our time tidyin' up after Miss Lisanne.'

'I hated to see it so untidy. I hope she won't mind.'

She laughed. 'Mind, Miss? Nay, she'll hardly notice. Some folks 'ave it too easy, they don't appreciate it when they've got it.'

I stared at the pile of clothes ruefully. I couldn't hope to finish them in one day and I couldn't think that my aunt would let me make a habit of visiting the Hall to get on with the rest of them. I decided I would ask Miss Lisanne if I could take some home with me.

My opportunity came in the middle of the afternoon when she returned to the room to change out of her riding habit.

'How are you getting on?' she inquired brightly.

'I've finished two of them but I can't possibly finish all the others today.'

'Oh that doesn't matter, Ellen, you can come back tomorrow and the next day until they're done.'

'I won't be able to come again, Miss Lisanne, my aunt won't allow it.'

'She seemed all right about your being here when I talked to her. I'll have another word with her, I'm sure her bark's far worse than her bite.'

'She might be all right with you, Miss Lisanne, I'm the one who has to live with her.'

'But Ellen, I can't possibly wear them like that, when are you going to finish them for me?'

'I was going to ask you if I could take them back with me.'

The frown left her face as quickly as it had appeared.

'Well of course. I'll find you a suitcase and Lance and I will deliver you at your aunt's shop on our way to the Palmerstons'.'

I watched her flinging open the wardrobe doors. I had never seen such clothes, ranging from long ball gowns to silk afternoon dresses, but Lisanne stood looking at them with a frown on her pretty face.

'I'm so fed up with them,' she muttered. 'None of them are new, but I've got to look decent tonight, the Palmerstons are throwing a party for their youngest daughter so I've got to keep my end up. What do you think, Ellen, which of these will be suitable?'

She threw three of them on to the bed: a cornflower-blue taffeta, a cherry-red chiffon and another in black lace which she picked up suddenly and held against her.

'This is the one I love, Ellen, but even Mother was doubtful about it and Granny will be scandalized. I know it's probably too old for me and too sophisticated, but don't you just adore black even if it does make me look a Jezabel?'

'Which do you think your cousin Lance would like to see you in?'

'Oh, you know what men are. He'd love the blue, or that white one there with the blue streamers. My cousin Gervase would like me in black. Did you like Lance?'

'He seems nice. He's very attractive.'

'He is, isn't he? Did you know that the de Belleforts

always married their cousins? Both Lance and Gervase are very handsome, I don't much mind which of them I marry.'

I stared at her in amazement and she trilled with laughter.

'I've shocked you, Ellen. I expect you've been brought up to believe that people only marry the people they're in love with whereas I've been brought up to believe that the de Belleforts marry for expediency, to keep the money in the family and in the hope that love might come later.'

'Then you're not in love with either of your cousins?'

'Oh I love Lance, of course. I love him because he's nice and fun to be with. I haven't see Gervase since I was ten and I thought he was horrid. He wasn't the slightest bit interested in me, he was impossible to talk to and he spent all evening chatting up some woman whose husband was playing bridge in the card room.'

It was all a very different world to me. Talking of marriage to one man because he was fun to be with, and the other who would probably be indifferent. By this time she was rummaging through the dressing table for silk stockings.

'If Lance comes in do chat to him, Ellen. I'll wear the red chiffon and I'll take everything I need into the bathroom. Will you be able to get the dresses into this?'

She threw a leather suitcase on to the bed and without waiting for an answer went into the bathroom, slamming the door after her.

I spent the next few minutes carefully folding the dresses I intended to take with me. While I was busy with the straps Lance came into the room. He was wearing evening dress and I thought again how handsome he was. The sombre evening clothes gave him a peculiar distinction, more mature and strangely distinguished, and after a brief smile he said, 'Isn't she ready yet? We're going to be late, it's quite a drive over to the Palmerstons'.'

He eyed the suitcase I was struggling to put on the floor and came forward immediately to help me.

'What have you got in here, Ellen?' he demanded.

'Only dresses for alteration. Miss Lisanne said you would take me to my aunt's shop.'

'Come along then, I'll take you now. I doubt if there's room in the car for the three of us and that suitcase.'

I tripped beside him down the wide curving staircase where a maid was polishing the rail, and I could have smiled at her open-mouthed curiosity.

Lance's car was a low-slung open tourer with a bonnet that seemed to go on for ever and with precious little room in the back once the suitcase was in.

He drove fast down the long drive and once when I stole a look at his face he turned to smile at me.

'You'll have to tell where you live, Ellen, I don't know the village very well.'

'I live halfway down the high street, at the draper's shop.'

'With your aunt, I believe?'

'Yes.'

'And what do you do all day, serve in the shop and set out the window?'

I was aware of a strange resentment and yet there was nothing condescending in his tone of voice. How mundane he made my life sound in my own ears, serving in a shop, setting out the window, tasks that required no special training.

My heart sank when I saw Alec Devlin at the window of the baker's shop, his eyes almost popping out of his head with curiosity. Then I saw my aunt hurrying across the road from the pavement where she had been chatting to Alec's mother.

Both women stood on their respective pavements waiting for me to get out of Lance's car, watching him walk round to open the car door for me before he handed out the suitcase. They continued to watch while he smiled down at me and then got back into the car in the most unhurried manner, raising his hand in farewell before he drove up the street to turn round at the village hall and drive back, waving again as he passed the shop.

Aunt Liza strode into the shop with disapproval evident in her straight stiff back, leaving me to follow with the suitcase. She said acidly, 'Yer've taken yer time leavin' me on mi own all day. What's that yer bringin'?'

'There was a lot to do, Aunt, I couldn't possibly finish all these in one day. I asked if I could bring them home.'

'That means you'll spend every day workin' on 'em and expectin' another day to take 'em back to the 'All when they're finished. And who was that who brought you back?' she inquired shortly.

'It was Mr Lance, Lady de Bellefort's grandson.'

The frown grew more prominent. 'Don't ye be gettin' any fancy ideas, Ellen, men in 'is walk o' life are not lookin' for girls in yours.'

'I have no ideas at all about Lance de Bellefort, Aunt Liza, he was kind enough to bring me home, that's all.'

'Well, just as long as ye remembers that. Now I've got a meetin' to go to and I'm late as it is, thanks to you. Mrs Devlin's gone off without me, I'll 'ave to 'urry to catch 'er up. Lock up the shop when I've gone. I'll be back about ten.'

I watched her pulling her black straw hat down over her hair before snatching up her big black bag and marching out into the shop. I always wondered what was in that bag which she took everywhere, little realizing that I was soon to find out.

When the sun went down it was dark in the small room behind the shop and I was glad to put a match to the fire and light the gas jet. I worked steadily, sitting in Aunt Liza's velvet chair near the window, the only sound the steady ticking of the clock on the mantelpiece and the chattering of the birds in the tall elms. I was about to make a cup of tea when I heard somebody knocking loudly on the front door and I jumped to my feet, startled.

It was just nine o'clock, not nearly time for Aunt Liza to come home and although it was a sleepy quiet place, from time to time there had been trouble from village louts with too much to drink in them. Nervously I went into the shop and tried to see who was at the door from the window. I was hampered by the piles of wool Aunt Liza had stacked in the window so I went to the door and in a trembling voice called out, 'Who's there?'

I was relieved to hear the vicar's voice, even though the tones were undeniably urgent.

'It's your aunt, Ellen, she's been taken ill. Can you come at once?'

I unlocked the door with trembling fingers and there he stood accompanied by two members of the committee, both elderly women and decidedly agitated.

'We couldn't bring her home, Ellen,' the vicar explained. 'We've laid her down on one of the benches and Mrs Devlin's gone for the doctor, I expect she'll catch him at home at this time. Can you come right away?'

'Of course, Vicar, just let me get my keys. Is she very bad?'

'We couldn't bring her round, Ellen, she just passed out in the middle of an argument she'd been taking part in. One minute she was her usual forceful self, the next she was gasping for breath. I don't like the look of her at all, but perhaps by the time we get back she'll have come round.'

We hurried through the dusk to where the lights from the village hall streamed out into the night, and as we arrived we saw the doctor and Mrs Devlin at the door before us. Mrs Devlin eyed me unhappily, saying, 'She didn't look 'erself when she arrived, Ellen. Late she was and no doubt she'd been hurrying.'

I felt suddenly very guilty, and that her eyes were hostile as well as accusing, but the vicar hurried us into the hall and my eyes immediately took in the group of women clustered at one side of the hall while the doctor bent over my aunt. I stood with Mrs Devlin and the vicar while he conducted his examination, then at last he turned to take stock of us before addressing me.

'As far as I can see she's had a stroke. Are you the niece?'

'Yes, Doctor.'

'Just the two of you I suppose?'

'Yes.'

'Well I'll get her into the village hospital, they won't be pleased at this time of night but you'll not be able to cope on your own. She's a dead weight, you'll not be able to lift her and I'm not sure how severe the stroke is as yet.'

'Will I be able to go with her to the hospital?' I asked him.

'I'll drive you there myself after they've taken her away.'

'I'll come with you to the hospital,' Mrs Devlin said sharply.

It seemed to me that the next half hour happened like something in a dream. The ambulance chugged down the street and two men carrying a stretcher jumped out and hurried inside the hall. Aunt Liza lay as one dead, her face grey, her hands lying limply at her sides until I tucked them carefully under the rug, then we were climbing into the doctor's trap for our journey to the hospital.

'Never seen 'er ail a thing in all the time I've known 'er,' Mrs Devlin was saying. 'She'll not be a good patient, 'er sort never are.'

'How old is your aunt?' the doctor asked suddenly.

'I'm not sure, sixty perhaps.'

'Fifty's more like,' Mrs Devlin snapped. 'Nay, Ellen, whatever made ye think she was sixty?'

'I never really knew, she just seemed sixty, that's all.'

I realized I didn't know much about Aunt Liza at all and I hoped fervently that he wouldn't ask me any more questions. Mrs Devlin was the person to ask, not me.

It was after two o'clock when we were entering our respective dwellings having left Aunt Liza at the cottage hospital, still unconscious. The doctor said we could do nothing more that night and I would be allowed to visit the following day.

On parting, Mrs Devlin whispered, 'I don't like the look of 'er, Ellen. Mi mother died from a stroke and she never did regain consciousness – just like Liza, she was. What are ye goin' to do if she doesn't get over it, and what are ye goin' to do if she needs nursin'? Can ye manage 'er and the shop?'

'I don't know, Mrs Devlin, I don't know what will happen.'

'I suppose the shop'll 'ave to be sold. That niece of 'ers in Ripon'll not want it. 'Ave ye the money to buy it?'

'No.'

'Mm. Make a nice little tea shop it would. Mi 'usband's offen said we could branch out across the road 'ere. But these are early days, luv, I 'opes Liza'll get better and come 'ome.'

The fire had long since died in the grate and the room looked untidy with my sewing. I felt cold with shock and my hands trembled as I filled the kettle but all thoughts of sleep had deserted me. There was too much on my mind.

I was sorry about Aunt Liza, sorry without loving her, without really liking her very much, but once more I was burdened with insecurity. If she died my whole life would be changed and once again my father's figure loomed large, to be feared and to escape from. I prayed fervently for my aunt's life, that it might be spared both for her own sake and for mine, at least long enough to afford me the few years that would place me irrevocably beyond his jurisdiction.

My prayers were not to be answered. At eight o'clock the next morning a message came to me that Aunt Liza had died during the night without regaining consciousness, and during the next few days I had so much to do that my immediate future was the last thing I thought about.

I hated going through her things, and I hated even more my preoccupation with the rough diary she had kept in an old manuscript book. Right from the day she made me leave Liverpool there were references to me, most of them uncomplimentary, but two of them I was destined to remember most vividly.

The first one was written only a few days after I came to live with her and it read: 'I can't believe what Ellen tells me about her father who I've allus believed to be an upright God-fearing man, nor what she tells me about that girl from her village. One day I'll make it my business to find out, and if she's been lying to me she'll have to go, I'll have no further truck with the girl.'

The second entry was made on the night she came back from her brother's house in Ripon:

'Ellen's been to Liverpool, she hasn't said so but I know, and she's been to see that Kitty McGuire. I know now I've done the right thing by leaving everything I've got to my brother and his daughter. If I'd left some of it to Ellen she'd have been off seeing that Kitty and no doubt sharing whatever she'd got with her. My brother was right, I should never have doubted him.'

I stared at the pages filled with her small ill-formed handwriting, hearing her acid voice and seeing her thin-lipped doubting face. Then I started to cry, thinking how different it could have been.

I could have worked so hard in that little shop, made something of it, and I could have made Aunt Liza proud of me if she hadn't been so prejudiced and uncaring. Now my future was an empty place, I would be without a home or employment. But worse than that, I had to write to my father to tell him his half-sister was dead.

The village was in mourning on the day of Aunt Liza's funeral. The curtains were drawn in every window and all through the morning the women came and went from their front doors in order not to miss a solitary happening.

I altered one of Aunt Liza's black skirts to fit me and I wore my white silk blouse. It was a warm day so I didn't need a coat and I tied a black ribbon in my hair because I didn't possess a black hat, and I couldn't bring myself to wear one of Aunt Liza's.

Alec Devlin delivered balm cakes and boiled ham and tongue, and Mrs Devlin helped me to make sandwiches. Later he came again with huge slabs of fruit cake, and Mrs Devlin said, 'I suppose the brother'll settle up with mi for all this, Ellen. You'll 'ave nothin' to spare, I don't suppose.'

We spread the repast out in the kitchen and covered the plates with greaseproof paper, then she went to get ready for the funeral and I sat waiting. Aunt Liza lay in her coffin in the living room where they had brought her from the mortuary that morning but I had no desire to look at her, a fact which Mrs Devlin had regarded as unfeeling and unusual.

I hated to go into the room and when I did so I walked

with averted eyes and the thought that I would never again be able to sit there without seeing the coffin on its trestle across one corner. Because of my fears I was inordinately glad to hear voices in the shop and next moment four people entered the living room. I knew immediatley that these were my aunt's relatives from Ripon – her brother Simeon Ashington and his wife Martha, their daughter Jennie and her financé George. Although the two older people went immediately to the coffin, the girl and the man took stock of me.

Jennie was a pale girl with hazel eyes and light brown hair, and she clung on to the arm of the young man as though afraid to let go. I thought he looked like a bank clerk. He was correctly dressed and well scrubbed and he had pale protruding blue eyes and a receding chin. Neither of them seemed disposed to be civil towards me.

The father said somewhat sullenly, 'I suppose you're Ellen?'

'Yes.'

'Well we didn't expect this, to be sure. Our Liza seemed as fit as a fiddle when she stayed with us i' Ripon. Not bin doin' too much, 'as she?'

'No. I'm sure she hasn't.'

'Stroke was it?'

'Yes. The death certificate is on the table and the doctor said if you cared to visit him he would tell you everything you needed to know.'

'Ay well, I might just do that after the funeral. Is yer father and anybody else comin'?'

'I haven't heard but I've written to tell everybody I thought should know.'

'Well Cousin Edie won't be comin', she wont' leave that damn dog of 'ers, so there's only yer father and mother. If they intend comin' they should be 'ere anytime.'

At that moment the bell tinkled once more above the shop door and my heart leapt when I saw my father in the doorway.

Our eyes met across the room, but for all the

acknowledgement he made I might have been a marble statue instead of his daughter.

The pain of his rejection was acute, but almost immediately it was dispelled by the sight of my brother Peter and the warmth of his smile. I hoped we would be able to talk later, although there was little chance of it now because my father had placed a firm hand on Peter's shoulder and kept it there.

Mrs Devlin returned and introduced herself, and then the funeral coaches were outside and the men were coming in to close up the coffin.

It seemed that all along the long rambling high street people in black stood at their doors. Pulled up at the front of the shop was a black hearse with purple velvet curtains at the windows and purple plumes on the headgear of the black horses.

Two coaches followed, each pulled by two black horses, and into the first one my father climbed followed by Peter and myself, while the other five people piled into the other. When I questioned this procedure the undertaker said, 'Your father is the eldest brother, Miss Adair, and you are living in Miss Ashington's house.'

'I see,' I replied with a little smile.

All the same I didn't miss the haughty stare Jennie favoured me with and I sat miserably opposite my father's sullen face and Peter's embarrassed one. Just before we reached the churchyard, Father snapped, 'I noticed ye haven't asked about yer mother, Ellen.'

'I'm sorry Father, how is Mother?'

'Not well, not well at all. She needs somebody to look after 'er and I've got mi work to see to.'

I said nothing. Was this the preamble to asking me to return home, I wondered, and catching Peter's eyes on me I didn't miss the slight shake of his head.

My opportunity to talk to him came while we walked together towards the gates of the churchyard after the service.

'Is my mother really ill?' I asked Peter fearfully.

'No more than she always is, Ellen. You mustn't think of

comin' home, for if you do ye'll never get away again. Yer've made the break, Ellen.'

'But is she being looked after?'

'Our Mary's very good and I suppose Naomi does a bit. Mi father could do more.'

'You've left school, Peter, what are you doing?'

'There's not much work in the village, Ellen, but I'm doin' a bit of farm labouring. Mi father sez there might be a job goin' over at St Hilda's when old Mr Marshall retires but I don't want to be a sexton. I daren't tell mi father, though.'

'What will you do then?'

'When I'm eighteen I'm going to sea. It's something I want to do and next time Arnold Mason comes home he's promised to take me to Liverpool with him and get me on his ship. I'm countin' the days.'

'Do they know about it at home, Peter?'

'Nobody knows about it. I'll 'ave to do it just like you did, Ellen, a note left in the kitchen for 'em to find. It's the only way.'

'Then we'll both be outcasts, Peter, the sort of people nobody at home ever talks about.'

'I suppose so.'

For a few minutes we walked in silence, then abruptly I asked, 'Did you ever hear any talk about mi father and Phoebe Patterson?'

His face flushed and he looked acutely embarrassed, then he said softly, 'I got to watchin' 'im, Ellen, after I saw 'im goin' into her cottage. I don't think anybody in the village suspects 'e's friendly with 'er, 'e's covered his tracks too well for that. I'm just glad mi mother doesn't know about it, she worships 'im just like she allus did.'

'Oh Peter, I could never come home, I'd have to confront him with it, I couldn't stop miself, and in his heart he doesn't want mi home. He'd never be sure of me, would he?'

'No, Ellen, he never would. What will ye do?'

'I honestly don't know. The shop's goin' to the niece and she'll soon dispose of it. There's no work in the village so

I'll have to think very hard of what I want to do and where I'm goin'.'

'I hope we get a chance to talk again, Ellen, but if not I'll write to you. We'd best be quiet now, 'ere they come.'

CHAPTER 16

As the afternoon wore on I could see there wasn't going to be much opportunity to speak with Peter again. The people from Ripon made short work of the sandwiches and I was kept busy brewing pots of tea while Mrs Devlin basked in their admiration of her husband's cakes.

My father maintained an austere silence and Peter sat beside him looking miserable until I engineered his help in handing round plates.

'It doesn't look as if we're goin' to be able to talk again, Ellen,' he whispered, 'we're goin' home on the four o'clock train.'

'Is there anywhere I can write to you when I'm settled – how about the vicarage?' I asked.

'Nay, the vicar'd hand yer letter to mi father. Ye can write to Mr Nelson, I 'elps out at the smallholdin' at the weekends, 'e'd pass yer letter on. Mr Nelson's no love for mi father, though Mrs Nelson'd feel she 'ad to give it to mi mother.'

'Then as soon as I'm settled I'll write, Peter.'

'Now then you two,' came my father's voice from the doorway, 'we're waitin' for tea in 'ere, and y'ed best look sharp, Peter, the train won't wait for us.'

In minutes they were shaking hands, saying it was a sad business. Then they were gone without a backward glance from my father and with a long sad look from my brother.

Mrs Devlin helped me to clear away, then Simeon Ashington said, 'Well, Ellen, there's things to talk over. I reckon we'd best make a start,' whereupon Mrs Devlin wished them all good afternoon and I went with her to the shop door.

'It looks as if he means business, luv,' she said. 'My 'usband'd be interested in buying the shop so just you see 'ow the land lies and if ye gets a chance tell 'im we'll be interested.'

They sat in a small bunch across the hearth from me. I soon felt sure they had come well prepared, that between Aunt Liza's death and the day of her funeral, matters to do with her shop had been well and truly gone into.

'Ye knew of course that the shop was to be our Jennie's,' her father began. 'Mi sister said she'd left ye in no doubt about that.'

I nodded, unable to trust the evenness of my voice.

'Well our Jennie'll be gettin' married next year and goin' to live i' Harrogate. George 'ere's got a transfer to the bank there and it'll be very nice with 'is folks livin' there. Naturally she won't want the shop so it'll 'ave to be sold. I suppose yer've no money to buy it?'

'No.'

'Ave ye somewhere to go?'

'Not at the moment.'

'Well obviously these things can't be done in a day so there's no reason why the shop can't go on tradin'. I'll pay ye a wage for lookin' after it and it's a roof over yer head. How about the same money that Liza paid ye – does that seem fair to you, Ellen?'

'Did my aunt tell you how much she paid me?'

'Two and sixpence a week she said, and yer board and lodgin'. I'll give ye four shillings, that sounds about right to me.'

'I think the Devlins might be interested in buying the shop.'

'Is that so? Why didn't she say somethin' when she was 'ere then?'

'I expect she thought you might think she was interfering. You could speak to Mr Devlin if you have the time.'

'What's 'e aimin' to do with the shop if he gets it? E'll not be keepin' it on as a draper's?'

'No. Mrs Devlin thought it might make a nice tea room, selling their confectionery of course.'

'Would he keep you on 'ere, has he mentioned that?'

'No. That has never been mentioned.'

'Well if the price was right and if he'll match whatever else I might be offered p'rhaps it would make a cafe. I can't see it payin' except on market days.'

'I think if it was here it would pay. Walkers and climbers come into the district and people come to look at Langstone Priory. There has been talk that Lady de Bellefort might throw open the gardens several days a week, and there's the old abbey up on the fell.'

His eyes narrowed with speculation, then turning to his wife he said, 'The shop's got possibility, Martha, if we'd bin a bit nearer you might 'a bin able to do somethin' with it. I haven't time to see Devlin today but I'll get mi solicitor to have a talk to im. Now, Ellen, yer'll keep the place lookin' nice and if folks want to look round yer'll treat 'em respectful and point out all the good things in the village. If ye does all that don't be surprised if there isn't a nice little present for ye at the end of it.'

'Can't we 'ave a look round, Father?' Jennie said. 'There might be somethin' George and me might want.'

'And 'ow are ye goin' to get it 'ome? We can come again, lass, and bring a suitcase and hire a trap from the station.'

'There's tablecloths and the like,' Jennie protested. 'Surely there'll be a suitcase we can put 'em in.'

'Oh well, ye might as well look while you're 'ere. P'rhaps Ellen'd show ye where our Liza kept things.'

Seething with anger I took Jennie upstairs where she went through Aunt Liza's bedroom. While I watched her I heard a sound from the other bedroom and went in, to find her mother rummaging through my things.

'You'll find nothing in here, Mrs Ashington. This is my room and there are only my things in it,' I said firmly.

'Oh well, I was just savin' time,' she said, and without a look in my direction went on to the landing. 'Ave ye got everythin' ye want, Jennie?' she called out.

Jennie appeared with several tablecloths, two pairs of new bedroom slippers and a roll of white damask.

'There's more,' she said, 'but we couldn't put it all in the suitcase. I thought we could put these in the carpet bag I saw in the kitchen.'

'What's 'appenin' to Liza's clothes?' Mrs Ashington asked as her daughter tripped lightly down the stairs.

'I have no idea. Is there anything you want?'

'Well I never much liked the things Liza wore but she did 'ave a new 'at for that weddin' she went to. I'd like to 'ave a look at that.'

Together we returned to Aunt Liza's bedroom where Mrs Ashington helped herself to the wedding hat, the new blouse and several items of underwear wrapped in tissue paper and unworn.

'Liza was a great one for black,' she said, 'but it doesn't suit mi. This 'at'll do very nicely for our Jennie's weddin', I can find a costume to wear to it and it'll save mi a bit o' money.'

At just before five thirty I saw them depart carrying two suitcases and the carpet bag, watched from their upstairs window by both Mr and Mrs Devlin, and by Alec from the front of the shop.

They were still marching down the street when the doctor's trap drew up at the front door and he alighted with a conspiratorial smile.

'I see the vultures have gone, Ellen, and not empty-handed by the look of things.'

I smiled. I liked Doctor Jarvis, he was always friendly and with a ready smile, and I liked his sense of humour which leaned towards dryness.

'Have they sorted your life out for you, Ellen?'

'For the next few weeks yes, Doctor. After that I'm on my own. Have you time to come in for a while, Doctor?'

'Well I'm due up at the Hall, the old lady is indisposed today but it's only the usual sick headache she suffers from. A few minutes is neither here nor there.'

He followed me into the living room which still smelled sickly of flowers and I hurried into the kitchen to put the kettle on.

'No tea for me, Ellen,' he called out, 'but I'll have a tot of your aunt's whisky if you know where to lay your hands on it.'

I grinned at him across the room. 'I don't rightly know that I do, Doctor.'

'Well I'll show you, Ellen. Second drawer down, pushed away at the back. If they'd discovered that it would be on its way to the station along with the other loot.'

I poured out a generous dram for him, and with a wink he raised his glass, saying, 'Good health to you, lassy, and here's to your future. Now did your aunt leave you any money?'

'Not a penny, Doctor. I'm to stay in the shop and work 'til its sold, then I have no plans.'

He shivered delicately.

'Heaven preserve us from such a project. Women gossipin' over their teacups and hikers queuing up for tables at the weekends. I'll be telling my wife to keep clear of the street on market days, I can tell you.'

'So, Ellen, you're likely to be leavin' us in the near future, and no place to go.'

'Something like that.'

'Well I'll keep my eyes and ears open. Have you thought of going into service, Ellen? There's not much else for a girl these days unless its shop work and you'd have to go to one of the big towns for that. By the way, I've got your aunt's big black bag, but I didn't want to deliver it while the funeral party was here. It's in the trap, Ellen, I'll try to hand it over without the nosy parkers seeing what we're about.'

The high street was quiet. The men would be home from the fields by this time and families sitting down to their evening meal, even so the doctor looked quickly along the street, then up at the Devlins' before he handed out Aunt Liza's bag wrapped in newspaper, then with a gay wave of his hand he picked up his whip and urged the ponies on.

Back in the house I took out the bag and stared at it curiously. It was bulky and I had sometimes wondered idly what she carried in it and why she took it everywhere. At the same time I was reluctant to open it and I could imagine her standing watching me, grim-faced and accusing.

I laid it on the table and went into the kitchen to make

a cup of tea. Whatever the bag contained, I had no right to it. Instead I should have been racing down the high street, trying to catch the Ashingtons before they could board the train. Then glancing briefly at the clock I saw that it was six thirty and by this time they would be on their way.

I picked up the bag gingerly, turning it this way and that, then taking my courage in both hands I pulled at the clasp and opened it.

It was full. Two pairs of leather gloves and a woollen scarf lay on top, and under them was a pair of scissors and a small cash book showing the shop's day-to-day takings. There was a rolled copy of the church magazine and two tickets for the Harvest Fair, then I opened the middle pocket and stared incredulously at a roll of banknotes.

With trembling fingers I took it out and started to count. There was over a hundred pounds, a hundred and seventeen to be precise as well as several pounds in loose change, and if at first my heart leapt, it immediately sank when I realized the money was not mine. At first I wanted to rush out of the house to share my secret with the Devlins, but something held me back. I needed to think and I didn't think they were the right people to advise me.

I decided to sleep on it. Tomorrow I would tell Doctor Jarvis what I had found and accept any advice he cared to give me, and in spite of all the trauma of the day I was surprised how well I slept that night.

CHAPTER 17

I viewed the shop the next morning with many misgivings. When my aunt was alive I had felt my interest in her shop was a way of repaying her for giving me a home. Now I felt no allegiance whatsoever to her relatives in Ripon, and yet mechanically I set about tidying out the drawers and making the window seem a little more enticing.

Mid morning Miss Lisanne arrived on her horse and from my vantage point in the window I thought what a pretty picture she made in her dark habit, riding side-saddle on the big chestnut horse, her blond hair hidden under her attractive yet severe bowler and with the snowy white stock at her throat.

She smiled at me brightly and perched on the wooden seat before the counter.

'I came to see how you were getting along with my clothes, Ellen. My mother might be coming here any day now and if she wishes to take me back with her I'll be needing them.'

'Didn't you hear that my aunt died, Miss Lisanne? I'm afraid there's been so much to do I haven't been able to finish them. The funeral was only yesterday.'

Her pretty face took on a petulant air. 'Oh yes, Granny told me something about it, but I thought the funeral was days ago.'

'I've only had the dresses a few days, she died the night I brought them home.'

'Oh dear, what are we to do then? I suppose you're looking after the shop on your own?'

'Yes I am.'

'Does that mean you're not going to be able to do them?'

'I'll work on them in the evenings and during the day if I get a chance. I promise you'll have them as soon as I've finished.'

'Oh well I suppose I'll have to be satisfied with that. It's so inconvenient.'

Suddenly aware of my expression she said more contritely. 'You must think I'm an unfeeling little beast but it's the way I am, I suppose. I'm sorry about your aunt, Ellen.'

She smiled at me brightly across the counter, then with a gay wave of her whip she tripped lightly out of the shop and I watched her untying her horse while Mr Devlin came across the road to assist her into the saddle.

Business was slow. People came to look in the window and move on, almost as if they thought it too soon to be buying, and for want of something to do I sat in the shop stitching one of Lisanne's dresses.

There was a lot on my mind, particularly the contents of the black leather bag, and I wished it was time to shut up the shop so that I could seek Doctor Jarvis's advice.

My next visitor was Mrs Devlin, cheerful and conspiratorial, asking, 'Did ye mention we might be interested in buyin' the shop, Ellen?'

'Yes. Mr Ashington's putting it in the hands of his solicitors, but he did say if the price was right he'd have no objection to letting you have it.'

'We talked about it all last night. A little cafe'd do right well 'ere, Ellen, particularly if Lady de Bellefort opens the gardens for visitors. We'd not need the livin' room, we could knock that wall down to make more room, and the back kitchen's big enough to make tea and coffee and see to the cakes. We're not thinkin' about meals, only mornin' coffee and afternoon tea. The little cafe in Scarborough was makin' a fortune doin' things like that, and we 'ave a good name for our confectionary.'

I reflected cynically that this had been my aunt's best friend, now all she was interested in was how much Aunt Liza's death might benefit them.

While she chatted on the doorbell rang and I looked up gratefully to see Doctor Jarvis entering the shop.

Wrapped up in her ambitions Mrs Devlin didn't turn round so he stood patiently waiting for her to conclude her fantasies, then when she did turn round to see who my visitor was she blushed as red as a beetroot and I did not miss his sharp twinkling eyes.

After that she beat a hasty retreat and he said with a wry smile, 'So she's got the cafe already has she, Ellen, and where do you come into all this? Has she asked you to run the cafe for them?'

'I don't come into it all all, Doctor, but I'm very glad you've called. If you hadn't I'd have called to see you.'

'I suppose it's your aunt's black bag?'

'Yes, Doctor. Can we talk in the living room? I'll hear the bell if anybody comes.'

He followed me into the living room, and although it was mid morning I helped him to a tot of whisky and he sat in Aunt Liza's big chair drinking it with obvious enjoyment.

'Now then, Ellen, what did she carry in that black bag? Ye never saw her without it.'

I took it out and emptied the contents on the table.

He raised his eyebrows at the wad of notes.

'I always thought there'd be money in there, Ellen. Is the bag empty?'

'I think so.'

'Well we'll just make sure, it would be like your aunt to keep money and jewellery stitched into the lining.'

I watched his hands exploring the inside of the bag and the innumerable pockets, then looking up with a smile he said, 'Hand me the scissors, Ellen, I didn't think I'd be far wrong. There's somethin' at the bottom here.'

'Damn!' he said suddenly. 'There's some sort of pin in there.'

Next moment he had brought out a heavy gold brooch and was sucking his bleeding finger ruefully. 'The blasted pin was open,' he said. 'I can't think why the woman didn't wear her jewellery instead of carrying it about in her handbag. Hold on awhile, Ellen, there's somethin' else in there.'

I picked up the brooch curiously. It was engraved with the initial 'L' and decorated with tiny embossed flowers, and I supposed it was valuable because it was heavy and obviously gold. Then there was a clatter on the table and the doctor was setting out a row of gold sovereigns as well as a gold chain and locket.

'Did she ever wear any jewellery, Ellen?' he asked sharply.

'She had a gold watch on a long chain and several small brooches. I never saw these before.'

'And where is her jewellery now?'

'She kept it upstairs in her chest of drawers.'

'Well nip up and see if it's still there. If it's gone then they took it yesterday.'

I searched every drawer in the bedroom but I didn't find the jewellery, and when I told the doctor he smiled grimly, saying, 'I guessed as much. Well, Ellen, I wouldn't let 'em get their hands on this lot. They ransacked this house yesterday and took what valuables they found. They know nothin' about this and I'd keep it that way.'

'But can I do that, Doctor, I haven't any right and I'm pretty sure she'd want her niece to have it.'

'Look, lassy, you're going to lose the roof over your head, and your livelihood. You'll have no home and no money and they'll get a fair price for the shop. I reckon they've done very well. Now what are you going to do with this money?'

'I've no idea.'

'I'll put it in my bank for you and you'll get interest on it. The bank's in Ilkley but that's no problem, you'll have the address and you can get what you want when you want it, and it's a better idea than leaving it in the village. If the nosy parkers sees ye going into the little bank in the high street they'll put two and two together and make five.'

'I don't know what to say, Doctor.'

'Ye mean you've got a conscience about this money, Ellen. Well you don't need to have, love. I knew your aunt a good many years as a cantankerous tight-fisted and very difficult woman. I could hardly believe my own ears when I heard she'd brought a niece home to live with her, I could never think it was out of Christian charity. My wife told me how nice the little shop was lookin'. What made you come 'ere, Ellen?'

'I was living in Liverpool and she came looking for me.

I couldn't get on with mi father and I ran away from home when I left school. I was happy in Liverpool. I didn't want to come here but I was under age and I didn't have much choice. I could never go back to living with mi father.'

'Was he at the funeral?'

'Yes, with mi brother Peter. He'll leave home too when he's old enough to join the merchant navy.'

He looked at me shrewdly but made no comment, then he wrapped up the notes in a page taken from the newspaper and after counting the sovereigns placed them in his pocket.

'There's fifteen of 'em, Ellen, a nice little nest egg, and I hope your aunt's somewhere or other bein' made aware of what we're doing.'

'If she is she'll haunt me, I just know she will.'

'Don't even think it, lass. She'll be so busy makin' her peace with her maker she'll have no time to haunt you, and if she haunts me I'll soon send her packin'.'

As our eyes met I suddenly felt very light-hearted and I laughed joyfully for the first time in days.

'That's better, Ellen, that pretty face wasn't made for tears. By the way, wasn't that Lady de Bellefort's granddaughter I saw leavin' the shop earlier on?'

'Yes, I'm doing some sewing for her.'

'You're very much like her, you know, I thought so the first time I saw you. Are there any skeletons in your family, Ellen?'

I smiled. 'No, I'm sure there's not. None of my family had ever heard of the de Belleforts and they didn't come from these parts.'

'Well perhaps way back there was a romance nobody these days knows anything about. These things happened, Ellen, some member of the gentry and a local lass, some baby born on the wrong side of the blanket and a whole village coverin' up the scandal. You and that lass at the hall could be sisters and it's my bet the old lady knows a thing or two.'

'She's remarked on the resemblance but that's all.'

'She's a shrewd one. Well I'd best be off, I'm overdue

on my rounds as it is. I'll see to your money for you, Ellen, and I'll be in touch.'

He grinned at me mischievously and suddenly I felt more light-hearted than I had any right to be, with a fortune that I had no right to and a fellow conspirator to aid and abet me.

CHAPTER 18

In the middle of the afternoon Alec Devlin appeared in the shop, jaunty and smiling. He said amiably, 'Well, Ellen, what's it feel like to 'ave the shop to yerself and be yer own boss?'

'I'm not quite used to the idea yet.'

'I suppose mi mother's told ye about our ideas for a cafe. What do you think, Ellen.?'

'It sounds like a good idea with more and more people coming into the village.'

'Well it'd be very handy with the shop across the way. All the bakin' could be done there, all we'd need to do is bring it across the first thing in the mornin'. It'd be a good thing on market days and we've heard they intend to 'ave a market on an extra day.'

'Will your mother be taking charge of the cafe?'

'They're talkin' about mi wife getting involved, but I don't think she'd take to that. She's not a good mixer and when the baby comes she'll 'ave 'er hands full. Did ye know we were goin' to be parents, Ellen?'

'No I didn't, Alec. Congratulations.'

'Well ye can see mi point, can't ye, Ellen? I can't see mi wife wantin' to come 'ere and mi mother wouldn't make a waitress, she'd spend all 'er time gossipin' to the customers. No, what it wants is a nice attractive young girl who'd look well in a frilly cap and apron, somebody who can talk nice to the customers and take a pride in settin' out the window and seein' to the tables. It might suit you, Ellen.'

I stared at him stupidly.

He grinned at me and sidled round the counter. 'Think about it, Ellen. I'd 'ave a word with mi father, I'm sure both 'im and mi stepmother'd soon see the sense of it. Ye could live upstairs and work down 'ere, and it's my bet 'e'd pay ye more than ever ye aunt did.'

I was on the point of thinking the idea had possibilities when I felt his arm slide round my waist and suddenly I was pushing him away while was was cajoling, 'Think about it, Ellen, you and me working more or less together, there's many a day we can get off to Harrogate or even to Ripon. I'm lookin' round for a little car and it'll all be in the line o' business.'

Angrily I pushed him away. 'You've got a nerve, Alec Devlin. In one breath you're telling me your wife's going to have a baby and in the next you're suggesting you and me might have something going for each other. I think you're despicable. I don't want to work in your wretched cafe and I don't want to have any more to do with you.'

His face was red and angry as he answered me. 'Well I don't see you've any cause to be so high and mighty, Ellen Adair, yer'll be out on yer ear when mi father buys this shop and I know for a fact yer aunt didn't leave ye any money. You thought ye were too good for mi 'afore I got wed, it seems ye still thinks so.'

'I don't, Alec, I just think you're a married man who's going to be a father. Why don't *ye* remember it?'

Sulky, like a small badly behaved child he flung out of the shop, slamming the door, and I stood dejectedly at the counter trembling with distaste.

Alec could be vindictive. Once his father got the shop I felt sure my days would be numbered.

It was a long wearisome day. I was glad when I could pull down the shop blinds and go into the back to prepare my evening meal.

I was still in the kitchen when there was a smart rap on the shop door, and I hurried to open it. I stared in surprise at the de Bellefort butler standing there tall and unsmiling, and even more surprised when he handed me an envelope.

'Her ladyship asked mi to give you this, Miss. I'm not to wait for a reply.'

I stared at it stupidly for several seconds, then he raised his hat and stalked off down the street. Across at the baker's Alec Devlin was pulling up the shutters, his round eyes bulging with curiosity.

A faint aura of perfume hung about the pale cream envelope, and as I turned it over I saw that the de Bellefort crest decorated the flap. It contained a single sheet of pale cream parchment and the handwriting was beautifully formed and flowing:

> Dear Miss Adair,
> I was very sorry to hear of the death of your aunt who was always most efficient at ordering my requirements. I shall miss her and would like to think that the shop will continue to function.
>
> I shall be much obliged if you will kindly call upon me one day soon to suit your convenience when I shall have a proposition to put before you. It is not necessary to make an appointment, I am invariably at home.
>
> Yours sincerely,
> Helena, Lady de Bellefort

For several minutes I stared at the letter. What sort of proposition could Lady de Bellefort possibly have to put before me? And immediately I thought of going into service. But I didn't want to scrub floors and clean vegetables, serve tea or wait on table in the Hall's enormous dining room. It would be a far cry from the mission but I'd had a surfeit of menial tasks, and yet I wasn't trained for anything else unless it was sewing, and I sewed because I needed the money, not because I wanted to spend the rest of my life doing it.

I thought distastefully of Alec Devlin's proposition, and it seemed to me then that anything her ladyship might propose would be preferable to looking after the Devlins' tea room and having Alec think he had a right to paw me because he was paying my wages.

I realized suddenly that I wasn't very hungry, so I let myself out of the shop and set off along the street at a brisk pace. I hadn't planned to climb the fell above the Hall, but unconsciously my feet led me on to it. The late afternoon sunshine lit up the mullioned windows until they blazed as if a fire burned in the rooms, and there was a timeless peace about the parkland and the shimmering mere. As I sat on the fell I saw two girls walking arm in arm from the direction of the house. I knew that they were servants from their attire, but they were chatting happily together and quite suddenly I felt an urge to belong in such a life.

What did it really matter what I did as long as it was good honest work? I had money at the back of me even if I still felt it shouldn't be mine, and I badly needed somewhere to live. At that moment I prayed that Lady de Bellefort might have the solution I was looking for, and then suddenly I thought about Kitty.

Kitty would have tossed her head at the idea of going into service. Service would never open the door to ermine and emeralds but it would put another meal in my mouth and find me somewhere to lay my head. It was high time I forgot about Kitty and her ideas of grandeur.

CHAPTER 19

It was Sunday afternoon before I could take advantage of Lady de Bellefort's request to visit her. In the meantime the shop was busy, and I was agreeably surprised when I totted up my takings on Saturday evening. Aunt Liza would have been highly gratified and no doubt her brother would be too.

I had finished all Miss Lisanne's alterations but was not looking forward to the journey up to Langstone Priory with a full suitcase.

On Sunday morning I attended church out of deference to my aunt and I was very glad I'd gone when the vicar said prayers for her soul and the congregation joined in singing her favourite hymn, 'Abide with Me'. After the service many came to offer their condolences and most of them wanted to know if I intended staying in the village and keeping open the shop. When I said I didn't know, one woman said, 'I suppose we could get by without a draper's, the wool on the market's much cheaper,' a remark which left me thinking that neither Aunt Liza nor myself would be much missed.

Doctor Jarvis and his wife walked down the church path with me, and he amused me by saying, 'Well Ellen, have ye given a good account of your week's tradin' to the folk up at Ripon?'

'Not yet, Doctor Jarvis, but I think they'll be well pleased.'

'And today's a day of rest for you.'

That gave me an opportunity to tell him about my proposed visit to the Hall and I was delighted when he said, 'I have to go up there myself this afternoon, Ellen, I like to keep an eye on the old lady. I'll give you a lift if you like.'

'I'd be very grateful, Doctor.'

'Good, that's settled then. I'll pick you up at two. I'll only be a few minutes with the old lady and I can tell her you're waiting to see her. I had a feeling she might be getting in touch with you.'

'Why is that, Doctor?'

'Well she asked a few questions about you and it's my guess she's curious about the way you look. You're too much like Miss Lisanne for it to be merely coincidence.'

I stared at him curiously, and Mrs Jarvis said with a smile, 'Have none of the villagers mentioned it, Ellen? I would have thought they might.'

'No, none of them, and I'm glad about that because coincidence is all it is.'

'Oh well,' the doctor said, 'you go along there and see what she has to say. I'd like to think she might be able to help you, Ellen, you badly need a friend just now and she carries a lot of influence.'

We parted at my front door with me wondering just how her influence could help me, and with whom.

I was glad of the lift, and when Doctor Jarvis picked up the suitcase he exclaimed, 'Gracious me, Ellen, what have ye got in here, the crown jewels?'

'Only clothes, Doctor.'

'Enough to last 'til she's in her dotage, I shouldn't wonder. That lass's been spoiled what with her father bein' killed when she was only a wee thing and her mother flittin' about from pillar to post, never settling long enough to give the girl a proper home or a steady education. First she was in one boarding school and then another, next she was abroad in a French convent school, then another in Switzerland. I'm surprised she's turned out as well as she has.'

'I wonder which of the cousins she'll marry, Doctor?'

'You know about that, do you? It's not a good thing for first cousins to marry, and the de Belleforts have always done it. I'm surprised there hasn't been more sickness, both mental and physical, in the family but there must be some good stock there somewhere.'

I was unprepared for the charm of the sitting room in which Lady de Bellefort received me, so overwhelmed had I been by the great rooms we had passed through to arrive there.

The doctor gave my arm a gentle squeeze as I passed into the room through the door he held open for me. 'Take heart,' he whispered, 'she's not going to eat you.'

It was a room overlooking the mere, decorated in gentle pastel colours, with a delicate Chinese carpet and exquisite watercolours. On that day I was only aware of its beauty without knowing anything of the value of the pictures and porcelain around me, and Lady de Bellefort, sitting in a rose-coloured velvet chair at a long low window, received me graciously, indicating that I should take the chair opposite.

'I'm sorry I couldn't come before, Milady, but there was the shop to see to and the rest of Miss Lisanne's gowns to finish.'

She smiled. 'I understand, Ellen. I didn't expect you immediately, and have you finished my granddaughter's dresses?'

'Yes. I left them with the housekeeper.'

'And she must pay you for doing them, they have taken a great deal of your time. You are keeping the shop open until it is sold, I believe.'

'Yes.'

'And when the shop is sold?'

'I shall have to find something else.'

Her eyes were kind, so kind that I felt a lump rise into my throat and in my eyes the smarting of unshed tears.

'I would like to hear something about yourself, Ellen, how you came to be living in the village, something of your early life and your family.'

'There isn't much to tell. I left home when I was fourteen.'

'Then you shall tell me why you left home and what happened before you came to Langstone.'

So I told her about my schooldays, my parents and my brothers and sisters. I told her about my friendship with Kitty McGuire and my father's rigid principles and unyielding abhorrence of anything outside his own concept of right and wrong. I was aware of the bitterness that crept into my voice, the hatred and the fear that I could not escape from whenever I thought of him.

Gently she asked, 'Did your father never come after you, Ellen? And what about your mother in all this?'

'My mother never spoke against him, and I know how he would feel, I'd made my bed so I must lie on it. His pride would never allow him to take me back.'

I could have talked about his involvement with Phoebe Patterson but some strange sense of loyalty made me bite my tongue.

'Are you like your mother, Ellen?'

'I don't think so. My mother always looked so careworn and she was so thin. Some of the neighbours told me she was a pretty woman when she first went to live in the village, but she'd had a lot of children and my father wasn't an easy man to live with.'

'Your family hadn't always lived in the village then?'

'Mi father was born and brought up there but when he was a young man he went to work on the land over at Chantry. He only went back to the village when the old sexton died and he got his job at the church. Mi mother was living in Chantry, it was there where they met.'

I was aware of the gleam of interest in her eyes. 'So your mother lived in Chantry. It begins to make sense, Ellen. Tell me, what sort of a family did your mother have in Chantry?'

'She didn't talk about it much. Mi grandmother died when I was seven and mi grandfather wasn't much interested in any of us. I went once with my mother to visit but my grandfather hardly spoke to either of us and mi aunt and uncles seemed not to care if we ever went again. When I said as much to mi mother she said there was probably a reason for it, but she would never say anything else.'

'Do you remember your grandmother?'

'I remember that she was pretty, and I once saw a picture of her, lovely she was with dark auburn hair and eyes as blue as mine.'

'What was her name?'

'Sarah Welsby.'

'That was her married name?'

'Yes, she was called Sarah Saxton before she married, she came from a little village not far from here.'

She sat looking out of the window with a pensive smile, and seemed to have forgotten my existence, as though her thoughts were on the past and a long long way from her sitting room on that bright sunny afternoon. At last she turned with a small sad little smile which I found strangely appealing, the tone of her voice compelling.

'And now, Ellen, I am going to tell you something about myself and my family which you might feel you should have known about a long time ago. Some might think that it is better to let sleeping dogs lie, but not when you are going to be given the opportunity to concern yourself with the de Belleforts. The choice shall be yours.'

Our eyes met and locked, and I was not sure that I wanted to hear what she had every intention of telling me, for I knew in my heart that after today my life would never be the same again.

'I always knew that one day I would marry my cousin Roland de Bellefort and I saw no reason to quarrel with that. The de Belleforts always married their cousins or second cousins and although we had only met twice I had liked him. He was the younger of the two de Bellefort boys, not destined to take the title, and we were little more than children, so marriage was a long way off.

'My mother was a de Bellefort, my father a second cousin, the son of a country parson. When my father was thirty he came into a fairly substantial fortune left him by a maiden aunt who had been particularly fond of him, and we started to travel.

'I had an enchanted childhood and it continued until I was seventeen and approaching marriageable age. We lived in lovely cities for months at a time or until my father felt the urge to move on – Florence and Venice, Vienna and Saltzburg, Genoa and Sienna, Madrid and Grenada. I could speak German, Spanish and Italian fluently, and I was pretty. Quite suddenly when I was seventeen I realized I didn't want to come to Yorkshire and live the life of a country squire's wife in a draughty stone mansion where the weather was unpredictable and where nothing ever happened.

'I made my wishes known in no uncertain manner, but here I came across my parents' iron resolve. Not lightly were the laws that had governed the de Bellefort family since medieval times to be put aside. I would go to England when I was eighteen and I would marry Roland de Bellefort. It was my duty to provide strong heirs to an ancient lineage and neither tears nor tantrums would alter the course of my future.

'Fate plays some very strange tricks on us, Ellen, it was almost as though God sat there in his heaven saying, "Who are these de Belleforts that they should usurp my role in the order of things? Helena Cressey will not marry Roland de Bellefort, he will not live to make her his wife." Indeed we had hardly left our ship at Dover when my father received a message that Roland had died in an epidemic of typhoid while serving with his regiment which had just recently returned from Russia, and to my shame I inwardly rejoiced.

'I was sorry Roland had died. I remembered him as a nice, well-set-up young man I had danced with and laughed with and believed that one day I might marry, but in recent years he had taken on the mantle of a stranger, an unwelcome stranger.

'I hoped my parents would catch the next boat back to France and that would be the last I would ever hear of the de Bellefort family, but instead my father set out for Yorkshire, leaving my mother and myself in a comfortable inn in Dover. Several days later he returned with the news that the three of us were to journey post haste to Yorkshire, to this house where we were to meet Roland's parents and his elder brother William.

'You can imagine how my heart sank at the news. How I longed for the warm mellow cities of Europe, the sun shining on the Apennines, the azure sea, the sun-baked plains, while instead we travelled north towards these dark hostile hills, the unrelenting moorland and those lonely pines on the windswept crags.

'By the time we reached the house I was almost in tears and certainly in a deep sulk, but I hadn't imagined for one moment that William de Bellefort would be no more anxious to meet me than I was to meet him.

'My mother urged me to smile as we dressed for dinner on that first evening. She pinched my pale cheeks to bring some colour into them, and I was ordered to wear my prettiest gown and show some degree of delight at being there, tempered of course by my sadness at the death of my fiancé.

'We sat down to dinner in that great dining room on the ground floor, my parents affable and compassionate, William's parents sad at the loss of their younger son, but anxious, most anxious to see that William and I found each other's company agreeable. We did not.

'We hardly exchanged a word and I did not miss the look which passed between the girl who served us at the dining table and William. She was a pretty girl with dark red hair and blue eyes, a combination I found quite intriguing as, I have no doubt, did William. Later I saw him in earnest conversation with the servant girl.

'I don't propose to bore you with all the details, I will only say that both William and I were told in no uncertain terms that we would marry, and if I protested to my parents I am sure William protested to his. In my own misery I was able to sympathize with his.

'It did not take long for my sympathy to turn to impatience. William had no earthly chance of making the girl his wife, he had had no right to fall in love with her and fill her naive head with ideas that one day things might go right for them.

'I became cross when she waited on table with tearstained cheeks, when she looked at William with eyes filled with reproach, and at me with barely concealed envy. There were nights when I stood in the shadows on the stairs listening to raised voices coming from the study, William's voice coupled with his father's arrogant one, and more and more

I became angry. After all I was the one who wanted to return with my parents to the continent, if William didn't wish to marry me I most certainly didn't wish to marry him. But the de Belleforts named our wedding day and I found myself wearing the engagement ring which all the brides of the de Bellefort heirs were expected to wear. When my eldest son was born the ring was placed in the vault for safekeeping until he should choose a wife. My husband presented me with a copy, just as valuable but hardly as old.'

She held out her left hand so that I could admire the large emerald surrounded by sparkling diamonds.

'I fear that I may be boring you, Ellen, but it is a story you should hear.'

When I said it was a story which interested me enormously, she merely smiled and went on.

'We were married fairly quietly out of deference to the memory of Roland and we went immediately to County Wicklow to spend our honeymoon in a similar house to this one, surrounded by mountains and wild moorland, where the sea crashed on the rocks below the house and where William rode madly day after day along the shore to erase the memory of Sarah Saxton so that he returned to me spent and exhausted.'

At the mention of my grandmother's name I started and she nodded. 'Oh yes, Ellen, my husband was very much in love with your grandmother, but all I knew was that she had been sent away from the Hall with enough money to placate her family, and eventually buy her a husband. It was archaic, dishonest, but it was the way things were in those days.

'Months later I made inquiries as to her whereabouts but all I could find out was that she had left the village, married a farm labourer in another village, and that her family did not expect to see her again.

'One gets over many things in this life, Ellen, even love, and I was an intelligent girl and not unattractive. I had many admirers. I was a good hostess, a lively companion, and in due course I believe William came to care for me. Never perhaps with that foolish young love that believes all things are possible, but with a more intelligent, deeper understanding, and when our children began to arrive he was a faithful if somewhat undemanding husband.

'Four children I gave him, three sons and one daughter, and I believe your grandmother Sarah Saxton gave him one child: a daughter, and your mother.'

'Why are you so sure about that?' I asked quickly.

'Look in a mirror, child, and then look at Lisanne. Look in the picture gallery and you will see that face, that colouring again and again across the centuries. Why did your grandfather show little interest in either you or your mother? Because he was never your grandfather and was probably filled with resentment because your mother was not his child. In all probability his sons and daughters knew that your mother was not their full sister, and if your father knows perhaps that is why he was all too ready to attribute your grandmother's shortcomings to yourself. Perhaps he believed that one day you would be like her – he does not appear to be a man endowed with much Christian charity. What do you think of my story, Ellen?'

'I suppose it's true, but I don't understand why you had to tell me or why you asked me to come here.'

'Because I owe you something, because in my heart I always felt sorry for that girl Sarah Saxton. I took what she wanted, and I took him without love, my only excuse that I was upholding a law made centuries ago by people unconcerned with love and only with wealth.'

'But isn't it a law you subscribe to today, Lady de Bellefort? Is it any more right now than it was then?'

'No, Ellen, but are you prepared to come into this family and be a part of it?'

'Come into this family! How can I do that, how can I be a part of it?'

'By being my granddaughter's friend and companion. I can't suddenly turn you into a relative but I can give you employment, and Lisanne needs a friend very badly.'

I stared at her in stunned silence. Her face was grave and unsmiling, and for the first time that afternoon she seemed suddenly old, as though the talk of the past had taken its toll, and I felt a twinge of pity for this proud old woman who had bared her soul to me.

'I can't think that she so badly needs a friend, she has you and this lovely house to live in, she has money and education and position. I don't see that I can bring anything into her life that she hasn't got already.'

'You can bring more stability than she's ever known, and you can bring loyalty, the same loyalty that you had for that girl Kitty McGuire. You'll have more money than you ever earned, better clothes, the chance to travel and see something of the world, and in time Lisanne will come to think of you as her one true friend who she will always be able to rely on. You like Lisanne, don't you, Ellen?'

'Well yes, but I don't know her very well. I can't really think straight at the moment, all this is so new and strange to me. Are you wanting my answer right away? I feel it's something I need to think about.'

'Well of course you must think about it, Ellen, and take as much time as you like, but I believe you will come to see the advantages of the proposition I have put to you. I shall be very glad and relieved if you look upon it kindly, Ellen.'

CHAPTER 20

I had thought that running away from home was the hardest decision I would ever made, but Lady de Bellefort's proposition was causing almost as much heart-searching.

I thought about it while I was serving in the shop so that some of my customers grew impatient with wrong change and mis-matching of colours. I couldn't sleep for thinking about it and I could have wept with relief when Doctor Jarvis's trap pulled up outside the shop several days later just as I was closing.

'I just thought I'd call to tell you I've deposited your money in my bank in Ilkley, Ellen. I've got your bank book here and the money will be earning interest. You're lookin' a bit peaky, my girl, haven't you been sleeping well?'

So I poured out my problem and he listened without interrupting until it was told, then with a wry smile he said, 'I wondered what the old lady had up her sleeve. I've known her a long time, but although we get along and I can have a joke with her I've never really known what she was thinkin'. She's never had much time for her middle son, that's the one over in County Wicklow, and she thinks her eldest son's a bit of a dry old stick, but she's very fond of Lance. She sees more of Lisanne than the others but she's scathing about the girl's mother, now and again over the years she's let that much slip.

'Are you expected to be a maid to Lisanne?'

'A friend, a companion she said, so really it's neither one thing nor the other.'

'There's more to this than meets the eye, lassy: Why you, why is her ladyship being so philanthropic, is it the way you look?'

I might have known that Doctor Jarvis would be too astute to let it rest there, so haltingly I told him the story of my grandmother, and he chuckled delightedly.

'I knew it wasn't coincidence, Ellen, that you look like you do. So Sir William wasn't the stern and upright country gentleman everybody thought he was, but he got away with it, didn't he? It's funny how folk in these closeknit villages stick together. I've been in Langstone twenty-five years and I've never heard a whisper, not from the folk in four villages or from the Hall, and it took your aunt to bring you here from Liverpool to start it all up again.'

'But I haven't started anything up, nobody's said a word.'

'Not yet they haven't, but the old lady's jumping in first by taking you out of the village and planting you in the Hall.'

'Isn't that likely to open more mouths than if she'd left me here hoping I'd go away?'

'Yes, but then she has a queer streak of honour in her and perhaps you'll learn more as time goes by. Have you decided what you're going to do?'

'No. I'm very tempted but being somebody's servant isn't really what I want.'

'Well if you're not happy there ye can always move out, you've a bit of money behind you. I think I'd take it, Ellen, out of curiosity maybe, but certainly out of self-preservation.'

In the end my mind was made up for me by the arrival of the Ashingtons. They came early on Saturday morning, with several suitcases.

'Things is quiet in the street, Ellen,' Mr Ashington remarked. 'I would 'ave thought Saturday'd be busy enough.'

'It's very early. It was busy yesterday. I have the takings for you, they're quite good.'

'I'm pleased to hear it. There's one or two things we couldn't take after the funeral, mi wife and our Jennie'll take a look upstairs.'

I sat while he counted the money in the cash box, and across the table George the fiancé sat scanning the account book. At last he looked up, saying, 'It seems all right, Mr Ashington,' whereupon he handed the book over for Mr Ashington's scrutiny.

After nodding briefly he said, 'The shop's sold, Ellen, I've decided to let the Devlins 'ave it for their tea shop. Course it'll take a few weeks 'afore its properly finalized, so ye can continue to work in it. No doubt the Devlins'll be spendin' a fair bit o' time 'ere so I'll be glad if yer'll be accommodatin', Ellen.' I expect yer'll want to start lookin' round for work but there's not much ye can do 'til the shop's turned over.'

'If I find something soon I won't be able to stay on here.'

He looked at me sharply. ''Ave ye anythin' in mind Ellen?'

'I might have.'

'I don't know why ye didn't make it up with yer father. Ye had every opportunity on the day of the funeral.'

I didn't speak and irritably he went on, 'What are those two doin' upstairs? I 'ope ye haven't bin getting rid of yer aunt's things, Ellen.'

'I haven't even looked at them,' I answered sharply.

Eventually Mrs Ashington and her daughter came down carrying blankets and sheets, table linen and numerous cardboard boxes containing heaven knows what.

All these articles were unceremoniously dumped on the table top before Jennie returned upstairs for more. I stared at the pile of blankets and linen but almost immediately Jennie came back carrying hats and dresses. Her mother asked, 'Did you bring the shoe boxes, love?'

'I'm goin' back for them, Mother, I couldn't carry 'em all.'

'Yer'd best get packin' the suitcases if we're to get that train home,' her father said, then turning to me: 'You'll not have much call for any of Liza's stuff, Ellen, seein' as 'ow yer've no place to go to and the Devlins'll want this place cleared so that they can make a start. I thought ye said our Liza had nothin' in the way of clothes that you wanted,' he ended, addressing his wife.

'Nor do I for miself, but mi sister might be able to make use of them and what she doesn't want we can give to the church for their appeal.'

'I rather think our vicar was hoping he might be given

something for his appeal,' I couldn't resist saying. 'Aunt Liza was a very prominent member of the church.'

'Ay well, if there's nowt left 'e'll be disappointed, won't he?'

At that moment I made up my mind. I would go to Langstone Priory. There couldn't be anything in my future worse than my past, and there couldn't be people more mercenary or grasping, more unkind than those I had already met.

Time was to prove that I could be wrong on both counts, but I was not to know that as I faced my father's half-brother. 'I shan't be staying on at the shop, I have a job to go to but I'll stay on for a bit until you find someone else.'

My words sounded terse even in my own ears, but one look at his angry red face made me tremble with fear. I felt I was looking at my father after one of his tirades, his eyes narrowed dangerously, his lips set in a thin straight line.

'What's that, a job did ye say! 'Ow long 'ave ye known about it and 'ere's me thinkin' ye'd be glad of these next few weeks. You've not bin straight with mi, Ellen, ye could 'ave told me you were lookin' for work.'

'I'm sorry but I have to think about myself. I need somewhere to live, and I doubt if you'd concern yourself about that.'

'It seems to me our Liza was right when she called ye an ungrateful girl, you were ungrateful to yer mother and father and now it's my turn. Well if ye feels like that about it, Ellen, the sooner ye gets out the better I'll like it.'

'But what about the shop, Father?' Jennie asked anxiously. 'Who's goin' to look after that? We'll lose money if it's closed.'

'You and yer mother can stay. Yer'll soon get the 'ang of things.'

'But I don't know anythin' about wool and bobbins o' cotton.'

'Ye're not too daft to learn, I 'ope. Me and George'll go back to Ripon tonight and we'll be back next weekend. In the meantime learn as much as ye can from Ellen 'ere. I don't suppose she'll want to take up 'er new job today.'

He looked at me sharply for an answer and quickly I said, 'No of course not, I'll be glad to show them where everything is and how much they cost.'

'Well then, that's what yer'll do, and I'll thank ye not to look so sulky, Jennie. What yer makes in this shop'll help to pay for yer weddin' finery with a bit to spare for that 'ouse yer intent on buyin' in 'Arrogate.'

Jennie's face brightened visibly and just then the bell went over the shop door and her father said, 'You go into the shop with Ellen to see 'ow things are done, yer'll soon pick things up.'

It was a day I wanted to come quickly to an end. Jennie had little patience with customers who couldn't make up their minds and she quickly forgot where things were kept. I doubted if the account book would fare any better in her hands, and her mother must have thought so too because she quickly decided that the accounts would be her province.

Mrs Devlin and Alec appeared in the afternoon and they spent a long time taking measurements and chatting to the men in the living room. As they left Mrs Devlin said, 'I hear you've got another job to go to, Ellen.'

'Yes.'

'In the village?'

'No.'

'Does that mean yer'll be leaving the village then?'

'In a manner of speaking it does.'

'Well it's not like me to ask questions but I must say I'm surprised, I didn't think there was that much work about. Where 'ave ye managed to find somethin'?'

'I'd rather not say until I'm absolutely sure, if you don't mind, Mrs Devlin.'

'Oh well, if ye feel like that about it,' she snapped, shrugging her shoulders. 'Come on, Alec, there's work to be done.'

Alec would dearly like to have stayed to ask more questions, but one look at his stepmother's set face and he decided against it.

I was over the first hurdle. It was almost five o'clock, in

another half hour Mr Ashington and George would have left, and there would only be his wife and daughter to suffer.

As I watched Simeon Ashington departing up the street he reminded me strongly of my father. He had the same tall spare figure, and his eyes had been cold and peevishly vindictive, like my father's eyes after one of his beatings.

Tomorrow I would tell Lady de Bellefort that I would accept whatever plans she had for my future. My life as Ellen Adair had come full circle.

BOOK II

CHAPTER 21

There were times during the next two years over which I would dearly have liked to draw a veil, but there were other times that I would hold close to my heart for ever.

There were difficulties, right from that first moment when I arrived in Doctor Jarvis's trap with my one suitcase, and there were other times when I seemed as much a part of Langstone Priory as those others who call themselves de Belleforts.

Often in those early days I found myself staring at William de Bellefort's portrait, reassuring myself that whether they liked it or not this was my grandfather, and my grandmother had been the woman he loved, not Lady de Bellefort for all her patrician beauty and her social graces.

The servants were told that I was a distant relative and that she had inquiries made about my family when she realized how closely I resembled her granddaughter. I have never been sure how much of that they believed, particularly Cook and the housekeeper who had lived in the village most of their lives.

They knew better than to gossip openly or disbelieve what they had been told, and I was accepted in the capacity of poor relation. This was not her ladyship's fault. She was always kind to me and most gracious, but it was Lisanne who one minute treated me like her dear friend and the next like some child who had been swept in from the storm. For weeks, months even, we were close companions, more like sisters than friends, and then after one of Lance de Bellefort's visits we were like strangers.

I never quite knew if I was happy, only that I was there to learn. How to dress and speak, how to walk and ride. At first I was frightened of the horses, they seemed so large and temperamental and Lisanne laughed at my fears in a situation where she was so confident.

I came in for the clothes Lisanne no longer wanted and I had no difficulty in changing them to fit me and improving on them. I was a little taller than she and slimmer so there was always plenty of material to play with. In the company of visitors we were told we looked like sisters and it was then that Lisanne would say airily, 'Oh, we're actually not related at all. Granny arranged all this because Ellen was soon to lose her job at the draper's shop and it entertained Granny to see how alike we were.'

I never missed the discreet looks that were exchanged between those present, and Lisanne was careful not to make such remarks when her grandmother was present.

There were times when I could have quarrelled with her but I bit my tongue, thinking about my small fortune in the bank at Ilkley and of those other times when she was away from the house with Lady de Bellefort, visiting friends and relatives. Then I would borrow books from the library which I read avidly, tracing the history of the family which went back to Norman times. There had been a Sir Roland de Bellefort on the first Crusade, and another who had been decorated on the field of Waterloo. Sir Geoffrey de Bellefort had been present at the signing of the Magna Carta and a Sir William de Bellefort had perished in the Charge of the Light Brigade. As I read I became more and more involved. This was my family, my grandfather's family.

One day the butler came across me sitting cross-legged on the window seat in the library with my head buried in a book and he came across to shut the window.

'There's a storm brewin', Miss Ellen, you'd be warmer in the sitting room.'

'I'm not cold, Mr Carstairs, and the books are so heavy.'

He smiled. 'I doubt if Miss Lisanne's opened one of those books in all the time she's spent here. I can't think what you find so interesting.'

'The family's interesting.' And there and then I began to recite to him all the achievements of the de Belleforts across the years.

'They might be your family, Miss, you're so interested,'

he remarked, and then thinking I had said too much I smiled and continued to read.

That the servants talked among themselves I felt sure, but in the main they were respectful. It was only the young servants who showed some reluctance at waiting on me, a girl from the draper's in the village, but as these servants left and others took their places the antagonism became less and less.

'Why are you always reading those stuffy old books?' Lisanne asked one day. 'Granny says you know more about the family than I do.'

'I love reading about them, I love anything connected with history.'

'Then it's a pity you didn't receive a good education so that you could make use of it,' she said caustically.

'I agree with you. It would have been nice to be educated like you were. Why don't you make more use of it?'

'Because I don't have to. I've been born to riches. I'll never want for money and I know that in five hundred years my descendants will be in exactly the same position as I'm in now. That's more then you can say, Ellen.'

I bit my lip angrily and turned away, then with a little laugh she said, 'I'm sorry, Ellen, I didn't intend to be mean but you're always so superior when it comes to reading. We're supposed to be companions, why aren't you more interested in learning to ride, and the latest dance steps?'

'I am interested, I'm not nearly as afraid of the horses as I was and I love dancing. But we never go to places where I can dance so I really don't see why I should bother.'

'Does that mean you'd like to dance if I took you to parties with me?'

'Yes, but you really don't have to. Your friends always ask so many questions, wanting to know if we're related and where I come from?'

'And you always prevaricate, Ellen, by saying a little and leaving so much unsaid that they think there's more to it than meets the eye.'

'I often wonder if it was a mistake for me to come here when you say things like that, Lisanne.'

She threw her arms around me impetuously. 'Well of course it wasn't a mistake, Ellen, we're very good friends and when my mother comes at the end of the month and Grandmother holds her usual family party you shall come to all the functions and set everybody's tongue wagging.'

'Your mother is coming?' I asked in dismay.

'Well of course, she does come periodically and I'd love to see her face when she sees you. I'm so fed up with the Priory, I'm going to persuade Mother to take me back with her to wherever she's going. Granny won't like it but I can usually bring Mother round to see things my way.'

'How long will you be gone for?'

'Well I haven't gone yet, have I? But hopefully for months. Why do you ask?'

'I was wondering what there would be for me to do while you're away.'

'Oh, the usual things. Hold Granny's knitting wool, read to her, sit for hours poring over those dreary old books, and – oh, I forgot to tell you, Lance will be here for the celebrations and my cousin Geraldine, Aunt Alice's daughter. We haven't met since I was six years old, I don't even know what she looks like.'

Lance would be coming! That was the only thing that registered in my foolish tormented heart, and it was agony to be in love with Lance when I knew that one day he would be married to Lisanne or Geraldine and I would have to look on while Lady de Bellefort engineered it all.

They came at the beginning of December when snow lay thick on the ground, the north-east wind swept across the moors from the sea, and the Pennine hills cast their dark shadows across the parkland and the churning mere.

I heard voices in the hall, and laughter, then Lisanne's mother swept into the old nursery, staring at me with wide quizzical eyes while Lisanne looked on delightedly.

'Gracious me,' her mother murmured, 'I didn't believe it when you wrote to tell me, now I feel I gave birth to two daughters instead of just one. Ellen, isn't it?'

'Yes, Ma'am.'

'Don't call me Ma'am, Ellen, I prefer you to call me by

name. Either Mrs de Bellefort or Mrs Roland, like the rest of the servants call me.'

'Ellen isn't exactly a servant, Mother. Granny says she's much more than that, she's a distant relative.'

'What sort of relative, for heaven's sake, and how is she related?'

'You'd better ask Granny about that. We are alike though, aren't we?'

'Yes indeed. Come over here, Ellen, into the light, let me take a good look at you.'

I felt like some prize poodle as she took hold of my shoulder and turned me around. I was glad that I was wearing my good black skirt and a pretty cream lace blouse, and that my flaxen hair was tied back simply by its black watered-silk ribbon, but if Mrs Roland de Bellefort appraised me I did likewise.

She was tall and slender and incredibly fashionable. Her hair was a bright golden blond and it was impeccably set and styled. She was wearing a rich dark fur coat over her pale cream gown. My first thought was that Lisanne was not like her mother, she was a de Bellefort while this woman was a socialite, a breed old Lady de Bellefort classes as inconsequential, a butterfly.

Satisfied with her appraisal, she smiled. 'Well obviously my mother-in-law had her reasons for putting you two together. Are you very good friends?'

With a laugh and petulant toss of her head Lisanne said, 'Oh we get along, Mother. Granny's almost as good at choosing friends as she is at choosing husbands. Lance is coming, and Geraldine. I suppose we'll know over Christmas which one of us he's going to marry.'

'Don't you mind, darling?'

'Will it make any difference if I do?'

I had gone to sit on the window seat wishing they would carry on this conversation out of my presence, but over the last two years I had become accustomed to people behaving as if I weren't there. It wasn't because they considered me family, but rather that I suddenly became invisible.

Now Mrs Roland sank gracefully into one of the easy

chair while Lisanne perched on the edge of the table, facing her mother with some degree of petulance.

'I can use my influence,' her mother said gently. 'How well do you know your cousin Lance?'

'Better than I know Gervase, I don't really know him at all.'

'Well of course not, he's too far away and I don't suppose he comes here. After all his father never got along with your grandmother and his mother died when he was just a child. It would be interesting to know how Lance feels about marriage.'

'We've never discussed it, but we're good friends, Mother. He's such fun to be with and we like the same sort of things. Oh, you know, horses and dancing, and he doesn't talk to me like he talks to Ellen.'

'He talks to Ellen!'

'Well yes. They talk for hours walking in the park. Of course they both know it can never be more than that. Ellen's a friend, that's all.'

'I see.'

With a blushing face I applied myself to my reading, but I was aware of Mrs Roland's close scrutiny across the room before she rose to her feet to show that the conversation was at an end.

'We'll talk about this after dinner, Lisanne. By that time both your cousins will have arrived and I'll be able to make my own judgement. Will Ellen be dining with the family this evening?'

I looked up quickly. 'Oh no, Mrs Roland, I hardly think so. I shall have my meal in here or in my room.'

'I'm accustomed to my mother-in-law's vagaries, she decrees what goes on in this house and the rest of us acquiesce if we know what's good for us. Come to my room, Lisanne, while I change out of these travelling clothes. I have a present for you from Rome, I want to see if you like it.'

Lisanne jumped off her perch gleefully. 'I do hope it's something to wear,' she said gaily, 'all my clothes are ancient.'

A fine snow was falling, obscuring the hills, clinging like dust to the ivy which climbed outside the window. I shivered in the draught that came through a chink in the window frame, and then my heart lurched painfully as I saw Lance's long low tourer arriving. He had assisted two women out of the car when, as if aware of my scrutiny, Lance suddenly looked up. His face broke into a smile and he raised his hand to me in greeting. The younger of the two women looked up briefly and I was aware of a pretty face surrounded by cloudy dark hair. She was totally unlike either Lisanne or myself.

I received Lady de Bellefort's invitation to be present at dinner as if it were a royal command, delivered by her butler with a half smile of amusement. As we sat round the heavy ornate dining table groaning under its wealth of silver and glass, waited on by deft servants, I was unable to banish my wayward and cynical thoughts.

How in the years to come would I be able to describe that evening? Lady de Bellefort sat at the head of the table, slim as a reed in her black gown heavily beaded with jet, her thin claw-like hands occasionally fingering the pearl choker round her throat, her fine eyes missing nothing.

At the other end sat Lance, dark and inscrutable in his sombre evening clothes, occasionally inclining his head to hear the remarks passed by Lady Alice Vernon on his left and her daughter Geraldine on his right.

Totally unlike her mother, Lady Alice was comfortably plump, and her chatter brought a glance of impatience from the woman at the head of the table. Lady Alice wore a gown in an indeterminate shade of yellow and she was well corseted and had a healthy appetite. Her daughter was lovely. She dimpled prettily at Lance's remarks, looking strangely ethereal in a white delicate gown, her dark hair framing her face, and when she laughed she showed small even white teeth.

Lisanne picked at her food. She had a mutinous look and appeared not to like the attention Geraldine was getting, attention which was merely the attempt of a chivalrous man endeavouring to put at her ease the girl sitting next to him.

Lisanne's mother chatted amicably to the only other man present, Lawrence Hartington, the de Belleforts' estate manager, and from the way he responded I was sure he admired her. She was indeed a very attractive woman and she knew how to dress. Her magenta gown was elegant and fitted her tall slender figure as though she had been poured into it, a fact that her mother-in-law seemed to disapprove of.

I sat opposite Lisanne, her face so like mine I might have been looking into a mirror, except that she wore her hair on top of her head whereas mine fell on to my shoulders, unadorned by either ribbons or jewels. I wore no jewellery, but the blue dress I had chosen was the colour of my eyes and it flattered my tall slender figure in its simplicity.

Lisanne was wearing pink, not a colour that I cared for with our pale hair and porcelain skin, and I noticed round her throat a necklace of tiny opals which I assumed was the present her mother had brought from Rome.

As our eyes met she fingered the necklace and smiled, confirming my assumption. I was so intrigued by those sitting round the table I didn't at first hear Lady Alice's remarks and, confused, asked her to repeat them.

'How long have you been living at Langstone Priory, Ellen, and where did my mother find you?'

'Just over two years, Milady. I was living in the village.'

'I see.'

Quite obviously she didn't see, and I felt sure that either her mother or myself would be subjected to further questions at a later date. I found Lance watching me, and as our eyes met I knew that a rich red colour had dyed my cheeks and I looked away quickly, embarrassed and confused. When I glanced up again I found Lady de Bellefort staring at me, her face a polite mask.

After dinner we retired to the drawing room for coffee and Lance came to sit with me while Geraldine played the piano, some light tinkling tune that I had never heard before. I had no accomplishments and it seemed that every day of my life I was being made aware of the fact. I had no skill with a watercolour brush and although I loved music I was no performer. And I was an indifferent horsewoman.

Later when Lisanne suggested somebody should put on a gramophone record I watched miserably while Lance danced first with her and then with Geraldine. I loved dancing. My feet tapped in time to the music under cover of my long skirt while Lady de Bellefort and her daughter looked on indulgently, and Mrs Roland and the estate manager chatted together.

I was unprepared for Lance standing before me holding out his hand.

'Will you dance with me, Ellen? I can't leave you sitting here alone and looking all forlorn.'

Like one in a dream I moved into his arms and I felt until that moment that I had never been alive. Suddenly the music came to an abrupt end and we stopped in some dismay to see that Lisanne had lifted the arm on the gramophone and was snapping peevishly, 'Oh can't we do something else? There's not enough men to dance with.'

'Don't be so tiresome,' snapped her grandmother, 'I was enjoying the music.'

'Well, Lance can't dance with everybody and I hate sitting here like the proverbial wallflower.'

Lance was looking at her with a small frown and I left him to return to my seat. I wished it was time to go to my room. I thought desperately that I might excuse myself on the grounds of a headache but one look at Lady de Bellefort's tight-lipped face made me think again.

Didn't Lisanne realise that these few days were to be a testing time and that in them her grandmother would make up her mind which granddaughter would be the future Lady de Bellefort: Geraldine sitting quiet and demure beside her mother and regarding Lisanne's show of bad temper with something akin to dismay, or Lisanne, her blue eyes flashing, her voice raised in petulant annoyance.

Lisanne's mother sauntered across the room and poured herself another sherry, then in a light airy voice she said, 'Too many women and too few men have always been a problem. Thank heavens it's never been a problem whenever I've invited people to my house.'

'I doubt if you are ever in a house long enough to invite anybody,' said her mother-in-law caustically. 'It seems to me that for the past twelve years you have moved about Europe like an aimless moth, gathering too many acquaintances and very few friends.'

'But of course. The de Belleforts never remarry so what is the use of putting down roots and making commitments one can't keep? As long as I remain as I am I'm entitled to whatever money the family gives me. It isn't inconsiderable, and up to now I've found nothing worth giving it up for. But you must confess, Mother-in-law, the limitations are endless.'

'I hardly think this is the time or place to air the limitations, and certainly not in front of your daughter, Delia.'

'On the contrary, I think both these girls should be made aware of what it means to be a de Bellefort wife. Presumably we're all here to decide which one of them is to marry which grandson, all except Ellen that is. None of this concerns her. I expect she's mighty glad about that.

Across the room my eyes met Lance's and I surprised in them a sudden misery, while my own eyes blazed.

Why doesn't he tell them all here and now, I thought, that he doesn't want to marry either Geraldine or Lisanne, that he objected to being treated like a prize stallion instead of a human being. How long did it take for someone in this high and mighty family to cut and run, to tell this indomitable old woman that she wasn't God, that she had no right to ordain people's lives as though they were puppets without wills of their own? But as he turned away I knew that as yet he had no will that was not her will, no future that had not been nurtured and determined by others of his family across the centuries.

I decided at that moment that I had had enough of the de Belleforts. I would leave Langstone Priory where I was nothing more than a whim, leave the first man I had ever been in love with to one or other of the women he was expected to marry, and I would make a new life for myself.

What had I once said to Kitty McGuire? 'When one door shuts another opens,' then with a wry smile I remembered her answer: 'Ye mean when one door closes another slams shut.'

I asked Lady de Bellefort if I might be excused to go to my room, aware of her steely blue eyes and set gracious smile.

'Of course, Ellen, but I want to see you in the morning, first thing after breakfast. I have something to discuss with you.'

There it was again, the cool assumption that I would be here after breakfast, waiting with some trepidation to hear what new plans she had for my future. Like the rest of them I squirmed with resentment at her high-handed belief that she had only to say a thing for it to be so, all the same I knew that I would be there outside her door waiting to be received, with my heart thumping like a wild thing, my palms sticky with anticipation.

CHAPTER 22

I lay sleepless for hours, then stood at the window.

The snow had stopped, and a full moon showed a scene of indescribable beauty. The park shimmered silvery white and snow clung to the trees like blossom. The mere was frozen over but through the trees the deer moved silently, and as they came out into the open I could see the proud head of Jupiter the stag, crowned with magnificent antlers raised towards the moon.

It was no use. I was not going to sleep easily so I went down to the library for a book.

Lance was reading at one of the long tables. He looked up sharply as I entered, then he smiled, a smile that always had the power to touch my foolish heart. 'Why Ellen, what's this, can't you sleep?'

'No. I came to find a book. It seems you couldn't sleep either.'

'No, and it seemed a golden opportunity to catch up on our family history.'

'I can tell you all about the de Belleforts: honoured by royalty, brave in battle, honourable in conquest. Ask me anything you need to know.'

He laughed. 'Then I wonder if you can tell me, Ellen, which one of my ancestors decreed that for ever more his descendants should marry one another. He must have been a bitter man who was afraid of life – terrified of losing his wealth and desperately afraid of falling in love.'

He was not smiling now, but looking down at me with sombre searching eyes.

'You won't find any mention of it in the book you were studying.'

'So you've looked for it too, Ellen?'

'No.'

'You're not curious about it?'

'No. I was curious once. I agonized about how your grandfather could love my grandmother and yet allow her to go from his life, and I wondered if he ever thought of her afterwards.'

'I'm sure he did, Ellen, a great many times.'

'But it isn't enough, is it, Lance? Just to think about somebody with regret and a degree of kindness, even feeling relief perhaps that he'd had the courage to let her go, that she had no power to interfere with his nice comfortable ordered life with his wife and children. It seemed so odd to me that all that loving, all that passion could turn into complacency.'

Suddenly he put his arms around me. 'Oh Ellen,' he groaned, 'is it my grandfather you are despising, or me?'

He was kissing my hair, my face, my lips, and God help me I was kissing him back with all the passion that was in me. I felt him pick me up in his arms and carry me across the room, putting me down on the long low velvet settee before the fireplace, but as his lips came down once more on mine my eyes fell on the portrait above the mantelpiece of his grandfather surrounded by his wife and children. A happy, respectable family group, permanent and inviolate. With all my strength I pushed him aside and struggled to my feet.

He put his arms around me again but fiercely I said, 'No, Lance. No. I love you and I want you but I'm not my grandmother, I won't let you make love to me then toss me on one side to marry one of your cousins. Save your loving for her, you'll have no memories of me to look back on with kindness or regret.'

I tore myself from his arms and fled to my room, where I lay sleepless until the dawn.

I presented myself in Lady de Bellefort's sitting room immediately after breakfast the following morning. I had lived in her house for two years but I still felt the distressing tightening in my throat in those first few moments of our meeting.

'You are punctual as always, Ellen. Don't look so anxious

child, I have not asked you to come here to be scolded. How well do you get along with Lisanne?'

'Quite well I think, considering that I am the companion you found for her.'

'You resent my interference in such matters, Ellen, you think my grandchildren should be allowed to chose their own companions and partners in life.'

I didn't answer her, but sat with lowered head and every expectation that I should hear more. I was not disappointed.

I was unprepared however for the compassion in her voice and the touch of her hand over my clenched fist.

'I am not a fool, Ellen, I saw how it was with you and Lance last evening. You think you love him, and I can well understand why you think it. Lance is young and tall and handsome, and totally unlike any other man you have ever met. But you are a sensible girl, Ellen, you know he can never be yours.' With a little sigh she went on. 'It is not in my power to alter things that have been asked of this family for generations, Ellen. Lance knows this, that is why he will not attempt to change anything, why I have decided that he will marry Geraldine and why I must let you go away.'

I looked up quickly, my heart thumping with anxiety. 'I am to go away?' I cried.

'Don't look so tragic, Ellen, I am not sending you away as your grandmother was. My daughter-in-law wishes to take Lisanne with her when she goes and I have said I have no objections if she takes you also.'

Resentment burned in me and I could feel the hot blood burning my cheeks while a new and desperate courage made me burst out, 'Why should Mrs de Bellefort be asked to take me? I won't be treated like a parcel.'

She smiled gently. 'My dear, I have put it very badly, perhaps I should explain. Delia is a flibbertigibbet. She is my husband's sister's child and a more spoilt child you could never have imagined. I was not happy that she married my favourite son but I had hopes that she would mature, that life in India would teach her responsibility and stability. It did neither.

'From time to time over the years I heard stories of their

life in India. While my son was serving his country on the North West Frontier his flighty wife was indulging in all sorts of fleeting affairs in Calcutta and Bombay, then when Roland was killed in a skirmish on the Khyber Pass I insisted that Delia should return to England with their daughter.

'She was happy enough to leave the child in my care. I got Lisanne into a good school in this country, and then two years later right out of the blue her mother removed Lisanne from the school and took her to France, so I stopped her allowance. I thought she would come running back but she found some man to finance her. It didn't last, Delia is selfish and imperious. She would be a liability to any man over a long term and this man was no exception. The affair was over and Delia came running back here to ask for the restoration of her money. By this time Lisanne was in school in Zürich but before I restored Delia's money I made her promise that Lisanne would spend all her school holidays with me, and she gave her word.

'I have watched Lisanne closely over these last two years while her mother flitted unconcerned from one gay European resort to the next. Now for some quite unknown reason she wants Lisanne to return to Europe with her.

'I do not want Lisanne to marry Lance. She is not the wife for him, she is too much like her mother. When she is twenty-one I wish her to marry Gervase, they are probably two of a kind if he is anything like his father, my middle son. Together they will have a gay old time, spending money like water, and I shall be happier thinking that one day Lance and Geraldine will make this their home. Lance's father is a sick man, and one day, anyday I expect to hear that he is dead. I have never liked the house at Mowbray, nor has Lance. When he has the title I hope he will reside here.'

I knew that I was staring at her with desperate awareness. It seemed incredible to me that this slight silver-haired woman could wield such power simply because she held the purse strings. As though she read my thoughts she suddenly rose and walked over to the window, where she turned and held out her hand to me.

'Come here, Ellen. Let me explain something to you.'

Mechanically I joined her at the window.

'I too felt like you when first I came to Langstone Priory. I rebelled at all that obsession with land and property and it took me a long time to accept what generations of de Belleforts had accepted before me. Now in my mid seventies I know that these are the only things that last. The young are obsessed with trivialities, they do not know that even love is transient, that they will recover from the trauma and tragedy of loving, or even move on to other loves just as conflicting and hurtful. But what you see out there, Ellen, remains sure and unchanging. That is the rock on which we build our lives, not the littleness of love.

'I came to that belief slowly and painfully over the years, and at last I understood why we de Belleforts are as we are. I shall not be the one to change things, Ellen, that is why I am sending you away. I could wish that you were my granddaughter, wish you were the woman to marry Lance, for you would bring to him loyalty and courage and devotion, but you are not my granddaughter.

'Geraldine is sweet and pliable. She has not been blessed with too much imagination and yet I think that like their grandfather and me they will be contented and in the years to come consider themselves well blessed.'

There was nothing to say. No words of mine could change this old indomitable woman's thinking, and like the rest of them, like a leaf in the wind I was going to allow myself to be blown in whatever direction she desired. I stood with bent head waiting to be dismissed and for several moments there was no sound in the room.

I thought: I will not go with Lisanne, I have a little money, I'll make my own way, go where I please, find work and show the de Belleforts that I am not beholden to them, that I am Ellen Adair, a free spirit, not a puppet to be worked by strings. As if she read my thoughts she said gently, 'Don't fight me on this, Ellen. Try to see what advantages there are in it for you. You will travel, see new and exciting places, wonderful cities, beautiful lakes and mountains. And who knows who you might meet? You are intelligent and beautiful, and you will not go empty-handed. I will arrange for an allowance to be paid to you so that you will not feel like a poor relation, and all that I ask from you is to provide the stability Lisanne will lack in the company of her mother. I am giving you the power to mould Lisanne into the sort of woman who will make Gervase de Bellefort a fitting wife when the time comes. When she goes to Ireland for her marriage, your task will be done. A lump sum will be paid to you and you will be free to make your own life. I think your grandmother would approve of what I am doing for you, Ellen, while I feel that my debt to her will have been fulfilled.'

Our eyes met and her smile was filled with appeal. Against all my better judgement and in spite of all the reluctance in my heart I found myself promising to do what she asked.

That is not to say that I did not agonize over my acceptance in the days which followed. In spite of the deep snow and icy winds I tramped through the parklands. I avoided Lance as much as I could. If we met in the corridors we smiled politely and I knew with some chagrin that he was obeying his grandmother and seeing as much as possible of Geraldine.

I seethed inwardly at her dimpled smiles and the way her eyes followed him across a room. Geraldine was already in love with him, but when Lance looked at me his eyes were sombre and filled with a strange hunger.

I did not often visit the village, largely because the villagers' tongues wagged too easily, but on market day some perverse obstinacy made me leave the house immediately after breakfast to go there. I told Lisanne I wanted to buy some embroidery silk but she merely said, 'Oh well, you would have been on your own anyway, I'm going with Granny and Mother to see the Rawlinsons and you wouldn't want to play gooseberry with the lovers.'

I didn't answer, and in a light teasing voice she said, 'It does bother you, doesn't it Ellen? Oh I know you go around as if you don't in the least care but I've heard you prowling about your room in the middle of the night and all that tramping about in the snow can only be because you have to get something out of your system.'

'I haven't been sleeping well but it has nothing whatsoever to do with Mr Lance or Miss Geraldine.'

'Mr Lance! I've heard you address him as Lance often enough.'

'Then it must have been a slip of the tongue.'

'He'll never fall for that sweet simpering Geraldine. Lance is too much of a red-blooded male for that.'

I was in no mood to discuss Lance or Geraldine, on the other hand Lisanne was in no mood to let the subject drop.

'One day she'll be just like Aunt Alice, far too fat with masses of diamond rings on those too podgy fingers, and Lance will be miserable.'

'He deserves to be miserable if he's not prepared to do anything about it.'

'What can he do, what can any of us do without money? We've not been brought up to be poor. Right from the very beginning we've all known what our destiny was to be. We're proud to be de Belleforts, and we all want what rightly belongs to us. Love is something quite different and apart.'

'So you're going to marry Gervase without knowing him or loving him, and it doesn't worry you?'

'Not in the least. I met him first when I was about six. He came here with his father and I hated him. He was bold and attractive. He pulled my hair and threw my favourite doll through the window, I didn't speak to him for days and granny made him apologize and he was sent to bed without supper.'

I stared at her curiously and she dissolved into peals of laughter. 'You think I must be mad to even think of marrying a man I disliked so much as a boy.'

'I know I couldn't do it.'

'Well of course not. You're not a de Bellefoprt and you haven't grown up with the knowledge that one day it will happen. I always rather hoped it would be Lance, but granny could never really stand my mother so she's wishing me on Gervase.'

'I think it's archaic.'

'Of course, it's equally archaic to have you accompany me to Europe in the role of a watchdog.'

'I have no intention of being a watchdog. Your grandmother hasn't asked me to spy on you, only provide some sort of companionship because she feels your mother might neglect you.'

'I want to be neglected, I want to go off on my own – and don't foget, I know my way around most of Europe.'

'I can't think that's true. You were only a schoolgirl, Lisanne.'

'There are schoolgirls and schoolgirls. We didn't spend all our time sequestered in the schoolroom or the dormitories. We led some of those nuns a terrible dance, I can tell you.'

'Perhaps your grandmother has heard somcthing of your escapades and thinks you need a watchdog. I can assure you it won't be me.'

'I'm glad about that, Ellen, it would have spoiled our friendship, such as it is. You can take the trap into the village if you like.'

'I thought I would walk, the pony doesn't like a lot of people and the high street will be crowded today.'

I left her petulantly looking through the clothes in her wardrobe. Outdoors the keen wind hit me like a lash so I dug my hands deep in my pockets after pulling my woollen scarf round my throat. I kept to the drive where the snow had been flattened, but even so it was tiring with the wind against my face and my feet slipping and sliding.

It had been a mistake to come to the village. I mingled with the crowds around the market stalls but I was not one of them. The old Ellen Adair had gone, to be replaced by a new alien being, but I was not a de Bellefort either.

My whole being rebelled at the laws which governed the de Belleforts. The rigidity of those medieval beliefs made me want to scream from the housetops that they were cruel and degenerate, and the pain in my heart was so intense I viewed the village street through a haze of stinging tears. To cover my distress I pretended to be interested in the fruit and vegetables on the stalls, and if people stared at me curiously I dabbed at my eyes, hoping they would think it was the wind that had brought the tears.

The Devlins had transformed Aunt Liza's little shop. A gaily coloured canopy decorated the window and the tea room was doing a steady trade. Through the net curtains I could see that the room had been enlarged and was filled with small tables and chairs.

Across the road the bakery seemed much as usual. It was the busiest time of the morning and a queue had formed outside. I could see both Alec and his father busy at the counter. Lowering my head I made as if to pass on, but my arm was seized firmly, and looking round I found Mrs Devlin staring at me.

'I wasn't sure if it was you, Ellen. We don't seem to see ye in the village these days.'

'No. I don't often get here. How are you, Mrs Devlin?'

'Well enough. We're grandparents ye know, we 'as a little granddaughter over twelve months old, lovely she is, we've called her Ruby.'

'That's nice, Mrs Devlin, I'm so pleased for you.'

'What do ye think of the tea shop? We does very well on market days. Come on in, Ellen, and 'ave a cup o' coffee. I allus 'ave a table reserved for mi.'

Reluctantly I went in and she led me to a table near the window. The shop and the living room were now one big room. A middle-aged woman sat at the cash desk near the door, and two younger women in dark dresses and white aprons and caps were taking orders. Mrs Devlin commanded immediate attention and in no time at all coffee and biscuits were placed in front of us. I sat back in anticipation of the inquisition to come.

'Ye did very well to be taken on at the 'all, Ellen. There was a lot o' talk, particularly with ye lookin so much like the granddaughter. What exactly are ye doin' there Ellen, 'ousemaid is it?'

'Not exactly, you could say I'm looking after Miss Lisanne.'

'Lady's maid?'

'Sort of.'

'Yer'll 'ave yer 'ands full then, I see 'er mother's arrived 'ere. There was allus a lot o' talk about Mrs de Bellefort before and after her husband was killed.'

'People will talk about anything.'

'Ay well, there's no smoke without fire, and scandal in small communities gets milled over.'

When I remained silent she pursed her lips and set off in another direction. 'I don't suppose ye hears from yer family, Ellen, or from the folks at Ripon?'

'No, I never hear from them.' I didn't tell Mrs Devlin that I couldn't understand why my brother Peter hadn't written, and could only think that my father had intercepted his letter.

Bitterly Mrs Devlin was saying, 'That Jenny and 'er mother took everythin' Liza left in the house. That wasn't right when Liza's church got nothin'. I made sure they knew 'ow I felt about it afore they left.'

When I didn't reply she went on, 'We're allus busy like this on market days and on the other days a lot o' the villagers come in for a cup o' tea and a bit of a gossip. The vicar says the cafe's as much a part o' the village now as the inn and the village hall itself.'

I smiled. The people in the cafe were all strangers to me, market day shoppers, and I was unprepared for Mrs Devlin's look of utter dismay when a man stopped at our table. I gasped with surprise at seeing Lance looking down at me with obvious relief.

'So here you are Ellen, I've been looking for you along the street.'

He spoke as if it was the most natural thing in the world for Lance de Bellefort to be searching the high street for me on market day, then looking at Mrs Devlin with an all-embracing smile he said. 'I hadn't realized Ellen wasn't alone.'

She struggled to her feet and I performed the introduction. She could barely contain her amazement, and I felt sure she would think I had taken the first step towards perdition. Oblivious to her surprise Lance took the seat she had vacated and asked brightly, 'More coffee, Ellen? I've left the trap at the inn with instructions to feed the pony. He'll not miss us for half an hour.'

Mrs Devlin had taken over the cash desk from where she could watch the room, and our table in particular.

Unconcerned Lance reached out and covered my hand with his own.

'Ellen, we've got to talk and it can't be here.'

'I don't see that there's anything to talk about,' I said shortly.

'Lisanne tells me you are going to Europe with them, is that true?'

'Your grandmother has decided and we all obey, don't we?'

'And you, do you want to go?'

'I have very little option. If I don't go I'm on my own looking for work, if I do go at least I'll be seeing something of the world and getting paid for it.'

'You make it sound very mercenary.'

'It is mercenary, isn't that what it's all about? Nobody should know that better than you, Lance.'

'Let's get out of here, Ellen, damn the coffee.'

'But you've ordered it.'

'Then I'll pay for it, we don't have to drink it.'

Mrs Devlin's disapproval was very evident until Lance explained that we hadn't time to wait and she mellowed considerably when he left a handsome tip for the waitress, at the same time bestowing a charming smile on Mrs Devlin herself.

He took my arm and as we hurried up the street I was only too aware of Alec Devlin's round eyes watching us from the baker's shop window. The pony and trap stood outside the inn and the pony's nose was thrust into his nosebag with evident enjoyment. 'We'll drink a glass of sherry until the pony's finished his lunch,' Lance said.

Shortly afterwards we set off back to the Priory and after

leaving the pony with one of the stablehands we were walking along the path which edged the frozen mere. The swans, dejected and ungainly waddled ponderously through the reeds, occasionally endeavouring to break the ice with their beaks.

'Poor things,' Lance said softly. 'How does one explain these things to birds and animals?'

His face was pensive, with that sensitive remote expression that I loved. We stood hand in hand watching the swans, then he turned and smiled down at me.

'If you're not too cold, Ellen, we could walk as far as the boat house.'

We walked in silence until we reached the boat house, sheltered between trees heavy with snow and out of sight of the house.

'We can talk here, Ellen, I don't think we shall be disturbed.'

I waited. In my heart I believed that anything Lance had to say could only be irrelevant, there was no room for Ellen Adair in his life and I felt a fierce satisfaction that he was finding the words difficult to say. At last he looked straight into my eyes and I stared back solemnly, determined not to help him.

'Ellen, I think you must hate me,' he said at last.

I shook my head sorrowfully. 'I could never hate you, Lance. I don't understand you, that's all. I don't understand any of you.'

He was looking at me helplessly and I felt that he hardly understood himself. Then his eyes swept the mere and the snow-covered acres before him and resolutely he seemed to square his shoulders.

'Darling Ellen,' he said gently, 'it would all be so simple in your world, wouldn't it? Girl meets boy and they marry, as easy and straightforward as seeing and breathing. But now you're caught up in a tradition that has ordained our lives for centuries. If there have been rebels they have gone their ways and been unheard of again.

'Gervase's father was a rebel in his youth. He quarrelled with his parents and for much of his life went his own way, but in the end he came back to the fold. Money and possessions brought him back, if nothing else. He conformed. And like me, Gervase will conform, however reluctantly.'

'Then why are we talking like this, Lance? You have nothing new to tell me.'

'I want to make you understand, Ellen.'

'I do understand. You care more for all this than you could ever care for me. You say you love me, but you are not prepared to give anything up for me. I know you will marry Geraldine and she will give you children to carry on the tradition, and if I want you I can be like my grandmother, your mistress, nothing more.'

'What would you be giving up to be my mistress, Ellen?'

I stared at him dumbfounded, then anger took over. 'I can answer that question, Lance: my self-respect and every dream I ever had that one day a man might love and want to marry me. Oh I know that seems very trivial against all you would be giving up for me, but it isn't trivial to me. I don't want to talk any more, Lance, you will never understand me and I shall never understand you. It's a good thing I'm going away, I want to forget I ever knew you and loved you, as I'm sure you will quickly forget me in the life your ridiculous ancestor planned for you.'

I turned on my heel and ran towards the house with my feet slipping in the snow, then my feet slid from under me and I went sprawling.

He was there at once, gathering me into his arms, his voice breathing endearments against my frozen face, and I do not know which hurt the most, the pain in my ankle or in my heart.

Gingerly I put my foot down on the path and hobbled a few steps with his arm holding me close. Then I struggled free and, still limping and writhing against my loss of dignity, made my way painfully towards the house.

My face was wet with tears of pain and from the biting wind, and when he took my arm again I had no strength to tear it away.

'I'll get the housekeeper to see to your ankle, Ellen. You'll have to rest it for a day or so if you want to be fit to travel at the end of next week.'

The end of next week! A lump came into my throat and I wanted to fling myself onto the snow and sob my heart out. I loved him and he was letting me go. Then as though he knew how I was feeling he gathered me into his arms and kissed me savagely.

I knew that later I would despise myself for responding passionately to his kisses but I had no will at that moment that was not his, no thoughts of the future. Only the present mattered, only the joy of his arms round me, his lips exploring mine.

I have no memory of the dusk coming down across the parkland, I knew little until icy hail whipped my face and I looked away from Lance in dismay to see that we were caught in a world of whirling whiteness. Once more the paths had become obliterated and the lights from the house were faint.

'Lance we must go,' I said anxiously, 'it's so late.'

Without another word he picked me up and carried me. At the front door he set me on my feet and for a moment we stood staring at each other, his eyes sombre and strangely pleading, mine swimming with tears.

CHAPTER 23

The room was cold and I was glad to pull the curtains to shut out the night, even so the hail rattled against the windows and the wind moaned eerily. The gas lamps flickered fitfully and I thought savagely, what is so wonderful about this draughty old house that makes a man believe it is more important than people, than love?

A young maid entered carrying a bowl of hot water and I realized Lance had made arrangements for my aching ankle to receive attention.

It was swollen and discoloured, and the pain was excruciating when I removed my short leather boots and woollen stockings.

'Oh Miss,' the maid cried, ''ow did yer manage to do that?'

'I was hurrying through the snow, I slipped and fell.'

'Mr Lance said as 'ow ye 'ad to rest it. 'E's asked the 'ousekeeper if ye can 'ave some food up 'ere in yer room, and I 'as to light the fire.'

While I eased my foot gently into the water I said, 'I don't remember seeing you before. What is your name?'

'It's Jemima, Miss. I'm new 'ere but mi grandmother worked 'ere 'afore she were married. Mi grandfather worked in the stables, and mi mother was a parlourmaid afore she married mi father, who was a gardener 'ere. All mi family's worked 'ere at some time or another.'

'And who will you marry, Jemima?'

She blushed and dimpled prettily. 'I reckon I'll marry Algy, 'e's only a stable lad now but there's plenty o' time.'

Plenty of time. Generations of time for entire families to serve this one great family. It was feudal, I told myself angrily.

'Can ye manage to bathe yer foot, Miss, while I go and see to yer meal?'

'I can manage, Jemima. Will you light the fire? It *is* cold in here.'

Gently I applied a soft face towel to my sore ankle and already the soothing warmth was easing the pain.

The door opened sharply and Lisanne stood on the threshold staring at me curiously.

'Lance told me about the ankle,' she said lightly. 'That's what you get for cavorting in the snow with my cousin. I don't suppose you'll be able to walk on it for days. If Doctor Jarvis sees it he'll probably tell you to rest with it up.'

'I don't intend Doctor Jarvis to see it, it isn't broken.'

'You don't really know that. There are so many bones in one's ankle, it could quite easily be broken without your knowing it.'

'If it was broken I couldn't stand on it, and I did manage to walk on it. You sound as though you'd *like* it to be broken, Lisanne.'

'Well it would let you off going to the continent with us at the end of next week.'

She came and perched beside me on the bed.

'Lance and Geraldine are to be married in the spring and Granny has decided we are to be back by then. I'm to be her bridesmaid along with two half-cousins I've never met. What granny doesn't know is that my mother is quite determined we are not coming back. She'll make all sorts of excuses to stay in Europe and I don't suppose you want to come back here to see Lance married.'

'Why should I care?'

'You shouldn't, but you do. You care so much it's making you waspish and quite unlike yourself. If you'd any sense you'd be asking yourself all sorts of questions.'

'What questions?'

'It's not for me to tell you, Ellen, you'll tell yourself sooner or later. Just think about it, that's all.'

She smiled brightly and left just as abruptly as she had entered, and several minutes later the maid came back with my evening meal. It was beautifully cooked but I had little appetite. I ached after Lance. I felt worthless and rejected, my ankle hurt and I was glad he wasn't there to see me with my foot in a bowl of water and a tray of uneaten food in front of me.

How long would it take to forget him, I wondered. I knew I must forget him, a girl was a fool to yearn after a man who didn't yearn after her. Then unbidden I found myself answering the questions Lisanne had posed.

I was Ellen Adair, a country girl without education, self-taught from listening to others, and although I was intelligent and honest the only money I had in the world was that taken out of Aunt Liza's bag. I was pretty, but so were a million other girls. What right had I to expect Lance de Bellefort to forsake the conventions he had sworn his life to?

All night long I agonized about Lance, alternately loving him and hating him, but with the first cold light of day I realized, with that peculiar honesty of being able to see both sides, that I understood him.

I slid out of bed and put my foot gingerly on the carpet. There was still some pain in my ankle but nothing like before. I looked out at the frozen mere and the forest behind: as far as I could see the land belonged to the de Belleforts, and I, Ellen Adair, had had the temerity to think I might matter against all that.

I rarely ever thought about Kitty these days because it made me miserable. Now, however, I found myself thinking of her tight-lipped gamin face on the street in Liverpool when she stated adamantly that she would never go into the city again without enough money to buy what she wanted. I had not properly understood her then, but now I understood her only too well.

My life stretched before me like a battleground. I was being given opportunities that had been denied to Kitty but they were opportunities surrounded by barriers of wealth and class. If I lived to be a hundred they would always be there, and the longer I stayed close to the de Belleforts the more I would be aware of them.

Kitty had sold her soul to the devil to achieve her desires. I could not live like that, but I made a silent vow that I would serve the de Belleforts and take what they offered. I would listen and learn, and whatever sum of money Lady de Bellefort settled on me I would save and add to what I had in the bank in Ilkley.

There would be no more ecstatic meetings with Lance. It was finished, and somehow or other I would make the barren waste of the years before me blossom, even if at that moment I did not know how.

I was accustomed to watching Lisanne opening her mail. There was never anything for me, so I was more than surprised when she tossed an envelope across the table, saying, 'This is for you, Ellen. It looks a bit battered, as if it had been around a bit.'

The envelope was decidedly battered. The ink was smudged as if by rain and the paper was torn in one place. Even so my heart lifted with joy when I recognized my brother's handwriting. Lisanne was looking at me expectantly so I said. 'It's from my brother Peter, I've been hoping he might write.'

Impatiently I slit the envelope and took out two sheets of paper which I read eagerly.

Like me he had left home, and was joining a ship sailing from Plymouth. I guessed he had been carrying the envelope about in his pocket for several days before he posted it.

The heartache he had suffered at leaving home was evident, but he had been unable to stand it any longer. My father was impossible to live with, and my mother was ailing. More and more Father was becoming careless about his affair with Phoebe Patterson, so that there was gossip in the village. If it got to the vicar's ears his job would be in jeopardy.

Peter had remonstrated with him and received a cuff about his ears for his pains, and that had been the deciding factor. I was glad he'd had the courage to leave. His letter made me feel that I too had made the right decision, and strangely enough I felt cheered by it.

I folded the letter and put it in my pocket. Lisanne was uninterested in my correspondence, she was too immersed in her own, and I sat watching her, wishing she would find me something to do. It was the inactivity of my life at Langstone which caused me the most heart-searching.

At last she looked up casually to remark, 'I'm waiting for Mother, she's in with Granny at the moment. They're probably talking about when we are to leave here.'

Oh God let it be soon, I prayed silently, and just then Mrs de Bellefort swept in and went to stand staring out of the window while Lisanne and I sat startled. She seemed preoccupied. There was a frown on her beautiful face, though as always she seemed to be the epitome of grace and elegance.

'Is something wrong, Mother?' Lisanne asked at last.

She spun round and eyed us stonily. 'Lance's father is very ill and probably won't last the week out. Lance is leaving here this morning and your grandmother thinks we shouldn't travel until after it's all over. I hate funerals, and I'm quite sure Gerald wouldn't be bothered if I didn't attend his. We never really hit it off, he was always a dry old stick. Steven was the gay one, we had a lot more in common.'

'Is he really going to die, Mother?' Lisanne asked petulantly.

'Darling, he's been a creaking gate for years. I suppose it could be another false alarm but this time I don't think so. There'll be all those mourners from all over Yorkshire and further afield than that, all the pomp of opening up the family vault, and Granny will be there to lord it over the proceedings like some ancient potentate. I don't think I can stand it.'

'Then why can't we go away like we planned?' Lisanne said anxiously.

'I'm in trouble with your grandmother as it is. I don't want my allowance docked, you know what she's capable of.'

'Why does she arrange everything, why can't we have our own money, why does everything have to be ploughed back into the family? Why does she always know best?'

Mrs de Bellefort shrugged. 'Why indeed?' she said cynically. 'Oh well, I can't afford to antagonize her, Lisanne, we'll just have to hope that Gerald doesn't linger on. I can't think they'll be coming over from Ireland for the funeral, neither Steven nor Gervase came to Cousin John's funeral.'

'If he dies Geraldine's going to be Lady de Bellefort when she marries Lance, isn't she Mother? She'll be no match for old Lady de Bellefort.'

Her mother laughed. 'No, I don't suppose she will, but quite often the shy sweet ones are the most dominant. It will be very interesting to see how she develops, and it will serve the old girl right if Geraldine plays her at her own game. Don't worry, Lisanne, we'll hang on for a few more days. By the weekend we shall know if Gerald is going to survive yet another heart attack.'

We knew before the end of the day. Lance arrived home in time to be with his father when he died, upon which he became the fourteenth baronet. And Geraldine had every expectation of being the next Lady de Bellefort.

I watched the funeral cortege arriving for his interment in the family vault at the church in Langstone. I had never seen such an array of black coaches, black horses and purple plumes. Lady de Bellefort disdained limousines as being unsuitably decadent for such an occasion.

I walked to the village church as a mark of respect and stood in the crowded churchyard wearing a thin black veil over my face, my feet becoming colder by the minute. If my eyes followed Lance's tall figure with considerable longing nobody could see behind the veil, but it was at old Lady de Bellefort that most people looked. She stood beside Lance, slender and upright, her tightly clenched hand resting on her tall umbrella, and when he offered his arm she declined, walking slowly with head held high behind the coffin of her eldest son.

Geraldine walked behind with her mother, and as she passed there were smiles of sympathy and curtseys from those lining the paths. It seemed that already it was understood that this was the girl Lance would marry.

Lisanne's mother looked conspicuously elegant in her black. This was not the attire brought out of mothballs for a funeral, but rather the sort of fashionable black she might have worn for Ascot. The large sweeping brim of her hat was adorned with ostrich feathers and just once I saw her mother-in-law glance at her with cynical impatience, an impatience the younger woman treated with maddening unconcern.

They came back to the Priory for the funeral breakfast in the great hall while I sat alone in Lisanne's small sitting room overlooking the fells. It was not surprising they forgot to serve a meal to me, I knew the servants were run off their feet, so after two o'clock I went down to the kitchens in search of a sandwich.

Cook was busy at the long black range, her face flushed with exertion, issuing orders to the kitchenmaids who scurried about as if their life depended on it.

I stood hesitantly in the doorway wishing I hadn't come, and I was about to make a retreat when Cook spotted me.

'Did they forget ye, love? I'm not surprised, there's so much goin' on. There's hot soup in the tureen there and ye can no doubt find some bread and cheese if ye looks round for it. Yer'd think some o' them folk up there 'adn't eaten for months.'

I helped myself to soup and found newly baked bread and Wensleydale cheese and settled myself at the kitchen table. At the first lull in the proceedings Cook came to sit opposite me.

'Things'll be changin' round 'ere, now,' she said gloomily. 'I can sense it in mi bones. Did ye go down to the church?'

'Yes, the church and all the roads were crowded.'

'Ay well, they would be. Out o' curiosity if not compassion. Sir Gerald was allus a quiet sort o' man not like Master Steven who were never averse to chattin' up one o' the servants. Right caution he was and led 'er ladyship a merry dance. I thought one of 'em might 'ave come over from Ireland for the funeral, but they 'aven't.'

'It's a long way to come for a funeral.'

'I suppose so, and I've heard Master Steven 'asn't been all that well. Still, there's that son of 'is. Not a bit like Master Lance 'e wasn't, that lad sure 'ad the devil in 'im.'

I didn't speak and Cook sat pensive, remembering. At

length shc looked up and said, 'I suppose it is Miss Geraldine who'll be the next Lady de Bellefort?'

'I think so.'

'And Miss Lisanne'll be packed off to County Wicklow to wed that limb o' Satan. Oh well, like as not 'e's changed a lot over the years.'

I didn't speak, but finished my tea and with a smile and a word of thanks left the table and edged towards the door. At that moment the butler came in rattling his keys and saying in a cross voice. 'They want more port. I thought I'd laid out enough to supply a regiment, but apparently not.'

Cook smiled at me across the room. ''E watches that port as if 'e'd paid for it.'

I made my escape up the back stairs and returned to the sitting room. It had turned cold so I built up the fire and drew my chair up before it. I tried to read but the warmth made me sleepy and I started up guiltily at hearing a sharp knock on the door. I was surprised to find Lance standing hesitantly outside it.

We stared at each other for several seconds before he said with a small smile, 'Aren't you going to invite me in, Ellen?'

I stepped back and held the door open wider. He followed me to the fireplace and stood looking down into the flamcs while I sat back in my chair, waiting for him to speak.

It seemed a small eternity before he looked at me again and when he finally spoke his voice was tired and remotely sad.

'My aunt tells me you hope to travel on Wednesday. I couldn't let you go without saying goodbye. I shall miss you, Ellen.'

I didn't speak.

'I wish all those people would go home. It seems somehow indecent to see them wading through all that food and wine, more like a celebration than a funeral.'

'I'm sorry about your father, Lance. Were you very close?'

'No. My father was a solitary man, he liked books and collecting pictures and bronzes. He'd never been a great traveller and he disliked field sports. After my mother died he retreated more and more into his shell. They were very close.'

'In spite of being closely related?'

'Yes. They were fond of each other as children. It can happen, Ellen.'

'Of course. I hope you and Geraldine will be very happy, Lance, and that in time you too will be close. You're to be married in the spring, I believe?'

'Yes.' He looked at me keenly.

Sharply I said, 'I shan't be here, Lance. Mrs de Bellefort is hoping to stay away some time, I know that your grandmother is expecting that Lisanne will be Geraldine's bridesmaid.'

'I've told my aunt I'm not expecting her to return for my wedding. She thinks I'm merely being considerate, I couldn't tell her it was because I couldn't bear to see you at that time.'

'If this is to be your home Lance, you can rest assured I shall never return to it.'

'Ellen, if ever you want for anything – money, anything – will you promise to let me know?'

'I shan't want for anything, Lance, your grandmother has been very generous.'

I wouldn't tell him that he was the last person I would ever ask for anything, not even if I were old and destitute.

He seemed ill at ease, he wanted to touch me but was afraid of the passion I would arouse in him, and he wanted to be gone. I too wanted him gone, I wished he had never come, and I was more than relieved when he finally said, 'I must go back, Ellen. I am after all the host of that affair downstairs.'

I stood up and walked to the door. He made no effort to take my hand, instead with a brief smile he passed in front of me and I closed the door behind him. I stood with my back to it while the tears flowed from my eyes unchecked, then fiercely I rubbed my face clean and returned to the fireside.

Wednesday couldn't come quickly enough. I wanted to be gone from this place, never to return. I would have been astounded if I had known then how fate would shape and change my destiny.

I had one more meeting with Lady de Bellefort, the night before we left for London. She seemed more fragile, her aristocratic fine-boned face almost transparent, and her hands were nervous. As always she was gracious, inviting me to take the seat opposite, but she came quickly to the point.

'It may be that we shall not meet again, Ellen. I am hoping Lisanne and her mother will return for the wedding but knowing my daughter-in-law I cannot be sure, and I am too old to argue with her.

'Do you have a bank account?'

'I have a little money in the bank in Ilkley.'

'If you will give me the details I will see that it is added to. I have also given my daughter-in-law money for your upkeep and for anything you wish to buy. I don't know what sort of life you will live abroad. No doubt you will have a great deal of time to yourself but you are an intelligent girl, I am sure you will spend your leisure time wisely. Europe is a treasure trove of culture, my dear. Visit the art galleries and the museums, walk in the parks and along the water fronts. Real education begins after one has left the schoolroom, Ellen, life is the educator.

'Lisanne does not understand that any more than does her mother. She believes education for itself is not important because she will have enough money to ignore it. I disagree.

'My grandson Gervase might enjoy having a social butterfly for a wife. On the other hand Lisanne could exasperate him beyond all measure. It will not concern you, Ellen, by that time you will undoubtedly have sorted out your own future. I wish you well in it.'

The interview was at an end and I thanked her for the time I had been allowed to spend in her house and for the chance she was giving me now, all of which she waved away with a graceful move of her hand.

From a small table beside her chair she took up a dark blue leather box and handed it to me.

'I would like you to have this, Ellen. No, do not open it now, wait until you are in your room. My husband gave me what you will find in that box soon after we were married. I always had the feeling that he would have preferred to give it to your grandmother.'

Suddenly compassion flooded my being for this proud old woman who had for a brief moment allowed me to feel sorry for her. Then raising her head imperiously she said, 'That is all, Ellen, I wish you a pleasant journey and a happy life.'

I sat on my bed with the leather box unopened. I had been careful to lock the door, I didn't want Lisanne bursting in on me as she was wont to do and asking too many questions. Gingerly I opened the box then gasped with delight. Inside was a gold chain holding a single beautiful pearl, and matching earrings. I determined to have my ears pierced at the first opportunity.

I felt sure that Lady de Bellefort had never worn this jewellery, knowing it had not really been meant for her. I wished I had known my grandmother. My mother said she had not had an easy life. There had been too many children too soon and not enough money, but she had worked her fingers to the bone to keep them decently dressed and fed. I thought unhappily of the hundreds of times she must have remembered the love affair of her youth, particularly when she looked at my mother, and all those times when she had to shield her daughter from her husband's resentment.

I set about packing my suitcase. I needed to take everything I had because I would not be coming back. Most of my clothes were hand-me-downs from Lisanne. I packed the leather box in the same cardboard box which contained Aunt Liza's jewellery, and left the suitcase undone for last-minute things in the morning. It would not be heavy, nor would it be strictly full, a thing which I was pleased about when later that evening Lisanne asked if she could find room for things she couldn't fit into her own luggage.

She perched on my bed with evident enjoyment.

'Aren't you absolutely thrilled to be going in the morning?' she trilled. 'We're spending four days in London, then we're going to Paris. You should learn some French, Ellen, it's so silly and so British to think everybody should talk to us in our own language. Mother speaks French and Italian quite fluently. I only wish I'd paid more attention to Madame Buchard at the school in Switzerland.'

'French was something they didn't teach at my school, I'm afraid.'

'Oh well, there's no reason why you shouldn't start to learn it, it will give you something to do in Paris. We're to stay with Aunt Julie. She has a lovely house not far from the Opéra and I just know she'll fill it with dozens of her exciting friends. I adore Paris. There'll be no Christmas festivities here with Lance's father dying, but we can look forward to Paris in the spring.'

'Where do we sail from?'

'Oh Dover, or Folkestone I expect. Will this be your first boat trip, Ellen?'

'I've crossed the Mersey on a ferryboat from Liverpool to New Brighton.'

She dissolved into laughter. 'Oh Ellen, you're going to have your eyes opened, I shall enjoy seeing them fill with wonder at all the new experiences. Mother's downstairs talking to Granny, who'll be full of advice, that I hope Mother ignores. They packed me off and told me to get to bed early but I'm far too excited. The way Granny treats me one might think I was still a schoolgirl. Did Lance come to say goodbye?'

'Yes, after the funeral.'

'Did you melt into each other's arms and vow undying love?'

'Of course not.'

'Whyever not, for heavens sake? There doesn't look to be much passion in Geraldine. I can't think she'll add any lustre to his life.'

'You don't know that, Lisanne.'

'I can guess. What clothes are you travelling in?'

'My tweed coat, it's the only one I've got that's decent.'

Suddenly the laughter died out of her eyes, and after giving me a little hug she said. 'You can try my grey one with the fox collar. Grey's not really my colour – come to think of it, it isn't yours either – but the coat is lovely. I'll wear the blue, it's newer.'

'Oh Lisanne, I can't keep wearing your clothes. What will your mother say?'

'She'll never notice. I'll bring it in the morning, and there's a darling little velvet hat to go with it. In that tweed coat you look like somebody's nanny or governess, and I'm too old for either. I'd much rather you looked like my friend than my poor relation.'

After she had gone I looked at my tweed coat ruefully. It was warm and serviceable. It would be perfect for those moments when I was out on my own, and I felt sure they would come often in the weeks ahead. Lisanne's grey coat was a dressed-up affair, suitable for drinking tea in elegant salons, not for tramping through the parks or along the city streets.

She was in my bedroom before it was properly light next morning, cramming things into my suitcase so that we had to sit on it to fasten it.

'What shall I do about my tweed coat?' I asked. 'There isn't going to be room for it.'

'Didn't I promise you the grey one, Ellen? You're surely not thinking of taking that tweed thing with you. Leave it for one of the maids. It's very suitable for tramping across the fields, but absolutely hopeless for Paris.'

She brought the grey coat and hat and laid them on the bed. 'We're to have breakfast around nine, Ellen, then Major Hartington will take us to the station.'

I wore my best dress, a fine cornflower-blue wool which looked pretty against the grey coat, then I went down to the breakfast room. While I waited for Lisanne and her mother I stood absorbing the view of the distant snow-covered fells and the forest of evergreens which I believed I was seeing for the last time.

They arrived together, Lisanne wearing blue, her mother elegant as always in pale beige. We sat down to breakfast together. Mrs de Bellefort leafed through her mail, occasionally handing envelopes to Lisanne, and there was no conversation. It was strange that I felt more at a disadvantage with Lisanne's mother than with her grandmother. She made me feel nervous, I was afraid of her sophistication, the way she smoked her cigarette through a long ebony holder, the manner in which she flicked her eyes over me as though I didn't exist. I felt that she regarded me as an encumbrance, and my antagonism towards her mother-in-law grew minute by minute.

As she swept from the room she said, 'Ten minutes girls, and I want you both in the hall. Major Hartington won't want to be kept waiting.'

After she had gone Lisanne grinned. 'Ten minutes is long enough for them to bid each other a fond farewell.'

I didn't speak. I had seen the Major and Mrs de Bellefort riding together in the park. I had seen him pick her up in his car one evening. It seemed Lisanne was reading more into their association.

Jemima was in my bedroom when I entered it but the luggage had gone. She turned with a bright smile on her pretty face and I went to the bed to pick up the coat and hat.

The hat was a pretty thing, a tiny velvet tricorn with a cluster of grey feathers framing the face, and as soon as I put it on I knew it suited me. The coat's fox-collar fell soft around my shoulders and looked expensive and elegant over the blue dress.

Jemima gasped with admiration. 'Oh Miss Ellen, ye do look lovely, I've never seen ye lookin' so nice.'

'Thank you. Jemima, would you like to have my tweed coat?'

Her eyes opened with pleasure. 'Are ye sure, Miss?'

I took it out of the wardrobe and handed it to her. 'Try it on, see if it fits.'

It fitted the girl beautifully and she stood in front of my mirror smoothing her hands along the collar and her hips, her eyes shining excitedly.

'This is one coat mi sister's not goin' to get 'er hands on,' she said smugly. 'Thanks ever so much, Miss Ellen, I'll look after it.'

I held out my hand for the girl to take otherwise she would have bobbed a curtsey, and curtsies I didn't merit from Jemima.

'Goodbye, Jemima,' I said, smiling down at her, 'thank you for looking after me so well.'

'But yer'll be back, Miss, yer'll be back for Sir Lance's weddin' in the spring.'

'I'm not sure, Jemima, our plans are uncertain.'

She was staring at me in a puzzled way and I knew my remarks would be repeated in the servants' quarters. Nobody would be surprised. The vagaries of Mrs de Bellefort were as much a puzzlement to those downstairs as they were to the lady of the manor.

CHAPTER 24

I became aware very quickly that I had embarked upon a great adventure. I revelled in the quiet luxury of the hotel in London and I was happy to find my way about alone. Lisanne and her mother knew people in the city, so largely I was left to entertain myself. I loved the mist that hung low over the river, and the theatre crowds. I went to the art galleries and the museums and I bought myself a dark brown coat which seemed less ostentatious for such meanderings.

I was sorry to leave London but greater adventures were in store, the next one being the ferry across the channel. As soon as we boarded her Mrs de Bellefort and Lisanne went to their cabins with Lisanne saying, 'I must get to sleep before the boat sails otherwise I'll be awake all night just thinking about being at sea. You should do the same Ellen, that trip on the Mersey ferry didn't prove you're a good sailor.'

Needless to say I didn't go to my cabin, instead I stood at the rail of the ship until England faded into the distance, and I discovered that I was a good sailor. Then I discovered the lounges and the companionship of fellow travellers. Indeed it was after two in the morning when I finally went to my cabin and even then I was too excited to sleep.

Although I was not the seasoned traveller it was I who ate the hearty breakfast. When Lisanne and her mother finally joined me they both seemed pale and languid, and for the first time since I had met her Mrs de Bellefort seemed less than elegant. They revived on the train to Paris, and by the time we arrived they were both eagerly looking through the window. As we stepped down a woman came hurrying along the platform followed by a uniformed chauffeur and then there were embraces and much laughter while I stood back waiting for it to subside. At last Lisanne turned to me, saying, 'This is Aunt Julie, Ellen.' I found myself being appraised from head to foot in some surprise and I was glad I was wearing the grey coat and hat.

At last Aunt Julie said, 'Well it's easy to see you're related, darling. Now come along with me, all of you. I've brought Leon to see to your luggage.'

We followed in her wake obediently and Lisanne whispered, 'She's so very French, Ellen, she never stops talking and like all French people she talks with her hands as well as her lips. I love Aunt Julie, she's so chic.'

Aunt Julie was small and slender. Her dark hair was fashionably shingled under the tight fitting velvet toque and there was dark fur round the hem and cuffs of her beige coat. Her shoes were the same colour as her coat, with ridiculously high heels, and as she tripped daintily along the platform she chatted animatedly to Mrs de Bellefort, her hands gesticulating excitedly.

She led us to a long black car and soon afterwards the chauffeur appeared with porters carrying our luggage.

I was too preoccupied with the streets of Paris to pay much attention to the conversation. Now and again Lisanne would point out buildings of interest, particularly the Eiffel Tower, a gigantic landmark against the blue sky.

As the car moved into the most beautiful boulevard I had ever seen, Lisanne whispered, 'The Champs Elysées, Ellen. And look, up there on the hill, the church of the Sacre Coeur.'

It was all too much to take in in one day: the warm pulsating heartbeat of the life along the streets, the laughter and chatter from the pavement cafes, the sound of bells and smell of roasting chestnuts, the children's carousels at almost every street corner. Whereas London had seemed as solid and eternal as the white cliffs of Dover, Paris spoke to me of laughter, as gay and feminine as a woman's smile.

I had only just arrived in the city but already I was in love with her, and I hoped anxiously that I would be left alone to discover her at my own pace. I need not have worried.

In those early days I was forgotten. There was always somewhere for them to go with Aunt Julie, people to meet at the race track or at cocktail parties. It was a strange new world to me who had never heard of cocktails before the arrival of Mrs de Bellefort in my life, now I was being initiated on second-hand terms into the opera and musical comedies, expensive nightclubs and horse racing. Lisanne and I took morning saunters along the Grande Boulevard where the fashions defied description, and there were times when, perhaps unkindly, some of them left me helpless with laughter.

Left to myself I discovered the parks and gardens. I took boat rides on the Seine and gazed in rapt admiration at the many bridges. I visited the tomb of Napoleon where I stood looking down at it from the gallery and was told by one of the attendants that even in death, all entering would bow to the little emperor. I gazed in awe at the beauty of Notre Dame even when I deplored the ugliness of the gargoyles and the flying buttresses, and there were other days when I climbed the steep streets of Montmartre and from the Sacre Coeur looked out with aesthetic pleasure on the sprawling city beneath me.

Christmas came and went and it didn't seem like Christmas at all. I received presents from Lisanne, her mother and Aunt Julie – a silk scarf, perfume and toilet water – and I presented each of them with a silk handkerchief. They were pretty and so expensive they had taken most of my money, and I felt even as I received their polite thanks that my gifts had been totally inadequate.

It was two weeks later when Mrs de Bellefort remembered my existence and sent for me.

She sat at her dressing table in a frothy pink negligée, brushing her blond shingled hair, and I stood near the door hoping she would soon acknowledge my presence. At last she turned and for a few seconds sat eyeing me with a small frown.

'How are you for money?' she surprised me by asking.

'I have a little, Mrs de Bellefort.'

'What do you mean by a little?'

'Lisanne changed five pounds into francs for me the day we arrived here, I have a little left.'

'You mean you have been in Paris two weeks and have only spent five pounds?'

'Not quite five pounds, Mrs de Bellefort.'

'But what have you done all day?'

'I've been to the museums and the art galleries, they cost very little, and I've walked for miles around the city. The boat trips were the dearest but it was lovely on the river and I met the nicest people.'

'I could wish my daughter was as thrifty,' she snapped, then in a more friendly tone, 'Has my mother-in-law written to you since you arrived here?'

I stared at her in surprise. 'Why no, Mrs de Bellefort, I'm not expecting a letter from her.'

'Lady de Bellefort gave me a sum of money for your keep and for other things that you might want. I can't think why she didn't give it to you, you are a far more economical proposition that either my daughter or myself. However, I propose to give you an allowance each month, and if for any reason I forget I would like you to ask me for it.

'In time you will want to buy clothes and accompany Lisanne to the theatre. Up to now she has gone everywhere with me but I have my own friends here in Paris and she should see that it won't always be possible for me to invite her to join us. You are here as her companion, perhaps it is time you started to earn your money.'

I could feel my face flaming with colour and in some indignation I said, 'I shall be happy to be Lisanne's companion, Mrs de Bellefort, I want to earn my money.'

She seemed irritable and ill at ease as she played with one of the brushes on top of the dressing table, then in a more conciliatory manner she said, 'I'm sorry, Ellen. It hasn't been your fault that you have been left too much on your own. Lisanne is demanding and we havn't seen too much of one another over the years, so I can't really blame her.

'I'm asking you to take her off my hands for a while. You are much of an age whereas she's far too young to be with my friends, and some of the men are flirtatious where a young girl is concerned. I intend to be generous. Go to the theatres and the opera and for heaven's sake see that she absorbs a little culture. I haven't seen Gervase de Bellefort since he was a schoolboy but I hardly think he will want an ignoramus for a wife. The girl has had every opportunity to study, she went to the best schools and a very expensive finishing school in Switzerland, but until now she's frittered away her advantages. I don't suppose you had many of those.'

'I didn't have any of them.'

'It seems very strange to me that you are as you are and Lisanne is as she is.'

'It isn't really so strange, Mrs de Bellefort. If I wanted to survive I had to work at it, for Lisanne everything came too easily.'

'You could be right. Well, that's all, Ellen. You'll find Lisanne in her room, probably in a temper. Try to think of something you can do together. I'm dining out, it will be quite late when we get back.'

She reached into a drawer and took out a wad of French francs which she handed to me.

'I don't know exactly how much is there, Ellen, but it will last for a while. When it runs out ask me for more. That money is yours. As for Lisanne, try not to let her spend more than she needs to.'

When I still stood hesitantly near the door she nodded briefly. 'That's all, Ellen, but I'm relying on you.'

CHAPTER 25

Lisanne behaved as if her mother had abandoned her. Like the spoilt child she was she threw one tantrum after another until, unable to stand it any longeer, I snapped, 'Really, Lisanne, I wish you'd grow up. You're twenty years old, and in twelve months you hope to be a married woman. Can't you make a life for yourself apart from your mother? This is a wonderful exciting city. Why do you need to have your mother with you?'

She turned on me viciously. 'Because she goes to all the right places with the right people. You're not getting me into any museum or art gallery.'

'You mean you actually like being with all those dilettantes she surrounds herself with?'

'What do you know about them?'

'I've heard them, each one trying to talk a little louder, laugh a little wilder than the rest. I shouldn't think most of them have a brain in their heads.'

'What do brains matter? They know how to enjoy themselves. They have so much money they don't need brains.'

'Then I don't understand your mother. She's beautiful and cultured, why does she need those silly ineffectual people around her?'

'They amuse her, besides they're friends of Aunt Julie.'

'Well, your mother has asked me to go with you wherever you want, and I've given her my promise. Where is it to be, Lisanne?'

'We can't go to the tea dances or the nightclubs without an escort so I suppose we'll just have to go to one of the pavement cafes and watch the world go by. If this is to be the pattern of our time in Paris I shall die of boredom.'

So we went out and looked into the shop windows, and were drinking coffee at a pavement cafe when we were accosted by a dapperly dressed man wearing a monocle.

'Darling Lisanne, what are you doing here and where is your mother?'

Her face lost some of its sulky expression and she dimpled prettily. 'Why Henri, why aren't you out at Deauville with the others?'

'I had things to do in the city.'

He was looking at me expectantly and Lisanne said, 'This is Ellen Adair. Ellen, this is Henri, Comte d'Aubriet.'

He lifted my hand and brushed it with his lips, then sat at the table. Before I knew what was happening Lisanne was pouring out her woes to him.

'I'm going to be so bored, Henri. Mother's decided she doesn't want me around all the time which means there's absolutely nothing for Ellen and me to do.'

'You don't feel like visiting the museums or the galleries?' he asked quietly, and I gave him a grateful look.

'I had quite enough of museums and the like when I was at school, I've outgrown such things. We're in the most exciting city in the world, can't you think of anything else?'

He was studying us in an amused fashion and I was studying him. It was difficult to guess his age but I would have thought him to be well into his forties. He was slim and elegant and good-looking in a faintly foppish way. The monocle was an affectation, but somehow it suited him and he spoke English with only the faintest foreign inflection.

'I can think of a hundred different ways to amuse two charming girls, but would your mother approve?'

'I don't care about my mother, she doesn't care about me.'

'I don't think that is strictly true, my dear, but tomorrow if you agree I will bring along a friend and we could drive out to Fontainebleau.'

'More culture?' she pouted.

'Can you think of anything else in the middle of the afternoon? The drive there is through beautiful scenery, the house is exquisite and we could have tea at a very charming restaurant on the way back. What do you think, Miss Ellen?'

'Thank you, Monsieur le Comte, perhaps if we were to ask Lisanne's mother,' I replied unhappily.

'Perhaps I should explain that Ellen is the watchdog my grandmother insisted came abroad with us,' Lisanne put in angrily.

'A more charming watchdog I have never seen,' he replied gallantly, 'but perhaps she is right, we should ask your mother.'

'If you do I shan't come. Can't I just for once do as I please? I'm sure neither you nor your friend have designs on us, isn't that right, Henri?'

He laughed. 'Well of course not, and you will find my young friend Anton charming and knowledgeable. We will call for you at ten o'clock in the morning and have lunch on the way.'

'Please, Henri, can't we meet you somewhere else? I don't want you to call at Aunt Julie's for us. I wouldn't be in the least surprised if the servants haven't been cautioned to keep their eyes open.'

'You mean your mother wouldn't think I'm respectable, Chérie?'

'I mean she doesn't want me to enjoy myself.'

He shrugged his immaculate shoulders, and with a wry smile said, 'Very well, it is as you wish. We will look for you here at ten.'

He rose to his feet and smiled down at us, kissed Lisanne's hand and mine, gave a polite bow and walked off down the boulevard.

'For heaven's sake don't look so doubtful, Ellen. We're going to have a marvellous time. Henri's amusing and he finds you attractive, I can tell. I wonder what the friend's like, I hope he's young and good-looking, I'm long overdue for an escort of that calibre.'

I was beginning to realize the enormous responsibility that had been thrust upon me. Lisanne was strong-willed and determined when it came to her own amusement, and if I were the more responsible, she possessed a sophistication that made my homespun philosophy seem childishly immature.

She had got her own way, she had something to look

forward to, and the rest of the day passed without further incident.

In spite of my many misgivings I began to enjoy the next few weeks. Henri and Anton were charming, fun to be with and knowledgeable about everything we saw. We took boat trips on the Seine and I learned a lot about architecture. I was educated into choosing a good wine by the year it was laid down, and I came to appreciate works of art which before had been merely judged on whether or not they appealed to me.

To say that Lisanne was bored by much of this is an understatement, so to offset her boredom we were taken to concerts in the evenings, and when this did not satisfy her to discreet nightclubs Henri vetted most carefully as proper for two young English women.

Lisanne was not impressed.

'Oh Henri, why can't we go to one of the more risqué places? Mother's not likely to find out, and in any case she isn't interested just as long as I don't interfere with her pleasures,' she cried petulantly.

'The risqué places are not for girls of your age, chérie, why can't you be content with the clubs that put on a decent floor show and have a good pianist?' he said gently.

'Because I can stand all that when I'm eighty, right now I want to see one of the naughty shows, somewhere Ellen and I couldn't go on our own.'

Across the table his eyes met Anton's, and with a shrug the younger man said, 'Why not, Henri? This is Paris, why shouldn't the girls see what all the tourists come to see?'

'But these girls are not tourists in the accepted sense,' Henri said firmly, 'and you are forgetting that I am a friend of Madame de Bellefort.'

'Oh Henri, please don't be such a spoilsport, my mother needn't know anything about it. I'll make a deal with you: two concerts to one club with a reputation. That's a fair exchange, I think.'

He laughed. 'Let me think about it, chérie, but tomorrow

we are going to Versailles. I find your total lack of knowledge about our history most deplorable.'

She pouted prettily. 'All right Henri, tomorrow you shall tell us all about your French kings and queens, and that terrible revolution when you took off their heads. But the day after, or rather the night after, we shall expect you to take us slumming.'

Henri merely smiled, but not displeased with the conversation Lisanne maintained her good temper for the rest of the afternoon. That evening when we returned to the house however she said, 'You really should ask Mother for some more money, Ellen. You need some decent clothes, you've worn that blue thing three days over the last week and I know for a fact Grandmother gave her an allowance for you. And you always wear that jewellery Granny gave you. Does that mean you haven't anything else?'

'Nothing I want to wear, and it doesn't seem very long since your mother gave me some money, if I ask her for more so soon she's sure to want to know what I need to buy clothes for and you've said over and over again that I mustn't tell her.'

'Don't you have a bank account back in Yorkshire?'

'Well yes, but that's for later on when I'm no longer with you. You'll go off and marry your cousin, I'll need that money then.'

'It's quite ridiculous to have money in Yorkshire when you're living in Paris. It's a long time before I go off to marry Gervase, and a great deal could happen before then. Besides, when Mother gives you more you could always put it in the bank to replace what you'd taken out.'

'I don't know,' I murmured doubtfully.

'Well I am a bit sick of you looking like a poor relation, Ellen, I really do wish you'd spend a little on some pretty dresses. You're a lovely girl, if you set your stall out who knows who you might capture.'

When I still looked doubtful she flounced towards the door petulantly. 'If you decide to have your account transferred here I can tell you how to go about it. After all I'm not asking you to spend the lot, only enough to make you look a little more attractive. I'm sure Henri's noticed that your clothes are quite dreary, and a worldly sophisticated man likes to be seen with a fashionable girl.'

After she had gone I surveyed my wardrobe with the utmost disenchantment. They were not the clothes of a fashionable young lady in the Paris of nineteen thirty-nine but I was a Yorkshire lass brought up to recognize the desirability of money in the bank for a rainy day.

The money in the bank in Ilkley was along way away but before I did anything about that I decided to ask Mrs de Bellefort for a little more and hoped she wouldn't ask too many questions.

I heard her come in with Aunt Julie in the late afternoon and went to the top of the stairs to look down into the hall. They were laughing together as they separated their parcels, and from the looks of them they had both spent a great deal of money. I ran lightly down the stairs and she favoured me with a slight, absentminded smile.

'Perhaps you would help me to carry some of these upstairs, Ellen.'

I followed her up the stairs carrying a number of her parcels, and together we laid them out across her bed.

'I was hoping to have a few words with you, Mrs de Bellefort,' I said.

She was busy taking out gown after gown and laying them across the bed wherever there was an inch of space. For a few minutes I stood watching her until she said irritably, 'Well, Ellen, what is it?'

'You said I should ask you for more money when I needed it, Mrs de Bellefort. I am getting rather short.'

She frowned. 'It doesn't seem all that long since I gave you some, Ellen, I hope you're not spending it rashly. It isn't a bottomless pit, you know.'

'I do know, and I have been very careful. Lisanne says I need to buy clothes, those I have are really quite old and she is tired of my looking shabby.'

'Is she indeed?'

She stood on the other side of the room eyeing me and my attire with maddening condescension, then picked up her handbag and handed me a roll of notes. 'If there isn't enough to get something decent, ask me again.'

'Thank you, Mrs de Bellefort, I won't spend money needlessly.'

As I moved towards the door I began to think I had got away remarkably lightly and my hand was on the knob when she called out, 'Where do you and Lisanne spend your time? It seems to me I should have asked before.'

'We go to the art galleries and the shops, we take boat trips on the river and we walk in the parks. Tomorrow we're going to Versailles.' She stared at me in some surprise. 'My daughter was never interested in art galleries or places like Versailles. You've done very well to persuade her to visit them. I take it there are just the two of you?'

I could feel the warm blood colouring my cheeks, and sharply she said, 'Who is taking you to Versailles, Ellen, some young men you have become entangled with?'

'Oh no, Mrs de Bellefort. Actually this gentleman is a friend of yours. He's been very kind in showing Paris to us.'

'Who is he?'

'The Comte d'Aubriet.'

For a few moments she simply stared at me, then she threw back her head and laughed with delighted amusement.

'Henri! Well neither of you will come to much harm with Henri. He's a dear little man but quite averse to females. Oh, he likes to be seen with them, to pet and flatter them, but that's all. So the three of you have been taking in the cultural sights of Paris?'

'Henri brought along a friend, Anton. They have both been very kind.'

The laughter died and her eyes became strangely thoughtful.

'Anton Gourin. Young, handsome and supposedly Henri's live-in lover.'

I stared at her, shaken. In my innocence I knew nothing of men who loved other men, to me Anton had merely been a young friend of Henri's, a friend who shared the same sort of interests.

My shocked expression suddenly registered with her and she said quickly, 'I'm sorry, Ellen, obviously you are a child in such matters. Anton Gourin is a young man without means. When he came to Paris from Dijon he was the complete gigolo, escorting wealthy old women to the opera, the race course and dubious nightclubs where they could not go alone. He has certain charm and is obviously handsome. In no time at all Henri took him under his wing and installed him in his apartment. They were seen everywhere together and I must say I am not at all happy about the situation where Lisanne and you are concerned.'

'But Mrs de Bellefort, I can assure you Henri and Anton are always most polite and kind, if they had been otherwise neither Lisanne nor I would have gone with them again.'

'You are not as sophisticated as Lisanne, Ellen. My daughter knows well the sort of men she is dealing with and I am not convinced that Anton is of the same persuasion as Henri. It could well be that he admires women, particularly younger women, and merely goes along with Henri for what he can get out of him. If that is so there can be undercurrents and repercussions you cannot be aware of.'

I stared at her helplessly, miserably aware that she was deeply disconcerted by Lisanne's association with Anton and unsure what she could do about it. Of course she could forbid us to go with them again but that would interfere with her own pleasure, and while Lisanne was being entertained and kept amused she was less likely to demand attention from her mother. I was beginning to realize how infantile I must appear to this worldly woman, but while I fretted and worried she suddenly appeared to make up her mind.

'Oh very well, Ellen, there's nothing I can do about tomorrow, but I have put you on your guard. Stay together, don't let Lisanne wander off with Anton and don't be tempted to wander off with him yourself. I don't want either of you to become involved in a lovers' quarrel between the two men. In the next few days we must think seriously about moving on, I'm getting a little tired of Paris anyway and there is an atmosphere in the city I don't particularly understand.'

I stared at her. I sensed no atmosphere. Paris was gay and airy, a city obsessed with life and enjoyment, but Mrs de Bellefort showed no inclination to explain her sudden disenchantment with the city.

'I wouldn't say anything to Lisanne about this conversation, Ellen,' she said, 'she will give me a thousand reasons why we should stay here and I intend to make my own mind up about that. Enjoy Versailles and bear in mind what I have said.'

The following day I found myself watching Henri and Anton with new eyes, and realized I should have seen something not quite normal in their relationship from the beginning.

Henri's pernickety behaviour exasperated me. The complete dilettante, he liked to be seen and acknowledged by painters and actresses, members of the new nobility, and to be fussed over by the curators as an authority on everything in the palace of Versailles.

My head spun with paintings of the French kings and queens, their lovers and their mistresses, and if I was dutifully appreciative, Lisanne was plainly bored. She and Anton lagged behind, whispering and giggling together, and Henri's irritation was plain. Eventually they decided they would saunter out into the gardens, and while warning bells sounded in my head, Henri stubbornly persisted in escorting me from one ornate hall to the next.

For an hour or more we wandered through the palace, and Henri became more and more preoccupied. He seemed relieved when I suggested we should go outside but the gardens were extensive and we couldn't see Lisanne and Anton.

By this time we were walking in silence, a strange menacing silence, and Henri constantly consulted his watch as though to assure himself that time was moving slowly. How I would have loved those gardens if the atmosphere had been more amenable. As it was my shoes had started to pinch and I suggested that we should sit for a little.

He sat beside me with ill-disguised impatience, his eyes constantly raking the paths on either side, and I could have wept with relief when at long last Lisanne and Anton came into view, walking arm in arm, so intent on each other they failed to see us until they were almost level.

Relief made Henri snap at them but Anton merely raised his eyebrows maddeningly and Lisanne smiled so coyly I could cheerfully have slapped her. The day was spoiled, and I wanted to get back to Paris as quickly as possible. It soon became apparent that Henri had the same desire.

Anton prevaricated. 'Why should we rush back to the city when it's so beautiful out here?' he said angrily.

'I have matters to attend to in the city,' Henri snapped. 'matters I have totally neglected over the past few weeks.'

Lisanne looked from one to the other uncertainly and at last began to realize that her unfortunate behaviour was making Henri think twice about his association with us. She left Anton to link her arm through Henri's, all charm and girlish affection.

'Darling Henri, you've been so good,' she simpered, 'surely you can't mean you are going to desert us now?'

'I simply want to get back to the city,' he said stolidly. 'Perhaps some other day soon we could meet again.'

'But Henri, you promised. What about the nightclub?' she wailed.

'I did not promise, Lisanne, I only said maybe.'

The tears came readily to Lisanne when she was in danger of not getting her way, and today was no exception. Henri and Anton stared at her helplesly and after a few minutes Anton said coldly. 'Now see what you have done, Henri? Besides, you *half* promised to take the girls to a nightclub.'

Henri was not proof against Lisanne's tears and Anton's rebuke. With that small shrug I had grown familiar with over the past weeks he said resignedly, 'Oh very well, there is a small nightclub that has a reputation for good food and a singer who is making a name for herself.'

'Not one of those too-proper places, Henri, you promised,' Lisanne said appealingly.

'The nightclub is neither too proper nor too obscene, please allow me to know what is suitable for two English girls and do not forget your mother is a friend of mine. I do not want to lose her friendship because of some silly whim of her daughter's.'

'You really are cross, aren't you, Henri?' Lisanne said gently. 'I'm sorry we were so late, the time simply went, there was so much to see.'

Slightly mollified, Henri said, 'Come along then, let us get back in time for you to dress. We will pick you up at the house at eight o'clock.'

Back at the house Lisanne trilled lightly, 'Wasn't he cross, just because we left you for an hour? Poor Henri, it's my guess he loves Anton but Anton doesn't love him.'

'How can you say that?'

'It's true, Ellen. I've known about them for some time, I've heard Mother's friends talking about them. Anton would leave Henri like a flash if he found some girl with plenty of money to latch on to.'

'Some girl like you, do you mean?'

'Well yes. Unfortunately for Anton I'm already spoken for and he knows you haven't any money, he's only got to look at the clothes you've been wearing. Did Mother give you some money?'

'Yes, but I want it to last me for a month.'

'What nonsense. Paris is expensive, nobody knows that better than Mother. Have you thought about having your account transferred here?'

'Yes. I suppose it isn't much use to me back in Ilkley but I still can't afford to be extravagant with it, Lisanne.'

'Well of course not. We'll do it tomorrow, and tonight you shall borrow something of mine. We must do Henri proud, it's the only way to restore a smile to his face. Otherwise the evening will be spoilt.'

Lisanne wore a gown I had never seen her in before. It was black, shimmering with tiny bugle beads and, I privately considered, far too old and sophisticated for her. When she saw my doubtful expression she laughed airily. 'It's not mine, Ellen, I've borrowed it from Aunt Julie. She said I might look in her wardrobe for anything I needed.'

'Don't you think it's a little old for you?' I said anxiously.

'I suppose it is, but I'm fed up with pastels and frills and flounces. Let Henri and Anton see that we know how to be sophisticated and soigné. Now what can we do with you?'

I waited while she ran her fingers along the clothes in her wardrobe, then she pulled out a dark blue chiffon gown.

'That's the one, Ellen, blue is definitely your colour. I'll lend you my saphire pendant and earrings.'

I had never worn such a gown before. It shimmered and swirled around my feet and gave me a shape I had never thought I possessed. As I fastened the pendant round my neck I knew that I was beautiful. That was the moment I decided to transfer my money from the bank in Ilkley to Paris, a decision made in a moment of euphoria, elated by the sight of my reflection in the mirror.

Lisanne gasped with admiration when she came into my room carrying an armful of furs.

'You look wonderful, Ellen, I knew you would. Now which one of these goes best with that gown? This one, I think.'

She draped a soft luxurious stole round my neck. The fur was dark and rich and my fingers sank into it. I stared at her helplessly. 'Is it yours?' I whispered.

'No, it's Mother's. She won't mind. I'm going to wear the ermine, it looks better with black.'

I stroked the fur, my fingers seeming reluctant to part with it, and Lisanne laughed. 'It's sable, Ellen, don't you just love it? You should, the man who gave that to Mother was an Indian prince or something.'

'Honestly, Lisanne, I feel I shouldn't wear it. Haven't you a silk stole or a shawl you could lend me?'

'Don't be so tiresome, Ellen, tonight we're going to have the time of our lives. We're going to make Henri wish he preferred women to men, and I'm going to make poor Anton see the error of his ways.'

'Lisanne, be careful. You saw what happened this afternoon, that should be a warning to you.'

She laughed delightedly. 'Wasn't it funny, Ellen? Just like a man and a woman being jealous of each other.'

'I didn't think it was funny at all, I thought it was very sad.'

'Sad!'

'Well, yes. Can't you see that?'

'No of course I can't. Henri will do well to realize that Anton is merely using him, he'll come to his senses much quicker if he does, and there must be other men who are really like him, not one who merely pretends to be.'

'I still don't think it's up to you to enlighten him.'

'Oh well, I'm not going to argue with you, Ellen, I just want to enjoy every moment tonight. Was that the doorbell?'

Henri and Anton waited for us in the salon, both of them in faultless evening dress and both enthusiastic about our appearance.

Gallant as ever, Henri said, 'We shall be very proud to escort such elegant ladies.'

It felt so wonderful to be driving through the city in Henri's chauffeured limousine. The perfume from the sable fur rose to my nostrils and I knew instinctively that the sapphires gleamed attractively against my throat and in my ears.

Lisanne was wearing a diamond necklace and there were diamonds in her ears, borrowed no doubt from her mother or Julie, but it was the ermine wrap which sent my mind back over the years: diamonds and ermine, not emeralds and ermine.

It was in a badly lit street where the car pulled up, and Lisanne pouted a little as we were escorted into a narrow passage and finally into a dimly lit room. At one end was a small stage where a Negro sat at the piano playing softly. The tables were set back from the floor space and we could see immediately that most of them were occupied. A man wearing a dinner suit with a bright red cummerbund escorted us to our table, which was in an alcove with a good view of the stage and the floor.

Lisanne whispered, 'Couldn't we have sat nearer the floor, Henri?'

'This is better, chérie, if the dancers get too enthusiastic they are not likely to fall over us here.'

'Oh well, I suppose you know best,' she admitted grudgingly.

There were candles and bright red and white checked cloths on the table. Looking round I soon realized that though some of the men were in evening dress, the women were not dressed as flamboyantly as Lisanne and myself. I caught Henri's eyes and knew that he had guessed my thoughts.

'This is Paris, chérie, nobody cares how the next person dresses or behaves. The men will look at you with admiration, the women with indifference.'

'Nobody is going to see how we look in this dim light,' Lisanne complained.

'The night is young, Lisanne,' he answered patiently. 'The food is good, it is said the entertainment is different, we should wait and see.'

'What is the entertainment?' I asked, hoping to relieve the tension.

'A man and a woman who perform the apache dances better than anywhere else in Paris, the Negro pianist you are hearing now and a girl who is making quite a name for herself with her singing.'

Henri was right about the food. We dined on deliciously cooked duckling and tender young vegetables, followed by pastries I had never dreamed of. By this time I was enjoying the piano – haunting, faintly sad French music listened to by those around us appreciatively – and I thought how pleasant and civilized it was not to spoil it by chatter and laughter.

Anton was on his best behaviour. He danced first with Lisanne and then with me but in both cases Henri watched our progress round the floor with tense narrowed eyes.

I was glad that we were sitting well back when the apache dancers began their show. The woman was flung from one side of the floor to the other and the people occupying the front seats had to move back to avoid the spirited exhibition. It was a display of male domination, cruelty set to music, and it was not to my taste although I could not deny the artistry of their dancing.

I could tell that Henri was not impressed, he would have preferred a concert or the opera, but Lisanne and Anton applauded enthusiastically.

Once more the lights were dimmed and the Negro returned to the piano amid much applause, then a girl came towards the centre of the floor. She had bright red hair and was wearing a black satin dress that clung tightly to her slender figure. The dress showed an ample amount of bosom, and although the skirt reached the floor it was slit at the side and showed a shapely thigh. She carried a bright emerald-green feather boa and her only jewels were long green earings.

I couldn't take my eyes off her. In some strange way she reminded me of Kitty, even though her hair was brighter, her figure more slender, her walk more sinuous. From all around us the applause and cheering rang out.

'Who is she?' I whispered to Henri.

'She calls herself Emerald but I don't suppose that is her name.'

I was about to tell Lisanne that she reminded me of Kitty but when I turned to speak to her I saw that she and Anton were in deep conversation. I also saw that he was holding her hand.

The tune was haunting and the girl's voice low and melodious. She sang in French which immdiately dispelled any idea that she might be Kitty.

I had learned a smattering of French, but it was not sufficient to follow her words. I knew when the song was risqué from the titters and laughter that came from the tables around us, and I knew when there was pathos from the expressions that flitted across the audience's faces.

After she had finished the applause was deafening. They stood on their feet and cheered her and she picked up a vase of roses from one of the tables and tossed them around the room. She was laughing, her eyes shimmering with bright green eyeshadow sparkling with enjoyment, and for one breathless moment they met mine. I saw them open wide in startled surprise, then I thought I had imagined it for in the next moment she flung the emerald stole around her neck and after making several low bows disappeared behind the dais.

Of course it wasn't Kitty. Kitty had no French and would surely never have taken the trouble to learn any. Besides it was a far cry from the streets of Liverpool to a nightclub in Paris. It was then I became aware of the atmosphere around me, and saw that Henri was watching Anton and Lisanne closely.

We danced a little more, then Henri stated that he did not wish to be late since he had an early call to make in the morning, and disregarding Lisanne's cry of protest and Anton's scowls he rose to his feet and indicated that we should follow.

In the car, disconcerted by Henri's coldness, Lisanne said quickly, 'I hope we are going to see you tomorrow, Henri?'

'Alas no, I expect to be out of the city all day.'

'Tomorrow evening perhaps?'

'I am making no plans for tomorrow, Lisanne, I do not know what time I shall be returning from Rouen.'

'But I'd love to go to Rouen, Henri, we both would. I've read so much about Joan of Arc, wasn't she burnt in Rouen? And you're always saying I should pay more attention to French history.'

Her voice was persuasive, and at one time Henri would not have been proof against it, but tonight was different.

'I'm sorry, chérie, but I shall be too busy at Rouen to entertain two ladies.'

'Well couldn't Anton do that while you attend to your business?'

'Anton is not coming with me, he has things to do in Paris.'

I did not miss the surprise on Anton's face or the sudden glee in Lisanne's.

Henri's goodnight was unusually cool but in Anton's

smile there was promise, and as we let ourselves into the house Lisanne seemed well pleased with herself.

For myself I was glad we were not seeing the two men in the morning, I had decided to transfer my money from Yorkshire to Paris and I hoped Lisanne would tell me how to go about it. This she did the following morning with something approaching impatience.

'Honestly, Ellen, you've had all these weeks to do something about your money, now you're bothering me today when I particularly wanted to be out of the house early.'

'Why, where are you going?' I asked in surprise. 'I'm meeting Anton at the cafe soon after ten. He's at a loose end all day and so am I. I don't want you to come with me, you can find something else to do, I'm sure.'

'When was this arranged and why didn't you tell me last night?'

'I don't have to tell you everything I do or take you everywhere I go. If that was my grandmother's plan then it's not going to work.'

'I don't expect it, I only know you are flirting with dangers. Surely you must have seen Henri was angry with both of you at Versailles.'

'Henri's a foolish man if he thinks Anton will stay with him. I like Anton, he's lively and amusing and there's absolutely nothing wrong in our wanting to spend a little time together. If Henri doesn't like it then he should have asked Anton to go to Rouen with him.'

'Your mother wouldn't like you to go off with Anton on your own.'

'What has my mother got to do with it?' Her eyes narrowed dangerously and suddenly she caught hold of my arm in a grip like iron. 'You've been talking to her about us, haven't you, Ellen? What nonsense have you been telling her?'

'She asked me how we were spending our time, I didn't see why I should lie to her.'

'When did she ask you?'

'When I asked her for money. She doesn't think much

of Anton and she said we should be very careful not to cause trouble between the two of them.'

'Having you around is like having a gaoler, if I'd wanted my mother to know how we spent our time I'd have told her myself. I'm spending the day with Anton whether she likes it or not and if you say just one more word to her I'll make you wish you'd never heard of any of us. I'll ask her to get rid of you and it won't be very pleasant being left stranded in Paris where you don't know the language and haven't any money. I mean it, Ellen.'

She was too angry at that moment to reason with, and stunned into silence I watched while she slammed out of the house.

For several minutes I felt shaken by the force of her anger, then pulling myself together I went slowly to my room. The house was quiet. Mrs de Bellefort and Aunt Julie invariably slept late if they had been out the evening before, and I made up my mind to be out of the house before they surfaced.

I wrote to the bank manager in Ilkley asking for my money to be paid to me in Paris, then went out. It was a warm sunny spring morning. The trees along the boulevards had erupted into delicate leaf and people were already sitting at the cafes or standing in companionable groups at the street corners.

Boys on bicycles went by whistling joyfully and there was a smell of newly baked bread from the cafe at the corner of the avenue, and yet there was something strangely different about the way people were behaving. They sat at the tables in earnest conversation, they snatched newspapers from the stands and stood in groups poring over them urgently. I wished fervently that my French was better and as I waited to cross the road I tentatively asked a man standing beside me if there was bad news in the papers.

He spread the front sheet of his paper before my eyes, but seeing my puzzlement he said, 'It is war, chérie, very soon I fear.'

I stared up at him dumbfounded and in a soft voice he said, 'You are English, Mademoiselle?'

'Yes.'

'Then you should think about going home while it is still possible. Very soon I fear both England and France will be at war with Germany.'

He raised his hat and moved off across the road, leaving me staring.

I looked round at the gay bustling city, and in my innocence could not think that anything could change the city I had come to love. It was nonsense, of course there would not be war. It was quite ridiculous of the newspapers to fill their pages with such threats.

I posted my letter and stopped at a cafe for coffee. The day stretched before me and I realized that for the first time in weeks nothing was planned. I was alone with nothing to do. Then the idea took shape.

I had no idea where the nightclub was situated, but a taxi driver would know. When I found a taxi and asked for Le Chat Noir the driver stared at me curiously. It was a place one went to in the evening, not in the middle of the morning, and I thought he might be wondering if I was an entertainer. But shrugging his shoulders he applied himself to his driving while I tried to memorize the route.

Eventually we came to a less salubrious part of the city where the streets were narrower and less populated, lined with dingy shops and dingier houses. At last we stopped in front of a door I recognized from the night before and I paid the fare before stepping out on to the road.

The nightclub looked even less inviting than on the previous evening. Over the door a cardboard witch wearing a tall pointed hat sat on a broomstick while a black cat sat behind her, and the door was painted black and endorsed with silver stars. It was all a little crude but I remembered that the food had been good and the entertainment even better.

A glass case stood behind the front door, filled with photographs. There was a photo of the Negro sitting at the piano and smiling broadly, and another of the apache dancers, but there was none of Emerald. Disappointed I turned away, and then through a glass panel by the door I saw a life-size cardboard figure of Emerald staring back at me – the bright red hair, the poppy-red lips smiling tantalizingly, the bright emerald feathers and long emerald earrings. Once again my heart missed a beat when I thought how strangely she resembled Kitty McGuire.

From behind me a voice said, 'It is me, Ellen. I was hopin' you hadn't recognized me.'

I spun round and there was Kitty looking much like she used to without the theatrical make-up, and only her red hair more startling than I remembered it.

I took her hands and leaned forward to embrace her. 'Oh Kitty, I couldn't really believe the girl last night was you, but I had to be sure. Can we go somewhere to talk?'

'I have a rehearsal and I'm a bit late. You can sit and watch if you like, then we can go round the corner to a little cafe where the food isn't bad. I'll be rehearsing for about an hour, can you wait that long?'

'I can wait all day if necessary. Kitty, I've so much to ask you.'

'And I you, Ellen Adair. You could 'ave knocked me down with a feather, seein' you sitting in the nightclub with those posh folk. I knows the younger of the two men, he's been here somethin' an' often with different women.'

'He's a friend of a friend. I don't know him very well.'

Her eyes were smiling into mine, worldly cynical eyes that brought a blush to my cheeks.

Nothing I told Kitty would shock her. She knew Anton for what he was and probably Henri too. It was Lisanne and myself she would want to know about, and how I came to be in Paris in an atmosphere totally alien from the Yorkshire we had both known and the old life we had shared.

CHAPTER 26

I sat entranced at the back of the nightclub as Kitty went through her repertoire. She conversed with the pianist in English, which he instantly translated into French for the manager who sat near the dais.

She sang the songs with impeccable French aplomb and I was entranced, marvelling at her lively courage and with a mounting impatience for the rehearsal to finish.

After what seemed ages she turned to the pianist, saying, 'That's enough for today, I have a friend waiting for me.' She flashed him a bright smile and after a gay wave to the manager she was walking quickly towards me.

'Come on, Ellen, let's get out of here afore they produce a hundred and one new numbers for me to try.'

The cafe was only a few minutes' walk away and was crowded with ordinary working-class people. Kitty was met with smiles and greetings.

'It's cheap,' Kitty said. 'You might not like it now that you've become used to better things, but I don't waste mi hard-earned money on expensive food. It's good and plentiful here and it's what the local people enjoy.'

'I shall love it, Kitty. I can live without the expensive restaurants I've been to recently.'

Indeed the food was better than anything I had eaten for days. We dined off succulent onion soup and tender escalopes of veal, and shared a bottle of sweet white wine of no special vintage but which I found quite delicious.

She seemed reluctant to be the first to ask questions and, equally unsure, my first question was, 'What do you think of the war news, Kitty?'

'What war news?' she asked, opening her eyes wide with surprise.

'The papers are full of it, the people on the streets talk about nothing else.'

'I've heard nothing round here, and if I had a newspaper I wouldn't understand most of it. I'm going to take French lessons but I don't start until next Friday.'

'I thought of doing the same . . .'

'We're skating round the things we really want to know about, aren't we, Ellen? Suppose you start first. What are you doing here, and who was that girl you were with? She was a lot like you, one of your sisters was it?'

So I started to tell Kitty about my life since Aunt Liza died and in my own ears it sounded like a fairy story, starting with my grandmother and her lover and ending with my reasons for being in Paris. I could feel the bitterness in my voice when I told her about Lance and she listened without speaking. When I became silent there were tears in her eyes and then there were tears in mine, and we cried a little in memory of the years that united us and the traumas that had divided us.

'What's goin' to happen to you when this girl Lisanne goes off to marry her cousin then?' she wanted to know.

'Honestly I don't know, Kitty. I'll have to find work, that's for sure.'

'This Lady de Bellefort's done you no favours, has she, Ellen? You fell in love with her grandson and she took him away from you, she's made you a companion for her granddaughter who'll go off and leave you without a second thought. I wonder if this is her way of making you pay for what she suffered because her husband loved your grandmother. I reckon it's cruel she's been.'

I'd never seen it like that. I'd believed in the old lady's good intentions in giving me work and a home, now I was seeing her actions through new eyes and I too saw the cruelty behind it. But I couldn't believe that she had been deliberately cruel. Fate had taken me to Langstone where it had all begun, and there was no armour against fate.

'Tell me about you, Kitty. How can you sing so beautifully in French when you hardly understand a word of it?'

'I learn it like a parrot. I've always been a mimic, nobody knows that better than you. It used to get me into trouble at school. And I could always sing a pretty tune. It was my only accomplishment, learnin' was never easy.'

'But when did you leave Liverpool?'

'I got to hate it, Ellen. I hated the disdainful looks we got in the shops and on the streets. They knew us for what we were and I told Emmie if she wouldn't leave with mi then I'd go on mi own, but she wouldn't come. I don't know what became of her, but at any rate she had a mother in Liverpool. She could allus go home if the worst came to the worst.'

'Where did you go?'

'I went up to London. I joined the Salvation Army and stayed in some grotty hostel in the East End while I looked for work.' She grinned, the old infectious grin that had always brought a smile to my lips.

'In the weekdays I worked in a mission, like in Liverpool, and at the weekends I walked with the Army and carried one of the banners.

'We were singin' in the street near the West End one Saturday afternoon when I saw this feller listenin' and watchin' mi. I always felt safe from fellas in mi uniform, and he didn't look like a chap that was after pickin' a girl up. When I went round with mi collectin' box he gave me his card and said if I was interested in a job I could contact him at that address.

'I did nothin' about it for weeks, then one day we had a seaman at the mission much like Black Jake. Ye remember him, don't you, Ellen?'

'I don't think I'll ever forget him!'

'Well he made a nuisance of himself and he frightened me a bit. That week I dressed miself up and went into the West End to look this man up. The outcome was that he sent me to see the manager of a club who was lookin' for a girl singer. I sang one or two songs for him and he took me on trial singin' three nights a week. I found digs with two other girls who worked at the club and I stayed with him two years. Then one night a man came to mi dressing room and offered me a job in a new club that was openin' in the West End, singing five nights a week at double the money, and I moved on. I called miself Emerald, ye can guess why, and I allus wore black and emerald. The earrings are real, Ellen, I saved up for 'em. If no chap was goin' to lavish mi with 'em I was goin' to buy 'em for myself.'

'When did you come to Paris?'

'Some months ago. The same chap that owned the club in London owns this one and I've built up a reputation, you can see that for yourself.'

'I thought you were wonderful, Kitty.'

'I like singin'. I like the atmosphere, the dimmed lights and the cigarette smoke. I adore the applause and I enjoys bein' that bit disdainful which helps mi to keep mi distance, and the customers seem to like it that way.'

'Where will you go from here then?'

'Always to somethin'a little bit better, I hope. A better club, a richer audience. I'd like to become known all over Europe. I'd like to see the name Emerald in lights over the most expensive clubs in Paris. But it's early days yet, all that takes time. I always had such big ideas, I'm not surprised you got exasperated with me.'

'I never forgot you, Kitty. You were the only one who ever brought warmth and laughter into my life. When I lived with my aunt I couldn't think I'd ever see you again but I began to understand why you did what you did. As long as I'm in Paris I hope we can meet. We mustn't lose touch with one another ever again.'

She laughed. 'Oh Ellen, you were always such an earnest little thing, I don't think I ever really deserved you.'

'Is there anybody you're in love with, Kitty?'

Her face became strangely wistful, then with some bravado she shrugged it off, saying, 'I take love where I finds it, Ellen. I'm not the type to settle down with a man and a home and children, I like variety and I like independence. One day perhaps I'll feel different about love but for now I'm only interested in makin' somethin' of mi life as a singer. I have it in me to do well, Ellen, I'd be a fool to tie miself down.'

'Will you stay in Paris if there's a war? Everybody is saying it's inevitable.'

'Well if there is the Germans won't come to Paris. The French have got that Maginot Line no army could get through. Besides, there isn't going to be a war. Would all these people be sitting at the cafes laughing and joking if they thought war was comin'? Surely you don't believe those rumours.'

I looked at her tense earnest face and hadn't the heart to say that I did believe them. Instead I brought the conversation round to something more light-hearted like the apache dancers at the nightclub.

'They're married,' she confided, 'and it isn't all make-believe when he throws her about. He's jealous of everything she does, the way she looks and the way men look at her. You can hear 'em rowing in their dressing room night after night, Desmond says one night he'll kill her for sure.'

'Who is Desmond?'

'The pianist. He's helped me a lot, if I move on I'd like to think he'll move on too.'

'Are you very good friends, Kitty?'

'If you mean are we lovers the answer's no,' and there was something in her face that prevented me asking more.

It was late afternoon when I made my way back to Aunty Julie's, promising Kitty that I would see her again in a few days. I could make no definite arangements until I had spoken to Lisanne.

The house was quiet. I had not expected Mrs de Bellefort or Aunt Julie to be in but I had hoped Lisanne would be back from her meeting with Anton. When eight o'clock came and went and she still had not returned I became anxious.

I dined off a tray in my room and afterwards I tried to get interested in a book Lisanne had passed on to me. It was a light frothy novel, entirely predictable, and failed to hold my interest so that I laid it aside and thought about my talk with Kitty. I found her life far more interesting than any novel, for how could I ever have believed that I would find Kitty McGuire entertaining fashionable Parisian society in the improbable name of Emerald?

It was considerably later when I heard the slamming of

the front door and hurrying footsteps followed by the crashing of Lisanne's door and I leapt to my feet, startled.

For several seconds I stood outside her door but inside there was silence, then I heard sobbing.

Cautiously I opened the door. Lisanne lay prone on the bed, crying into the pillow, and anxiously I went to sit beside her. Her face was red and swollen from weeping, and when I touched her gently a fresh flood of tears shook her slender body.

I waited patiently for them to subside, then gently I asked, 'What is wrong, Lisanne, is it Anton?'

Her voice came to me muffled by the pillow. 'It was horrible, Ellen. He told me to get out.'

'Who did, Anton?'

'No. Henri.'

My heart sank dismally and in some exasperation I said, 'Tell me what happened, Lisanne. I can't hear you properly.'

She struggled into a sitting posture and for the first time I saw the fear as well as the anger in her face.

'He was there all the time, sitting in the dark waiting for us to go back there, just like a spider. I couldn't believe that Henri could be so sneaky, he'd said he would be in Rouen all day.'

'You went to Henri's house?'

'Well yes. We were so tired of walking in the parks and drinking wine at the cafe. Anton didn't seem to have enough money for anything else so when it got dark he said we should go to Henri's house and he would make coffee. Honestly, Ellen, we weren't doing anything wrong, just a few kisses and caresses, that's all, but then suddenly Henri was there, accusing us, and he looked so terrible, not like himself at all. When I started to tell him we hadn't done anything wrong he told me to get out, just like he would speak to some woman off the streets. I was so furious I ran out without my coat and I daren't go back for it even when I was freezing.'

'What about Anton, what did he say?'

'Nothing. At first he was flippant, then when he saw how

furious Henri was, he looked frightened. Don't you dare say I told you so, and don't you dare tell my mother.'

'Perhaps in a day or two Henri will be in the mood to listen to explanations.'

'I don't ever want to see Henri again, I'm just afraid he'll tell my mother. If he does she'll pack me off home to Grandmother and you know what that'll be like.'

I could quite cheerfully have slapped her. Just when I'd found Kitty and there was a chance of renewing our friendship, just when I was beginning to see all the advantages the coming months might bring. She had started to sob again and suddenly I felt sorry for her. It wasn't her fault that she was spoilt and wilful, but she had to learn her lessons some time. Sooner or later she had to learn that mistakes had to be paid for, that takers needed to be givers also, and if she learned it the hard way so much the better.

Lisanne seemed to have recovered her high spirits when she came to my room the next morning. If she had wept during the night careful make-up had obliterated all signs of it, and she was wearing a bright poppy-red skirt and white organdie blouse which seemed to demonstrate her restored equilibrium.

'I heard Mother and Aunt Julie going down to breakfast so I thought we might join them,' she said brightly. 'They might have some suggestions about how we should spend the day.'

We were halfway down the stairs when Aunt Julie came out of the breakfast room and crossed the hall. She gave us never a look but ran past us up the stairs dabbing at her eyes with a lace handkerchief. Meeting my eyes Lisanne shrugged, saying, 'Now what? Do you suppose there really is going to be a war?'

Mrs de Bellefort sat at the table with the paper open before her and she was very angry. A spot of colour burned in each cheek and her eyes were cold and hard.

We approached uncertainly and she snapped, 'Sit down, the pair of you.'

'Is it war?' Lisanne whispered anxiously.

'War! War is all I need, I doubt if even that catastrophe will cause more consternation among my friends than this. Where were you yesterday, Lisanne? And don't lie to me.'

'We walked in the gardens and went to the Louvre.'

'Who is we?'

'Ellen . . .'

'I told you not to lie to me, Lisanne. You were not with Ellen yesterday, indeed you were seen drinking wine at a cafe near the Opéra with Anton Gourin.'

'Well what of it? We were doing no harm. Who saw us anyway?'

'Somebody of sufficient note to see that it appears in the press.'

'You should be glad that I've made the society column then.'

'Don't you dare speak to me like that. You are not in any society column, indeed you will be lucky if you escape being interviewed by the gendarmerie before the morning is over.'

The bombast was suddenly wiped off Lisanne's face. 'Why the gendarmerie, what has happened?' she asked fearfully.

'Your friend Anton Gourin is dead, he was shot early this morning by his friend Henri who is now in the hands of the police.'

We stared across the table in horrified silence and Mrs de Bellefort had the satisfaction of seeing her daughter put her head in her hands and sob helplessly.

Neither of us attempted to comfort her. For my part I felt too stunned, and in a little while when Lisanne saw there were to be no words from either of us she moaned, 'It isn't my fault, Mother, I had nothing to do with it.'

Mrs de Bellefort directed her attention to me. 'I warned you about this, Ellen. Did you not see fit to warn my daugher?'

'I tried to warn her, neither of us believed it would end like this.'

'I told you Henri could be as jealous as any woman. The shock of discovering that he was being used by Anton was evidently too much for him, that and his involvement with my daughter. Do stop snivelling, Lisanne, any amount of tears is not going to undo the damage. What we have to think about is your grandmother.'

'Grandmother?' Lisanne murmured.'

'Well of course. If this gets into the English papers, and she does seen quite capable of getting to know most of my business, she will demand that I return you to her immediately. And what is far worse, she will not countenance any shopsoiled girl marrying her grandson.'

'I'm not shopsoiled,' Lisanne stormed. 'If the papers say I am then they're lying. Nothing, absolutely nothing happened between Anton and me.'

'I believe you, strangely enough. But would your grandmother, and would Gervase de Bellefort?'

'I don't care about him, how do we know what *he's* been doing all these years?'

'It is a fact of the times, my dear, that what a man does before he is married, and sometimes afterwards, bears little relationship to how a young woman is expected to conduct herself.

'If the police wish to interview you, you will tell them the honest truth, that you and Ellen were friends of both Henri and Anton, that they had been kind enough to escort you around the city and to Versailles, and that is all. Where were you yesterday, Ellen, in case the police wish to know why you were not together?'

'I went to the shops and I had lunch with a friend I once knew in England. I didn't know she was in Paris until the day before.'

'A woman friend?'

'Yes of course.'

'Had you arranged to meet her?'

'No. I met her by chance.'

'But *you* had arranged to meet Anton Gourin, Lisanne.'

'Well yes. Henri said he had to go to Rouen and Anton was all alone all day. Honestly, Mother, all we did was walk in the park and sit at a cafe.'

'Are you sure that is all that you did? Did you return with him to Henri's house?'

'Yes, but only for a little while. Anton made coffee and we drank it in the salon.'

'And I suppose Henri found you together?'

'He was so sneaky, Mother, waiting in the dark just like a big spider, and he looked so strange. His eyes were staring and he started shrieking at us like some old harpy.'

'I can't believe that you were such a fool, Lisanne. I can't believe that I'm saddled with two girls who don't seem to know what damage they've done. Go to your rooms and wait there until I send for you. I don't want you together concocting some story for the police. Henri d'Aubriet is a man of some consequence in Paris. Everyone will be talking about this terrible thing this morning and I very much fear that neither of you will come out of it smelling of roses.'

'I don't see why anybody can blame us,' Lisanne insisted vehemently. 'They must know that Henri was a silly vain little man who was queer to say the least. Why should he shoot Anton for spending thc day with a girl? Men are meeting girls all over Paris.'

'Go to your room, Lisanne, and begin to think a little. I suspect it's something you don't do very often. And stay there until I send for you.'

Lunch was served to us in our separate rooms and we heard nothing more until we were summoned to the salon about four o'clock. Once more we faced Mrs de Bellefort but this time Aunt Julie too sat before the fire, though she would not look at either of us.

'You may sit down,' Mrs de Bellefort said.

'It appears we are not to be troubled by the police, as whatever statement Henri has made does not apparently include you. He may indeed be a vain little man who is unlike other men but in your case he has behaved impeccably by sparing you a great deal of harassment. He probably wishes he had never heard of you, and the French can be surprisingly sympathic in a crime of passion. You would do well to put the whole matter behind you.'

For the first time I began to agonize over my position. I had asked for my money to be sent to me here in Paris, but suppose Mrs de Bellefort decided to move on and send me back to England. Where would I go and who would I go to? As if she understood my anxiety she said, 'Do you wish to go home to England, Ellen? If you do I cannot stop you.'

'I have nowhere to go to in England.'

'You have no family?'

'None who would welcome me.'

'And you could not go to Langstone, there is nothing for you there. What do you propose to do then?'

'I don't know,' I said in a small voice.

Almost immediately Lisanne said, 'I don't see why Ellen can't stay with us. At least she'd be somebody of my own age.'

'Would you be prepared to travel with us, Ellen I feel we should leave Paris for a time.'

'Oh yes, Mrs de Bellefort, I promise to behave and not be any trouble.'

'I would prefer those promises to come from my daugher, she's the one most likely to cause me trouble.'

For days we scanned the newspapers in case something of Anton's death should be reported but there was nothing.

I chose a day to visit Kitty when Lisanne was out shopping. I was astonished to see closing notices splashed across the door of the club, which was closed and padlocked.

I had only a vague idea where Kitty was living, but I had come so far, I couldn't go back without trying to find her.

The streets around the club seemed unnaturally quiet and the cafe where we had eaten lunch was almost empty. I recognized one of the men who had spoken to Kitty, and when he saw me he rose to his feet and smiled.

'You wait for your friend?' he said, and I was surprised that he addressed me in English.

'The club is closed, can you tell me where she lives?'

'Ze club ees being transferred to anozer part of zer city, better, much better. Come, I veel show you where she lives.'

So we walked together down the narrow cobbled streets and at last he pointed to a small courtyard and some steps leading to a narrow veranda behind which there were small-paned windows.

'Zat ees 'er door, she may be in, I do not know.'

I thanked him warmly and hurried across. A fat tabby cat sat washing its face on the bottom step and there were plant pots on each step and along the balcony.

Before I reached the door I was aware of laughter, and then the deeper tones of a man's voice. Tentatively I knocked on the door and from inside came a man's muttered curse but I knocked again, more loudly this time.

After what seemed ages the bolts were drawn back and the door was opened only a fraction. A man stood at the door wearing a robe over his trousers but the robe was open to reveal a tanned hairy chest. He was dark, with tousled hair over a handsome inquiring face, and slowly he eyed me from head to foot, bringing the hot blood to my face.

'May I speak to Kitty, please? Tell her it's Ellen.'

Maddeningly his eyes appraised me for several seconds before he said, 'Kitty, who ees Kitty?'

Nonplussed and at a great disadvantage, held as I was by his bold dark eyes, I stammered awkwardly, 'Emerald then, please tell her it's her friend Ellen Adair.'

Suddenly he found the door taken out of his grasp and it opened wider to reveal Kitty, her red hair hanging in great curls on to her shoulders, her hands hastily tying the thin silk cord which girdled her robe. For a moment she seemed embarrassed that I should find her in the company of a man in a state of undress, then with that old take it or leave it shrug which I remembered so well she said, 'I wasn't expecting you, Ellen, and the room's a mess.'

'I don't want to come in, Kitty, I only came to tell you that we might soon be leaving Paris. I didn't want to leave without seeing you again.'

'Is it the war that's making you go?'

'That amongst other things.'

'Like the shooting of Anton Gourin for instance?'

'That is one reason, yes.'

The man's voice came from inside the room, saying, 'Must you stay there all afternoon?'

Kitty merely smiled, her eyes filled with cynical amusement.

'Who is he?' I asked curiously.

'Didn't you recognize him?'

'No.'

'You saw him dance with his wife at the club the other evening, the apache dancer.'

I stared at her incredulously, then I burst out with, 'But you told me he and his wife were jealous of each other, is it any wonder?'

'He came to me for sympathy, he often does, and if it ends with us making love, no love in involved. We both know that.'

'Oh Kitty,' I murmured, and again the small sardonic smile came back to her lips.

'Men have used me in the past, a great many of them, but it was Kitty McGuire they used. Emerald is something different, she takes them and leaves them to please herself. I give them no illusions, and I promise nothing. I wonder if your upright moral little soul is capable of understanding that.'

'I would like to understand it better.'

'You've been hurt by a man, Ellen. You loved that man Lance and you could have been his mistress, you could have stayed together on his terms. What sort of life would it have been for you, always in the background, somebody he came to see when he wasn't busy, when he didn't have to appear with his wife in all the right places and with all the right people?'

'I told him I couldn't live like that, but I couldn't live like you either, Kitty. I'll always care about you, I'll always want to see you no matter what you do, but that man isn't worthy of you, Kitty.'

We stood for a while saying nothing, then she said, 'You know I'm moving to a new club?

'To some grotty little street in Montmartre. It's fashionable, but there are so many nightclubs in the area I just hope the people will come to mine.'

'I'm sure they will, Kitty, those people the other evening adored you.'

'One day, Ellen, the name Emerald will be set in lights

from one end of Paris to the other.' Then she laughed gaily. 'There I go again, daydreaming.'

'What will you do if war comes?'

Her face sobered rapidly. 'I don't want to think about it. They tell mi Paris is invulnerable and I believe them. It's like London, the Germans could never come here.'

'But if they do?'

'They'll be a new audience, won't they, Ellen? Different uniforms, different men.'

'Kitty, you can't mean that, you wouldn't entertain the Germans?'

'If I wanted to survive I would have to, wouldn't I? Besides, you seem to forget that I'm Irish, and England's done precious little for me.'

'It didn't even teach you any values, did it, Kitty?'

'Oh those. Yes I learned some of them but to live by them depends on what life does to you, doesn't it? I found out in Liverpool that I couldn't really afford values. Will you come to see me when the new club opens?'

'If I'm in Paris yes, I'll come to see you.'

'I've got two great new numbers you'll love. In no time at all everybody'll be singing them.'

'What are they?'

' "Love's Last Word is Spoken" and "I'll be Seeing You". I'm learning to sing them in French but I'll do them in English too. They'll be just the sort of things to go well if the men have to go away.'

It was a Kitty I'd seen so many times before, obsessed with herself, impatient for life and riches, a survivor even if everybody else went under. I couldn't relate to Kitty like this. All the same I embraced her and as I ran down the stone steps and across the courtyard she called out, 'Take care, Ellen. I'll be seeing you.'

CHAPTER 27

In spite of the threat of war the people seemed gay, too gay, and as Lisanne and I mingled with them in the cafes and the parks, talk of war seemed incongruous.

I was having French lessons ever morning but when Mrs de Bellefort suggested Lisanne should accompany me she refused, saying there would be little use for French when she married her cousin in Ireland.

There was nothing in the papers now about Henri who was still in prison awaiting trail, but Aunt Julie was convinced he would seen be relased. 'After all,' she said, shrugging her silk-clad shoulders, 'Anton Gourin was well known as a gigolo before Henri became fond of him, that surely is enough to stand Henri in good stead when he comes to trial. Poor Henri, he was more sinned against then sinning.'

She maintaned an aloof stance towards Lisanne and in some anger Lisanne said, 'I don't care what she thinks, I know myself that I did nothing wrong. Surely even in Paris it must be possible to spend an afternoon in the company of a young man without some idiot like Henri shooting him.'

In many ways Lisanne was very like Kitty. She only believed what she wanted to believe and was quite capable of closing her eyes and ears to unpleasant happenings.

Matters were brought to a head one morning over breakfast when a letter arrived for Mrs de Bellefort bearing an English postmark.

'From Grandmama,' she announced. 'No doubt to do with Lance's aproaching wedding when we shall be expected to swell the ranks of the de Belleforts. At least that is what I hope it is, and not about Paris's latest scandal which involves you, Lisanne.'

We watched anxiously while she read. Her expression conveyed nothing, and consumed with impatience Lisanne said sharply, 'What does she want, Mother?'

Her mother looked up with a half smile. 'She wants us to return to England without further delay.'

'For Lance's wedding?'

'Apparently Lance and Geraldine were married at the beginning of March, very quietly, and Lance is now serving with the Yeomanry somewhere in the south of England.'

'Lance is in the army, but why?'

'Apparently they are rather more concerned with the war news in England than we are in France's capital. Your grandmother informs me that gas masks have been issued and Langstone is populated by children from the large cities out of the way of air raids, and it is time we realized that our place is at Langstone, or at least in England where we can take some part in the war effort.'

'Is that all?' Lisanne asked dismally.

'She also says your marriage will in all probability have to be deferred since Gervase has seen fit to enlist in the Royal Navy. He has told her that he will not be available for matrimony or anything else until the war is over. Knowing Gervase, I expect it has afforded him a great deal of pleasure to tell her that.'

'If he's not anxious to marry me, I'm certainly not anxious to marry him,' Lisanne said angrily.

'Your grandmother's made very sure that Lance honoured his obligations, but at any rate we don't have to go rushing back to attend his wedding.'

'What will you do?' Lisanne asked anxiously.

'I can't go back to Langstone to sit out the war under your grandmother's watchful eyes, that's for sure. On the other hand we can't stay here in Paris.'

'Granny'll be furious if we don't go back after receiving her letter.'

'I know, but she's not to know we received it, is she? If we move on within the next few days she'll think her letter went astray. After all, in today's climate anything could happen.'

My own thoughts were in turmoil. One half of me wanted to go back to England, not to Langstone but to some place where I could find work in any capacity that might help my country, but the other half wanted to stay away. I had unhappy memories of my youth in England, memories that seemed quite alien to the woman I had become.

When Mrs de Bellefort told Aunt Julie the contents of her mother-in-law's letter, she burst into tears.

'But you can't go back to England, Delia, what shall I do all alone in Paris?'

'But Julie, you are never alone in Paris, you have a large collection of friends.'

'And most of them are talking about moving away. Besides, I'm half Jewish, they wouldn't want to know me if the Germans come. Hitler is fanatical about the Jews. I thought you and the girls would be staying on here in my house, or if not we could go somewhere together. There's the house at Antibes, you love it there, Delia, and the girls would love it too. Besides it's close to Monaco and the Principality will never go to war. You know, Delia, I have more friends in the south of France than I have ever had in Paris.'

'I was thinking of Switzerland, don't you have friends there?'

'Oh no, Mother, not Switzerland,' Lisanne moaned dismally. 'I vowed I was never going back there, all that snow and those dreadful cuckoo clocks.'

'If there is war what makes you all so sure that it won't touch the south of France?' her mother asked sharply. 'It seems to me we shall be jumping out of the frying pan into the fire.'

'Where else is there?' Aunt Julie sighed helplessly.

'We could go home, I suppose. Money is going to be my problem if we don't. My allowance would cease, there is no way Lady de Bellefort would send money out of the country during a war. Being entirely practical, Julie, it does seem as if that's the best idea for us. You could come with us.'

'I wouldn't be happy in England, I hate your beastly climate and it would be quite ridiculous to go there when I have a house in the south of France which is quite beautiful.'

'Money *is* important, Julie, I've never learned to live without it.'

'Delia, I have enough money for all of us, and so many people like and admire you. In no time at all we'll be feted and entertained without it costing you a penny.'

'Julie, I have to think about it. I don't want to live on charity and I won't be persuaded against my will.'

I had sat patiently listening, not having been invited to take part. Now as we left the room Mrs de Bellefort turned to me, saying, 'I would like a few words with you in private, Ellen. Perhaps you will come to my room.'

Now I am going to learn my fate, I thought anxiously as I followed her. She sat before the window and indicated that I should sit opposite.

'Your problem is my problem, Ellen,' she began. 'My mother-in-law sends money to me for your keep. I can ignore her letter and we can go south to Antibes. I can write to her from there and she will think we never received her letter. She will no doubt urge me to return, and may for a time continue my allowance, but if there is war it will stop immediately. I intend to withdraw my money from the bank here in Paris, but I don't exactly know what to do about you.'

'I have had my money transferred here, Mrs de Bellefort.'

'I'm not very sure if that was wise. Your bank manager in Yorkshire will have notified my mother-in-law that your account is no longer in his hands and she will assume that none of us had any intention of returning to England. I suppose Lisanne cajoled you into taking that step.'

I didn't speak. Any minute now she was going to tell me I must go home, and I had no doubt that she would see the anxiety in my face. While she pondered I could have cried with impatience. She started to pace the floor, while I sat with my hands clenched against my knees.

At last she stopped in front of my chair. 'You've said nothing of what you want, Ellen, but I must ask you. I can send you home to England, or you can throw in your lot with us. Be very sure that I can give you no promises regarding our future. Life will be very uncertain and in six months you might well be wishing you were safe in England with people you know, speaking a language you understand. How adventurous are you, Ellen?'

'Please, Mrs de Bellefort, I would much rather go with you and Lisanne, wherever you're going. I'll try not to be a burden, indeed perhaps I will be able to find work.'

'Work!' she said, raising her delicate eyebrows.

'Yes, of course. If there is war they will be needing people in the hospitals and the factories. I could earn my keep, I've never been afraid of hard work.'

'I have a much better idea, Ellen. You are a beautiful girl, talk of factories and hospitals seems a little incongruous besides my memories of the Côte d'Azure. Be a little aloof, remember that you are English, but not too aloof to prevent you being pleasantly charming to those rich men you will undoubtedly meet. And Lisanne must give you some of her clothes, I will see to it personally.'

There was doubt on my face, and she laughed delightedly. 'My dear child, don't look so alarmed. I am not asking you to sell yourself, only to be available as a charming companion. I am talking about survival, Ellen. As the months pass, particularly if war comes to Europe, you will begin to understand.'

'Does that mean that we are going to Antibes?'

'I expect so. Julie is well known in the area and the house is lovely, in the most beautiful place you can ever imagine. One could do worse than sit out the war in Antibes.'

'It seems so awful to talk about sitting out the war.'

'My dear girl, you are talking like a romantic child. I have seen war, the last one was terrible, and I lived through riots in India and China. Can you blame me if I never want to see another one? And count yourself lucky to be in a position to escape this one.

'I should withdraw your money from the bank in Paris, Ellen. We must take everything we have with us and we must make preparation to leave as quickly as possible, by the end of June at the very latest.'

Lisanne was waiting eagerly in my room to hear what had transpired between her mother and me.

'Well I'm so relieved not be going back to Langstone,'

she said firmly, 'and I couldn't have stood going to Switzerland. After all, we don't know how long the war will last, supposing it comes at all.'

'Your mother says we must be prepared to leave at the end of June, no later.'

'Oh well, why not? I'm fed up with Paris anyhow and Antibes is quite beautiful. I wish it was Nice or Cannes but neither of them is very far away.'

The end of June came and went and still we were in Paris. It was largely Aunt Julie's business commitments that kept us there. Her husband had had his fingers in a great many pies, and disposing of her assets in Paris at that time was a harrowing business. It was the beginning of August which finally saw us taking down pictures and shrouding furniture, packing great wooden crates with ceramics and porcelain over which Lisanne's mother remarked, 'I really don't know why we are doing all this, if the Germans come they'll take what they want regardless.'

'How can you say that, Delia?' Aunt Julia cried angrily. 'This is Paris, the Germans won't come and the servants won't let them lay a finger on my treasures anyway.'

Two days before we were due to leave another blow fell. Leon, Aunt Julie's chauffeur, was called up to the army. It was the final straw in a succession of calamities in Aunt Julie's eyes, and she sat in the midst of her packing cases with the tears streaming down her face, a pretty spoilt woman who was thinking only of herself while her world crumbled around her.

'What shall we do?' she moaned. 'I was taking all my most treasured things with us in the car and Leon was going to do the driving. How are we to get to Antibes now? We can't go on the train.'

'We shall have to do the driving,' Mrs de Bellefort said reasonably. 'It surely isn't outside our capabilities.'

'It's outside mine, I never learned to drive. Hermi always provided me with a chauffeur.'

'Hermi never allowed you to grow up, Julie. Thank God I can drive.'

'But it's so far, Delia. You're never going to drive all that way without somebody to help you.'

'I shall have to. We can stay over for the odd night, and France isn't at war yet. And we are leaving in the morning, not a minute later.'

'How can we possibly be ready to leave in the morning?' Aunt Julie wailed.

'We shall have to. This afternoon we shall have to pack the car with our clothes and everything else we want to take with us. Anything the car won't hold we shall have to leave behind. And please, Julie, don't take a lot of useless things merely because they're valuable.'

'It's because they're valuable that I am taking them.' Aunt Julie snapped.

'Our lives are more important than china, or jewellery too for that matter.'

'You are surely not suggesting I leave any of my jewellery behind?'

'No, I'm merely trying to point out the relative importance of things. Hurry, girls, collect your things and take them down to the garage. And that reminds me, Ellen, did you see about your money?'

'Yes, Mrs de Bellefort, I withdrew it all.'

'As soon as we get to Antibes you must put it in the safe, at this particular moment and in the forseeable future it will be safer there than in the bank.'

'You talk as if war is inevitable, Delia, and that we are going to lose it.'

'I don't mean to be defeatist, Julie, but I've lived with catastrophe too often not to see when it stares me in the face.'

It was a day of urgency, of running up and down to the garage below the house carrying suitcases and boxes which we stuffed into the massive boot of the limousine until there wasn't an inch of space for anything else, then we started to place things inside the car until Mrs de Bellefort said angrily, 'All of this stuff can't go. The journey will be a long one, we can't possibly spend it cramped like sardines. I'm sorry, Julie, but you'll have to leave more of it here and pray to God that it will be here when you return.'

For once Aunt Julie saw the logic of her argument, and sadly she began to retrieve her packages.

We ate dinner early. Outside we could hear newsboys crying out the latest war news.

As soon as we had eaten I said I must go out to say goodbye to my French teacher. Nobody was very interested so I escaped into the night, hurrying along the crowded pavement in the desperate hope of finding a taxi. In actual fact I had given up my French lessons, now I was on my way to see Kitty McGuire. I had found the club where she was working several weeks before but had not seen her since that afternoon at her apartment. I was lucky to pick up a taxi near the Opéra and soon we were climbing the steep meandering steets of Montmartre.

It was about nine o'clock when I approached the door of the club and with some trepidation the big burly man who stood there, and he gazed down at me moodily.

When I asked to see Emerald he said sourly, 'Emerald doesn't see anybody.'

'But I'm a very old friend of hers, I'm sure she will see me if I give you my name.'

'Zey all zay they are old friends. I tell you, Mademoiselle, she veel be madder zan a wasp eef I take you in zere.'

Helplessly I turned away but I had only gone a few steps when there were quick light footsteps along the pavement and then I saw Kitty.

She took in the situation at a glance and said to the doorman, 'It's all right, Emile, I know this one. I haven't got long, Ellen, I hope you won't mind chatting while I change.'

I was fascinated, sitting in her tiny dressing room watching Kitty McGuire disappear, to be replaced by the alien exotic Emerald. Her red hair was teased and pulled into a tumbling flowing mane. Bright emerald eyeshadow enhanced eyes that were a softer jade green, and artificial eyelashes hid their frankness, lending them a mysterious and sensual magic. Carmine lipstick changed the shape of her mouth and then her slender body was poured into the sequinned black dress, slit voluptuously to show one rounded thigh.

'Well,' she said at last, turning round for my inspection.

'You look so different, Kitty, it's not surprising I wasn't sure the first night I saw you.'

'The dress is new, Ellen. The club's bigger and better and we fill it night after night. I demanded a new dress – after all I'm the main attraction – and the manager agreed even if he is an old skinflint. And what do you think of this?'

She opened a large flat leather box and there shining against the satin lining was an emerald necklace. I looked up at Kitty with some awe.

'It's only paste, Ellen, I've not got the real thing yet although my earrings are real. A jeweller made it up for me and with the lights on it you should hear the cries of amazement from the women in the audience. And here, look at this. No more feather boas for me, this is fox, real fox.'

It was fox, two thick pelts dyed a bright emerald green, and there were black sequinned shoes with incredible four-inch heels.

She looked beautiful: beautiful, exotic and alien. Not the Kitty I knew and loved but some elusive threatrical being who only came alive beyond the footlights.

'Are the apache dancers in the floor show too?' I asked.

'No. They had a terrible row one night in the dressing room and she went for him with a knife, after that the manager told them to go.'

'Why did she go for him?'

She grinned at me. 'It had nothing to do with me, Ellen. It was always going on. One of these days, if she doesn't kill him, he'll kill her.'

'Why doesn't one of them just leave?'

'They're in love, that's why.'

'How can they be?'

'Oh Ellen, didn't love teach you anything? Didn't you love that man you told me about and hate him, all at the same time?'

'I left him, though. I didn't go on being with him.'

'Yes well, maybe you're stronger than the rest of us.'

'Have you stayed with somebody you hated?'

She sat silent staring in the mirror, then with a sudden bright smile she turned, saying, 'No, I never have. I don't know what it's like to really love somebody, I guess I'm only in love with me, but I've seen what it can do to other people. I don't ever want to be in love, Ellen, it's too punishing. Now tell me why you wanted to see me so urgently.'

'I came to say goodbye, Kitty, we're leaving in the morning.'

'You're going home then?'

'No, we're going to Antibes in the south, to Aunt Julie's house.'

'You think you'll be safe there?'

'I'm not thinking at all, I'm just flowing with the tide. Beyond tomorrow I don't seem able to think at all.'

Her face was thoughtful and when she didn't speak I cried anxiously, 'Shouldn't you be thinking of leaving Paris too, Kitty?'

'There's no hurry. I'm an Irish girl earning a decent living here, if the worst comes to the worst I'll have a new audience.'

I felt betrayed once again by Kitty, as betrayed as when I stood with Aunt Liza at the corner of the street in Liverpool looking back at her tight, closed-in face. I felt a desperate urge to get out of her tiny scented dressing room and into the clear air of the summer night.

I rose to my feet clutching my bag tightly in my hands, saying in a small distant voice, 'I'll say goodbye then, Kitty, I don't supose we'll see each other again.'

I didn't want to touch her, I just wanted to leave, and she too seemed to recognize that it wasn't the time for tender farewells or words of regret.

'Oh, you never know, I could end up on the Côte d'Azure myself if Paris gets to hot. Take care.'

Quite deliberately she turned her back on me and sat staring into her mirror. I opened the door and fled, startling the doorman when I took to my heels and ran, oblivious to the jostling crowds and the flashing lights from innumberable nightclubs.

CHAPTER 28

As long as I live I shall remember that long journey from Paris to Antibes, as much for its discomfort but more, much more for its beauty. All of nature was combining to colour the countryside with the exquisite tones of summer, the apple orchards and the red-roofed old towns, the grapes ripening on the vines and the long sun-baked straight roads lined with poplars.

I was enchanted with the chateaux in the valley of the Loire and the stone bridges that crossed the lovely meandering river. I would dearly like to have explored towns like Orleans and Nevers, but always Mrs de Bellefort said we must press on until Lisanne rebelled, saying, 'Oh Mother, we're so cramped in the back of the car, if I don't get out to stretch my legs I feel I'll never walk again.'

Pierre, Aunt Julie's poodle, was increasingly restless as we tried to accommodate him on the back seat, and at last Mrs de Bellefort decided we'd had enough, and stopped at a small country inn.

Before nine o'clock the next morning we were once more on the road, headed for Lyon, and here we encountered army vehicles driving north and we were delayed. Aunt Julie said, 'Why did we have to come through Lyon? The roads are always so busy and today they're worse than usual.'

'I want the girls to see Avignon,' Mrs de Bellefort replied, 'I loved it as a child and Lisanne has never been there.'

'I thought we were suposed to be in a hurry,' Aunt Julie said petulantly.

'We are, but since I am doing all the driving I should at least be able to determine the route we take,' Mrs de Bellefort replied firmly.

'I'm sorry, dear, of course you must fix the route, it's only that I'm so anxious.'

We found a hotel for the night at Avignon and Lisanne

said, 'We must go out tonight, Ellen, I want to see the bridge and the Palace of the Popes. Everything is going to be so beautiful from now on. Tomorrow we shall see the Mediterranean and so much more of Provence. Did you see those old women sitting at their doors knitting in those tiny villages we drove through? I had a friend at school whose home was in Arles and she said most of them lost their husbands in the last war and they'll wear black for ever. None of them will ever marry again, isn't that terrible? I'm glad I'm not a French peasant woman, it must be horrible to be in mourning for some man you've probably forgotten anyway.'

'You never talk about your cousin Gervase, and yet in a few months if all had been normal you would have been marrying him,' I said.

'Well it looks as though I'll be marrying him in a few years now, doesn't it? Always supposing we survive to marry each other.'

'Have you any feelings for him at all?'

'Well obviously, he's my cousin and blood's thicker than water, but I'll make the best of it when the time comes.'

'It doesn't seem to be a particularly good reason for marrying anybody.'

She stared at me reflectively, then with a small smile she said, 'I've got a respite, Ellen, time to look around and perhaps find some man to love, some man who'll love me. That way I'll have something to remember when I'm a staid married lady.'

'You don't think that's unfair to the man, or to you?'

'Darling Ellen, of course I do, it's diabolical, but you're only angry because of Lance and you. It didn't stop him marrying Geraldine and it won't stop me marrying Gervase. Just see to it that you forget him when somebody else comes along.

'Do come along, Ellen, we're missing all this heavenly sunshine.'

So we went out into the streets of Avignon and mingled with the holiday crowds who stood looking at the bridge even though only half of it was left. As we walked back into the town we burst into song and those we passed on the way sang with us. 'Sur le pont d'Avignon,' we sang, and suddenly I felt light-hearted and gay with the warm sun on my bare head and arms, and we ran laughing into the crowds that thronged the sun-baked pavements of the old town.

The first feeling of disquiet should have occurred when first we arrived at the door of the Villa Hibiscus in Antibes and an old man came down the steps to help us unload the car. With him were two middle-aged women who greeted Aunt Julie joyfully. She asked anxiously, 'Where is your son, Jules? You should not be lifting that heavy luggage.'

The old man shrugged, and his face became suddenly sad. 'He has been called into the army, Madame, I have not see him for three weeks. All the young men have been called and some of the young women also.'

'But who is left?'

'Only the three of us. We can manage, Madame, the house is no trouble.'

'What about the gardeners?'

'Gone too, Madame, and who knows when they will return? Not until after the war.'

'But there is no war yet, Jules. Oh I cannot believe that war will come here, look how beautiful it is. God will not allow it.'

'It is the devil who rules Hitler. I fear that God has washed his hands of the lot of us. We have seen this coming for too long and done nothing to prevent it. God only helps those who help themselves.'

My room overlooked the rock garden which tumbled down the hillside in a riot of pink and blue. It afforded me only a brief glimpse of the sea but I stood on the balcony breathing in the pine-scented air, thinking that war was a myth, a fantasy dreamed up by politicians who would soon be proved wrong. In a rush of delighted optimism I thought about Kitty and how very far both of us had come from those two country girls who had boarded the train on the first stage of their journey to Liverpool and a whole new life.

That night we dined on the terrace. A full moon sailed omnipotently in a star-spangled sky, silvering the sea, vying with the lights strung out like jewels along the coast as far as I could see.

It was warm, with only a slight breeze filling the air with the perfume of blossoms, and as we ate I looked round the table at my companions.

Lisanne had piled her pale hair on top of her head and she was wearing her favourite gown, a pale delicate turquoise which matched her eyes. I thought her mother looked pale and tired, but that was not surprising after driving all the way from Paris, coupled with her other anxieties about money. Aunt Julie on the other hand kept up a constant chatter about what we must do and see in the days ahead. She at least, I thought, semed confident that we were safe in Antibes.

CHAPTER 29

I was in love with Provence, enchanted with the narrow winding streets of her old towns, where steep crumbling steps led down to ancient harbours and to where warm stone villages clustered lovingly on impossible hills. How I loved the terracotta villas surrounded by dark stately cypresses, and every day the sun shone in a blaze of glory on scenes of enchanting beauty.

Aunt Julie's friends and acquaintances came trooping back, and night after night we entertained or were entertained by people unlike any I had ever met. Many of them had titles. Archdukes and duchesses, counts and countesses, none of them English. One elderly man who seemed like somebody out of a Viennese operetta commanded a great deal of respect and I was told he was Prince Vladimir, a survivor from a deposed royal family. Personally I thought him the most disreputable hanger-on of all.

He accepted all the adulation and largesse as a personal right and always sat in the most comfortable chair surrounded by fawning courtiers who combined to see that his glass and plate were filled.

'What will happen to them if France goes to war?' I asked Mrs de Bellefort, and smiling cynically she said, 'I rather think they'll try to move on, always supposing there is somewhere to move to.'

'But who are they?'

'Remnants of forgotten royalty. Many of them are Russian aristocrats who were lucky enough to get out during the revolution. All these years they have hung on, hoping that one day they would be invited back to take up their old lifestyle. It will never happen. People like that bred communism. How can they ever believe that Russia will take them back to behave like medieval lords?'

I found myself staring at them: aristocratic women in

their silks and chiffons, men who still wore silken orders across their chests. 'And the Prince?' I asked, looking to where the old man sat surveying the room through the monocle with a lordly air.

She laughed. 'He calls himseslf a Polish prince and tells me he is closely linked with the Polish royal family. You must ask Julie, she knows more about him than I do.'

The occasion came to ask Aunt Julie next morning over breakfast.

'I can only tell you that he is of royal blood, Ellen,' she informed me. 'It's so sad for these poor people to have lost their homes and their estates. Luckily many of them were able to bring valuables out and have been living on them ever since. It must be heartbreaking to see one's jewllery sold, simply to live.

'I know you think he's an old humbug, Delia, but I think he's a very charming man who has had a most unhappy life.'

'He appears to be doing very well for himself at the moment, Julie. He never entertains yet he gets asked everywhere. He's fetched and carried, he never gives presents and he never buys drinks. Tell me, when did he ever send you flowers after a night when he's eaten your food and drunk your wine? I don't believe he ever has.'

'But I don't expect flowers, Delia, it's an honour to have him here.'

'My mother-in-law wouldn't have given the old fraud house room. Over the years some of her acumen must have rubbed off on me, at any rate I have very little time for people like Prince Vladimir.'

'You're hard, Delia. How would you have liked to lose your country as well as your home?'

'I have the strangest feeling that I might find out about that very soon. Have you see this morning's newspaper? Hitler has ordered his army into Poland. They are already in Warsaw so it seems even less likely that our Prince Vladimir will be allowed back to claim his heritage.'

'Poland isn't France, Delia. We didn't help when the

Germans walked into Austria or Czcchoslavakia, why should Poland be any different?'

'Poor Julie, go on for a little while belicving that your world is inviolate. I haven't the heart to shatter your illusions.'

At night, when darkness came too suddenly after the sun went down, there were now no lights strung out like jewels along the winding coast of the southern sea, there was only darkness except for the raking fingers of the searchlights that probed the skies above the shoreline that reached down into Italy.

Complacent in their faith in the invincibility of their Maginot Line, the French refused to believe that war would be fought on their soil, but contemptuously the Germans ignored the Maginot Line and swept through the Low Countries and into France in a matter of days.

We hung round our radio sets in fearful disbelief as the Germans swept towrds Paris. Refugees thronged thc roads of Northern France, hampering the French and British armies. As soldiers and civilians alike retreated towards the coast they were forced to take refuge in ditches to escape the machine guns of the German planes.

It was with tearful disbelief that we heard that the British Expeditionary Force was fighting a last-ditch battle on the beaches of Dunkerque while miraculously an armada of small pleasure craft manned by weekend sailors waited off shore to pluck the soldiers from the jaws of death, and always across that narrow strip of water Britain stood defiant and waiting for the bombardment that was to rain down in the months ahead.

For over two years we lived in the limbo that was Vichy France – unoccupied by the Germans, in a kind of truce that gave no real peace. We carried on with the social round as before, almost as if no state of war existed, until the Germans decided to take over the rest of France. They came suddenly to Provence, their armoured vehicles and tanks disturbing the peace of the countryside, and overnight our familiar world collapsed into chaos.

Curfews were imposed, German soldiers strutted in the

streets, and hotels and civic buildings were annexed for their use. German officers came to inspect everyone, and I shall never forget the morning when every member of the household stood facing the officer who had come to interview us.

He sat in the salon wearing field-grey uniform, young and tall and arrogant, and we stood before him like supplicants for his favour and with deep resentment in our hearts.

'Who is the owner of this house?' he asked, staring at Mrs de Bellefort.

'My friend, Madame le Mauriac,' she replied shorly.

He sat with our passports in front of him, then singling out Aunt Julie's he said, 'You are Madame le Mauriac?'

'Yes.'

'Yes, Herr Kommandant,' he corrected.

He was leafing through her passport so slowly I could feel her trembling beside me, and instinctively I took hold of her hand.

'I see that your address is noted as Paris, how long have you been in Antibes?'

'Since August nineteen thirty-nine. Herr Kommandant.'

'Just before France declared war on Germany. Vy did you leave Paris, did you think to escape the war?'

'We always came to Antibes in the summer.'

'Who is ve?'

'My husband and me.'

'Vere is your husband now?'

'He is dead. He died five years ago.'

'Vat vas your husband's business?'

'He was a banker. He had many business interests.'

'And a great deal of money if you could afford a house in Paris and this one in the south of France. Vas your husband Jewish?'

'No, Herr Kommandant, he was French.'

Her voice trembled and her face was so pale I felt that if he questioned her further she would have fainted, but instead a sadistic half smile curled his lip and in a distant voice he said, 'I shall keep your passport, for further inquiries. Now you Madame,' he said, addressing Mrs de Bellefort, and singling her passport out from the rest.

'You are vell travelled Madame,' he said, raising his eyebrows.

She didn't speak, and he began to recite the names of the countries she had lived in. 'This is a British passport, Madame, why are you in Antibes?'

'Madame le Mauriac is an old friend, I often stayed with her in Paris, Antibes also.'

'You did not think to go back to England then, you preferred to hide here in Provence?'

'I consider we are in more danger here than we would have been in England, Herr Kommandant. France has fallen, England is still at war and as yet the Germans are not on her soil.'

'Ve vill be, Madame, and very soon,' he said sarcastically, his lips curving in a scornful smile, but she met his eyes without flinching. 'You have not answered my question, vy did you come to Antibes?'

'It was an extension of the summer, to find a little more sun and the sea.'

'You vere wery complacent, Madame, you evidently did not think that war would come. Isn't that so?'

'I thought it possible that somebody somewhere might come to the realization that civilization was not prepared to destroy itself.'

'Oh, the var vill not last long, Madame, ve have conquered most of Europe, and England vill be no match for us. The Führer had promised an early peace – but on our terms, Madame. I fear that things may never be quite the same for you and people like you, but peace is to be prized. De Bellefort is not an English name, vhere did it originate?'

'In Normandy, the de Belleforts have been in England since the Norman invasion.'

He laughed. 'In nine hundred years, Madame, there will be others in England bearing proud German names. Are these two young vomen your daughters?'

'This is my daughter Lisanne, the other is her friend Ellen Adair.'

'But they are related I think?'

'No, Herr Kommandant, they are friends.'

In something approaching disbelief he took up our passports and scanned them closely, but made no further comment.

'Ve Germans are a magnanimous people, obey our rules and ve shall not trouble you.'

'Your rules, Herr Kommandant?' Mrs de Bellefort asked.

'Vy yes, Madame, you vill obey the curfew and for the time being confine yourselves to the villa.'

'Is it permitted to shop for food? We must eat.'

'The servants vill shop for food. You there,' he said, addressing Jules, 'for one hour every morning you are permitted to leave the villa to go to the shops. If you are accosted by a German soldier you must show him your identity card, is that understood?'

'Yes, Herr Kommandant.'

'Are these all your servants, Madame?' he said to Aunt Julie. 'You have no gardeners, no younger men on the premises?'

'No, they all went to the army.'

'If any of them should return you vill notify us immediately.'

She nodded dismally, then he gathered his papers together and walked towards the door. There he turned, and said in the friendliest manner, 'You need not vorry, the curfew will not last long. The coming months could be quite pleasurable, and you, Madame de Bellefort, might come to think you were fortunate to come to Antibes instead of returning to England.'

He left us, and Aunt Julie sank trembling into a chair. 'Oh, the disgrace of it, what is to happen to my beautiful France?'

'He will be back, Julie,' Mrs de Bellefort said scornfully, 'and the more frightened you appear the more he will bully you.'

'I can't help it, Delia. Why did he take my passport when he didn't take any of the others?'

'Because you were the most afraid. They've been well

trained, those interrogating officers. If he comes again you must try to be calmer.'

'I'll try,' she said without much conviction.

Three days later he returned but this time he did not wish to see the servants. He seemed friendlier, but it was a manner more terrifying than before.

He invited us to sit while he presided at the table before us, flanked by two German soldiers. He was smiling genially, and almost absentmindedly brought out a passport which he tossed to Aunt Julie.

'Your passport, Madame,' he said. 'You may keep it for the time being although we may vish to see it again at a later date. Tell me, Madame, you have been known to keep open house here for a great many of your friends, are they all vell known to you?'

'Why yes. Many of them live in the south of France permanently. My husband and I came here every summer. We visited our friends and they visited us, it was wonderful.'

'To hobnob with faded royalty, people without roots, drifters.'

'I felt sad for them, it wasn't their fault that they had beome exiles from their own countries, and largely I found them kind and hospitable.'

'What do you know about the Caspards?'

'The Caspards?' she echoed, and this time her voice lost its conviction and trembled slightly.

'Vy yes, Madame, Joseph and Marie Caspard. You knew them in Paris did you not?'

'Yes, Joseph Caspard was in banking like my husband.'

'But he was not French.'

'I don't know, I believed him to be French.'

Again his thin lips smiled, wolfishly, without mirth.

'Joseph Caspard vas born in Latvia and came to Paris in nineteen twenty-one but he vas not French. His wife Marie vas born in Hungary and likewise made her way to France via Austria and Germany vere she met up with the man who became her husband. Surely, Madame, they must have discussed their history with you.'

'Why should they? I accepted them for what they were,

he a business associate of my husband, she a charming woman and a good friend.'

'It vould be best for you to be frank with me, Madame le Mauriac. Ve have reason to believe that the Caspards are both Jewish. Did you know that, Madame de Bellefort?'

'If I had known it I would not have thought anything about it. I have friends in many walks of life, some of whom are indeed Jewish. But in actual fact I only knew the Caspards from holidays in Paris and here.'

'I see.'

He continued to smile, pressing his fingers together, looking from one to the other of us. Three of us met his eyes bravely, but Aunt Julie was pale and quite obviously distressed. Suddenly he straightened up and, jumping to his feet, said affably, 'Vell, for the time being ve vill leave matters as they are. The good times are coming back, ladies, and ve are here to enjoy them with you. France has been defeated, accept it and she vill survive, reject it and ve shall have to show her who are the masters here. I bid you good day, ladies.'

We sat stunned until Lisanne at last said, 'Does he mean that we can go out of the house now, Mother, are we no longer prisoners?'

'I think we should wait a little while, Lisanne. I can't think that life is going to be that simple.'

'What is going to happen to the Caspards?' Aunt Julie maoned. 'I didn't tell him anything, did I, Delia, nothing I said could possibly affect them?'

'No of course not.'

'If they found out about the Caspards they'll find out about me.'

'Why should they?'

'I don't know, but they will. Look how they've traced the Caspards, all their journeyings, where they came from. They can do the same thing to me.'

'Julie, stop worrying. He knows nothing about you as yet, let us hope it remains that way.'

Three days later an invitation came from the German

Embassy in Monaco to attend a garden party in the grounds of the Sporting Club.

CHAPTER 30

One of Lisanne's dresses lay across my bed but I had no wish to attend the function, and I said as much to Mrs de Bellefort.

She said sharply, 'I told the Kommandant you were my daughter's friend, Ellen, and it's about time you stopped thinking of yourself as her paid companion.'

'What else am I?'

'You are somebody who will share whatever calamity befalls us, but you will also accompany us to the German Embassy. It is a matter of survival, Ellen.'

So I dressed myself in Lisanne's rose chiffon and stuck an artificial gardenia in my hair to match the ones on the shoulder of my gown. Lisanne wore her favourite turquoise and Aunt Julie her usual beige, and Mrs de Bellefort a grey and rose frothy confection with a large rose-coloured hat.

Faced with our amazement she laughed, saying, 'I wore it as a whim, I want to show the Germans that a garden party is a garden party whoever gives it.'

Promptly at two o'clock a large limousine arrived at the door to collect us, driven by a German soldier. As we drove along the wide sweeping corniche road to Monte Carlo I thought I had never seen the sea so blue or the mountain slopes so green. Something of my thoughts must have communicated to Aunt Julie who said wistfully, 'How beautiful it all feels. The world must seem like this to a cage bird who escapes.'

Mrs de Bellefort smiled cynically. 'Personally I think we are still caged, except that the cage has become a little larger.'

The garden party was a glittering affair. I recognized several people, some who had come to the Villa Hibiscus and others whose homes we had visited. Prince Vladimir stood at the buffet table happily piling large helpings of caviare on to thin slivers of toast and holding out his glass to be replenished.

It seemed to me that everybody who was anybody was there, and I couldn't help thinking: What would Kitty McGuire say if she could see me now, in my borrowed plumes, hobnobbing with the enemy – and wishing I were ten thousand miles away?

Mrs de Bellefort was engaged in gay and vivacious conversation with a high-ranking German officer who was looking at her with some admiration. Lisanne said hotly, 'She needn't look so pleased about, I think it's quite dreadful to be talking to the Germans as if they were our friends.'

'I can't think she's enjoying it, Lisanne, but she intends to survive.'

'She looks as though she's enjoying every minute of it. I've never been able to understand my mother, I'm not surprised she never got along with Granny.'

It was dusk when we were finally driven home and in the car there was silence, each one of us no doubt busy with our own thoughts.

Once inside the villa however Aunt Julie burst into tears. 'Nobody's seen the Caspards for days,' she sobbed. 'They were taken away for questioning and they haven't returned. The rumours are that they've been taken to Vichy for questioning.'

'But they're old,' I protested, 'what have they to do with the war?'

'Nothing – how can they have? – but they are Jewish. Oh, I am so afraid for them, and for me. What shall I do if they take me for questioning?'

'Julie, they won't,' Mrs de Bellefort reassured her. 'You were invited to the function today, which proves they don't suspect you. And we must all behave in such a manner that they have no reason to complain. I know, it sticks in your throat, as it sticks in mine, but there's no alternative.'

'The curfew has been lifted, so we go about our business as usual. We entertain and we visit our friends, we go to the casino and the nightclubs openly to show we have nothing to fear. Is that understood?'

'What about money?' Aunt Julie complained mournfully. 'Our finances are not a bottomless pit, it takes money to do the things you say. I was never any good with money, you know my husband always handled our financial matters and we can't get money from the bank, the Germans have seen to that. Delia, we only have the money we brought out of Paris with us.'

'Then we must start to sell our jewellery – or better still, try to be a little nicer to our lords and masters. I made a considerable effort this afternoon, I didn't see any of you contributing to the success of the occasion.'

'Mother, how *could* you laugh and chatter to that German officer? You can't expect Ellen and me to do the same.'

'I can and I do. Before all this is over you will both have to forget a great many of your prejudices. Now I am going to get out of this ridiculous dress and into something a little less flamboyant.'

Just then Jules came in carrying a crate of champagne and a large spray of white roses. His face was inscrutable as he handed her an envelope.

She said, 'It is from the German general you saw me talking to this afternoon. He hopes I will accept his gifts with pleasure, and invites us all to a ball at the German Embassy in Monaco next Friday.'

She looked at each one of us with pointed authority before sweeping out of the room, while Jules shook his head sadly and shuffled after her.

That was the start of a merry-go-round that went on and on. We entertained and were entertained. We went to the casinos in Monte Carlo and Nice. We sauntered along the boulevards of Cannes and explored the shops and in the evenings we went to the nightclubs and to dinner parties in dimly lit restaurants.

Mostly we went together, although there were other times when a German staff car came for only Mrs de Bellefort and she left the house in her evening gown and furs, but the jewellery she wore became less and less.

Aunt Julie too was parting with her jewellery until the day when Mrs de Bellefort said, 'You didn't tell me you were selling your opal necklace, Julie. That was the last present your husband gave you.'

'It caused me a great deal of pain to part with it, but there was no alternative.'

'I told General Eisfeld a little of our circumstances, and I asked him to retrieve the necklace for you, Julie. Please don't ask any questions, just be grateful to have it back.'

Aunt Julie took the leather case from Mrs de Bellefort's hands with an expression of wonder, and across the table I saw Lisanne's eyes become hard and resentful.

'But Delia,' Aunt Julie said softly, 'you too have parted with jewellery, what of that?'

'I have decided that we should not invite so many people to the villa. People like Prince Vladimir and some of the others are not real friends, they wouldn't lift a finger to help us if we were in trouble and we have to think about ourselves. The General has promised to help us with obtaining food, and I can't think we should be too proud to accept.'

'Every mouthful will stick in my throat,' Lisanne cried hotly.

'In that case you'll probably starve yourself into an early death,' her mother snapped, 'but it would be more intelligent to be realistic. I'm not asking you to like the General, only to eat his food.'

I was glad to have evenings when my face could relax from smiling, when I could walk in the garden and breathe the pine-scented air, when I could read or sew, any of the simple pleasures I had once considered boring but which now were preferable to the socializing I had become used to.

It was hot in my bedroom with the shutters drawn, and for hours it seemed I had tossed and turned. Unmindful of mosquitoes lurking in the garden I rose from my bed and flung the shutters wide. For a long while I stood looking out to the calm and unruffled sea, I then heard the soft closing of a door. Jules came creeping silently along the path, pausing now and again to listen and look round fearfully.

I waited, stepping back a little. When he reached the

shrubbery he paused, peering intently, then I heard a long low whistle and a small rustle in the shrubbery. Next moment another man stood beside him, somebody younger and slimmer, and they were embracing one another and whispering together. The younger man drew Jules further into the shrubbery and they were lost from my view.

I waited but neither of them reappeared, and after a few minutes I returned to bed. The episode had disturbed me strangely. Jules was always polite, always subservient, but there were times when I sensed his anger that he had to be polite to German officers who visited the house, opening doors for them, serving them drinks. Now I wondered who he was meeting and what plots they might be hatching.

Aunt Julie was worried about her friends the Caspards, who had not been seen again.

'I wish you could find out what has happened to them, Delia,' she said unhappily. 'Couldn't you do it very discreetly?'

'No, Julie, I don't want the Germans to think we are interested, that is what they are waiting for. If we appear uninterested it might put them off.'

'But it's so awful to think they've just disappeared and that nobody is in the least concerned.'

'They're not the only ones, Julie. Other people from Cannes and Nice have been taken away – many of them shopkeepers, Jewish no doubt – people who have been in Provence for a great many years. Julie, you have to think about yourself, it would be dangerous to show concern'.

Coupled with all our other woes I was desperately concerned about money. My nest egg, drawn from the bank in Paris, was almost gone, spent on the clothes and other expenses essential to the way of life we were leading. I felt I was living on charity when I listened to Aunt Julie bewailing her lack of ready money, and with this in mind I approached Mrs de Bellefort to ask her advice.

'You were foolish to transfer your money from the bank in England, Ellen and it was more foolish still of Lisanne to attempt to advise you.'

'But I feel I'm living on charity, Mrs de Bellefort, I need to contribute but I don't know how.'

'There is no way you can contribute, Ellen, and I don't expect it. I've always accepted gifts of jewellery with the utmost complacency, the right of a woman men thought attractive, even desirable. Now more than ever before I look upon such baubles as a lifeline for all of us. We won't speak of money again, Ellen. I feel responsible for our being here, we should have gone home to England.'

We learned little about the war since newspapers were heavily censored and I wished I could have asked Jules. I was sure he knew more about the war than any of us.

One day after lunch Mrs de Bellefort said, 'We are invited to the new nightclub in Nice. Apparently it's one of the smart places to be seen in and the girl singer is particularly good. There will be a party of us and we are being picked up around nine, You two girls must think what you are to wear, we shall probably be staying to dance.'

'It's quite immoral to be opening up new nightclubs in these times,' Aunt Julie said with some anger. 'People are suffering and dying and all we can think about is a new nightclub.'

'It will take your mind off of peoplc suffering and dying, Juile.'

The new nightclub was plushy, with red velvet seating and a preponderance of crystal chandeliers, and on the dais stood a white grand piano. Our party was at the largest table in the room, with waiters hovering behind us deferentially.

The German general took his place at the head of the table with Mrs de Bellefort on his right and Aunt Julie on his left. At Mrs de Bellefort's place rested a long black leather box, and the German general smiled as he invited her to open it. On a bed of blue velvet rested a diamond and sapphire necklace and long earrings, and she gasped with pleasure while Lisanne exclaimed, 'Mother, it's your necklace! Whenever did you part with it?'

The General leaned forward with a smile, saying, 'Some time ago, Fräulein. I have retrieved it for your mother with instructions that she should part with nothing else. Now, Madame, will you allow me to fasten it for you?'

Across the table Aunt Julie's eyes met mine with an unfathomable expression before she turned to speak to her companion. Over the laughter I could hear the piano, the haunting air of a French tune, and I turned to look at the pianist. I had recognized his touch and was not surprised to find it was the Negro of Le Chat Noir.

His music was unobtrusive, a melodious background to light-hearted laughter and lovers' whispers, and I for one wished they would all be silent so that I could hear this true artist better. I took no part in the conversation. Was Kitty the singer we had all come to hear, and would we be treated to a display of apache dancing?

Suddenly the lights were dimmed and spotlights shone on the raised dais and from the shadows a girl appeared, gliding sinuously into the light, and I caught my breath sharply in amazement.

Her hair hung in great waves reaching below her shoulders, startingly red, and her gown, glittering with beads, caught the light as she moved so that it changed alternatively between jade and emerald. It was split provocatively to the thigh and there were trails of ostrich feathers round the hem. Green stones sparkled in her ears and round her throat, and behind her she trailed from one slender hand a white ermine coat. By fair means or foul Kitty McGuire had acquired her emeralds and ermine.

When she started to sing I realized her voice had taken on a new maturity. It was deeper, richer, more throaty and she sang in French, making me glad that I now understood it well. The tune was slow, haunting: 'Was it the spell of Paris, or the April dawn, Who knows if we shall meet again, But when the morning chimes ring sweet again, I'll be seeing you . . .'

The applause was rapturous, and she sang several more, all in French, then to the gratification of the Germans she lapsed into their language and the more martial tones of 'Lili Marlene.'

They whistled and stamped their feet, and she moved

from table to table, her green eyes under their glittering jade eyeshadow tantalizing and enticing, yet at the same time miraculously distant. Then her eyes met mine and became filled with a strange nostalgia.

She came back again and again for yet another song, and then for the first time she sang in English, in a voice so sad and filled with memories I felt the tears rolling unchecked down my cheeks.

> Ah the apple trees,
> Blossoms in the breeze,
> That we walked among,
> Lying in the hay,
> Games we used to play,
> While the rounds were sung,
> Only yesterday, when the world was young.
>
> Ah the apple trees,
> Sunlit memories,
> Where the hammock swung,
> On our backs we'd lie,
> Gazing at the sky,
> 'Til the stars were strung,
> Only last July, when the world was young.

At last she was bowing and smiling her farewells. The audience was cheering her enthusiastically, as she moved from table to table, then she was at ours. The General was on his feet inviting her to join us but she only met his invitation with smiles and in a French accent totally different from her native Irish brogue she said, 'I'm sorry, Herr General, but I nevaire seet at ze tables.'

Her smile embraced the rest of us, then she reached across the table and handed a rose to me.

She returned to the dais, trailing the ermine, without looking back. Then the pianist started to play, laughter and chatter broke out around the room and I stared down at the red rose lying in my hands.

'I wonder why she gave it to you,' Lisanne whispered, 'why not one of the men?'

I didn't answer. People were starting to dance and at the door there was a small stir as three or four German officers came into the room. They were taken to a table set against the wall, and one of them surveyed the room and our table in particular.

He was tall and slender, blond, good-looking and arrogant as he crossed the room and stood before me, clicking his heels and bowing his head before asking me to dance.

I should have smiled my acceptance of the honour he clearly believed he was bestowing upon me, I should have allowed him to lead me on to the floor and dance with every appearance of enjoyment, but I did none of those things. Instead my eyes met his icily and in a voice devoid of emotion and speaking in English I said, 'I'm sorry, but I'm not dancing this evening.'

I couldn't believe that I had said those words. I saw his face change, coloured by rich red blood which made his eyes seem startingly shocked and blue, then I was aware of the silence around us.

It took Mrs de Bellefort only a few seconds to recover her poise before she said quickly, 'You should have said you didn't feel well, Ellen. The poor child didn't really want to come with us tonight, she's not been well all day. Perhaps you should think of going home now that you've heard Emerald sing. Lisanne will go with you, won't you, darling?'

'Oh no, please,' I said, jumping to my feet, 'I'll go alone, I don't want to spoil the evening for Lisanne.'

I was more than relieved when a young French man rose to his feet, saying he would drive me home. As we drove, he said, 'I'm glad you refused to dance with him, Mademoiselle. We have lost our identity – day after day we swallow our pride, we pretend in a world of makebelieve that everything is the same. Tonight you made me see that it can never be the same, that we cannot be coerced and pushed into doing the thing we hate. Mademoiselle, I salute you.'

I grasped his hand gratefully but the comfort was short-lived.

When the rest of them returned to the villa my bedroom door was thrown open unceremoniously and Mrs de Bellefort snapped, 'Ellen, I wish to see you in the salon immediately. Please don't keep me waiting.'

I struggled into my robe and hurried down the stairs.

Aunt Julie sat next to Lisanne on a couch pulled up near the dying fire but Mrs de Bellefort stood in the centre of the room filled with a strange nervous anger.

'Ellen, whatever possessed you to behave so disgracefully at the nightclub?' she began. 'We are foreigners living in a conquered country. We have no rights, the Germans are our masters whether we like it or not, and your behaviour tonight must surely have undone all I have tried to do.'

I didn't speak, and in some exasperation she went on, 'Why couldn't you have danced with him? That young officer, Major Klaus, will not forgive a slight like that and he has a reputation for thoroughness in his investigations, or he is much maligned.'

'What investigations?' Lisanne asked.

'Why do you suppose I've made myself charming and polite to the General and indeed to every other German officer I've met if it wasn't to protect Aunt Julie? Have you forgotten that she is half Jewish, that they have requested her passport not once but three times, and that a host of our friends have disappeared from the area and have not returned?'

The enormity of my behaviour was suddenly brought home to me but with head held high I said, 'I'm sorry if you think it will injure Aunt Julie, Mrs de Bellefort. I wasn't even thinking of her when I refused to dance with him.'

'What *were* you thinking of then? That is if you were thinking at all.'

'I was thinking that my country was at war with Germany, that they were sinking our ships, killing our men, bombing our cities, and I have a brother in the Royal Navy. I couldn't bring myself to dance with one of the men he was fighting. Besides I hated his arrogance, his assumption that he only had to ask and I would jump at the chance to dance with him.'

'I told them you were ill, that you hadn't been well for days, but whether they believed me or not I can't say.'

'Perhaps it would be advisable if I didn't go in their company in future. I would prefer it, Mrs de Bellefort.'

'Well certainly in the immediate future it would be just as well if you stayed at home. That way they might begin to believe that you are unwell. When you do eventually accompany us, and the officer asks you to dance again, I suggest you comply with his request.'

'Surely he will never ask me again.'

'To make you squirm, perhaps. Oh yes, I think Major Klaus is quite capable of that.'

'I didn't mean to hurt or embarrass anybody but him. Please believe that, Aunt Julie.'

'Oh, my dear, I do. One half of me applauded your courage, the other more cowardly half made me desperately afraid. I understand your feelings. Now can we please have done with the matter?'

Mrs de Bellefort nodded curtly. It was a nod of dismissal and I was glad to escape to my room, where I lay sleepless for most of the night.

In the time that followed I was much alone, and happier than I had been in months. I helped Jules in the garden and caught up with my reading, and I knew I had the servants' approval by the way they cosseted me.

One afternoon in the garden Jules said, 'You listen to the radio, Mademoiselle. You are anxious about the war?'

'We only listen to what the authorities want us to hear, and sometimes I don't believe a word of it,' I answered him shortly.

'You are right not to believe it, Mademoiselle. It will cheer you to know that the Allied armies have returned to France in force.'

'Who tells you these things, Jules? How is it you know and we don't?'

'That, Mademoiselle, I am unable to tell you, and it will be a secret between us. Say nothing of what I have told you.'

'Well of course not, but I would like it to be true.'

He laughed. 'It is all true, so it would seem that the good God is on our side after all.'

'Oh, I do hope so.'

'Well of course. You were brave to behave as you did with that German officer, but he is known to be a vindictive man. I fear there might well be repercussions, so be on your guard at all times. His reputation is a bad one, even among the Germans.'

'I hope I never see him again, Jules, I am happier here working in the garden with you. Perhaps I shall soon be able to walk in the hills again or along the shore.'

He smiled. 'Perhaps, Mademoiselle, if you are vigilant.'

I loved Provence. I seemed to have lived there for much longer than four years and I believed it was the climate which made it so timeless. Winter melted into spring, and spring into summer and yet there were many times when I recalled our northern winters with nostalgia. And how I missed the twilight, long country twilights in what seemed like another life.

Then came the morning when Mrs de Bellefort said, 'There is a tea dance this afternoon, Ellen, and I think you should come with us. Your illness has lasted quite long enough, it is time to emerge from your chrysalis. If anyone asks if you are better, answer them politely but don't embroider on your condition. I have merely told people that you were indisposed, something quite trifling.'

After she had gone Lisanne asked, 'What will you do if Major Klaus asks you to dance?'

'Dance with him, I suppose. I owe it to your mother and Aunt Julie.'

'You'll lose face, which will delight him.'

As it turned out, nobody asked me to dance. I thanked people for inquiring after my health, and I sat listening to the music while people danced on a tiny crowded floor. Lisanne, passing by in the arms of an officer, grinned wickedly in my direction.

I longed for the affair to be over, but there was one more humiliation in store. Just before the dance finished a party of German officers entered and stood at a long bar at the edge of the floor. My heart sank when I recognized Major Klaus, standing nonchalantly scanning the room, with one arm resting along the bar, the other holding a glass of wine. Across the room our eyes met and held, and next moment he was striding in our direction.

I thought I would suffocate. I was conscious of the warm red blood colouring my cheeks, but he passed me with never a look and went directly to Lisanne. He bowed in front of her and next moment she was in his arms and he was laughing down at her with obvious admiration.

Beside me I heard Mrs de Bellefort saying, 'I told you he would make you squirm if ever the opportunity presented itself, Ellen. I hope he considers his action this afternoon puts an end to the matter.'

'Are you happy to see him dancing with Lisanne?' I asked her sharply.

'No more happy than I was dancing with several of them this afternoon, but surely by this time you are beginning to learn something about survival, Ellen.'

'I'm learning a great deal, Mrs de Bellefort. Most of it makes me very sad.'

'We're all sad, Ellen. I feel the rest of my life might be sad, none of us is in a position to fight it.'

On the way home Aunt Julie said tremulously, 'Did Major Klaus say anything of any importance, Lisanne?'

'He said it was a pleasure to dance with me, that I danced very well, and he hoped I would give him the pleasure of dancing with me again. All terribly polite and stilted.'

'He didn't mention Ellen?'

'No. He was pointedly rude to Ellen.'

'It doesn't matter,' I muttered.

'He asked if we were attending the General's ball at the Sporting Club on Friday evening. I said I didn't know, and he said he would make sure we received invitations.'

The following day a messenger arrived with invitations for Lisanne, her mother and Aunt Julie. Noticeably there was no invitation for me and I saw Major Klaus's hand in this.

Shortly before they left for the ball Lisanne said, 'Do you fancy doing some sewing for me?'

'Yes of course, what is it you want?'

'I'm so sick of that white georgette dress. I hate those handkerchief things hanging from the skirt, they're so dated. Would you mind taking them off and doing something with the neckline?'

'I'll have a look at it. Personally I like the effect of those handkerchiefs, they're very graceful.'

'I'm fed up with them, Ellen, they shriek out how long I've had it. You'll find it in my wardrobe, be a dear and see what you can do.'

They left at last and I went to her room for the gown. The material was delicate. Every handkerchief was edged with one tiny drop diamante and the overall effect was charming, but I knew from experience that no power on earth would make Lisanne wear something she felt was dated.

I hunted high and low for a pair of scissors but finally had to go down to the kitchen where Marie handed me a large pair of kitchen scissors which I looked at in some dismay. They were hardly suitable for cutting delicate stitches but they might comc in useful for trimming the hem.

I sat under a lamp in the salon. There was music on the radio and occasionally I could hear the distant rumble of thunder.

At shortly before ten o'clock I was surprised to hear a car driving up to the house. It was too early for them to be returning from Monte Carlo, and late for visitors. I heard the doorbell, and the feet of one of the servants crossing the hall, then Marie's startled face looked in on me. Before she could say a word Major Klaus pushed her aside and closed the door in her face.

I jumped to my feet but he didn't look at me. Instead he wandered round the room, picking up objects here and there, observing the pictures on the walls, leafing through magazines, taking up several gramophone records to look at the titles.

I could stand it no longer. 'If you want Lisanne,' I stammered, 'she has already left for the ball.'

'I know that, I sent the car for them.'

'Then why are you here?'

'I thought it would be nice to see you. Ve could perhaps dance in private since you appear not to vish to dance in public.'

'I'm sorry, I wasn't feeling well.'

'So you said. I didn't believe you. Vat vould you like to hear, a valse, a tango perhaps, vat are you best at?'

'This is ridiculous. I have said I'm sorry for what happened, surely that is enough.'

He slammed the records down and came to stand in front of me. His face was flushed and vindictive, his eyes so cold that I shrank back, afraid.

'Tell me,' he said, 'vat are you and the others doing here in the home of a Jewess?'

'Aunt Julie is French.'

'Ve know all about the Jewess, it is only a matter of time before ve have her.' His voice sank into a tone more infinitely menacing. 'Tonight, however, I intend to have you, Miss Ellen.'

Before I could gather my scattered wits he had me by the shoulders in a grip that made me cry out with pain. As I stepped backwards I fell over a footstool and he was on top of me, his hands tearing at my dress, and I was struggling with all my strength to push him away.

Suddenly as my hands flayed and thrashed about me they encountered the kitchen scissors lying on the floor, and with all my strength I plunged them into his back, not once but twice, and in that instant I saw surprised incredulity in his eyes. He was gasping and clutching at his back, and as I wriggled out from under him and stood unsteadily I saw that my hands were sticky with blood. I moved away, but obscenely he came after me, crawling on his knees, his hands clawing at his back, his eyes never leaving my face. Then one bloodstained hand reached out for me again and I ran towards the window. But still he came after me, crawling unsteadily like a crab.

I did not hear the door open, suddenly Jules was there, and taking in the situation at a glance he called out and a much younger man was in the room. I watched in horrified silence as he advanced towards the German kneeling on the floor, then he produced a thin shining length of wire which he threw round Klaus's neck. There was a horrible gurgling sound and his face became scarlet, his eyes protruding horribly before he fell forward. He lay with his head strangely twisted, the scissors still buried in his back.

I stared in horror at Jules and his companion, but by this time they were covering the body with a piece of sacking. Jules, looking up suddenly, said, 'Don't worry, Mademoiselle, he will be taken away. Only you and the servants are to know he was ever here, and they will say nothing.'

I stared at the younger man who by this time had bundled the body into the sacking and was busy tying it with ropes. He looked up with a grin, and incongruously I thought to myself that he was good-looking, but there was no fear or compassion in his dark smiling eyes.

'My son André,' Jules said. 'We saw the German enter the house and I knew immediately he was trouble. It is fortunate that André came to visit me tonight.'

The younger Frenchman picked the German up and slung him over his shoulder, then with another smile he said, 'Don't worry, Mademoiselle. Just remember you have not seen him, if they come asking. When they find his body they will not suspect you or my father.'

Jules left with his son and it was then I saw that Lisanne's dress was torn and stained with blood, and there was blood in a long heavy smear across the carpet. I was still looking at it when Jules came back into the room, taking in the situation at a glance.

'Don't worry,' he said gently, 'Marie will see to the carpet. The dress, I fear, is beyond redemption.'

'It is Lisanne's dress,' I murmured stupidly. 'She asked me to alter it.'

'You have not seen it, Mademoiselle. You looked for it and when you couldn't find it you sat for a while listening to music, you read a little, then you were tired and went to your room. Mademoiselle Lisanne will be made to think she made a mistake, she must have left the dress in Paris.'

'But she told me it was hanging in her wardrobe, Jules.'

'Then she was mistaken, Mademoiselle. It was another white gown she saw and not that one at all.'

'Jules, what is your son doing here?'

'He is in the Resistance. There are pockets of them all over France. France is still at war, Mademoiselle, she will never be defeated. Now go to your room and rest, and in the morning you must pretend as you never pretended before.'

He took the dress from my helpless fingers, then Marie ushered me upstairs. No sooner was I there than Annette appeared with hot milk, turning down my bed while I scrubbed my skin clean in the bathroom.

'Drink your milk, Mademoiselle,' she counselled. 'Zere ees brandy in eet to 'elp you sleep.'

I slept like a log, and when I awoke I lay motionless for some time, my mind refusing to face the realities of the night before. Then suddenly I was wide awake, sitting up and trembling like a leaf, and all the trauma of the night before brought me the realization that I had been capable of murder in the cause of self-preservation. How could I hide it, how could I go downstairs and join the others with a bland face and lies on my lips? How could I ever go into the salon without seeing Major Klaus crawling after me, reaching for the scissors I had plunged into his back?

After a brief good morning nobody paid much attention to me. They were talking about the ball, the gowns of the women, the gossip of the moment. Then Lisanne said, 'Did you manage to do anything with the dress, Ellen?'

I gulped nervously. 'I looked for it but I couldn't find it, Lisanne.'

'But it's there in the corner of my wardrobe. I'd have got it out for you but I was sure you'd find it for yourself.'

'I looked, but I couldn't see it.'

'Oh really, Ellen. After breakfast we'll go and look for it together, it was probably staring you in the face.'

Aunt Julie was saying, 'Did the General send the car for us, Delia?'

'Why no, apparently Major Klaus sent it, but it was strange that he didn't come to the ball.'

'He said he would be there,' Lisanne said sharply. 'He asked me to have the supper dance with him, and in view of Ellen's behaviour I promised I would.'

'Oh well, he was probably busy elsewhere. We shall see him again, I have no doubt, he seems to have formed an attachment to us,' her mother said dryly.

Immediately breakfast was over Lisanne invited me into her room.

'Now I'll show you where to find the dress, Ellen. I hope you can do something with it so that I can wear it. I'm so tired of my wardrobe.'

She flung open the doors, disclosing several evening gowns including two white ones. I watched her hand moving along the rail, her frown becoming deeper, and at last she faced me with a look of incredulity.

'I could have sworn I saw it hanging there yesterday, I could see those ridiculous handkerchiefs.'

'You must have been mistaken, Lisanne. Are you quite sure you didn't leave it in Paris?'

'Well of course I'm sure. And the servants wouldn't take it, neither of them has the figure for it anyway. You haven't borrowed it, have you, Ellen?'

'Well of course not. For one thing I wouldn't borrow anything of yours without telling you, and for another I'd know where to find it, wouldn't I?'

I was amazed at how glibly the lies were forming on my tongue as once more she searched the wardrobe before going through the drawers in her dressing table. At last she straightened up, saying, 'Then I must have left it in Paris. Oh well, I didn't like the thing, I don't suppose it's any loss.'

When I was alone I breathed a sigh of relief. It had been too easy, I couldn't believe that I had got away with it. But there was one more moment of anxiety in store.

That evening we went into the salon after dinner and

immediately my eyes were drawn to the faint stain on the pale carpet which all of Marie's ministrations had been unable to remove. Aunt Julie noticed at once.

'I wonder what's been spilled on the carpet?' she said in some annoyance. 'It looks as if it's been scrubbed, the pile is rough.'

She pulled the bellrope near the mantelpiece and almost immediately Jules came in answer.

'There's a stain on the carpet, Jules. Do you know how it got there?' she said.

He gave the carpet some attention, then straightening up he said calmly, 'I'll ask the servants, Madam. One of them will know.'

'It has obviously been scrubbed.'

'Yes, Madame, it would appear so. I will ask them now.'

In a little while he was back. 'Annette said there was a soiled mark on the carpet from someone's shoe, something brought in from outside, she thought. She has tried to remove it, and will try again when it is thoroughly dry.'

'Really, I would have preferred to have had it done professionally. This is a very valuable Chinese carpet which needs special treatment. Telephone Le Bourget's, they will send somebody out to look at it.'

His face inscrutable, Jules bowed and left the room, while I sat trembling, thinking that the man from Le Bourget's would know immediately what had caused the stain.

He came the following morning. Jules brought him into the salon while we were reading the morning papers, and immediately he went to the stain and bent down to examine it.

Over his head my eyes met Jules', and he smiled, allaying my fears.

'What is it?' Aunt Julie asked the carpet cleaner curiously.

'Probably moss from the garden, Madame. It is always difficult to remove, and this carpet has a very deep pile. On any other carpet the stain would not be so pronounced.'

'Can you remove it?'

'Oh, I expect so. Perhaps you would go into another

room, ladies, there will probably be fumes from the cleaner I intend to use.'

We all rose immediately and trooped into the morning room. In a little while Jules appeared to tell us the stain had been removed and the firm of Le Bourget would send their account.

Later I asked Jules if the man had not known that the stain had been blood.

'He knew of course, Mademoiselle. He asked no questions and I gave him no explanation.'

'Will he say anything if Major Klaus's body is discovered?'

'He will say nothing, Mademoiselle, he is a good Frenchman.'

His answer, delivered so calmly and so staunchly, helped considerably to ease my troubled mind.

That night after I had put out the light in my bedroom I pulled back the curtains and looked out into the garden. It was then I saw Jules and his son standing in the shadows deep in conversation. They talked for a long time. I could not hear their voices but I could see that their talk was earnest, then at last they embraced and Jules walked back to the house alone. Again I became afraid. Had Major Klaus's body been discovered and were the German authorities already searching for his killers?

The following morning I saw Jules working in the garden and immediately I joined him there, my eyes searching his anxiously until he smiled.

'The Germans have enough to occupy their minds this morning, Mademoiselle. There is heavy fighting in the north, it would seem they are being repelled on all fronts.'

'Oh Jules, I'm glad. Is there no news about Major Klaus's body?'

'We shall know as soon as he is found, in the meantime I suggest you learn to be a little happy at the good news I have given you. I do not need to ask you to keep it to yourself.'

'No, of course not. What happened to Lisanne's dress?'

'Marie burnt it. It was a pity, such a beautiful dress. Mademoiselle Lisanne accepted that you could not find it?'

'Yes. I hated lying to her, it made her doubt her memory.'

'Ah well, Mademoiselle's memory is ever elusive. She is a young lady who only remembers the things she wants to remember. She will soon forget about the dress, you will see.'

CHAPTER 31

The German Kommandant returned to the house the following week, bringing with him two Gestapo officers, who were infinitely more sinister and with none of his urbanity.

We were assembled in the salon and seated in a row facing the questioners, who began with Lisanne.

'I believe Major Klaus is vell known to you, Fräulein. Did you not have an appointment to meet him at the General's ball?'

'No. He asked me to save the supper dance for him and he sent a car for my mother, my aunt and myself.'

'Did you not think it strange that Major Klaus failed to keep his appointment?'

'No, I merely thought he was engaged elsewhere.'

'Did it not surprise you that your friend Fräulein Ellen vas not included in the invitation?'

'Not really. Ellen had been ill.'

'Indeed. And yet she found energy to work in the garden, hardly an occupation for an ailing young woman.'

Lisanne didn't speak and I could feel my heart fluttering while beside me Aunt Julie's face was pale and I could smell her fear.

'And on the night of the ball, Fräulein Ellen, perhaps you had a visit from Major Klaus?'

'There was no need for Major Klaus to come here when he had arranged to meet my friend at the ball. Why should he?'

'It has been told to me that you were impolite to Major Klaus previous to that evening. It could be that he intended to teach you your manners while the rest of the household was elsewhere.'

I felt everybody staring at me, and heard Aunt Julie catch her breath nervously. I made myself stare at him in surprise without answering, and in a more cajoling voice he continued, 'Come now, Fräulein, Major Klaus vas interested in you before ever he became aware of your friend. Vat vas more natrual than to send a car for the others to get them out of the vay and then make it his business to see you? Vat happened between you on that evening?'

'Nothing happened, I have told you, I read for a little while and went to bed early. I did not hear what time they came in from the ball.'

'So you slept vell that night, Fräulein, and with a good conscience?'

'Why shouldn't I?'

'Vat if I vas to tell you that Major Klaus's car vas seen climbing the hill outside this villa not long after these other ladies left the house?'

'There are a great many villas along this road, why should you think he was coming here?'

'Because of vat ve know of the Major himself. His reputation for retribution upon those who have offended him. Major Klaus vas not the man to forget or forgive an insult. And you, Fräulein, insulted him before a roomful of brother officers. Vat time did he leave here?'

'He was never here. Why don't you ask the servants? They would know if he was here.'

'I have every intention of asking the servants but before I do I should tell you that Major Klaus's body was discovered yesterday morning on the hillside above Gagnes. He had been strangled, but vat vas more surprising, he had also been stabbed in the back. The vound in his back vould not have killed him, so obviously some other person had to make sure that he died. You had an accomplice, Fräulein?'

For the first time Mrs de Bellefort spoke, calmly and contemptuously.

'Really, Herr Kommandant, must we listen to these wild accusations? Everything in this house was perfectly normal when we returned from Monte Carlo, and again the next morning. If such a thing had occurred Ellen would never have been able to keep it from me, she would have been terrified, and the mere idea of Major Klaus coming here to intimidate a young girl is nauseating.'

'We must explore every avenue, act upon every piece of information – and the information ve have received does not absolve this house. Now, Madame le Mauriac, I vish to question your servants.'

'Lisanne will bring them here, Sir.'

'My officer vill bring them here, Madame. I vish them to receive no promptings or varnings.'

Minutes later the three servants stood with us before the officers. Marie looked down stolidly at her shoes, but Jules and Annette faced the Germans with straight eyes, unperturbed.

The officer leading the questioning addressed himself to Jules. 'You remember the night of the ball in Monte Carlo?' he asked, watching him keenly.

'I remember it well, Sir.'

'Vy particularly?'

'It was a stormy night. I had to hold an umbrella for Madame and her guests as they got into the car.'

'Is that all you remember about that night?'

'Only that Mademoiselle Ellen did not go with them.'

'And vhen they had left for Monte Carlo, some time later you had a visit from Major Klaus.'

'No sir, we had no visitors that night.'

'And Fräulein Ellen, vat did she do?'

'She sat in the salon here and I know she went to bed early.'

'How do you know?'

'Mademoiselle Ellen had not been well. Annette took hot milk to her room after she had retired.'

'Vat time?' he snapped, addressing Annette.

'Soon after ten sir,' she answered.

'Vat makes you so sure?'

'I'm not sure, Sir, I only think it was soon after ten. It was not long after they left for Monte Carlo.'

'You did not think that it vas strange she retired so early?'

'No, Sir, she had not been . . .'

'I know, I know, she had not been vell. Do you ever hear from your son, old man? Many of the men who served in the French army returned by devious means to their homes

and are even now in the Resistance. Is your son one of them?'

'I do not know where my son is. I have had no news of him since the morning he left Provence. I would give everything I have to know where he is and to know that somewhere he is safe.'

The Kommandant's eyes moved over each one of us in turn, and at last he said coldly, 'There is to be a curfew. Nobody vill be allowed on the streets after dusk and there vill be no calls on friends or neighbours, no visits to other places in the area. You vill stay close to the villa and you vill receive no visitors. These restrictions vill extend until ve have Major Klaus's killer. And Madame le Mauriac, I should tell you that ve have found discrepancies in your passport. One day soon ve shall vish to see you for questioning.'

'But why?' Aunt Julie stammered. 'What discrepancies? My passport is in order.'

'It is not relevant to vhy I am here this morning. Ve shall come here again.'

In a body they rose to their feet, clicked their heels, and raised their right arms, said 'Heil Hitler' and departed.

Aunt Julie left the room in tears, with the others endeavouring to comfort her. Jules turned to me, saying, 'Mademoiselle, you will lie and lie to save all our skins. They must learn nothing otherwise many brave men will die, my son among them. Do you understand?'

'Yes I do. They will learn nothing from me.'

He smiled and clasped my hands in his.

'You must be brave, Mademoiselle, and you must have faith. These dark days will not last for ever. Europe is awake and fighting back. One day, perhaps sooner than we think, real freedom will be ours, and not this shameful travesty of freedom we have today.'

For weeks we were prisoners in the house and gardens, with a German soldier posted at the gates. Once a week Jules was allowed out to obtain groceries, and I felt rather more comfortable when he arrived home to say we were not the only house under surveillance.

From the terrace we could see German soldiers marching in columns along the roads, clambering down towards the harbours, or combing the hills.

The inactivity bothered Lisanne the most. Never a reader, she spent most of the morning lying in the hammock and the rest of the day going through her wardrobe again and again to look for clothes in need of alteration, a task which kept me busy when I was not helping Jules in the garden.

We worked together in silence, aware of the eyes of the soldier peering at us through the gates, occasionally served cups of coffee by Marie – who adamantly refused to take coffee to the soldier.

All Mrs de Bellefort's persuasions failed and in the end it was Lisanne who took coffee out to him. Jules said, 'Marie is a peasant. All she understands is that the Germans are keeping us prisoners in our own house.'

Mrs de Bellefort played endless games of patience while Aunt Julie read, but there were entire evenings when she sat staring into space without turning a page. It was a game of cat and mouse until the morning the Kommandant returned to tell us a man had been taken and would be shot.

I saw the colour drain out of Jules' face but it was Mrs de Bellefort who asked, 'Who is he, a local man?'

'Yes, Madame, a local man,' he replied, 'Armand Rochefort.'

'But you must be mistaken,' Aunt Julie cried, 'Armand Rochefort would not be capable of killing anyone. He is an old man, a good kind old man.'

'Nevertheless, Madame, the death of a German officer must be avenged. Ve have not got the man who killed him, therefore ve must take the life of a man of Provence. It is a warning to the men who killed Klaus. For the life of every German some man of Provence will forfeit his own. It is justice, Madame.'

'It is not justice,' I found myself crying, 'it is murder. This poor man had nothing to do with Major Klaus's death.'

'Then perhaps, Fräulein, you vill tell me who had. It is not too late to save his life.'

'I don't know, how could I know?'

He bowed, a cynical inclination of his head. I became aware of Jules' eyes fixed on me in desperate appeal and I was sure he had been afraid I would tell the Kommandant all I knew.

Instead I cried, 'Oh, this is a terrible war when innocent people have to die.'

Aunt Julie wept, 'Oh, that poor old man, always so kind, so much loved by everybody.'

The Kommandant faced us sternly. 'Exactly, madame. If ve had taken a vagrant, a man who was not loved, it vould hardly have mattered. But if ve take a man who is esteemed, loved you call it, that might be a lesson the men who killed Klaus would not forget. They vill think twice before they take another German life. Now, the curfew has been lifted, and you may now take up your life as previously. The sentry will be removed from your gate.'

Later that afternoon Jules found me in the summerhouse in tears. It was all my fault that Armand Rochefort must die, my fault that Major Klaus was dead. Why oh why hadn't I swallowed my pride and danced with the man?

I sobbed out my remorse with the tears rolling down my cheeks and Jules listened to me calmly, allowing me the luxury of self-pity, self-recrimination. Then he said gently, 'Mademoiselle, it is not your fault that you are caught up in a war that has made victims of us all. It is not your fault that Klaus behaved like a monster or that my son killed him. He would have killed the German on the mountainside, in the streets, wherever they had come face to face.

'Come, you must dry your eyes. They must not see you so distressed or they will ask questions and you may reveal more than you intend. We must protect poor Madame le Mauriac. They are playing with her like a cat plays with a mouse before he kills it. I fear for that good lady, she is very afraid.'

Those words calmed me as nothing else had done, and by the time I returned to the house I was composed.

Life took up its pattern, but it was more subdued than before. We learned that the General had left Provence and were told that he had a more important role to play in the north. Consequently, without her escort Mrs de Bellefort stayed away from the casino and other establishments, and I for one was glad. In those days it seemed Lisanne and I grew closer as we roamed the countryside while the slow leisurely pace of Provence entered my soul, ridding it of much of the bitterness accumulated over the years of war.

It was a world remote from war-torn Europe, but whenver Jules brought news I rejoiced at the victories of the Allies and cried at their losses.

Aunt Julie was like a cat on hot cinders. She jumped when the telephone or doorbell rang, she grew thin and nervous in spite of all our attempts to console her. And my admiration for Lisanne's mother grew.

I felt old Lady de Bellefort would now have approved of her daughter-in-law. She, more than any of us, remained calm, showing to the world an indifference, a stoicism nothing could shake, and more and more I modelled myself on her while her own daughter became petulant and desperate for entertainment.

'Why can't we go to the casino?' Lisanne complained. 'Women do go there on their own.'

'I prefer to go with an escort,' her mother replied. 'The German general was charming and entertaining, I have no wish to go anywhere with any of the others.'

'Do you suppose Emerald is still singing at the nightclub?' I asked, for I had neither seen Kitty nor had news of her for weeks.

'Apparently so,' Mrs de Bellefort said. 'She is the toast of the Côte d'Azur. The Germans love her, they entertain her and send her flowers. She is now to be seen at the casino wearing fabulous jewels and expensive furs. And not only with the Germans. It is rumoured there are several Arab princes buzzing like flies around the honeypot. She is obviously a girl on the make, delighted with her success and eager to extract every last ounce of profit and pleasure from it.'

How could I argue with her? I knew it to be true, but

Mrs de Bellefort knew nothing about the poverty and hardship that had prompted it.

Only days later I was shopping in Antibes when a German staff car was briefly stopped by oncoming traffic. Kitty sat in the back with a German officer. She was beautifully gowned in black, with a small black hat trimmed with osprey feathers, and silver fox furs round her neck. She was throwing coins to the children clustering round the car. She didn't see me, nor, later, the looks of contempt on the faces of the villagers as they forced the children to part with the coins, which were promptly thrown over the hillside.

Several days later it was a very different Kitty I saw in earnest conversation with a young Frenchman near the harbour. This Kitty wore a trenchcoat and had a scarf tied over her head. There was nothing the least flamboyant about her, she might have been any village girl meeting her lover. But this man was not her lover, their conversation was too intense.

I turned away and had almost reached the harbour when I heard my name called, and saw Kitty running lightly down the steps.

She had taken off the scarf and her hair flamed wildly about her vital gamin face. She was smiling, greeting me as if we had met the day before. 'I thought it was you, Ellen. Are you alone?'

'Yes. I saw you talking to a man, Kitty, I didn't want to interfere.'

'Oh he's just some man who comes to the club. An acquaintance, that's all.'

Afterwards I wondered why I didn't believe her, but almost immediately she was saying, 'You've never been back to the club, Ellen. Didn't you enjoy my performance?'

'Yes of course I did, we all did, but there was some trouble afterwards, it's all been pretty terrible.'

'You refused to dance with Major Klaus, I heard about it.'

'It was a silly thing to do, I should have danced with him and forgotten about it. I'm beginning to realize that one can't afford to be noble or cling too closely to old values.'

'And didn't I spend most of mi youth tellin' you that, Ellen Adair?'

How easily the Irish came back into her speech, but next moment she was saying, 'You know of course that the Major was murdered?'

'Yes. We had a sentry posted at the gate for weeks. Why they think we had anything to do with it I can't imagine.'

I was watching her carefully, choosing my words, and incredibly I didn't trust her. I couldn't reconcile the Kitty I had seen throwing coins from a German staff car with the girl I had just seen with the young Frenchman.

'You know that they intend to execute one of the men living in Antibes, I suppose?' she said casually.

'Yes. A man who had nothing to do with the Major's death, a good, kind old man. It is terrible.'

'But expected. They have to make very sure that the French know who are the masters here. I'm very much afraid there may be more killings before that lesson is learned.'

'Whose side are you on, Kitty? Surely you can't approve of the killing of an innocent man.'

'I'm not on anybody's side, Ellen. I'm Emerald the singer, nothing more. I have my living to earn and I'm doing it in the best way I know.'

'So it doesn't really bother you, all the cruelty and persecution of people like Aunt Julie and many of her friends who have been sent away and not heard of again?'

'If it bothers me, what can I do about it?'

My bitterness must have shown in my face because next moment she said lightly, 'What are you going to do when the war's over, Ellen?'

'I don't know, I don't see how any of us can know.'

'Could you live in an England under German rule?'

I stared at her in horror. 'How can you even think such a thing?' I said angrily. 'Germany isn't going to win this war, it's unthinkable,'

'Why not? She's already defeated most of Europe. We have to face facts, Ellen, you must see that.'

'I don't believe it can happen. Germany can't win the war.'

'Why are you so sure? What do you know that I don't?'

Once more I was wary. In my indignation had I said too much? She was watching me closely with a half smile on her lips, and I was quick to say, 'I don't know anything, how could I? But I don't believe England will be defeated, nothing will make me believe that.'

'One hears rumours, of course,' she said. 'We'll hear nothing from the Germans but there are pockets of resistance everywhere. I suppose news trickles through from them.'

'We get to hear nothing at the villa, and none of Aunt Julie's friends seem to know anything,' I replied, then looking at my watch I exclaimed, 'Gracious, Kitty, it's late, they'll be wondering where I've got to.'

'Do they monitor your hours then?'

'Well of course not, but life here is difficult. I don't suppose Armand Rochefort expected to be plucked off the street for a murder he didn't commit.'

'They're not very likely to do that to you, Ellen.'

'They questioned me at the villa and more or less accused me of his murder.'

She laughed. 'I can't see you murdering anybody, Ellen. If I hear they've accused you again I'll use whatever influence I have to tell them they're barking up the wrong tree.'

I looked at her sharply to find her eyes filled with a strange cynical humour before I turned away. 'Are you walking back with me, Kitty?' I asked.

'No, I'm staying down here for a little while. I like the cafe across from the harbour.'

She smiled, then digging her hands in the pockets of her trenchcoat she set off towards the harbour while I climbed up towards the town.

The road wound round the hillside and for a time the harbour was obscured from view. When I reached the top of the hill I paused to look down. Kitty stood at the harbour wall looking out across the forest of masts and then I saw a man crossing the square towards her. I thought it was the same man I had seen her talking to earlier, and as he reached her side she turned and together they walked towards the cafe.

As I reached the road I saw that I was not the only person to be interested. A German officer accompanied by two soldiers was standing looking over the wall, and in spite of the warm sunshine I shivered at the menace in his cold scrutiny.

I was dreading the evening before me, watching Mrs de Bellefort playing endless games of patience, Lisanne's restlessness and Aunt Julie's fears, but the atmosphere of gloom had vanished and I was met in the hall by Aunt Julie brandishing a letter, her face registering a happiness I hadn't seen for ages.

'Isn't this marvellous, Ellen? We have received invitations to the opera, just when we thought everything was going to be so terrible.'

'The opera!' I echoed stupidly.

'*Madama Butterfly*. The new German general is inviting a great many people to attend in aid of charity. It will be heavenly to sit in the opera house and listen to glorious music again. Singers from La Scala in Milan, it says. Don't you just love *Butterfly*?'

'I've never been to the opera. I love music and I've heard arias from *Butterfly*, but seeing it performed will be a new experience for me.'

'You'll love it, Ellen. How strange never to have seen an opera.'

The following day the new German general paid us a visit. He was a small, slender man with a toothy smile, overly polite, and I disliked him intensely: his narrow hooded eyes which seemed to be appraising us, the smile which never reached his eyes. He made quite a ceremony of kissing our hands in turn before he departed.

Apparently my dislike was shared by Mrs de Bellefort, who said dryly, 'He had a smile like that on the face of the tiger. Against all my better judgement I quite liked his predecessor, but I don't trust this man.'

'That's most unfair, Delia,' Aunt Julie argued. 'He's trying to be nice, he's invited us to the opera and he's paid us a social call. One can't really go by appearances.'

'Oh well, I suppose we should give him the benefit of the doubt, but I've always been pretty good at sizing people up.'

Never in my life had I expected to be involved in quite such a glittering occasion. Aunt Julie and Mrs de Bellefort were greeting friends and neighbours on either side and I stared in admiration at the jewels worn by the women – in their ears, round their throats and on their hair. It was like something out of a fairytale.

Lisanne whispered, 'Ellen, your eyes are popping. Do try to look as though you're accustomed to moving in such exalted circles.'

'But I'm not,' I hissed. 'Who are they all?'

'Germans, Italians and a sprinkling of French. I suppose we're the only English here, and sticking out like sore thumbs.'

It was an experience I would remember all my life. I would tell my grandchildren how once I had sat on a red plush seat in a box adorned with flowers watching the stalls being slowly filled by exquisitely gowned women and men in impeccable uniform.

Suddenly my reverie was shaken by Lisanne hissing, 'Up there, Ellen, in the box opposite.'

I looked across and my heart missed a beat. Kitty had swept into the box wearing an emerald gown. Her red hair was lifted on top of her head and adorned with white gardenias. She wore long emerald earrings, and as she took her seat she removed her ermine stole to reveal a stunning décolletage.

She was in the company of two high-ranking German officers who appeared to be vying for her attention.

Mrs de Bellefort observed, 'It appears the invitations have encompassed a varying selection of society. Isn't that the singer from the nightclub?'

Across the vast glittering space for a moment our eyes

met but Kitty was so far away I could not read her expression, and after the slightest inclination of her head in our direction she turned away to speak to her companions.

After that I forgot Kitty and everything else in the beauty of the music, the glorious voices of the singers as Puccini's exquisite melodies flooded the night with joy and pathos telling the bittersweet story of a love affair that turned sour and ended in tragedy.

It was over at last, the most exciting night of my life, and as we drifted out into the scented darkness, people were exchanging their thoughts on the performance, friends promising to meet soon, and none of them prepared for the nightmare to come.

Before the opera house stood a group of men in Gestapo uniform, watching the descending audience with more than a passing interest. In turn they stepped forward to address some man or woman on the steps, then to our horror one of them approached us.

He bowed to Aunt Julie, and in a cold officious voice said, 'Madame le Mauriac, I must ask you to accompany me.'

I could smell the fear that erupted all around us as women cried out in terror, clutching the arms of the men who were being taken, or in other cases refusing to be parted. Aunt Julie stood pale and shaken while Mrs de Bellefort said icily, 'Why must she go with you? Surely you can come to the villa?'

'It is not your concern, Madame,' he answered her. 'Kindly do not interfere.'

'Then I must go with her. Can't you see that she is very frightened?'

'You can not go with her, she must come alone.'

'But how long will you keep her, when will she be able to return home?'

'I do not know Madame, ve are taking them to Avignon for questioning.'

'Avignon!'

'To headquarters, Madame, now please stand aside. You, Madame le Mauriac, come vith me.'

We watched helplessly as about a dozen men and women were bundled into cars and driven off into the night.

From all around we were jostled by the crowds as we made our way to our car. At one time we were separated and as I looked around me wildly I found my arm taken in a fierce grip and I was staring into Kitty's jade-green eyes.

'I saw what happened,' she whispered urgently, 'I'll see what I can do to get news of her.'

Next second she was gone and the last I saw of her was a fleeting glimpse of bright red hair over an ermine wrap as she stepped into a long black car.

Mrs de Bellefort broke the news to the servants. The two women left the room in tears while Jules stood with bent head and clenched hands.

'Go about your duties as normally as possible,' Mrs de Bellefort advised him. 'I fear we shall be watched during the next few days.'

'I told them she was innocent of any crime,' Jules answered her savagely, 'I said that she was a kind good lady who had lived in Provence for many years. She was happy here, happier than she ever was in Paris, and those other people they have taken tonight were her friends. I knew when they came here after you had left for the opera that something terrible would happen.'

'They were here, Jules?'

'They tore everything out of her desk. Some papers they threw about the bedroom, others they pocketed.'

'But what sort of things?'

'Letters, photographs, business papers. They knew exactly what they were looking for. They will not let her return, Madame. God knows what will happen to her.'

There were no outward signs that we were prisoners in the house, no sentry at the gates, yet I had the distinct feeling that we were under observation and Lisanne's mother was sure the telephone was being tapped.

Jules shopped for groceries and we sat in the garden overlooking the exquisite coastline until I felt I knew every blade of grass. Once in the distance we heard what seemed to be thunder until Jules said it was gunfire. We stood with eyes straining out to sea until the sky turned from brightest blue into mauve and shooting flames.

Weeks passed and Aunt Julie did not return. We saw nothing of our neighbours, and any information we had came from Jules after one of his shopping trips.

None of the people taken had returned to their homes. The towns were quiet and there seemed not to be so many Germans in evidence.

'Either they have been taken for service elsewhere or they have been ordered to keep a low profile,' Jules said quietly.

That afternoon I decided to walk down to the harbour. For one thing I ached to get away from the house and for the other I hoped I might see Kitty since she had not been in touch with me.

I strolled down to the cafe near the harbour and sat at one of the small tables drinking coffee. The bartender eyed me curiously while in the harbour a tiny boat darted between the large yachts which had been anchored there since the start of hostilities.

Disconsolately I paid the man and wandered across to sit on the harbour wall.

I had the strangest impression of being watched. I could feel the hairs in my neck prickling, and as unconcerned as I knew how I sauntered across the square. The barman was sitting at a table under the awning but he paid no attention to me and I reached the steps and started to climb up to the town.

It was so silent, so dark in the narrow streets, and my footsteps seemed to echo hollowly on the old cobbles. I was frightened. I had reached a junction in the road when I felt my arm suddenly taken in a firm grip and I was pulled into a shop doorway. Gasping with terror, I looked up into the smiling face of the man I had seen talking to Kitty in this very road weeks before.

'Do not be frightened, Mademoiselle,' he whispered, 'I am not going to 'arm you. I 'ave a message for you from Mademoiselle Emerald. Eet is to do with Madame le Mauriac, you understand?'

I nodded mutely.

'She 'as been taken from Avignon with ze ozers, possibly to some prison camp in the north, or even in Germany. Zat ees all we'ave been able to discover.'

'Why didn't Kitty come to tell me this herself?'

He smiled. 'Mademoiselle Emerald has zere confidence, why jeopardize eet for a woman who is already doomed? Eet was not safe to telephone you. Eet is not safe for us to be seen talking together, I can tell you no more. Now go quickly, Mademoiselle, and I will wait a leetle while until I move out into the street.'

Still I was staring at him fascinated, then in some anger I said, 'Why do you say Madame le Mauraic is doomed, what will they do to her?'

'Go now, Mademoiselle, go while eet ees safe.'

He gave me a little push which sent me out on to the cobbles, and I had no choice but to turn away and climb up to the town.

One thing in our encounter had given me hope: that Kitty seemed to be playing a double game. She had the confidence of the Germans and, it seemed, of the man I had just met. I felt sure he was involved with the Resistance. It was the one good thing in all the hopeless sorry business of Aunt Julie that gave me renewed faith.

When I told Mrs de Bellefort what I had heard, without mentioning Kitty's name she said sharply, 'But why should this young man be concerned about Julie? Who was he?'

'I have no idea. He only said they had taken her away from Avignon.'

Jules said quietly, 'The man is obviously a member of the Resistance, Madame, he knew we would be anxious about the mistress.'

'There are times, Jules, when I suspect you know more than you are telling me,' she replied. 'One feels so helpless, it is wrong that we are living here in Julie's house when she is heaven knows where, and probably suffering terrible hardship.'

'Nay, Madame,' he murmured, 'I only know what my eyes and ears tell me. The Germans are only maintaining a small garrison here now, they are up in the north fighting the Allies, and perhaps for the first time they are losing. Why else would they send their soldiers away? I tell you Madame, my ears and eyes tell me all I need to know.'

They made their presence felt in the next months, those few men who had been left in Provence to prove that Germany was still our master. If the Resistance was more active the revenge was more terrible.

Men, women and children were taken and shot in the streets in front of their families, but it was the last desperate defiance of a nation facing defeat. The news came pouring into Provence, in spite of the curfews and the tapped telephone wires, in spite of the radio news fed to us by a defeated and degenerate government. Paris had been liberated, one by one the countries of Europe were being freed as the victorious Allies swept onward, and soon in Provence we were dancing in the streets, the Tricolour was being hoisted once more over public buildings and to shouts of derision and hysterical glee Swastika flags were being ceremoniously burnt at every street corner.

Lisanne threw her arms around me in an ecstasy of weeping. 'We're free, Ellen, free to go home, free to go to Langstone. I never thought I'd ever long to see those dark Pennine hills again or hear Granny de Bellefort telling me what I should or shouldn't do.'

It was a thought that sobered me up as nothing during the last few days had done. Langstone Priory was not my home. It belonged to Lance and his wife Geraldine, it belonged to that implacable imperious old woman who had shaped my life as indomitably as she had shaped the lives of her own kith and kin. Now they were talking of going home and I had no home to go to.

'We can't go home yet,' her mother said sternly. 'We have to find out what has happened to Julie. Just be patient, Lisanne, and in the meantime try to enjoy Provence which is slowly coming back to life, back to how she used to be.'

So day by day and hour by hour we got back on the merry-go-round, but a very different merry-go-round it was. Now people's faces were lighter, their smiles more meaningful. It was like the sudden golden shining of the sun through clouds of rain.

The authorities were desperately trying to find the people who had been taken from their homes but they were experiencing acute difficulties. Documents and papers had been destroyed as the Germans were pushed back, and although we were aware of the atrocities that had been committed against the Jews in the prison camps in the north we could not believe that Aunt Julie had suffered a like fate.

Not Aunt Julie with her fashionable clothes and gay lively wit, her childlike assumption that life was for living, sometimes extravagantly, but whose warm heart had always been the first to give where it was most needed.

It seemed incredible that those people should have disappeared into thin air after the opera. Then Jules came with the incredible news that one by one they had been shot on the outskirts of Auxerre when it became plain that Germany would lose the war.

We wept inconsolably for Aunt Julie and I realized that I too had loved her. Together we helped Lisanne's mother to sort out her belongings. The servants were asked to choose what they wanted from the house and I was surprised at the things they took: ordinary everyday things from the kitchens. A brass cooking pot or a geranium from the kitchen window. A favourite pair of embroidery scissors or a lace-edged handkerchief. In the end Mrs de Bellefort handed out items of furniture and other household effects.

'What are we to do about the house?' Lisanne asked curiously.

'The lawyers will decide that. Possibly they may find a copy of her will, or even her husband's will. Jules will stay on here for the time being. I suppose eventually he will go to live with one of his children.'

'When are we leaving for England, then?'

'I am going to telephone Langstone this evening, it's possible now to do that. After I've spoken to them we can start to make plans.'

Lisanne was impatient while her mother telephoned Langstone from the study.

'I just hope we can shop in London. Granny will insist on my marriage taking place as quickly as possible and she'll want it at Langstone, I'm sure,' she said airily. 'We shall need some money, most of what we brought here has gone. I don't suppose you have much left, Ellen?'

'No.'

'Oh well, Granny will see you don't go short. You'll be coming to Langstone with us, I suppose.'

'I shouldn't think so. There'll be nothing for me there.'

'Well I hadn't actually thought you'd be leaving us, but I suppose you're right. I'll be going to live in Ireland and I shan't need a companion when I have a husband.'

'No.'

'Oh well, something will turn up for you, Ellen. After all you're an accomplished lady now. You speak French and you're very pretty. That alone should secure a husband for you, hopefully a rich one.'

Lisanne seemed to think life at Langstone would be as she remembered it in spite of the years of war, and I don't suppose it had even entered her head that her husband to be might not have survived it.

Her mother's face was thoughtful when the returned to us. 'Fortunately Lance was there,' she began. 'He still hasn't got his release from the army but he is stationed nearby so was visiting the Priory. Your grandmother's health is failing and she has cataracts on both eyes, so she doesn't see very well.

'Geraldine is expecting her first baby in a week or so, and it all sounds too dismal for words. Most of the servants at Langstone have been either in the services or on war work and only a few of them have trickled back, indeed Lance has suggested that we stay anywhere except Langstone in the immediate future.'

Lisanne looked at her in dismay. 'But what about my marriage? Hasn't Grandmother anything to say in all this?'

'Lance will break the news to her that we are safe and living in Provence. I don't suppose she's too infirm to dictate policy, but we shall have to wait a while.'

'How about money?' Lisanne demanded.

'I told Lance that money was in short supply and he promised that something would be done immediately on that score. Oh, I'm sure when your grandmother is told she'll give instructions regarding our future. She's never failed before.'

So for several weeks we waited in Provence. Many of the wealthy people who had yachts in the harbour returned to claim them, and day by day life along that fabulous coast recovered its gaiety.

Lance kept his word to send money but I felt I was living on charity. There was none for me so I had to depend on Mrs de Bellefort's generosity. Entertainment however was there in plenty. I was included in any invitations that came our way and there were a great many of them – dining out, sailing, the opera and the theatre. But it was an empty existence. Then the letter arrived from Yorkshire.

My heart missed a beat when I recognized the crest on the pale parchment envelope and Lisanne too leaned forward eagerly while her mother slit the envelope.

'It's from your grandmother,' she announced. 'It isn't her writing, she's probably dictated it.'

She read it through without another word, and unable to bear it any longer Lisanne cried, 'Mother, what does she say?'

'She says she is pleased that we are safe and well, that she was very disappointed that we didn't return directly home to England from Paris before the war, and we will be pleased to hear that both Lance and Gervase returned safely.

'She was hoping your marriage could take place from Langstone but now she doesn't think it will be possible. She herself will not be well enough to attend and Gervase is reluctant to leave his estate in Ireland because he is too busy. His father died during the war and Gervase arrived home to be faced with a great deal of work. She suggests your marriage takes place quietly in Ireland and no doubt you will be able to visit Langstone at some later date when things are back to normal. I'm afraid my mother-in-law doesn't mention you, Ellen.

Lisanne stormed and raged. She would not marry Gervase in Ireland. She would marry him at Langstone or not at all, and nothing, absolutely nothing would make her change her mind.

Mrs de Bellefort eyed her with cynical impatience, and I knew that none of Lisanne's wishes would count. The tirade would end, her mother would talk to her logically and earnestly, and the outcome would be that she would go to Ireland to marry her cousin on his terms and her grandmother's. As for me I was living in limbo. My future was shrouded in uncertainty, and while the life and entertainment went on around me I felt I was floating on a cold and hostile sea.

As I had known, Lisanne accepted her grandmother's wishes, but with poor grace. She began to look for her trousseau in shops that were rapidly becoming exclusive, and one day she surprised me by saying, 'I'd like you to be my bridesmaid, Ellen.'

'Have you mentioned this to your mother?'

'No, but I know she won't mind. After all it is my wedding, I should be able to choose my bridesmaid even if I don't get my own way about anything else.'

Still doubtful, I approached Mrs de Bellefort to see if she approved, but she seemed quite resigned to thc fact. 'I don't see why not, Ellen. Most of Lisanne's friends are probably scattered all over the place by this time and I think you will make a very pretty bridesmaid.'

'Thank you, Mrs de Bellefort, I shall try to play my part.'

'I think we should go back to London for a few days before sailing for Ireland. There's a boat leaving Marseilles at the end of the month so I propose to book passage on it for the three of us. There is nothing we can do here, and if I was never keen to stay in England before I find I want to see London again. As soon as we arrive in England I will make some provision for you. If my mother-in-law is too frail to be concerned I am sure Lance will understand your predicament.'

'I shall be able to find work in England, Mrs de Bellefort,

I don't wish Sir Lance to be troubled,' I said more sharply than was necessary.

She looked at me with a half smile. 'My dear girl, you are in no position to be too proud. Let Lance help you, let him ease his conscience.'

Soon we were busy packing our belongings. I tried several times to telephone Kitty, but without success. Apparently she was still not taking telephone calls, but she now had a new and equally enthusiastic audience. I saw her one day in the company of a dark-skinned man in a luxurious motor car. They were talking animatedly so that she had eyes for no one else, and I thought with grim amusement that once again she seemed to have fallen on her feet.

Two days before we were due to sail Lisanne said that Kitty's pictures had been taken down from outside the nightclub. She had heard that Kitty was returning to Paris.

For what seemed like the tenth time I told myself that I would probably never see Kitty again. In that I was wrong, but it was fortunate that I couldn't know the circumstances that would throw us together once more.

CHAPTER 32

Lisanne's mother had been correct in her assumption that the boat would be a crowded one, indeed she was lucky to obtain two first-class cabins some distance apart.

I shared with Lisanne while her mother had a cabin on another deck, and we met for meals and for whatever entertainment there was in the evening. I was loving every minute of it. This was the sort of life I had envisaged when sitting on the seawall at New Brighton watching the big steamers sailing out from Liverpool. Now I was a part of that life.

We danced in the arms of the ship's officers night after night until the stars paled, and not even the weather in the Bay of Biscay could dampen our enthusiasm. Lisbon was a joy with its beautiful shops hardly touched by the war and Lisanne shopped wildly for household linen and exquisite underwear until her mother put a stop to it by saying firmly that the money Lance had forwarded was not limitless, and would have to see us through the voyage and probably for some time in London.

Our first surprise occurred the second night out after dinner when the master of ceremonies announced that he had a special treat for us all, a lady who had entertained all Paris and the Côte d'Azur with her singing. Then he went forward to bring Kitty out of the shadows into the light of the ballroom.

Those people who had boarded the ship in New Zealand and Australia had never heard of her, but those of us who had lived in France applauded rapturously, me among them, and she smiled like a queen as she acknowledged the applause.

She wore black, simply cut and expensive. Round her throat and in her ears were emeralds, and her red hair flamed under the lights. Her songs, filled with nostalgia and a sad longing in her deep throaty voice, brought tumultuous applause and calls for encores, until she kissed her hands to the audience and retired from the stage.

I knew she had seen me, and the young officer who was my companion whispered, 'She's really something, isn't she? Would you say she was French?'

'I've heard she's Irish.'

'I suppose she could be, with that lovely red hair and green eyes.'

'She's very successful.'

'You've heard of her before?'

'Yes, in Paris and again in Monte Carlo.'

So we talked for a while about life in Provence during the war, and then for a time Kitty was forgotten as we started to dance.

All the next day I looked for Kitty on the decks, in the lounges and the bars but I couldn't find her. I didn't even know if she was travelling alone and it was obvious she had no intention of entering into the life on board the ship.

On the last night there was to be a gala dance and notices went up that those who wanted to wear fancy dress were invited to do so.

'I can't be bothered to think of anything,' Lisanne said. 'I shall wear my prettiest dress and you must do the same.'

I wondered privately what she considered my prettiest dress considering they had all been bought before or at the beginning of the war, so it would have to be blue. The colour suited me and it was a pretty dress. Lisanne on the other hand was fretting and fussing about hers.

'What do I do with this thing?' she complained as she twisted the long chiffon ties that fell from her shoulders.

I was hunting into my cardboard jewellery box at the time and somewhat petulantly she came to look over my shoulder.

'What have you there?' she asked, sitting beside me on my bed.

'Nothing very much, I'm afraid. I shall wear the pearl drop and earrings.'

'How about the locket? It's pretty and I've never seen you wearing it.'

'I never have. It belonged to Aunt Liza.'

'And this brooch is beautiful, Ellen. Why have you never worn it?'

'It isn't my initial, that too belonged to Aunt Liza.'

She was holding it in her hand, turning it this way and that, then she started to arrange the ties on her gown, finally catching them with the brooch to her entire satisfaction.

'This is just what it needs, Ellen, It's my initial too. Can I borrow it?'

'Of course, you can keep it if you like.'

'Do you really mean it?'

'Yes of course. Look upon it as a wedding present, I think it's quite valuable and I could never wear it.'

Impulsively she bent down and kissed me. 'It's lovely, Ellen, and every time I wear it I'll think of you. Are you quite sure you don't want it?'

'Yes, I'm sure. I never felt I had any right to it anyway, and I'm sure Aunt Liza would never have given it to me. I've always felt guilty about having it with me.'

'Well I'm sure you don't need to. She treated you like a skivvy and she didn't care what became of you, it was that niece of hers who had to have everything. But for Granny you'd have been out on your ear looking for work.'

I didn't speak. I wasn't all that sure that her granny had done me any favours.

People were gay that night, the pent-up gaiety of people who had experienced long years of war, forgetting that in the Far East war still raged. We danced and drank champagne, and people paraded in ridiculous costumes they had obviously made up on the spur of the moment. I hoped that Kitty would come to sing to us but she didn't make an appearance.

Later when I lay sleepless in my cabin I thought of Kitty again. It was very hot in the cabin, airless, although Lisanne was sleeping like a baby. We were due to dock in the early afternoon and I lay staring up at the ceiling with my thoughts turning this way and that as I tried to think what my future might be.

It was no use, I had to get out for some air. Slipping my

arms into my dressing gown I tiptoed out of the cabin, closing the door quietly behind me.

Moonlight flooded the deck and silvered the sea, and I stood at the ship's rail with the wind in my hair and the tang of salt on my lips. If I had known the number of Kitty's cabin I would have gone there in the hope that she would talk to me, but I could not be sure that she was alone and I didn't want her to think that I was curious. After a while I grew cold in the freshening wind, and returned to the cabin.

Lisanne switched on the light over her bed, saying, 'Where on earth have you been? It's after four.'

'I couldn't sleep, it was so hot in the cabin. I stayed on deck until it turned suddenly cold.'

'Oh well, after tomorrow we'll be back to English weather. I've loved every minute of this voyage, it'll probably be my last chance to flirt for years. Those officers do it so beautifully.'

'On the voyage back they'll be flirting with other girls, have you thought about that?'

'Are you always so practical, Ellen?'

'I suppose so.'

'But you weren't very practical about Lance, were you?'

I didn't speak, and provocatively she said, 'You were in love with Lance, Ellen, however hopeless it was.'

'He would always have married Geraldine, so you're right, it was hopeless.'

'Or me. What would you have done if he'd married me?'

'Nothing at all. We would never have gone to Paris, our lives would have been quite different and we would probably never have met again.'

'Granny de Bellefort was a strange one, wasn't she? I've never quite been able to understand why she was so insistent that you went to live at the Priory. Oh I know she had that thing about your grandmother, but lots of men have affairs with women they're not married to, and vice versa. Everybody said my mother had lovers when we were living in India but I honestly never saw any of them.'

'You didn't live in India for long.'

She chuckled. 'That's true, Mother soon shipped me out so that I didn't interfere with her social life. Heavens, but it's hot in here. I wonder why that girl singer's going to England. Do you suppose she's singing in London?'

'I've no idea.'

'She looked much prettier in that black dress without all the emerald eyeshadow. I suppose she wears that for effect in her cabaret act.'

'I suppose so.'

She reached out to the table beside her bed and picked up the brooch she had worn the night before.

'I'm thrilled with this, Ellen, it's lovely. Mother said I shouldn't accept it until you were quite sure.'

'I'm sure.'

'I must ring for the steward and ask him to bring some iced water.'

I heard her get out of bed and move towards the bell, then there was a crash that sent me flying out of my bed and next moment Lisanne was lying on top of me, thrown across the room by the explosion.

The lights went out and although we struggled to our feet the floor was already listing and we had great difficulty in reaching the door. Winded by the fall we were gasping for breath, and all around us were the sounds of rending metal, hysterical screaming and the crackle of flames. There was chaos in the passage as men, women and childen fought to reach the companionway. I cried. 'Hold on to me, Lisanne, don't let them separate us.'

Somewhere a child was screaming, 'Mummy Mummy,' and the stewards were asking for calm, trying without much success to keep our pathway to the deck clear and the procession moving in an orderly direction.

Lisanne clung to my waist and it seemed to me as we moved forward inch by inch that the deck shifted terrifyingly under our feet. The wind hit us like a knife and we had great difficulty in staying on our feet since the deck was sloping at an alarming rate. Towards the prow of the ship flames were leaping upwards into the night.

Lisanne caught the sleeve of one of the young officers

we had danced with only hours before. His jacket was grimy with soot and his eyes were bloodshot.

'Hang on to the rails, girls. We're trying to do something with the boats but the list isn't helping.'

'What has happened?' Lisanne stammered. 'I can't see for the smoke.'

'We've struck a mine. All those miles of ocean and we have to strike a bloody mine within sight of England. Half the ship's gone.'

He shook himself free and we watched helplessly as he made his unsteady way through the crowds. Lisanne turned tortured eyes on me, crying, 'We must look for my mother, Ellen. She must be on deck somewhere.'

We started to move along the deck but it was hopeless. Our feet were slipping and sliding from under us as the ship listed further and further, and all around us people were screaming or praying, weeping or trying to claw their way towards the stern. Suddenly I thought: We're going to to die, we'll never get out of this alive. Even as I thought it there was a shudder that seemed to reverberate through the entire ship and I found myself falling down and down until I hit the icy water and I was thrashing about wildly looking for Lisanne.

The sea was alive with floating debris and others who had been thrown into the water with us. Suddenly I saw a steward with his arm round Lisanne, attempting to keep both of them afloat, and I made my way towards them. I was not a powerful swimmer, but he helped me to hold on to a floating table and I saw then that Lisanne was unconscious, with the blood pouring down her face from a blow she had received on her head.

'We must get away from the boat,' he gasped, 'or she'll take us with her when she goes down. 'Ang on to that table and I'll 'elp ye.'

My arms ached from holding on to the table and I was so cold I couldn't feel my feet, then to my horror I watched him let Lisanne go. For a few moments she floated away from us, then she sank from my sight.

I felt myself screaming, then clawing at him wildly. I

struggled until he slapped my face hard, hissing, 'Lie still, you little fool. I 'ad to let 'er go, she was done for.'

Shocked and hurting, I felt him take hold of me. He was a powerful swimmer, and bit by bit fought his way through the churning sea away from the ship, cautioning me all the time to hold on to the table. I wanted to die, it seemed too pointless to try to keep afloat, but self-preservation is a powerful thing. Then I heard him shouting, and he was waving wildly.

I found myself being lifted up out of the water by strong arms which laid me down on something hard. It was a boat, and as I struggled to sit up I saw a scene I shall never forget. The ship suddenly slid beneath the water in a haze of flame and smoke, and my last thought was that surely the sky was lighter, it was almost dawn.

I lived through the next few days in a haze, with people wearing white moving fitfully through my conscious thoughts. At times I heard voices, I felt hands moving me, and there were even times when I thought I saw faces looking down at me – Lisanne and her mother, Kitty and Aunt Liza. But my mind didn't want to remember, it was so blissful to lie in limbo with no past, present or future to agonize over. Then suddenly I opened my eyes to a white clinical room and a pale sun endeavouring to shine through the open window.

A woman stood beside the table holding something in her hands, and painfully I turned my head, moaning a little with the pain of it. She turned and came to the bed.

'So you're awake at last. Sure and oi thought you'd be comin' out of it today.'

My first thought was that she sounded like Kitty McGuire, but it wasn't Kitty, it was some woman I'd never seen in my life before. Then I realized that she was wearing nurse's uniform and memory came flooding back to me. I struggled to sit up.

'Oh no you don't,' she said, pushing me back gently. 'Toime enough for that when you're feeling stronger. Now what do you say to some nice hot soup, and after you've eaten oi'll get the doctor to take a look at you?'

'Is this a hospital?' I murmured.

'That it is.'

'Where?'

'Plymouth.'

'I don't remember them bringing me here.'

'No, of course ye don't. Now just lie still 'til I get the soup, then after the doctor's been I'll tell that friend of yours yer've come round.'

'Lisanne,' I murmured.

'Yes, love. I'm glad ye remembers yer name. Now just lie still for a while. You'll get stronger every day now and in no toime at all ye'll be sittin' up and takin' notice.'

Something was wrong but I didn't know what. Memory was elusive and as I lay in bed I allowed my eyes to rove round the room. There were flowers on the table near the bed and a large basket of fruit on the chest of drawers. I puzzled fretfully: Who knew me well enough to have sent them? There was no time to puzzle further because the nurse came back with a steaming bowl of soup.

'Now let me see if ye can sit up to eat yer soup, love. I'll see to the pillows. I've done mi best with your hair but I reckon there's still plenty o' salt in it. My, but it's my bet you'll not be forgettin' that sea voyage in a hurry. Now come on, love, lie back on the pillows and I'll bring over the soup.'

I was too weak to hold the spoon so she fed me the hot soup and gradually I began to feel warmer, more alive. She laughed, saying, 'Now what did oi tell you, sure and the colour's comin' back into your cheeks already. In a few days you'll be able to have visitors.'

'Visitors?'

'Why yes, Miss de Bellefort, you have a friend just up the passage there. She's been in every day to see how you were gettin' along.'

'Why do you call me Miss de Bellefort?' I murmured stupidly.

'Why sure and it's your name, love. Don't say yer've forgotten your name along with everything else?'

I was too weary to argue with her and she plumped the pillows after I had eaten and laid me back among them.

'I'll fetch the doctor now, love. He'll be pleased to see you've decided to enter the land of the livin'. Moi, but you've kept us entertained these last four days.'

'Entertained?'

'Sure, with yer talk about somebody called Emerald, and Aunt Julie bein' taken away and shot. What an imagination, I said to miself. Ye were dreamin', of course.'

Dreaming! I didn't want to remember, memories would be too painful, too hurtful, yet unbidden they came creeping back to me, the most terrible one of all seeing Lisanne slowly drifting away to drop almost gently beneath the waves.

The doctor came, kindly, solicitously, assuring me that I would soon regain my strength. He told the nurse to give me a sedative, that I must sleep some more.

'When you wake up next time you'll feel foine,' she assured me. 'Now drink this, love, and off ye go to sleep.'

When next I woke it was night and the curtains had been drawn. I felt more alert and my bones ached less. I struggled to sit up but hesitated to ring the bell beside my bed. My watch was missing, instead there was a plaster tape round my wrist bearing the name Lisanne de Bellefort. Once more memory came flooding back and impatiently I rang the bell, waiting anxiously to put the matter straight.

It was a different nurse who came in this time, an older woman, brisk and businesslike.

'So you're awake again, Miss de Bellefort. I'm busy in the ward at the moment but I won't be long.'

'I must talk to somebody, please. There's been a terrible mistake.'

'A mistake?'

'Yes. Please can I talk to the doctor?'

'Not at this time you can't my dear. It's almost eleven o'clock.'

'But I must talk to somebody.' I was almost in tears and she was impatient.

'I'll see if your friend is awake, she'll talk to you. You really must try not to get distressed, Miss de Bellefort. I'll be with you as soon as I've finished what I'm doing, we're very short staffed and the hospital is full. Now be a good girl and I'll send somebody in to you.'

I stared at the door which she had closed with some annoyance. Who was this friend she intended to send to me, who was there to tell me I was Lisanne de Bellefort?

I didn't have to wait long. There was a light tap on the door and then Kitty's red head appeared round it.

She was smiling and she reminded me of the Kitty I had known as a child with her red hair and freckles, freckles that had been well camouflaged by theatrical make-up.

'Oh good, the nurse said you were awake. My but I thought you'd sleep for ever like the sleeping beauty. I was on the point of askin' Lance de Bellfort to come down to kiss you awake.'

'Lance de Bellefort!'

'Sure, I've bin talkin' to him on the telephone. His wife's just had a baby girl and his grandmother's on her deathbed.'

'Kitty, they think I'm Lisanne. I've got to make them see, I can't think straight. How have they made such a mistake?'

'Well for one thing when they plucked you out of the sea you were clutching a gold brooch engraved with the letter L. I was in the lifeboat that fished you out of the sea, and I said I was your friend. They had a copy of the passenger list in no time and they put two and two together and made five.'

'But you knew, Kitty. Why didn't you tell them?'

'Why should I? Look, Ellen, both Lisanne and her mother lost their lives when the ship hit that mine. You've nobody to care a hoot about whether you're livin' or dead and you've no money. You haven't even a coat to stand up in and the de Belleforts owe you somethin'.

'I telephoned Lance de Bellefort. I told him Mrs de Bellefort was dead and so were you. I said only his cousin Lisanne had survived and she was unconscious. If he'd come tearing down here he'd have seen things for himself and I could always have said I'd made a mistake. But he's not comin', Ellen. He's still officially in the army, and what with his grandmother dyin' and the baby, he can't get away.

What he has done is send you the flowers, the fruit and the letter in that drawer there. I expect there's some money in it. Seems to me the de Belleforts are good at dishing out money, to them it solves everything.'

'Kitty, it's dishonest, I can't accept it and I can't go on calling myself Lisanne. How long do you think I'd get away with it?'

'For ever, if you're sensible. Look, there's only me who knows any different and wild horses wouldn't drag it out of me.'

'There's my family, my parents, my brothers and sisters.'

'And when are you likely to be seein' any of them? Read the letter, Ellen, see what he has to say.'

Cream parchment and the de Bellefort crest. I'd seen it so many times it seemed incredible that on this occasion it was for me. Nervously I slit the envelope and took out three pages of parchment covered in Lance's flowing handwriting, and my heart fluttered wildly with a remembered pain.

Dear Lisanne,
I am so relieved that you are safe, but saddened to hear that your mother and Ellen did not survive. Regretfully I am quite unable to visit you in hospital but I know you are in good hands. I have spoken with the doctor who assures me you will soon be well and strong and fully recovered.

I have also spoken with your friend on the telephone and explained to her why I am unable to make the journey to see you. Geraldine gave birth to a daughter just four days ago. It was a difficult birth and she is far from well. Worse than that, Grandmother is very ill and unlikely to recover. She is of course very old and has not been able to see well for several months. I have not told her of your mother's death, I doubt if she would be fully able to take it in.

I have written to Gervase in Ireland to tell him all that has happened. No doubt you will soon be hearing from him since your marriage was to take place quite soon in Ireland. I wish you well, Lisanne. I have very happy memories of those times we spent together at Langstone. So much has happened and it all seems so far away.

I wish you a quick and full recovery, dear cousin. Perhaps one day we might meet, although I have no wish to visit Ireland

and Gervase has even less desire to visit the Priory. I do however wish you well in your marriage.

Your ever loving cousin,
Lance

The letter fluttered on to the bedspread and I stared at Kitty helplessly, then I passed it over for her to read.

'What did I tell you?' she said firmly. 'He's not going to visit and he's no intention of visiting Ireland. If Granny de Bellefort gets better she can't see and she won't be visiting Ireland either, so I really don't see what you're worrying about.'

'Kitty, don't you understand, for the rest of my life I'd be living a lie, just waiting for somebody to say, "That isn't Lisanne." I can't spend the rest of my life married to a man I don't know, somebody I've never seen, somebody who thinks I'm somebody else.'

Suddenly she leaned forward and gripped my shoulders, holding them so firmly I cried out in pain.

'Don't be such a little fool, Ellen. I didn't ask them to fish you out of the sea to see you flounder on the rocks of life. I lived a lie every night of mi life when I paraded in front of all those people in my finery, smilin' when I never felt less like smilin', pretendin' to love somebody when I hated his guts, hating the Germans but hatin' miself more. It was a game called survival, Ellen, did you never know that?'

In my mind I was hearing Mrs de Bellefort's clipped upper-class tones saying, 'If we wish to survive in the harsh world we find ourselves in, Ellen, perhaps for a while we should forget our prejudices, even our honour. It is all a matter of survival.'

Something of all this must have registered on my face because Kitty pressed home her advantage. 'Ellen, think. Never to be short of money again, never needing to kowtow to people. Besides, you *are* a de Bellefort, even if your mother was born on the wrong side of the blanket.'

'I'll never get away with it, Kitty.'

'Oh yes you will. You and Lisanne were like sisters, you

had the same colouring, sometimes the same mannerisms. I can tell you it fascinated me whenever I saw you together, and you said yourself she'd not seen her cousin Gervase since they were children.'

'But he'll know, he'll sense it. How can I marry him? It's like prostitution.'

'You'll try that too if you're destitute. Oh come on, Ellen. How much money did Lance send you?'

'I don't know.'

I picked up the envelope again and looked inside. There was a folded cheque wrapped in a short note. I stared at the cheque in amazement. It was for two thousand pounds and the note informed me that an account had been opened in my name at the National Bank of Ireland in Dublin and all my money transferred into it. The statement showed that I was the richer by over a hundred thousand pounds.

Kitty gasped in amazement. 'Ellen, you're rich,' she said, 'you can't afford to say no to all that. Lisanne's dead, she isn't ever coming back, so who'd get all that money? Gervase or Lance. And it's my bet they've got more than enough already. Besides, I reckon Lance owes it to you, you loved him. And I know you, Ellen Adair, you don't fall in love very easily. That man made you suffer. Think, Ellen, think. You'll never get another chance like this one, never.'

Just then the nurse came back and Kitty sprang to her feet, saying, 'Miss de Bellefort seems much better. I expect she'd like something to drink.'

'I've only one pair of hands and we are short staffed. Thank you, Miss McGuire, you can go back to your room now.'

Kitty winked and waved to me from the door, while the nurse inquired if I wanted milk or cocoa.

'You'll be able to get up for a while tomorrow,' she said sharply, 'even if it's only to sit in the chair. You'll soon find your sea legs.' Then with a little titter, 'That was a stupid thing to say, I don't expect you'll ever want to find your sea legs again.'

She brought hot milk and I sat back to drink it. The enormity of Kitty's suggestion filled my thoughts to the exclusion of anything else. How could I ever get away with it, and would Gervase know? What would happen if he ever found out, if Lance ever found out? I lay sleepless for the rest of the night, and once I took Lance's letter out of its envelope and read it through.

He was sorry his aunt had not survived the wreck, sorry too about Ellen. But in being sorry for Ellen did he just once think that he had professed to love her years ago?

As the long night wore on I began to speculate whether I could get away with it. I told myself angrily that the de Belleforts owed me something, owed my grandmother something. That I had been loyal and served them faithfully, that I had tried desperately to save Lisanne. But the thought of marrying a stranger filled me with fear.

I tossed and turned in my narrow hospital bed and morning brought me no nearer to a solution. Kitty was bolder than I, she would never have had any hesitation in similar circumstances, but then Kitty's sights had always been set higher than possibilities. Even now she would probably know what her future was to be.

By the time the sun thrust its first tentative fingers into the room I began to know what my future would be, for better or worse. Ellen Adair had met her end in a watery grave and I was for the rest of my days destined to be Lisanne de Bellefort.

BOOK III

CHAPTER 33

Day by day I grew stronger and now I was able to walk in the gardens. Kitty had been discharged from hospital but was staying close by in a new hotel that had been recently completed.

'It's costing me the earth,' she complained, 'but I thought I'd stay on here until I know for sure what you're about. Besides, I'm waiting to hear what's happening in Paris.'

'Are you going back therc to sing?' I asked curiously.

'For a while. I was happy in Paris, it'll be the same again. I made friends there and if I'm lucky I'll get an apartment, something quite luxurious, not like the one I had before.'

'How are you for money, Kitty?'

'Well enough. I had a friend who managed my money for me. I'm quite well off, actually, and if I go back to sing in Paris I can command an extravagant fee. It's not really what I wanted but the war altered many things.'

'Will you ever get married, Kitty?'

'I might if I find somebody rich enough.'

'Oh Kitty, money isn't everything.'

'It is when you haven't got any. I want to return to Paris in the autumn, meantime I'm going up to Liverpool to see my folks.'

'Not to Yorkshire?'

'I've no folks in Yorkshire now. Mi mother's gone to live with Aunt Mary in Liverpool. Mi uncle was killed during the war so they've set up home together. There'll be a houseful of children and they'll be like pigs in muck even though I have sent mi mother money when I could spare it.'

'I'm sorry about your uncle, Kitty. Was he killed in the army?'

'No, at the docks when the Germans bombed Liverpool. He left mi aunt with six children to bring up, I expect she's takin' in sewin' again. I'll be glad to leave them some money and mi mother'll be glad to see me.'

'Oh yes, Kitty, I'm sure she will. Do you think we'll ever meet again? It's so funny, but every time we part I think it's for the last time.'

'I rather think this time it might be. You'll be off to County Wicklow to marry your cousin and I'll be off to Paris with one eye on the main chance. No, Ellen, this time I really think it'll be goodbye for ever. I must get used to calling you Lisanne but it seems so strange. It's just as well we shan't be meetin' again, I'll never get used to it.'

We walked on in silence and it was Kitty who eventually said, 'Have you had another letter from Lance?'

'No, just a huge bunch of carnations from Lance and Geraldine, with love.'

'No note to say how his grandmother was?'

'No.'

'And no word from Gervase?'

'No. That frightens me, Kitty. Wouldn't you just think he'd be eager to meet me? How can he ignore the woman he's going to marry, particularly when she's just survived a shipwreck?'

'It seems to me the de Belleforts can ignore a great many things. Most of them seem to have spent their lives riding roughshod over people's feelings. Won't it be funny if you have a son, Ellen, a son who inherits the title and everything else?'

I stopped in my tracks and stared at her open-mouthed. I could barely envisage a husband, but a child was something else.

'You *are* going to be married, you know,' she was saying with a tantalizing smile. 'Lance has a daughter, he might have another daughter. But if you had a son, what price the de Bellefort title then?'

'Oh Kitty, I can't think that far, when you talk like that

I can't even think straight. Suppose he doesn't like me, suppose he's in love with somebody else just like my grandfather was?'

'And just like your grandfather it won't make any difference. He'll marry the girl he's expected to marry. What he won't know is that it's a marriage of convenience for both of you. It wouldn't have been any better with Lisanne.'

'No, I don't suppose so.'

I was remembering Lisanne saying she hadn't really liked Gervase, that she found him overbearing and arrogant, and I wondered if I would find him the same.

'I think we should go back now,' Kitty was saying, 'I've got to pack a few things before catching the Liverpool train, and you've probably been out in the fresh air long enough.'

'Are you going to write to me, Kitty?'

'Oh Ellen, you know what a rotten correspondent I am. No, I don't think so. I don't know where I'll be, I don't intend to stay in Paris all that long and I've no idea where I'll move on to. I've got a good ear for music and I can sing in most languages without understanding a word of it – I learn like a parrot. I'd like to sing in Budapest and Vienna. I want to make money and travel, then when I've had enough I'll look around for that elusive man I might be able to live with for the rest of my life.'

'I wish you luck, Kitty.'

'I'll never forget you, Ellen. We did have some good times and we shared a lot. You were a better friend to me than I ever was to you.'

We parted on the terrace and I stood there while she walked quickly down the drive. She didn't look back.

I had only just reached my room when the Irish nurse bustled in, saying, 'You have a visitor, Miss de Bellefort, he's waitin' in the common room.'

My heart lurched sickeningly in my breast. 'A visitor, for me?'

'Yes, and he's not used to being kept waitin', from the look on his face.'

'Who is he?'

'A Mr de Bellefort. A relative, surely.'

For one desperate moment I thought: Lance. Lance, and the game was up. Then common sense came to my aid. He was now Sir Lance de Bellefort, so obviously it must be Gervase who waited for me in the common room.

'Here,' the nurse was saying, 'do something with your hair and I'll borrow a pretty dressing gown from next door.' She was soon back with a pale rose robe over her arm. The colour suited me, lighting up my wan face, but I was still trembling and she gave me a small exasperated push out of the door.

'Go on, love, he'll not be expecting Greta Garbo, he knows the ordeal you've been through.'

For a few moments I stood in the common room doorway looking at the tall slim figure of a man standing looking through the window, then I went in and closed the door.

He spun round and we eyed one another without speaking. My first thought was that he was surprisingly like Lance. They had the same shining dark hair and deep blue eyes, but there had been laughter in Lance's face while this one was remote. It was undeniably handsome but there was no warmth in it. Instead there was a sort of cynical aloofness in his eyes, and the finely chiselled lips were unsmiling.

I could not have spoken, my throat was too dry and my heart was hammering. At any moment I expected him to say, 'You're not Lisanne. Why are you posing as Lisanne? Instead he said in a voice which reminded me of Lance's, 'Have you no greeting for your fiancé, Lisanne, or at least for your cousin Gervase?'

I went forward immediately and held out my hand. He laughed before taking it, then dutifully he bent his head and gently brushed my cheek with his lips.

'I remember we didn't exactly get on the last time we met, and no doubt you've remembered it. How are you, better I hope?'

How formal it was. We were like two strangers asking polite questions, and if I shed no tears there were tears in my heart.

'Thank you, I'm much better,' I murmured.

Again the amusement flickered in his eyes.

‘I was out in the garden, have you been waiting long?’

‘About fifteen minutes. I should have brought flowers. I’m sorry, there wasn’t time to get any.’

‘Have you come straight here from Ireland?’

‘No. I’ve been in Yorkshire attending a funeral, our grandmother as it happens.’

‘Oh, I didn’t know. I’m so sorry, when did she die?’

‘Last Tuesday, she’s been ailing for some time. You really are sorry, aren’t you, Lisanne?’

‘Of course, aren’t you?’

‘I didn’t want her to die, but I never really knew her. She dictated policy from afar. She plotted and moved us about like pieces on a chess board and we obeyed on the strength of her promises. Money, power, land. With you I expect it was money, with me it was land, with Lance, heaven knows.’

‘Langstone Priory and the title,’ I murmured.

‘The title was his anyway, but I expect you’re right about the Priory.’

He said it casually, as if Lance’s ambitions didn’t really interest him, and in the next breath he said, ‘You look very pale, Lisanne. Perhaps we should sit down, here in the window.’

‘How are Geraldine and the baby?’ I asked dutifully.

‘Actually I began to feel rather relieved that it was not Geraldine I was to marry. She’s pretty and gentle, she’s also rather a bore. The baby is a girl, which no doubt disappointed our grandmother sorely. Perhaps we shall have a son, and somewhere beyond the grave Grandmother de Bellefort will rejoice with the angels.’

Would I ever understand this man, I wondered. He was amused by me which put me at an even greater disadvantage than I felt to begin with. Taking my courage in both hands I asked, ‘Did you have a very bad time during the war, Gervase?’

‘Didn’t we all, but then you were living in Antibes, weren’t you? What was it like under German rule? From what I remember of your mother she would be inclined to look upon it as a challenge, men were never a problem to her.’

'She was an inspiration to us all, and brave in the face of much provocation. I admired her tremendously.'

His eyes narrowed. 'Well well, I'm glad to see that you speak up for something or someone you believed in. Perhaps our life together might not be quite so tedious after all. When do you propose to join me in Ireland?'

'When are we supposed to be getting married?'

'Well, not too soon after Grandmother's death. I think we should let the dust settle for a while. Suppose we say November, that gives us five months.'

'November isn't exactly a nice month for a wedding.'

'No! Well, September then. I'll book a flight for you into Dublin, I'm sure you won't wish to take a boat so soon after the disaster. I expect you'll want to shop in London for all you need - the shops in Dublin are well enough but I doubt if they have the variety of London's.

'I hope you'll like the life in County Wicklow. The estate is quite large and it keeps me very busy although I do have an estate manager. We spend a lot of time fishing in the loughs, we hunt a lot and generally think a lot of our horses. You do ride, of course?'

'Not for a long time.'

'Oh, you'll soon fall into it again. I'll find you a decent mount. When you were a girl you rode quite recklessly, I seem to remember.'

Already it was going wrong. He would expect me to be an accomplished horsewoman when in fact all I had ever done was ride a docile and predictable mare around the park at Langstone. To be in Lisanne's class I would have had to live with horses since childhood.

Gathering my wits, I murmured, 'I had a bad fall, I rather lost interest in horses after that.'

'My dear girl, surely you knew you must get straight back on and ride. Don't worry, we'll soon lick you into shape. I suppose you lost everything on the ship?'

'Everything except a brooch. I haven't any clothes, the nurse said she would arrange for a girl to come in from one of the shops, just to help me out for the time being.'

'Good idea. Well, you'll need riding clothes, all sorts of

country clothes and the odd evening gown. You're looking very pale, Lisanne, you should get back to bed. I have to be going anyway, I have business to do when I get back to London tonight.

He rose and held out his hand to help me out of my chair. Together we walked to the door where he once more brushed my cheek with his lips. Then he was gone, striding away from me down the corridor.

In a bemused fashion I walked back to my room where the nurse was busily turning down my bed. She stared at me in amazement.

'My, but that didn't take long,' she said, smiling.

'No, he has to get back to London tonight.'

'Is he a relative?'

'Yes, he's also the man I am going to marry.'

The astonishment on her face was profound, indeed if it hadn't been so hurtful it would have been laughable. Then she said briskly, 'I don't much hold with cousins marryin', the blood gets thinner and they always throw up a weakling or two.'

'I don't think you need to worry about the de Bellefort family, they've been doing it for centuries without any dire results.'

'Is that so? Well if himself's an example I can believe you. Now come along into bed, you've been on your feet long enough.'

To my amazement and hers I got into bed laughing helplessly, wildly, and it was only when she closed the door behind her that my laughter turned into tears.

CHAPTER 34

I stayed in hospital for another week and received one letter from Gervase informing me that arrangements were being made for our wedding to be held privately. There would be few guests and after the ceremony we would be going back to the house for a reception. He asked me to let him know when I might expect to travel and he had arranged for me to stay with a Colonel and Mrs Jefferson until the day of our marriage. It was not the letter of a man to the woman he expected to marry within a few months, but rather that of a man honouring his obligations somewhat reluctantly. He hoped I was now fully recovered and sent me his love.

After leaving the hospital I went immediately to London and moved into a small hotel in Kensington. I thought it only correct to inform Lance of my movements but shied away from writing in case he thought there was something odd about my handwriting, so I sent him a telegram giving him my new address.

Within a few days a letter arrived from him saying he was pleased I was well again and that Gervase and I had decided our wedding plans. He also informed me that Geraldine was recovering from the birth of Catherine slowly, but the baby was well.

I sat on the edge of my bed in the informal hotel bedroom and thought about the enormity of what I had done, and that there was no going back. What would my marriage be like in a strange house in an environment I did not know? There would be no love to sustain me. Other women followed their husbands to the ends of the earth with love in their hearts, but that was not going to happen for me. Everything I would have would be superficial. I would be Mrs de Bellefort, the rich Mrs de Bellefort, but would that be enough for the rest of my life?

I tried not to think of the future in the joy of the present.

I loved London. I loved the park across the way, and the lovers lying on the grass and under the trees filled me with a sad nostalgia. I loved the shops and the tea lounges, the arcades and the museums, and for the first time in my life I could spend money extravagantly, knowing there was more.

I bought riding clothes and found stables near the hotel where I explained that I was an absolute beginner but was going to live in Ireland where I would be expected to ride.

They were kind and patient, and soon I was cantering in the park on a bright chestnut mare, taking lessons in dressage and even putting my horse over jumps that were not too formidable. My teacher expressed his delight over my prowess but I couldn't think I would ever be the horsewoman my future husband might be expecting.

I chose my clothes carefully. Elegant clothes that had a timeless air, and three evening gowns which seemed a ridiculous expense, but then I was unsure about the life I would be expected to lead.

I also bought my wedding dress, and if it wasn't exactly the dress of my girlhood dreams, it was expensive and elegant.

It was evident that Gervase was not a good correspondent, but two weeks before our marriage I received a long letter from him. It informed me that I would be met at Dublin airport, he didn't say by whom, and that I would be taken straight to the Jeffersons' house. He did not expect to see me before the day of the wedding as he had business to attend to in Cork and on the west coast. He also informed me that Lady de Bellefort had left all her grandchildren well provided for, but I was to have an additional sum which had been put aside for my mother. He thought I would be pleased to know.

Little did he know that that particular piece of information only made me feel very ashamed, but by this time it would need more courage to tell the truth than it would to act the part.

On the day I was to leave London I started to pack my clothes in the set of very expensive luggage I had bought.

Every case bore the initial L, and as I folded crepe-de-Chine underwear and soft leather skirts I reflected on how easily I had discarded the name Ellen for the more unusual Lisanne, and how easily I responded when hotel staff addressed me as Miss de Bellefort. A trunk containing most of my clothes had been dispatched to Ireland several days before and I was now packing the most expensive things I had purchased like evening gowns and afternoon dresses.

I had had my hair cut and styled at an exclusive new salon by a young woman who had enthused about its colour and texture. I had bought make-up, creams and lotions to pamper my skin, and bath oils in fragrant honeysuckle that reminded me poignantly of the countryside.

After my luggage had been taken to the foyer and I was dressed for the journey I took a final look in the mirror thinking that it was not Ellen Adair who faced me but a stranger, a fashionable expensive stranger in an exquisitely cut burgundy suit. On my fashionable bob was a hat of the same colour and round my shoulders a set of pale beige mink ties. There were soft kid gloves, and high-heeled burgundy shoes with a handbag of exactly the same colour. It was a fashionable, beautiful girl who faced me in the mirror and as I walked through the hotel foyer to the taxi heads turned to watch me.

I felt excited to be flying for the first time, but glad that the journey was a short one. Indeed I wasn't sure that I would ever again be a comfortable traveller.

After the customs I stood hesitantly in the airport lounge at Dublin surrounded by my luggage and feeling strangely deflated. People were milling all around me, many of them staring at the elegant woman who seemed lost and unsure.

Embarrassed, I was about to approach the desk when I felt my arm taken and looked up into the eyes of a man wearing country tweeds and an apologetic smile.

'I say, I am sorry but I was detained in the traffic on the way into Dublin. You're Miss de Bellefort, Gervase described you very accurately.'

I smiled, taking his outstretched hand.

'I'm Alan Harvey, Gervase's estate agent. I think he

explained that he would be away in Cork the day you arrived. My car's just outside. Here, I'll get somebody to help with your luggage.'

I thought he was nice. He had a boyish smile and he was trying too hard to be kind. Inwardly I wondered what he thought about this marriage. He must surely have heard Gervase's explanation of why he was marrying a cousin he hadn't seen since he was a child.

He seemed shy, and he kept up a running chatter while he eased the car through the late afternoon traffic. During our drive through the city he pointed out things like Nelson's Column in the centre of O'Connell Street, and the university buildings.

'It seems strange to see a monument to Nelson here in Dublin,' I said.

'Oh, one of these days they'll pull it down, there's nothing surer.'

'Are you a native of these parts?'

'Good gracious no, I'm from North Yorkshire, way up beyond Hawes. I could have sworn I detected a faint trace of the Yorkshire in your accent.'

'Oh well,' I said airily, 'I've spent a lot of my life in the Dales.'

'Of course, with your grandmother.'

He accepted it, and I in return began to realize how easy it was becoming to lie. Only I didn't want to lie. I prayed for the day when I wouldn't have to lie any more. When I really became Lisanne de Bellefort and stopped feeling guilty about remarks passed in all innocence.

We drove towards the mountains, beautiful and pointed like I'd always thought mountains should be, and my companion gave them names that I felt sure I would never be able to pronounce properly.

'How long have you known Gervase?' I asked him curiously.

'About twenty years. My family used to come over here for holidays when I was quite small, my mother had a brother who lived down there at Dalkey and we always loved the coast here, and the mountains. I met Gervase walking in the park with his father, I was trespassing and their gamekeeper caught me. They let me off with a lecture but I saw Gervase laughing and somehow or other we struck up a friendship, so that every summer I was invited to fish in their trout stream and ride in the park. When I left school I went to an agricultural college and learned estate management, Gervase's father took me on as under manager, and when my boss retired I was offered the job.'

'Are you happy working for him?'

'Of course. He knows what he wants and generally gets it. We understand each other and of course I've got a nice house that goes with the job, and a nice garden. I'm fond of gardening.'

'You actually live on the estate?'

'On the edge of it. Most of the labourers have cottages on the estate. The old man was more interested in the land than he was in the big house. I'm afraid it needs quite a bit doing to it, but now you're coming to live in it I expect Gervase will give you a free hand.'

'You mean it's decrepit?'

He laughed. 'By no means, but goodness knows when carpets and curtains were replaced. My wife says it needs a fortune spending on it.'

I hadn't realized he was married, and in the next breath he said, 'I married a girl from Bray only last year. We'd known each other a long time, also since we were chidlren.'

'I see.'

'I'm to take you to stay with Colonel Jefferson and his wife Edna. They'll make you very welcome. You do ride, I suppose?'

'Yes, but I'm not very expert.'

'Really? Gervase seemed to think you loved it, at least he told me you'd always had horses at your grandmother's place.'

'I haven't ridden for years, until I rode in London. I'm terribly out of practice.'

'Oh, one never forgets. Gervase will fix you up with a nice predictable mount and you'll soon get the hang of it again. And this is hunting country.'

My heart sank. I would not get the hang of it again, I'd yet to get the hang of it at all. I could already imagine how much I was going to disappoint my husband to be.

For a while we drove in silence, then he pulled the car over to the side and pointed down to the golden beach.

'That's Dalkey down there,' he said. 'Folk round here do say it's a lot like the Bay of Naples with Vesuvius rising across the bay. They're comparing the volcano to Old Sugar Loaf there, but you must admit it's very beautiful.'

I agreed. It was a pretty bay with the surf breaking on the soft sand and the exquisite shape of the mountain rising proudly in the distance.

'It's not far to the Jeffersons from here,' he said, 'I expect you're ready for a cup of tea.'

'Yes, that would be nice. Do I call you Mr Harvey?'

'I'd rather you called me Alan, Gervase does.'

'Very well, Alan.'

'You're not a bit what I expected, you know. It's funny, isn't it? I don't know why I imagined you so different.'

At that moment my heart missed a beat, and quickly I asked, 'Whyever not?'

'Well if you'll forgive me saying so Gervase described you as a bit of a brat, always wanting your own way, and probably a bit spoilt. I was expecting somebody rather imperious.'

'Gervase only remembers me as a child, I was probably all of those things.'

'How do you remember him?'

'Arrogantly insufferable, and when I met him in Plymouth I began to think he hadn't changed.'

He threw back his head and laughed. 'He can be all of those things. I suppose you'll both have to get to know each other all over again.'

'You're thinking that is hardly a happy augury for marriage.'

'I wouldn't presume to think anything of the kind. You've both known about this marriage for a very long time so I'm sure it'll work out. You know, in many countries marriages are still arranged, and surprisingly they do work out.'

He was reassuring me and I warmed to him. I was beginning to think I would find a good friend in Alan Harvey.

'The Jeffersons are just at the end of this lane here, the big red-brick house with the tall chimneys,' he said.

We drew up outside the front door and it opened immediately. Several dogs rushed out, followed by a tall spare man wearing tweeds and a pretty middle-aged woman in a tweed skirt, twin set and sensible shoes.

If she was surprised at seeing a distinctly elegant woman step down from the car she showed no signs of it. Her smile was welcoming and as the dogs were called to heel we all moved into the house.

'You'll stay for tea,' she called out to Alan.

'Actually no. I'll help with the luggage, then I've things to see to on the estate. I've been too long away already, and Gervase is in Cork.'

'Oh well, if that's the case we won't detain you. Give our love to Maureen,' Mrs Jefferson called out.

I was shown into a sitting room which I thought entirely charming, with pretty faded chintz covers on the large couches pulled up before the fire and chintz curtains at the windows. There were bowls of flowers here and there about the room, and gold-framed oil paintings.

I had noticed the hall as we passed through and thought to myself that I was in the home of hunting people. There were several hunting horns decorating the wall, a case filled with guns and rifles, and several fox masks.

'Take off your hat and anything else you want to get rid of, my dear,' Mrs Jefferson said, 'we'll have tea and then I'll show you up to your room.'

Almost immediately a small fresh-faced country girl came in carrying a tray set out with scones, butter, jam and an enormous fruit cake, followed by another girl carrying a tray arranged with a silver tea service.

The Colonel was poking the fire into renewed life, then he turned to me with a smile. 'The days are getting shorter and it was cool this morning. Is this your first visit to Ireland, my dear?'

'Yes, I'm afraid so.'

'Very pretty country round here, good hunting country. You do hunt, I suppose?'

'No, not since I had a bad fall several years ago.'

He raised his eyebrows in surprise. 'Is that so? I could have sworn Gervase told me you were into horses and hunting.'

I smiled politely and his wife said with a little laugh, 'I knew that was the first thing he'd ask you, he thinks of little else. Now I'm going to call you Lisanne, and my name is Edna. My husband's is George. Both very ordinary and easy to remember.'

'Yes they are, not like Lisanne.'

'But it's the prettiest name I ever heard. We were both so sorry to hear about the shipwreck, dear. How terrible to lose your mother in that way.'

'Yes, she was a very special person.'

'I'm sure she was, and how awful to have lived through the war under German rule and die on the way home to England. I don't suppose you'll ever forget it.'

'No.'

'And we don't want to go on talking about it,' her husband said sharply. 'It's something the poor girl wants to forget as quickly as possible.'

'Darling, don't be silly, of course she won't forget it.'

'No, and she doesn't want to talk about it either. Now come along, my dear, show us what a healthy appetite you've got.'

George was heavy-handed and kind, his wife fluttering like a little bird, but as the evening wore on I felt relaxed in their company and they asked few questions.

They talked about their neighbours, the countryside and the fishing, but never once did they mention Gervase or my approaching wedding day.

I was happy with the Jeffersons. I tramped the country lanes with them and sat in silence on the banks of the trout stream watching him fishing. I went with Mrs Jefferson to the country shops and was introduced to the people we met on the way, and I was always aware of their heads close together in small groups after we had wandered on.

'Country people gossip,' Edna said, smiling. 'They've been agog to know what you looked like. Of course they've known for years that one day the squire's son would marry his cousin from England. You'll be the topic of conversation for weeks.'

'Is the church where we are to be married near here?'

'You'll be married in the small chapel in the grounds of the house, dear. You needn't worry, it's properly consecrated and it's very pretty.'

'Does that mean that there will be nobody watching the wedding?'

'None of the villagers, dear. But we are guests along with one or two other people. Gervase said he wanted a quiet wedding in view of his grandmother's death and your mother's death also. I thought it was very sensitive of him.'

Personally I didn't think sensitivity had had anything to do with it. Gervase hadn't struck me as a man given to too much sentiment and I felt sure he was hating this marriage as much as I, as much as generations of de Belleforts must have hated having brides and grooms chosen for them, and strangely unable to do anything about it.

My silence made her say hurriedly, 'You and Gervase will have to get to know each other all over again, my dear. I'm very fond of him, although he's a singularly self-assured young man who doesn't suffer fools gladly.'

I felt strangely miserable. How Gervase would despise me if he ever knew the truth, as much as he despised the strictures placed around him by a grandmother he had respected but never loved.

CHAPTER 35

Like every girl before me I had dreamed of drifting down the aisle in a froth of white lace on my wedding morning, indeed there were many times when Kitty and I had fantasized about it. I could hear her voice saying, 'Just as long as ye don't expect mi to wear pink, Ellen. It's death to my colouring.'

So we had agreed that Kitty would wear lemon and I would wear blue when we acted as bridesmaids, but now here was I staring at my refleciton in the long cheval mirror in my room at the Jeffersons' and thinking I was dressed for a garden party but never a wedding.

The cream wild silk dress was beautifully cut and at the waist were pale pink chiffon roses which trailed prettily to the hem. The skirt fell in long folds from a narrow waist and the cream white hat with its pink chiffon roses was undoubtedly elegant though not exactly bridal.

Gervase had sent orchids which did not go with the roses so I decided to wear them on a long satin ribbon in my ivory prayer book. I had borrowed the prayer book that morning from Edna and she had insisted on stitching a small blue bow on to my petticoat. My clothes were new, the prayer book was old, so it would seem all the traditional items which might bring me luck had been included.

I wasn't required to have a bridesmaid but George Jefferson was giving me away, and Alan Harvey was Gervase's best man.

For the very first time we drove through the vast ornamental gates and the grounds of Glenmoor with the large turreted house in the misty distance. I was amazed how far the grounds extended, and as we drove through a forest of evergreens George whispered, 'We'll soon be at the church, it's in a little clearing just outside the forest.'

A small cluster of men and women stood round the

church door, and again George whispered, 'Servants from the house and off the land, come to watch the squire's marriage.'

As we left the car they bobbed quaint country curtsies to me and I smiled back at them shyly. There were other servants and tenants seated at the back of the church and a handful of guests in the front pews but my eyes were drawn to Gervase standing tall and impassive before the altar with Alan at his side, both of them wearing morning suits which surprised me a little.

The organist began to play, some tune I was unfamiliar with, and slowly George and I drifted down the aisle and Gervase took his place besides me.

I remember very little although I must have made the appropriate responses. All I was conscious of was the tall man standing beside me, his low voice making promises, then he was placing a heavy gold ring on my finger and the vicar proclaimed that we were man and wife.

He bent his head and kissed my cheek. His lips felt cold, impersonal, and his eyes stared into mine like blue steel.

The rest of the day passed in a haze of unreality. There were speeches and laughter at the reception, but I couldn't have told anyone what was said. I was introduced to people I felt sure I would not remember when we met again, and the meal tasted like nothing although the table was festive.

Gervase sat at one end of the long oak table and I at the other. Occasionally he raised his glass to me with a look of cynical amusement, and once I saw Alan looking at me, puzzled and compassionate.

I was glad when the meal was over and people began to drift about the house. I wanted to change, get out of my wedding finery, but nobody had told me where I could go. By this time pride and anger had come to my rescue and approaching Gervase, I said, 'I'd like to change, Gervase. Where is my room?'

'Surely you must mean our room, Lisanne?'

'All right then, our room. I take it my cases and trunk have been taken there.'

'I'm sure they have, and probably unpacked for you. We

may be living in darkest Ireland but we do have a modicum of the refinements.'

'Why are you so defensive, I wonder?'

'Why are you not more defensive? Surely you haven't enjoyed being a sacrificial lamb.'

'Is that what you think we are?'

'You need have no worries, my dear, I intend to honour our marriage to the extent of providing an heir. How far do you intend to honour it?'

'I don't know what you mean.'

'And now is not the time to explain. Martha will show you to our room. Please change quickly so as not to keep our guests waiting.'

I don't know what devilment prompted me to change into the only black dinner gown I had. It was elegant, with its low-cut neck and trailing sleeves edged with sable. The only adornment was the long diamong earrings I had bought in London and charged to my account.

I looked far more beautiful in the gown than I had done in my wedding dress. Black suited my pale blond colouring, and if the guests looked somewhat askance at my choice of gown, they also looked at me with some admiration.

For one fleeting moment I saw admiration in Gervase's eyes also, but almost immediately it was quenched by the maddening cynicism I had almost come to expect.

The night wore on. People laughed, the men sang hunting songs, they ate and drank too much and already it was midnight and I was wondering when Gervase would call a halt to the merriment. At precisely twelve o'clock he said, 'Time to go home. Thank you, my friends, for coming to our wedding. I can only say how much my dear wife and I have enjoyed your company, now we must have one last drink and you must leave us to enjoy the rest of the night.'

There were titters of appreciative laughter among the men and several embarrased glances from the women in my direction. For my part I watched them drift into the hall, then slowly I mounted the stairs towards the bedrooms.

For the first time I began to take a real look at Glenmoor. The curving shallow staircase could have been beautiful but the gilded balustrade, intricately carved, had suffered much neglect. The gilt was sadly in need of renovation and the oak steps badly needed polishing to restore the original lustre of the wood.

In places the carpet was threadbare and there were cobwebs high up on the walls. The lighting from heavy bronze lanterns was dim, and I thought sadly of the crystal chandeliers that had adorned the hall at the Priory where everything had been beautifully maintained under Lady de Bellefort's jurisdiction.

I entered the great bedroom overlooking the long drive and really saw it for the first time. Before I had been too anxious to change out of my wedding gown, now I was unhappily aware of the dark embossed wallpaper and the heavy dark blue carpet.

The long drapes at the windows were drab. Perhaps once they had been beautiful since the material was good and rich, but like the carpet the blue had faded and when I shook them the dust that came out made me cough and splutter. The room felt cold and I looked with dismay at the huge four-poster bed with its blue drapes. Gingerly I turned down the bedspread which felt cold to my touch, but I was relieved to see that at least the bed linen was newly laundered and clean.

A log fire had been laid in the hearth but nobody had thought to put a match to it, and I was shivering with cold. It was only late September, but there had been heavy rain during the evening and I could smell the damp which seemed to permeate the entire room. Off the bedroom was a bathroom, but this was no better. The floor tiling was badly chipped and I wrinkled up my nose with distaste at the stained bath and dark blue and gold paper on the walls.

It was evident that nobody living at Glenmoor had taken much pride in the house, and I speculated on what Gervases's father had been like.

I thought about Lady de Bellefort's description of him: a spendthrift, wayward and independent, totally unlike Lance's father who had been predictable and malleable. She had expected the same sort of behaviour from Gervase, and my marriage stretched out before me like a battle ground.

I undressed and bathed in lukewarm water. I had spent money extravagantly on exquisite underwear, and the satin nightdress I lowered over my head fell to the floor in exquisite folds.

There were matches on the mantelpiece and I lit the fire. The logs sparkled and crackled, sending volumes of blue smoke up the chimney, and I could smell them, a strangely aromatic scent that quickly filled the entire room. For a few minutes I knelt on the rug extending my hands to the blaze, feeling the warmth on my arms and shoulders, and I started to brush my hair.

I didn't want to think of the night ahead of me. I did not associate Gervase with the love and tenderness I had always longed for. I knew even before he entered the room that our lovemaking would be clinical, a means to an end, an obedience test, joyless and practical. But did I really deserve any better?

If I was being cheated of all the dreams in my heart, wasn't I in turn a bigger cheat, didn't I deserve to suffer at the hands of the man I had married in another girl's name?

From downstairs I could dimly hear laughter and the sound of voices. Our guests seemed in no hurry to depart and my husband was evidently showing no eagerness to seek his bride.

I felt lost in the great bed. The sheets were smooth and cold to my limbs but the bed was comfortable and the pillows soft. Whether he came to me or not there would be no sleep that night, my mind was too active, or so I thought. Eventually however the warmth of the room and the comfort of the bed proved me wrong and I drifted off to sleep.

It was a slumber plagued by terrible dreams. I saw Aunt Julie standing against a warm stone wall on a day when sunlight shimmered over the fields and honeysuckle ran riot across the hedgerows. I heard the German commands ringing coldly as one by one Aunt Julie and her friends sank in crumpled heaps after the sound of rifle fire. Then worse, far worse, I felt myself falling down and down until I was thrashing wildly in a cold black sea, and in my dream I was screaming.

Somebody was shaking me, saying sharply, 'Wake up, Lisanne, wake up, you're only dreaming.'

I opened my eyes to find Gervase was holding my shoulders in a firm grip, his dark steel-blue eyes staring into mine. My eyes darted wildly round the room in an attempt to reassure myself that it had all been a dream.

He laid me back on the pillow and went to a side table where he poured sherry into a glass and brought it over.

'Drink this,' he commanded. 'You've been having a nightmare. I heard you calling out before I entered the room.'

'What did I say?' I whispered.

'You were calling, "Aunt Julie," then you started to cry out, "Lisanne, Lisanne." Was somebody threatening you?'

'I don't know, I don't remember, but I did dream about the ship going down.'

He nodded grimly. 'It is to be expected, it was an experience you will not easily forget.'

For the first time I saw that he was wearing a dark red velvet dressing gown, and the grim amusement in his eyes brought the hot blood to my cheeks.

'Would you like a sleeping draught?' he asked quietly. 'I can quite easily sleep in my dressing room tonight.'

'Just as you wish,' I answered shakily.

'No, my dear, it is as you wish. Do we get our wedding night over or do we postpone the occasion?'

Anger came suddenly to my rescue and with cheeks flaming I stormed, 'You must think me uncommonly unattractive to leave the decision in my hands.'

He threw back his head and laughed delightedly. 'That is more like the Lisanne I remember. Incidentally I do find you attractive, more attractive, more beautiful than I had envisaged, and perhaps in any other circumstances I would have longed to make love to you. As it is I can only think that you and I are here to play a part, obey a command. Don't you think, my dear cousin, that in this most personal thing we should have been allowed to choose for ourselves?'

'Yes I do. I have always thought so.'

'And doesn't it make you feel less than a woman to have obeyed without question? It has made me feel less than a man.'

'Then why have you obeyed, why didn't you rebel?'

He was sitting on the edge of the bed, a reflective look on his dark, handsome face. 'Why indeed?' he said at last. 'I saw what it did to my parents, what it did to my father when he rebelled. My parents never loved each other, they quarrelled constantly, hating each other. It was hardly an atmosphere for a sensitive child to grow up in, and in those days I was sensitive. It was a sensitivity that needed to be stifled throughout my schooldays.

'In other people's homes I saw love and tenderness, friendship and comradeship, in my own I saw only strife and bitterness. When my father rebelled he was rejected, he became a traveller over the face of the earth and eventually his money ran out and he came home, humiliated and scorned. I learned the lesson well. I keep what I have, even this old house to which my father and his family were banished because my grandmother couldn't bear to have him living near her in England. I hate this house, I've always hated it, and as time goes by you'll hate it too.'

'Why do you hate it?'

'Because it's not Langstone Priory, because it's a house my grandmother hated, and she paid my father back by giving it to him.'

'It seems to me the de Belleforts have been more interested in hating than loving.'

'I think you're right, but they have loved the land, land that has been the de Belleforts' for centuries – the enduring thing, Lisanne, the only thing that matters.'

I was staring at him mutely, but I was thinking about another day years before when I had stood with Lance in the snow looking down at the Priory and its acres. Their voices were similar and in the firelight even their faces were etched in the same mould, and now as then I was being made to see that I had no armour against the land. Lance had loved me and I had lost, Gervase did not love me but I could never hope to win.

The tears welled slowly into my eyes and rolled unchecked down my face, and in that moment I saw his expression soften and grow kind. Appealingly I reached out to him and without hesitation he took me in his arms, kissing my tear-stained face. Then suddenly I felt his arms grow tight like bands of steel around me and his mouth was on mine, kissing me with a passion I had never really known, and before I was aware of it I was responding with all the ardour in my nature.

It was the animal passion of a man for a woman, hurting and gentle, painful and ecstatic, and it was a passion that left me trembling and drained in the hour before the dawn, when suddenly I was alone. I had felt him tear himself from my grasp as if he could no longer bear to have me pliant in his arms, as if the act of love had degraded him, robbed him of his manhood. I heard the door of his dressing room close with a sharp click, then in all the house there was a stillness, like the stillness of an empty tomb.

I slept late, waking to a chill grey morning when the room looked no more inviting than the night before and the dead cinders in the grate gave it an additional neglected atmosphere.

I dressed leisurely. It was almost eleven o'clock and nobody had thought fit to waken me or bring me a cup of tea. I dressed in a tweed skirt and sweater and after reassuring myself that I looked well enough, I ran lightly down the stairs.

A servant girl was busy sweeping the hall and she bobbed one of the curtsies I was becoming accustomed to. 'Is the master in?' I enquired.

'No, Mrs de Bellefort, the master was out of the 'ouse 'afore eight o'clock. Sure and we shan't be seein' 'im 'til just 'afore dinner.'

'Is there a fire in the dining room?'

'No, Ma'am, but there be one in the mornin' room. There's allus a fire in the mornin' room at this toime. Can I get you some breakfast, Ma'am?'

'No thank you, but a cup of coffee would be nice. What is your name?'

'Oime, Mary, Miss, Mary O'Donnell. Oi'll get your coffee and tell the 'ousekeeper you're awake.'

I found the morning room on my own, glad to see the warm fire roaring on the hearth, but like the rest of the house the room had little character. I decided at that moment that when I next saw my husband I would ask him if I could have a free hand to go over the house. If I lived here, then I should be able to do something about implanting my own taste.

When Mary appeared with the coffee I asked, 'Are there any dogs about, Mary?'

'Dogs, Ma'am?'

'Yes, I thought I would walk in the park, a dog would be good company.'

'The dogs usually go out with the master, but old Danny moight be in the kitchen, oi'll 'ave a look.'

I can't think why I had suddenly decided that a dog might be a good companion, I had always been afraid of them until Aunt Julie's poodle Pierre. I had been fond of Pierre and upset when we had to leave him with Jules.

She soon reappeared with a shake of her head. 'The dogs are all out with the master, Ma'am. Mr Murphy sez p'rhaps the master'll let ye'ave one o' the pups from the stable.'

'I'll talk to the master when he gets home, Mary. Thank you.'

Again came the curtesy before she disappeared into the hall.

Immediately I had drunk my coffee I put on a tweed coat and scarf and let myself out into the park.

It was fresh and I tied the scarf round my hair and thrust my hands deep into my pockets. I headed for the forest and was soon walking briskly, revelling in the salty tang of the wind, and taking off my scarf I allowed my hair to blow freely.

I came across the church we had been married in only the day before. I was surprised at its smallness, a grey stone church with a small square tower and stout oak door studded with brass. I pushed it open and entered. There were only a dozen rows of pews but the altar was pretty, a fact that had hardly registered the day before. Slowly I walked up the aisle, looking at the stained-glass windows and the plaques in honour of long dead de Belleforts.

It surprised me that Gervase didn't have much love for the place. It must have been in the de Bellefort family almost as long as Langstone, because some of those plaques dated from the sixteenth and seventeenth centuries.

An open Bible lay on the altar and as I stepped forward to look at it my foot disturbed a single orchid lying on the step. It was from the spray I had carried in my prayer book the day before.

I picked up the flower, a perfect thing, strangely exotic and alien in that tiny Irish church, then I laid it gently on the open Bible before going out into the open air.

I carried on through the forest until I came to a small clearing set out as a burial ground. The graves were all old, some of them bearing stone effigies like knights in armour, and one of them in the garb of a priest or bishop. I looked for Gervase's parents but could not find them, and in a little while it started to rain, soft misty rain that clung to my face and hair in tiny drops and, I hurried back through the forest and across the park.

In the afternoon I roamed the house armed with a notebook and pencil, making copious notes of what needed to be done to make the house more in keeping with the grace of its architecture.

Mary informed me that fires would be lit in the dining hall and the sitting room, and the master liked to eat dinner no later than seven thirty. I was therefore waiting in the sitting room at seven o'clock wearing a soft woollen dinner gown, feeling conspicuously overdressed and so nervous I jumped at every sound outside the room.

CHAPTER 36

We dined in splendid isolation in the great dining hall and I thought with some exasperation how much more intimate it would have been if we could have used the morning room. Conversation was practically impossible as he sat at the other end of the long table, and the food was mediocre and none too warm.

He seemed preoccupied, excusing himself immediately we had eaten by saying he had a telephone call to make, so disconsolately I wandered into the sitting room alone. I was bored. There were magazines laid out on a side table but they were boring men's magazines.

He returned after about half an hour and came to sit opposite me. For several minutes he eyed me in an amused fashion over his whisky glass before saying, 'And how have you spent your day?'

'I walked in the park and went to the church.'

How stilted our conversation was, with neither of us making any real effort. I felt nervous, unsure of myself, and he was enjoying my discomfort. In some exasperation I snapped, 'Is this how you spend all your evenings, drinking whisky and staring into the fire?'

He stared at me in silence, then getting to his feet he said politely, 'You must forgive me, Lisanne, I am accustomed to spending my evenings alone without the need to entertain a wife. What would you like a drink, sherry?'

'Nothing, thank you.'

'You'll have to get accustomed to spending a great deal of your time alone. I'm kept very busy on the estate and I shall be away for the next few days. Why don't you get a car and drive around the countryside? You'll find it very beautiful.'

'I'm afraid I don't drive.'

He stared at me in amazement. 'You never fail to surprise

me, Lisanne. Surely my respected aunt must have insisted you learn to drive.'

I bit my lip angrily. Of course Lisanne had been able to drive. All sorts of dragons were rearing their ugly heads and once more the enormity of what I had done hit me like a sledgehammer.

'I haven't driven for years, I need practice,' I answered him.

'You don't drive and you don't like horses. Where is the Lisanne I knew?'

'I do like horses. You said you would find me a predictable mount.'

'And so I will. I'll speak to Alan, he'll go along to the stables with you in the morning and you can take a look around. As for a car, that can easily be arranged and you can begin by driving round the estate.'

'Thank you, Gervase. I would also like a dog, quite a small one, one that would be a good companion.'

'Very well, I'll see what I can do. Tell me, how well did you get along with Cousin Lance?'

I stared at him in surprise. 'Very well. Lance was always kind.'

'Where I am not.'

'I didn't say that.'

'Nevertheless, my dear, you will find out that we are very different. I have the strangest feeling that Lance is destined to be a man with daughters. See that you give me a son, Lisanne.'

I could feel my face burning with colour but with my head held high I answered, 'That is something neither of us can be sure of, we can only hope.'

'It is the one thing that might bring us closer together, the only thing. It's a great pity that in an arranged marriage such as ours the birth of a son and heir can't be arranged also.'

'I think this whole conversation is offensive.'

'Very well then, we'll change it. What shall we talk about?'

'We can talk about the state of the house.'

'The house?'

'Yes. It's a beautiful house which has been allowed to fall to pieces. It needs a great deal of money spending on it. The curtains are dusty and extremely dirty, there are cobwebs in the corners and the woodwork is disgraceful. That beautiful balustrade is in an awful state and the food at dinner was inferior, badly cooked and barely warm.'

He threw back his head and laughed.

'There now, you remind me of Aunt Delia. I can see her sitting there wrinkling up her aristocratic nose and telling me what is wrong with my home. Personally I don't see anything wrong with it.'

In some anger I jumped to my feet and pointing to the windows said, 'Take a look at those curtains then. All the colour is faded out of them, and look at the dust.'

To suit my actions to my words I went over to the curtains and shook them and immediately the dust was in my eyes and my throat.

He didn't speak, but simply sat there with a small smile on his face.

'Look at the fireplace,' I cried. 'It's the most beautiful marble, yet when did it ever get polished? It's lifeless.'

'If you want to spend your money on the house go ahead with my blessing,' he said calmly. 'As for the food, you're the mistress now, you have my full permission to talk to the servants.'

'How many servants are there?'

'Enough. I've always been satisfied, but then I'm often away and maybe they have been able to go in for self-determination. You must do what you think fit about the house and the servants, Lisanne, it will no doubt keep you fully occupied. Now if you will excuse me I have work to do in the study. I may have gone when you get up in the morning but I expect to be back by the end of the week.'

I stared after him in amazement. It was barely nine o'clock and a lonely evening stretched before me. Evidently he had no intention of sitting with me again and no doubt he expected me to be fast asleep when he sought his bed.

I couldn't sleep. I lay alone in the huge four-poster listening to the rain on the window, the sighing of trees and occasionally the distant hooting of an owl. Once I thought I heard the sound of a ship's hooter echoing dismally through the mist but later it became so insistent I realized it must be a foghorn.

I cried stormy tears into my pillow as I tossed this way and that through the early hours, then I heard a door close in the corridor and I sat up with my ears straining, my eyes looking into the darkness. I eased out of bed and went to the window to draw back the curtains. It was a dark moonless night and I shivered in the cold air which crept through the cracks in the window frames.

Nervously I returned to the bed, listening all the time for the sounds of somebody moving in the room next to mine, watching feverishly for the knob on the door to turn, but there was no sound. For what seemed ages I sat up in my bed hardly daring to breathe, and then realization dawned. Gervase was sleeping next door in his dressing room, he had no intention of coming to me.

I was eating breakfast before nine o'clock the following morning but Gervase had already left the house. I had no sooner finished breakfast, however, when Alan came into the room, and with his arrival something more normal entered my life.

'Gervase said you wanted to take a look round the stables, Lisanne. We'll go now if you're free.'

'There's nothing else to do round here, I'll be glad to go with you, Alan.'

The stables were several minutes' walk from the house and as we neared them I could hear the sound of laughter and men's voices.

A group of them stood chatting in the centre of the stableyard and as we entered they raised their caps respectfully. Several dogs came rushing towards us.

'I haven't seen any dogs around the house,' I said to Alan while they leaped and fawned around us.

'Well old Danny stays mostly in the kitchens and I expect Gervase keeps the others in his study. He doesn't allow them the run of the house.'

'What sort of dogs does he have?'

'Great danes, enormous chaps but they have a nice temperament. There's no need to be afraid of them.'

'What kind are these?'

'Retrievers, labradors and spaniels. I say, Lisanne, you're not really well up in dogs. I would have thought you would be.'

'I never had one of my own.'

'But you had them at Langstone?'

'My grandmother wasn't into hunting or field sports, she was quite an old lady, you know.'

His face cleared and he nodded in agreement, while I thought how glibly the words came, almost without thinking.

A row of horses stood with their heads over their stall doors and we walked past them, occasionally patting their noses.

'How proficient are you, Lisanne?' Alan asked.

'I enjoy riding but I'm not keen on hunting. I just need a horse I can ride around the estate or maybe into the villages.'

We paused in front of a stall where a grey horse looked at us gently from behind incredibly long eyelashes.

'This is Silver. He's a gelding with a placid temperament and can be relied upon to behave. I don't think you could do better, Lisanne.'

I was stroking his satiny neck gently, then he started to nuzzle my neck and I was loving him. Suddenly he was my friend, something of my own.

'Oh yes, Alan, I like this one. Will you have time to ride with me one morning just until I get used to him?'

'Yes of course, but better than that I'll ask Maureen to ride with you. She knows her way around these parts and she'd like a woman companion, I'm sure. If you like I'll call for you this evening and you can spend the evening with us.'

'I'd like that very much, Alan.'

'Gervase said you'd also like a dog.'

At least, I thought, Gervase has made a little effort on my behalf, and my heart lifted in gratitude.

‘I thought a dog would be a good companion around the estate.’

‘We’ve three cocker spaniel pups in the stable. The older dogs are trained to the gun and need to be with a gamekeeper, but if you get one of the puppies early enough you can mould him into the sort of dog you want.’

The puppies were adorable. I loved them all but finally settled for a black one with large soulful eyes and a too-affectionate disposition.

‘You’ll need to house train him,’ Alan laughed, ‘or I could ask one of the grooms to take him for a day or two first.’

‘Perhaps that would be best, I’m still feeling my way up at the house.’

‘What are you going to call him?’

‘I think I’ll call him Toby, what do you think?’

‘I like it. We have a black one we call Jet. You’ll find your puppy very faithful and affectionate. How are you liking the house, Lisanne?’

‘I’m hating it, Alan. It needs a fortune spending on it. Hasn’t Gervase ever seen what it’s really like?’

‘Gervase is interested in the estate, he’s never really liked the house. His father disliked it.’

‘But why, when it could be so beautiful?’

‘I rather think his grandmother hadn’t much time for the old squire. He was a bit wild in his youth and he always had the feeling that this was a place of exile. Gervase has grown up with that belief.’

‘But Lady de Bellefort had three sons, so they couldn’t all live at Langstone, that was to be for her eldest son. The younger one was in the army, he died in the army.’

‘Your father?’

I stared at him, then I looked away sharply. Of course, Lisanne’s father, and I had spoken of him as if he were a stranger, just somebody someone had mentioned to me.

‘Yes.’

‘I expect with three sons rivalry between them is to be expected. Gervase’s father always said his elder brother was as dull as ditch water and the younger one was your grandmother's favourite. Resentment doesn't get better with the years, if anything it only festers.'

'I don't know Gervase at all. You're his friend, you can tell me if he's worth knowing.'

He stopped in his tracks to face me. 'My dear girl, he's your husband. If you want your marriage to succeed you've got to make the effort.'

'Don't we both have to make the effort?'

'That too.'

'Is there any other woman in his life?'

I saw the blank look come over his face, leaving it expressionless. I would learn nothing from Alan, and impatiently I thought that men were like that, they kept faith. If my husband was the greatest womanizer between Glenmoor and Dublin it wouldn't be Alan Harvey I heard it from.

Ignoring my question he said normally, 'You can get busy with the house, Lisanne. I expect Gervase has given you a free hand.'

'Of course, and the suggestion that I use my own money.'

He laughed. 'Well, I suppose he's satisfied with it as it is, so if you want it altered then you should pay for it.'

'Do you think that's fair? It isn't me who's allowed it to get into such a state.'

'It's all the same money that's in the family. I've never had that sort of money, so what can I say? You'll enjoy tackling the house, Lisanne. If you want any help I'm sure Maureen will lend a hand, and Edna Jefferson.'

That afternoon I walked down to see the Jeffersons and explained about the house.

They both laughed and Edna said, 'I told Gervase you'd soon fall out of love with the house. I wouldn't live in it for a fortune, but it has possibilities, I'll give you that.'

'What's wrong with the house, old girl?' George said impatiently. 'It only wants a decorator in some of the rooms. You must admit it's a fair stately pile.'

'It's a disgrace,' I retorted. 'Peeling paintwork, dirty walls, and the curtains are as ancient as those old tombs in the clearing.'

They laughed again. 'Gervase told us what a determined

young woman you were. I'm sure it won't take you long to get things moving.'

'But will he approve, do you think?'

'He probably won't take much interest,' George said, only to be reproved by a hard look from his wife.

'Of course he'll take notice, it's his house as well as Lisanne's.'

'Sorry, Edna, but you know Gervase as well as I. He doesn't care how much money he spends on the farms, the land, even the stables, but the house is just somewhere to lay his head.'

'I want rather more from my home than that,' I said firmly. 'I'm just not quite sure how to go about it.'

Lisanne would have known, but not Ellen Adair who'd never had any money and hardly knew how to spend it.

'The first thing we must do, Lisanne, is to get hold of an interior decorator who'll take a look at the house and decide just what needs to be done,' Edna said. 'He'll come along with samples of wallpaper, curtains, carpets, the lot – all you'll need to do is look at them and decide colour schemes. It'll be enormous fun, I'd love to help.'

'I'll be glad if you would. Alan said his wife would probably like to help too.'

'I'm sure she would. You'll quite like Maureen, she's a good sort.'

At the end of the day I felt I was gaining ground. I had found myself a horse and a puppy. I had made some headway with the house, and I had spent a delightful evening in the home of Alan Harvey and his wife. I got on very well with Maureen. She had a nice bubbly sense of fun, and she quickly became enthusiastic about my plans for Glenmoor.

'I knew you'd hate it,' she confided in me. 'When Gervase said you'd lived in the lap of luxury all your life I thought how much you'd hate Glenmoor. I'm not surprised you intend to do something about it.'

'I'm not too sure about the servants. The place is dirty and the food is inferior and badly cooked. I don't want to come the heavy-handed mistress of the house but I do think they need knocking into shape.'

'You're quite right. Gervase has let them have too easy a time of it and if you intend to change things, Lisanne, you've got to start right away.'

'Would Gervase mind if I interfered with the running of the house? The housekeeper's been there a long time.'

'Yes, I know. She spends more time helping out at the church in the village than she does attending to her duties at Glenmoor, and it's said she tipples her whisky and anything else she can get her hands on.'

'I have to talk to her, I have to talk to all of them.'

'Talk to them soon, before Gervase comes back, and then tell him about it.'

'I don't suppose he'll be too pleased.'

'Oh, men are all alike, they don't like the tenor of their lives disturbed in any way. But there does come a time when things need to change.'

The opportunity came the following morning when I asked to see all the servants in the morning room directly after breakfast. I had not realized there were so many of them as they stood in a shuffling untidy line before me, looking down at the floor.

The housekeeper, Mrs O'Flaherty, was a big raw-boned woman with a red face, wearing a long black dress and a none too clean apron.

Mary I already knew, and one by one the others introduced themselves – Rosie and Moira, Paddy, Connah and Jonah – and I was careful to be forthright without being unkind.

I told them I appreciated that the house was a large one and old houses needed more care than modern ones, but I was displeased that there were cobwebs on the walls and dust in the corners. I told them I was intent on making changes, there would be decorators in the house and workmen of all descriptions, after that there would be new carpets and new curtains. And things had to change.

Mrs O'Flaherty listened to me in silence, arms akimbo and face becoming more ruddy by the second, and when I had finished she said stoutly, 'We does our best, Ma'am. Like ye said it's large, the house is, and we works our fingers to the bone to keep it tidy. If it's wantin' improvements you are, then there should be more of us.'

'Then there will be, Mrs O'Flaherty, but if I'm still not satisfied when the improvements are completed then I shall have to replace you with other servants who are more conscientious. There is also the question of the food – who does the cooking here?'

'Rosie and me does it between us.'

'I like my meals served hot, Mrs O'Flaherty, and I dislike watery vegetables and green mould on the cheese. If you are short staffed in the kitchen then I will employ others, but there are only the master and myself to cater for. Surely it isn't too much to ask that the food be served properly and hot.'

'It's a fair distance from the dining room to the kitchens, no wonder the food's cold 'afore it's served, Ma'am.'

'In that case, Mrs O'Flaherty, we must see about installing a food lift from the kitchen to the dining room. All this can be gone into when the decorators and workmen come in. The house is bound to be upset for a considerable time, but I'm sure we shall all benefit from the results. That is all, and I am very glad to meet you. Please don't be afraid to approach me if you have any problems.'

On that note they departed, and I heard them muttering amongst themselves in a disgruntled way.

I had surprised even myself. That I had had the temerity to lecture a body of Gervase's servants as if I were accustomed to it gave me a new confidence. Those years with Lisanne's mother had not been in vain, and with a certain grim amusement I thought: I am after all a de Bellefort. My grandmother might have been a servant girl but my grandfather was the master of Langstone Priory.

CHAPTER 37

It seemed incredible that four years had passed and I had become as firmly established at Glenmoor as Lady de Bellefort was at the Priory. I had transformed the house from something approaching a monstrosity into a house people came to gaze at.

Once every month the gates were thrown open to the public who came to wander in the parkland. They had picnics near the mere and gazed in wonder at the old tombs in the burial ground. They knelt in reverent prayer in the tiny church and gazed at the flowerbeds and smooth green lawns with delighted appreciation.

Occasionally I moved among them, chatting to them as they stood about in groups, and I took my small son with me so that he would know how to greet other children.

If I had transformed Glenmoor I had also transformed myself. I was aware of a new confidence and not unaware of the admiring glances of the men and women I met in the park. I knew how to walk, how to speak and how to dress, and although the house had cost me a fortune it appeared that my capital was well invested in substantial areas which paid me considerable dividends, enabling me to spend lavishly on the things I loved.

I had expected Gervase to object when I wanted our son to be called Lance but he seemed not to mind, and when I told him I was surprised that he had not objected he merely smiled, saying, 'Lance is very appropriate. One day he will no doubt inherit Langstone, and there have been many Lances at the Priory.'

'Why do you say that?' I answered sharply.

'Didn't I tell you that Lance was destined to have daughters?' Indeed Geraldine had presented him with three – one older than Lance, one the same age and one two years younger.

When Gervase informed me that probably one day my son would marry one of his cousins I turned on him sharply, crying, 'He will marry who he wants to marry, neither you nor I will make him marry a stranger.'

Gervase and I went our separate ways. I had my house and my garden, I rode every day through the villages with Lance beside me on his pony, and I was very much the lady of the manor.

The girl Ellen Adair belonged to another world, another life. I had largely forgotten her existence and there were only two regrets. I wished I could have seen my brother Peter again, and I longed for news of Kitty. Kitty would approve of the way I had coped, but how could I tell my brother that every day of my life I was living a lie?

I knew that Kitty was married, indeed her picture had been in the papers only months before showing a gay laughing woman wrapped in furs standing with the Nôtre Dame behind her, laughing up into the face of a tall swarthy man with evident enjoyment. Under the photograph I read that the singer Emerald had been married quietly that morning to Sheik Mohamed Isfara, and they would be honeymooning in the Bahamas.

That day I felt disturbed. A part of my life had caught up with me and found me strangely vulnerable. When I showed the picture to Gervase, saying that I had heard her sing in Paris and Monte Carlo, he merely said, 'He's probably got half a dozen wives already. The woman's a fool to marry an Arab.'

'He's obviously very rich.'

'Obviously, or a woman like that wouldn't have entertained him.'

'You don't know what sort of a woman she is.'

'Do you?' he said maddeningly.

In the eyes of the world our marriage was well enough. We appeared together at race meetings and horse shows. We danced together at hunt balls and we entertained and were entertained in the homes of the few friends we had in the area, but still between us was the resentment that I had largely forgotten but Gervase could not.

He adored our son and occasionally he sought my bed, when I despised myself for the ardour he aroused in me and when I knew full well it was not prompted by love, only by desire, and such a bitterness flared between us that the aftermath left me in tears.

I first became aware of Pamela Capethorn at the ball our friends induced us to give on completion of the house.

'You ought to show it off,' Edna Jefferson encouraged. 'The house is a showplace and if Gervase never entertained before, he now has a wife. So there's really no excuse not to.'

Lisanne would have known how to organize a ball of vast proportions but when I appeared doubtful Edna said, 'Nobody does it themselves these days, there are numerous caterers you could call in. Really, dear, all you need to do is the flowers.'

When I consulted Gervase about the guest list he said sharply, 'Do we really need to fill the house with all sorts of people who will tramp over your newly polished floors and leave their glasses to stain the tables?'

'Other people have balls, why can't we?'

'We don't go to their bunfights. They mean a lot of silly people milling around talking at the tops of their voices about nothing at all.'

'We don't go because we don't invite them here. There are times when I still feel like a stranger in the area.'

'If you want the ball, Lisanne, go right ahead and arrange it. Just don't expect me to take much interest in it. I have other things on my mind.'

So I engaged a firm of caterers who moved in on the day, and I arranged the flowers – huge bowls of chrysanthemums in shades of white to deepest bronze, and with them shining holly which was already bearing scarlet berries although it was only late November.

Satisfied that the supper table looked festive and that huge log fires burned in every grate, I went up to my room to dress. For the first time I wore the turquoise chiffon evening gown I had bought in London, and I adored it. It draped my slender figure tenderly like some ancient dress of a Greek goddess, and the skirt shimmered and swirled around my feet when I moved.

I went into my son's room to say goodnight and he sat up in his bed with round eyes as he took in the picture I presented.

'Mother, you look so beautiful,' he said, and I gathered him into my arms and held him close.

'You smell lovely too,' he said. 'Why don't you always wear that dress?'

I laughed. 'What, to ride in the park and walk across the fields? Whatever would the villagers say?'

'Has father seen it?'

'Not yet. I've told Mary to bring in your hot milk and biscuits around eight o'clock. Will the music keep you awake, darling?'

'I'll lie in my bed listening to it. I'll think about you dancing in that dress with Father.'

I kissed him again before pulling the covers round him, then I turned on the light beside his bed before switching off the others. He was still watching me with a happy smile when I closed the door.

Gervase stood in the hall with a group of his friends as I descended the stairs and they all turned to greet me. I was instantly aware of their admiration, and the long mirror across the hall told me that I was indeed a beautiful woman in a beautiful dress. I had dressed my hair high on my head, leaving only one heavy tress to fall over my shoulder, and I was wearing my long diamond earrings, my only adornment.

Gallantly Gervase stepped forward and took his place by my side. His eyes were dark and sombre as they gazed into mine and then in a low voice he said, 'You look very beautiful, Lisanne. I should appreciate my good fortune more.'

'Thank you, Gervase.'

'I think you know everybody here.'

I smiled and one by one the group of men took my hand, then Gervase whispered, 'Perhaps we should go to the door, our other guests are arriving.'

There were so many of them. Several of the men were in hunting pink mess jackets, others in sombre evening dress, the women in silks and taffetas, with jewels round their throats and in their hair, but not one of them was wearing a dress as fashionable or beautiful as my own until Pamela Capethorn arrived.

She entered the room with an elderly man and immediately I became aware of a moment of silence before the chatter broke out anew.

She was not a beautiful woman but she was decidedly striking. She was tall, with wide smooth shoulders, and she wore a topless sheath dress in white satin that showed off her high firm breasts and shapely hips. She was dark, but there were red lights in her hair and her eyes were a curious light hazel.

She smiled confidently as Gervase said, 'This is Colonel Capethorn, Lisanne, and his daughter Pamela.'

I smiled a greeting but at the same time I was aware of her eyes sliding from me to Gervase, and her smile became warmer and singularly more promising. By this time her father was gripping my hand and congratulating me on the improvements I had done to the house, and in the conversation that followed I was given to understand that they had been living in India, where Colonel Capethorn was finishing his time. I could only assume that their invitation had been sent by Gervase, who must have known of their return to the area.

They were the last guests to arrive and I couldn't help thinking that their entrance had been engineered by the girl. As we moved in a foursome to the ballroom where there was already dancing, I knew that people were whispering together and many of them were regarding us with the utmost speculation, even amusement.

Dancing with Gervase was a joy. He moved with graceful competence round the ballroom and we were looked upon admiringly. Indeed to those watching we must have looked a well-matched couple, he dark and I fair, he tall and handsome, myself slight and somewhat ethereal, and from some of the older people present there were smiles of approval as the dance reached its end.

I danced with many of our guests and Gervase did likewise, then just before supper I saw him dancing with Pamela and they were laughing together, enjoying each other's company like old friends.

From dozens of people as the night wore on I was complimented on the beauty of the house and the success of the ball, and showered with invitations which I felt sure Gervase would ignore. Indeed I said to one lady who was over-insistent, 'My husband isn't fond of socializing, he always makes the excuse that he has too much to do.'

'Oh, Gervase has always been like that – his father was even worse – but he has a lovely wife to show off, he should make the effort.'

'Perhaps you should try to persuade him,' I said, smiling.

'He'll take no notice of me. Have a word with Pamela, my dear, she could always persuade him to attend one function or another.'

For a moment there was an uncomfortable silence before Edna Jefferson said, 'How's your darling little boy, Lisanne? You haven't brought him to see us this week.'

'Lance is very well, Edna, but I've been too busy this week. He's missed you too.'

'The caterers were excellent, dear, it's all been wonderful.'

I smiled and moved on to another group and met the same praise, the same invitations. Then I saw Gervase and Pamela move out on to the terrace regardless of the keen frosty night. He was helping her to arrange her fur wrap round her shoulders and although there were others moving out on to the terrace with them I didn't miss the knowing looks from several people standing nearby.

People were dancing again and as I excused myself and ran lightly upstairs I was sure that between Pamela Capethorn and my husband burned the embers of an old love. I went straight to my son's room to find him sleeping soundly, one rounded arm under his head. Toby, curled up at the end of his bed, raised his head and eyed me soulfully.

'You shouldn't be on the bed,' I admonished him. 'Come along now, get into your basket.' I patted his head as he obeyed me, then I switched off the light and went to my own room.

One of the servants had drawn the heavy drapes but I pulled them back, letting in the moonlight. I could see people standing in groups on the terrace, see the smoke from their cigarettes mingling with the autumnal mist, and I saw Pamela and Gervase strolling along the path towards the sunken garden. They were in earnest conversation and she appeared to be doing most of the talking. At times I could hear their laughter and I reflected that I didn't often hear Gervase laugh, to me his amusement was always cynically inclined.

They came to a halt almost below my window and I could hear their conversation.

'Didn't you mind when she decided to knock the house to pieces, Gervase? I must say it's an improvement,' she said in a light, amused voice.

'No, I didn't mind. It kept her occupied and she was pretty lonely, I suppose.'

'She's very beautiful, or hadn't you noticed?'

'Well of course I've noticed, I am a man after all.'

'And doesn't her beauty do something to you?'

'If you mean doesn't it compensate me for being unable to please myself, I suppose perhaps it does in a way. But it's not enough, Pamela.'

'She's played her part, you've got the son you wanted and she's made this place a show house. Isn't that enough?'

He was gazing down at her, and for several moments he didn't answer while I stood at the window with bated breath, waiting for his answer as she was waiting.

'If you mean am I ready to take up our liaison as before, as if my wife didn't exist, I don't think that's possible, Pamela. We've had some good times, we've enjoyed ourselves together, but Lisanne's not just my wife. She's a de Bellefort, and between we de Belleforts is a strange sort of honour. I don't intend to open everybody's mouths by carrying on with you as though Lisanne didn't exist, she's my wife, the mother of my son. I owe her something even if she did come to me gift wrapped and with precise instructions as to what to do with her.'

'You'll not keep it up, Gervase, I know you too well. One of these days you're going to want me again as I shall want you. We've too much going for us, too much to remember, and we're alike: hard and greedy and selfish.'

'Thank you for spelling out my faults, my dear, obviously you never recognized that queer streak of honour in me. I'd rather you forgot about the past, Pamela. In any case my cousin Lisanne might prove to be something of a match for you, she is after all her mother's daughter.'

'Darling, there never has been a woman who's been a match for me where you're concerned.'

Although they laughed together, as her arms reached out for him he held her away. 'I mean it, Pamela, not here, not now.'

Angrily I pulled the cord that closed the curtains, shutting out the night. I was trembling, and I sank down on to the edge of my bed, gasping with the pain of it.

Gervase had said it was over, but I had heard the longing in her voice. Why should I care? I didn't love him, I had never professed to love him, or he me. If he spent every night of his life with Pamela Capethorn it shouldn't bother me – but the awful thing was that it did.

I didn't want to be a cheated wife, I wanted to be a loved one. I wanted my son to be part of a loving family, not to grow up as Gervase had grown up: aware of the bitterness between his parents, the quarrels and bitter recriminations that must have coloured his childhood.

Gervase had said that Lisanne de Bellefort would know what to do with Pamela Capethorn. But Ellen Adair did not.

CHAPTER 38

With the advent of Pamela Capethorn into my life I felt less assured. She was a superb horsewoman and she could enter into men's conversation with ease as they discussed horses and hunting, agriculture and the running of large estates.

She was a man's girl, a drinking pal, a sportswoman who could often beat them at their own game, and although she treated all the men in our circle with friendly comradeship it was Gervase she followed with her eyes, Gervase she smiled at over her brandy glass.

I tried to appear indifferent but whenever we were in the same room I could sense the atmosphere, the knowing glances of those around us, and I began to refuse invitations – it was easier to stay away than it was to face people.

One afternoon she accosted me in the village, saying, 'Why not turn out with the hunt on Saturday, Lisanne? Gervase gave me to understand that you were keen.'

'Gervase gave you to understand wrong, then.'

'But I've spent months in Yorkshire in the winter time. Hunting's a way of life there.'

I smiled politely and made as if to move on but she stood in my path, her light hazel eyes filled with a strange amusement.

'You're not a bit like Gervase described you. He expected you to be something of a handful, too spoilt and self-assured, instead he finds you calm and strangely gentle. I don't really think he knows how to handle you.'

'Did he say that?'

'No, it's an impression I get.'

'If he's puzzled by me perhaps it's a good thing. He might like to be intrigued.'

'I didn't say he was intrigued, Lisanne, he's not sufficiently interested to be intrigued. He's merely puzzled that his giddy, rather silly little cousin isn't living up to expectations.'

'Are you always so insolent to people you don't know very well?'

I watched her face colouring a bright brick red, and covered with confusion she said quickly, 'I say, Lisanne, I really didn't mean to offend you. I'd very much like us to be friends.'

'I'm sure you would, it would be nice to have my blessing on your efforts to steal my husband. Unfortunately, however, I'm not looking for your friendship, I prefer to choose my friends from women who have no ulterior designs on what is mine.'

Stung to anger she retorted, 'Gervase was never yours, you were always just a girl he needed to marry to hold fast to his heritage.'

'Exactly so. I agreed to marry him for the same reasons. I have played my part, I shall expect him to play his.'

'What exactly do you mean by that?'

'I expect him to keep up appearances and not to scandalize everybody by flirting with you.'

'Gervase does not flirt with me, it goes much deeper than that.'

'Then I shall give him an ultimatum. Either he puts a stop to it or I leave him, taking my son with me. The de Belleforts have always known, and it was spelt out in our grandmother's will, that if there is divorce or separation the guilty party would forfeit all rights to land and property. You will count as nothing when Gervase comes to weigh up the cost.'

'You wouldn't dare, he would despise you for it.'

'Surely you don't think I care about that? What he does in private is his own affair but in public I have the right to expect him to conform. Either way I think you will find that you are relatively unimportant.'

I left her staring after me with my head held high. My words were filled with brave confidence but my heart was fluttering wildly. I could not believe that I had had the courage to talk to Pamela Capethorn with all the confidence of an affronted wife.

I thought about Lady de Bellefort arriving at Langstone as a bride only to become aware of her husband's dalliance with a serving girl. How her proud spirit must have squirmed, even when she hadn't learned to love him herself. Now I was experiencing the same sort of anger. It was retribution planned by some omnipotent diabolical genie and I was being asked to pay for the waywardness of other years.

It was several days later when Gervase made me aware of his displeasure in no uncertain manner. I was sitting with young Lance in the drawing room. He loved books and was beginning to read remarkably well for one so young. His father burst in upon us unceremoniously, saying, 'I want to see you in the study, Lisanne. Alone.'

I stared into his face. It was white with anger and his dark blue eyes shone with a steely glare.

Unhurried I said to Lance, 'Go on with your reading, darling. You're doing very well, I won't be long.'

I followed in Gervase's wake as he stormed across the hall and when I entered the study he was standing near the fireplace looking down into the flames.

I went to stand opposite him, then when he didn't look up I sat in the nearest chair with my hands clenched in my lap, hoping my face was more composed than my heart.

It seemed like a year before he looked at me. All I was aware of was the ticking of the marble clock on the mantelpiece and the crackling of the coals on the hearth. When he did look at me his face was cold and his words fell like drops of ice from his lips.

'I don't expect my wife to insult my friends in the village street. If you had anything to say to Pamela Capethorn it was better said in private.'

'I didn't accost her, she accosted me.'

'I can hardly believe that.'

'You prefer to believe your mistress before your wife?'

'Why do you call her my mistress?'

'Because she told me the thing between you went very

deep. It was more, much more than a mere flirtation. And I believe her.'

'And if it did go deep what does it matter? We were both free, and even now I didn't promise my grandmother to love you to the exclusion of all others, I only promised to marry you.'

'You're never going to forget that you married me as a duty, are you? It's seethed and festered in you ever since you knew that one day you'd have to conform. You don't see me as a woman at all, only as some terrible curse wished on you by a grandmother you never really knew. Don't think I don't think about you in the same way.'

'In that case behave yourself with my friends, accept things the way they are and we might be able to get along together.'

'I will not have my son learn about his father's infidelity from strangers. In public I'm asking you to conform, surely you must remember what your own parent's marriage did to you.'

'And I am asking you, Madam, not to interfere in my life. Do what you like in private and I will do the same. The façade we show to the world will be as blameless as you wish it to be, what we do in private will be our own affair.'

That was the start of it.

In the eyes of the world we were a happy well-adjusted family and it was plain to see how much Gervase adored his son. He took the boy fishing in the trout streams that burbled and gushed their way from the enchanting Wicklow mountains. Already Lance was becoming good with horses, and one day I heard Gervase say to him, 'Don't be afraid to get right back on should you ever have a fall. That was your mother's problem.'

Every day of my life I was cheating my husband, but at least I had given him the son he loved and was proud of. As for myself, I entertained his guests and played hostess with grace and polish at intimate dinner parties and stately balls. We appeared together at horse shows and race meetings, and if Pamela Capethorn was attracting men because she knew how to drink with them and ride with them, I attracted them with my beauty and the way I dressed.

I was never short of admirers or escorts and the face I showed to the world was smiling and serene.

Not so Gervase. He was sarcastic about my admirers. He called them dilettantes because they understood art and music, and more and more I was invited to listen to music in Dublin and London and I spent a great deal of time away from home, particularly after Lance went away to his prep school.

I watched Pamela Capethorn change from a handsome shapely girl into a coarser blowsy woman with a frustrated air, and smiling grimly I told myself that I was winning.

It was April and I was alone in London on one of my cultural shopping trips. Gervase was fishing in Connemara and Lance had just returned to school so there was no pressure on me to return home.

I was enjoying myself hugely, with trips to the theatre and the art galleries, where by this time I had become a familiar figure with the curators. It was one of the curators who told me about a private exhibition in one of the smaller galleries by a new artist who was commanding a great deal of attention in the art world on the continent.

'I've been along to look at it,' he confided. 'There's some very nice stuff there which I think you'd be interested in, Mrs de Bellefort.'

That afternoon I took him at his word and went to the exhibition. To be honest I was a traditionalist and much of the artist's work left me feeling bemused and unsure. It was only when I entered the second gallery that my eyes became riveted on a picture of a red-haired girl in an emerald gown. The artist had dealt haphazardly with the background, pale misty people sitting at pale misty tables, but the girl stood out vibrant and enchanting, and her green eyes seemed to mock me.

There was a price tag on the picture of two thousand pounds but undeterred I hurried along to the gallery office to buy it. The gallery owner was not alone so I waited impatiently outside for the man who was with him to leave.

They came out together, and seeing me the owner smiled and I stepped forward immediately to say, 'I would like to buy the picture of the girl in an emerald dress.'

His smile became uncertain and he looked doubtfully at the man with him and they laughed a little.

'I'm sorry, Madam, you are just too late. This gentleman has bought it.'

'Oh but you can't have,' I cried. 'It is very important to me.'

'I am sorry, Madam, but I'm afraid it's true,' he said apologetically. 'I've had my eye on it all week, and this morning I made up my mind to buy it.'

The distress must have shown on my face and in some torment I cried, 'But why do you want that particular one? There are dozens to choose from.'

'Why do *you* want that particular one?'

'Because I know her. I've known her for years. The picture is terribly important to me and I don't suppose I'll ever meet Kitty again.'

'Kitty?'

'Yes, Kitty McGuire, that's her name.'

'You must be mistaken, Madame,' the owner put in, 'the picture is of the singer Emerald. She's quite famous on the continent, that is she was until she left the stage to marry some Arab prince.'

'She's Kitty McGuire nevertheless,' I insisted, then suddenly realizing I had lost, I said, 'I'm sorry, of course the picture is yours. I was just terribly confused at seeing it and I thought I must have it. Do forgive me.'

The owner was quick to say, 'If another painting of this lady arrives may I telephone you, Madam?'

'I shall only be staying in London a few days but I would be very interested. The name is Mrs de Bellefort and I am staying at the Savoy.'

I smiled at them both before making my escape. I had behaved like a petulant schoolgirl and no doubt they were even now congratulating themselves that the picture wasn't being bought by me. I had no further interest in the exhibition, no other painting was to my taste and I was glad to get out into the open air.

I hurried down the street but had not gone far before I found my arm taken in a firm grip and looking up in surprise I found the man who had bought Kitty's picture looking down at me with a half smile.

'I hope you know I've almost had to break into a run to catch up with you,' he said. There was laughter in his voice and in spite of feeling decidedly at a disadvantage I eventually laughed to.

'Why don't we talk about the picture over a cup of tea?' he said calmly.

'But what is there to talk about? The picture is yours, I accept that.'

'And I accept that it really does mean something to you. I am open to be convinced.'

By this time he had taken my arm and we were walking down the street together.

'Tea at Grimaldi's I think, and the most sensational scones in all London. Do you agree?'

'I don't normally drink tea with a stranger.'

'In that case I should introduce myself, my name is Mark Allenby. And yours?'

'Lisanne de Bellefort.'

'Any relation to the Yorkshire de Belleforts?'

My heart began to race as I replied, 'Well yes, do you know them?'

'I was at school with Lance, and I knew Gervase at Oxford. Which de Bellefort are you?'

'I'm their cousin Lisanne, I'm also Gervase's wife.'

'Of course, the de Belleforts have always married their relatives. I thought Gervase was living in Ireland.'

'We do live in Ireland, in County Wicklow. My husband is away fishing so I took the opportunity to visit London for shopping and the theatre.'

'I'm sure Gervase wouldn't mind my escorting his wife to tea. I knew Lance better than Gervase, but no doubt he'll remember me.'

So we drank tea together and he asked a great many

questions about Lance and his wife and daughters. He seemed to know Langstone Priory well and when I asked him if he'd ever been there he said, 'Several times when I was a schoolboy. I stayed with Lance and his family at their place but I was taken to Langstone to meet his grandmother. She was a remarkable woman, very intelligent and with a marvellous sense of humour. Lance adored her. I rather think I met you and Geraldine on one of those occasions.'

Again my heart raced until he said, 'I remember you as a bit of a tomboy, a pretty fair-haired tomboy. I must say you've grown up beautifully, Lisanne. You don't mind me calling you Lisanne?'

'Not as we seem to be such old friends. Do you remember what I was doing when you met me at Langstone?'

'I remember you were mad keen on horses. Do you hunt much in Ireland?'

'My husband does. I still love horses but I don't hunt.'

'I must say that surprises me. I don't much care for hunting either but I do enjoy a game of polo. I met your mother at Langstone. She'd just returned from India, I think your father had died out there.'

'Yes, that's right.'

'Is she still living?'

So I told him about the mine and a little of our life in Provence and he listened attentively.

'Are you going to the theatre this evening?' he asked.

'I haven't made plans to go, I should think about going home soon.'

'But not yet, not when we've just met and I feel as if we're old friends. Will you come to the theatre with me this evening? I'll try to get seats for something good and I could pick you up around seven. I'm staying at my club, it's quite close to the Savoy.'

For a moment I hesitated. I liked this man, he was obviously a gentleman and he had seemed like an old friend when he talked about Langstone. I wavered and he pressed home his advantage. 'I'm sure your husband would rather you went to the theatre with me than went about London on your own,' he said gently.

That was the beginning of an enchanting spring. I stayed on in London savouring the joys of being admired and cosseted. We went to the theatres and we danced in dimly lit exclusive nightclubs. We listened to music in the concert halls, we even went to the zoo, and every day I fell deeper in love with him and he with me.

My beauty blossomed with a new-found delight in living and in my stupidity I believed it could go on indefinitely. I need not make a decision, I need not think of returning home to Ireland, Gervase would not care. We had never professed to anyone that our lives were intricately bound, we had a marriage and a child, but we had never had the sort of love that held others together.

It was pleasant to drift, pleasant to have his eyes, warm and caring, gazing at me across the table, heavenly to drift in his arms without a single thought beyond the moment, until the day we walked in the park and I found him unusually silent.

I had been happily chattering away until I realized suddenly that he was not responding and I found his face grave and strangely sad.

'Is something wrong, Mark?' I asked quietly.

He smiled down at me. 'Something is terribly wrong, Lisanne. You must know that I'm in love with you, and it can't go on like this.'

'I don't understand.'

'I think you do.'

'But what can we do? Oh Mark, must we talk about it now? You know I love you, but must we spoil this heavenly day by talking about things we have no answers for?'

'There have to be answers, my dear. I love you, I want to marry you but you're married to somebody else. Are you prepared to ask Gervase for a divorce?'

'A divorce!'

He nodded.

'Oh Mark, I don't know. It's not as easy as that, I have my son to think of and Gervase will be difficult, I know.'

'And the de Belleforts do not separate.'

'That too. Gervase will never divorce me, the penalties

are too great. We agreed to go our separate ways but on the day he married me he made me understand that I would be a de Bellefort for the rest of my life.'

'And I too have a duty, Lisanne. I have my own family to think of. I need to marry and have a son. I too have a noble name and an estate I love – the de Belleforts are not unique in that.'

'You would marry me?'

'If you were free I'd marry you tomorrow. But you're not free, Lisanne, or ever likely to be. I've spent all night thinking about this. Obviously we can't go on as we are. I love you but I can't have you, you love me but you're married to somebody else. The longer we go on seeing each other the harder it is going to be. We should part now, Lisanne, while we're still strong.'

Tears came into my eyes and rolled down my cheeks and I clung to him miserably while his arms held me close and I could feel the steady beating of his heart.

'Poor Lisanne,' he murmured gently, 'I don't suppose you've ever had to part from somebody you loved before.'

Wildly at that moment I thought of Lance. I had loved him but he hadn't loved me enough. Now I loved Mark and he loved me too much, and once again I was being made to realize what I had done when I adopted the role of Lisanne. As Ellen Adair I could have gone with this man to the ends of the earth, as Lisanne de Bellefort I would have to see him walking out of my life.

We moved on in silence, oblivious to the sun shining on the grass, or other lovers walking hand in hand beneath the trees. At the gates he paused and I looked up at him doubtfully, unsure until he said, 'I'll get a taxi for you, Lisanne. I don't think we should meet again under these circumstances.'

'You mean I shall never see you again?'

'Lisanne, I must go home. I've been away from my estate too long already. If you feel like talking to Gervase about us I shall be happy to hear the outcome. This is my address in Leicestershire.'

'How cold and formal you sound all of a sudden,' I cried dismally, taking the card from his fingers.

'I'm trying very hard to be formal, Lisanne. I don't feel formal, I feel like it's the ending of the world.'

'I'll speak to Gervase, Mark, I have to. Oh, surely he won't hold me to a marriage as empty as ours. He must see that we can't go on obeying laws that were laid down centuries ago, there should be something we can do about them in this day and age.'

'The decision is yours, my dear, but I am not hopeful. I have known the de Belleforts too long. Here is your taxi.'

I wanted him to hold me in his arms and kiss me, but instead he merely kissed the back of my hand, and raising his hat politely stood back while I entered the taxi and was whisked away into the afternoon traffic.

For the first time I looked at the card in my hand and saw that he was Sir Mark Allenby of Galveston Hall in Leicestershire.

That night I packed my suitcase and paid my hotel bill. In the morning I would fly home to Ireland.

The house felt strangely impersonal as it always did after one of my absences. There were no flowers in the rooms, and there was a film of dust on the furniture. I went immediately up to my room and started to unpack. The room felt stuffy so that I was glad to fling open the window and let in the fresh air. The gardens and the park beyond them looked much as usual. The gardeners were busy mowing the lawns: they were interested in appearances even if the house servants were not.

I rang the bell and in a few minutes Mary appeared, wiping her hands on her apron, staring at me with round-eyed surprise.

'We didn't expect ye, Ma'am,' she said somewhat sourly. 'Ye usually lets the master know when ye'll be home.'

'I made up my mind suddenly. Has anybody seen fit to dust the house since I went away?'

'We're short-handed, Ma'am, Moira's left to get married an' we haven't got anybody in 'er place yet.'

'I see. Well, please see what you can do with this room. Is the master on the estate?'

'Yes, Ma'am. There was a big storm in the noight, uprooted some o' the trees it did. One of them fell on a labourer's cottage. Sure and it's a lot of damage it's done.'

'I'm sorry, was anybody hurt?'

'Two o' the men, Ma'am, hurt bad they were.'

'I'll walk over there. Is Toby in the kitchen?'

Her face coloured bright red, and she stammered, 'Oim sorry, Ma'am, but 'e got out o' the kitchen one day and 'e went berserk in the park, killed a lot o' lambs 'e did. The master 'ad to 'ave 'im put down.'

I sank down on my bed, staring at her. Toby who had never killed a thing, Toby who had been my dog, my companion. I couldn't believe it.

'I reckon 'e was missin' you, Ma'am. He fretted a bit, Joe said 'is temper was spoiled.'

I dismissed the girl curtly, then I dissolved into tears, sobbing wildly. I had lost Mark and I had lost Toby. At that moment I hated Gervase with all my heart. He kept me from the man I loved and he had destroyed my dog. I couldn't wait to tell him how much I hated him.

I heard him come into the house, heard his footsteps crossing the hall then men's voices in the study, and without a second's thought I ran down the stairs and burst into his study. He sat behind his big mahogany desk and Alan Harvey and another man stood facing him. Across the desk maps were spread out and all three seemed intent on these. They looked up in surprise at my hurried entrance and Gervase said coolly, 'So the mistress of the house has returned. When?'

'An hour ago. What happened about Toby?'

'I'm busy now, Lisanne, I'll tell you about it over dinner.'

'No. Now, Gervase. There must have been some mistake, Toby never killed anything, he was always too gentle. Why did you have to put him down?'

The two others were looking uncomfortable but Gervase said firmly, 'I had to shoot him. He had a dead lamb in his mouth and we'd seen him savaging four or five of them.

When a spaniel goes wild he means business, and I couldn't take a chance. If they kill once they go on killing.'

I stared at him stonily. 'Couldn't you have waited until I got home? He'd be with me after that, he'd never have been alone on the estate again.'

'That was a chance I couldn't take, particularly as I had no idea when you were returning. Now, Lisanne, if you don't mind I'd like to carry on.'

I hated him. I hated his calm condescending voice. He was like a brick wall against which I was battering my bruised palms. I wished he were dead. That night I would tell him about Mark, I would wipe that self-satisfied smile off his face for ever.

I did not see Gervase again that night. I dined alone in the vast dining room and was informed that the master had had to go out suddenly and would not be back until well after midnight. My pride would not allow me to ask where he had gone and I assumed in my anger that he was with Pamela Capethorn. It was only much later in the evening when I learned that he had driven into Dublin to see the two labourers who had almost lost their lives in the storm, and from there had gone on to Alan Harvey's house to discuss what should be done about the damaged cottage.

CHAPTER 39

The moment to confront Gervase came over breakfast the following morning. Normally he was out of the house long before I went down but this morning I was determined to speak to him. When I entered the room he raised his eyes maddeningly and as I helped myself from the side table he calmly went about opening his mail. As I took my seat he said without looking up, 'To what do I owe this honour? I hope you've not come to talk about the dog, the matter is closed.'

'I want a divorce, Gervase.'

He threw back his head and laughed while I stared at him astonished. I had not expected merriment on my announcement.

'I mean it, Gervase, I want a divorce, and as quickly as possible.'

'You know that's impossible.'

'Why is it impossible? Other people get divorced, even people in our exalted station.'

'We agreed to go our separate ways, we agreed to make a public show of our marriage if we maintained a private indifference, but divorce is something neither of us can think about. Who is it, some man you've met in London, one of those arty men you hang about with?'

'I don't hang about with anybody. I have met somebody. I love him and he loves me. We would like to marry. Gervase, why should you mind so much? You don't love me, there are times when you don't even like me. If you divorced me you'd be free to marry Pamela Capethorn. That's what you want, isn't it?'

Deliberately he went on opening his mail, then he laid it in a neat pile beside his plate before raising his eyes to meet mine.

'Lisanne, you're a fool. I have no wish to marry Pamela

Capethorn, or any other woman for that matter. I don't break contracts, business or marriage. I have a name for the utmost integrity in these matters and I intend to keep it. You are my wife and you will remain my wife. Divorce between you and me is quite impossible. There is too much at stake, too much I have no desire to lose simply because my wife thinks she's fallen in love with a man she's known for a few short weeks. Who is he, anyway?'

'I have no intention of telling you.'

'You mean he's somebody I would consider quite impossible.'

'No, I don't mean that at all. If I told you who he was it might conceivably shatter your complacency.'

'Then why not tell me. I like to be surprised.'

I sprang to my feet and ran from the room, and all the way across the hall his laughter followed me.

I felt utterly and completely helpless. He would never let me go, he didn't want me but he would keep me. Lance had wanted me but he had wanted the land more. Either way there was something inside both of them that would hold fast to what was theirs regardless of the feelings of others.

Anger filled me and agonized in me to the exclusion of everything else, and even Alan Harvey said, 'Is something wrong, Lisanne? You've not been like yourself since you returned from London. I know you were upset about Toby, but really Gervase had no alternative, the spaniel was caught in the act.'

'It isn't the dog, Alan. I loved Toby but I realize he had to be destroyed when he went about killing the lambs.'

'What is it then? You can confide in me.'

'But you're Gervase's friend.'

'Yours too I hope.'

'Alan, I want a divorce. Neither of us is happy in this marriage and I've met somebody else, somebody I love very dearly.'

'Divorce is impossible, Lisanne.'

'Why are you so sure, what has Gervase told you?'

'Nothing at all. I only know he's talked about the family

for as long as I can remember. He talked about it and railed about it. At times he despises himself for conforming, but he'll never let you go.'

I felt as helpless as I had when facing my father, facing Aunt Liza. It seemed to me that every desire of my life had been thwarted by other people I had been afraid of.

I couldn't sleep, I was nauseated by food and I began to lose weight so that my skirts slipped over my hips and I had to fasten them with safety pins. Gervase was amused. He commented sarcastically on my lacklustre appearance by saying, 'I wonder if your lover would find you as attractive as you were in London. You look decidedly seedy to me.'

'Don't you care that I'm unhappy?' I cried.

'I'm afraid I don't care, Lisanne. You entered this marriage with your eyes wide open, you knew the terms. Gracious me, girl, they've been spelt out for you just as they were spelt out for me all through our lives, and now you want to change them to suit yourself.'

'I can't live the rest of my life unloved and unwanted. Why can't you let me go? You're not happy in this marriage either.'

'I didn't expect to be happy, but neither did I expect to be moaned at night and morning by a wife who isn't prepared to honour her obligations.'

'Obligations that are monstrous and archaic.'

'I agree, but obligations nevertheless.'

It was no use, I could never win against Gervase's arrogant stand, and during one of the nights when I tossed and turned in my bed I made up my mind to tell him the truth. The idea came upon me so suddenly it left me shattered.

I would tell Gervase that I had deceived him, that I was not Lisanne de Bellefort but Ellen Adair who had survived the shipwreck and taken his cousin's place because I was alone in the world and destitute. A bold plan that had misfired terribly, and I could not visualize that Gervase would stay married to a woman who had cheated and wormed her way into his life.

The more I thought about it the more it became the only solution, but it carried with it a price. I thought about the contempt I would be subjected to from my friends: Alan and Maureen, Edna and George. And how Pamela Capethorn would gloat about the aristocratic wife who was nothing more than an adventuress.

And what about Mark? He would have to know, and would he regard me in a better light? I hardly thought so.

Yet the more I thought about the idea the more it became a necessity. It wasn't just Mark, it was my conscience. But how was I to tell Gervase, and when would be the best time?

He was seldom in for dinner, and he was too anxious to be out of the house at breakfast time. I would have to make an appointment to see him, incongruous thought it was.

I left a note beside his breakfast plate before I retired for the night, saying that I would like to see him in his study some time during the day. When I went down to breakfast there was a note beside my plate saying he would see me at noon in the study.

I couldn't settle to anything. I changed my skirt and blouse twice and made the best of my face. I had no interest in the flowers, and even the house over which I had spent such time and trouble failed to please me. I thought of it as a cage, a beautiful cage of my creation furnished with toys I had suddenly outgrown.

It was a relief to go outside where the wind swept through the park and soft Irish rain misted the horizon, obscuring the distant mountains which I had come to love.

Promptly at noon I went to Gervase's study. My heart was beating so painfully I felt sick and my knees were trembling. The door to the study was open and I could see the play of firelight on the furniture. Gervase was standing at the window looking out into the park.

He didn't turn as I entered but continued to stare through the window, and nervously I went to sit near his deak. In front of his chair I could see an opened envelope lying casually on the blotting pad and my heart skipped a beat when I recognized the familiar cream parchment bearing the de Bellefort crest.

It seemed like a small eternity before he turned. He

seemed bemused, almost unaware of my existence, then making an effort to gather his scattered wits he said, 'You wanted to talk to me, Lisanne?'

'Yes. Is something wrong?'

He stared at me morosely for a second before tossing over the letter.

I did not recognize the writing and before reading it I turned to the signature. It was signed, 'your loving cousin Geraldine'. He was watching me closely but offered no comment, so I turned the page over and started to read.

Lance de Bellefort was dead, killed in a hunting accident when his horse fell and rolled on top of him. Geraldine was a widow, her children fatherless, and we were asked to attend Lance's funeral at Langstone.

All thoughts of what I had been about to tell him fled. Now was not the moment for it, but my thoughts had certainly been unable to fully recognize the implications of Geraldine's letter.

'I suppose you realize what this means?' Gervase said stonily.

'Only that Lance is dead. It is tragic.'

'I agree, it is tragic. We never really liked each other, there never seemed the time or inclination, but I never wished him dead.'

'Well of course you didn't.'

'Not even when his death would give me all I ever wanted, Langstone and the title.'

I stared at him incredulously. Of course. With Lance's death Gervase would be Sir Gervase de Bellefort and I would be his lady. I would be the mistress of Langstone Priory. Even in that moment of agonizing stupor I remembered old Lady de Bellefort vividly, offering little Ellen Adair a home and a job. That I would ever take her place was a thing so remote neither of us could have envisaged it.

Gervase was saying, 'I shall have to get hold of Harvey as soon as he returns from Dublin. There's a great deal to be done on the estate, and heaven knows how long we shall be away. Can you be ready to travel first thing in the morning?'

'In the morning?' I echoed stupidly.

'Well of course, if we're to be there in time for Lance's funeral the following day. We should offer some support to Geraldine. We're her closest relatives.'

'Yes,' I murmured. 'I'll pack this afternoon. Will you arrange the air travel?'

'Of course. What was it you wanted to see me about, Lisanne? It must have been very important.'

'No, it wasn't really very important, it can wait.'

'Good. I've enough on my mind at the moment. How do you feel about being Lady de Bellefort?'

'I don't know, it hasn't registered yet.'

'I can almost see our grandmother sitting with the angels, shaking her head doubtfully. I shouldn't think she would be happy to see her precious Langstone and the title in the hands of her tearaway grandson and his pretty spoilt wife.'

'I don't see why childish labels should stick to us for the rest of your lives.'

'You don't?' Well, it's true that you're very pretty, Lisanne, even if at the moment you look like the very devil. And you're spoilt, forever falling out with your toys when they cease to amuse you.'

He was baiting me, standing before me with that maddening half smile on his face. Tossing my head, I turned away and walked out of the study, followed by a cynical chuckle.

Telling him the truth was as far away as ever. Now was not the time, not when Lance lay dead and his widow was devastated by grief for herself and her three little girls. Not when Gervase for all his bombast maintained a feeling of shame because he had wanted the things that were Lance's by birth. Now they belonged to Gervase, but not even he had wanted them quite this way.

My first shock was when Mary came to my room to say the master would be in for dinner, calling me Milady with round-eyed awe.

Facing Gervase at the dinner table, it seemed to me that with Lance's death had come a new maturity. He was thoughtful, and his eyes were no longer appraising me with taunting cynicism. He informed me quietly that we were to fly from Dublin the following morning and he had ordered a car to meet us at the airport. I must take enough luggage to last several days and he had informed Alan Harvey he would not be back for the Hunt Ball. When I raised my eyes at this piece of information, for the first time I saw the old amused glint come into his eyes and he said casually, 'You look surprised, Lisanne, but you must admit a family bereavement should take precedence over the delights of dancing with Pamela Capethorn and seeing my wife flirting with half the men in the county.'

I didn't speak and after a few moments the sombre mood returned and he appeared to be miles away, no doubt thinking of the ambitions which had never seemed possible until now.

I was thinking about Lance. Remembering how much I had loved him, remembering the passion that had flared between us in the library at Langstone, and my tears in the snow above the house. Our lives had been a mess, a tortuous meandering mess, and even now when I had thought to see some way out by the easing of my conscience something had happened to make it impossible.

CHAPTER 40

It was late afternoon the next day when we drove through the village of Langstone, and I was immediately shocked by the black drapes at the windows of the cottages which lined the main street. The flag flew at half mast above the old church and over the entire village was a dejected sombre air.

The cafe which had been Aunt Liza's shop was deserted, and here again black drapes hung at the windows and I remembered that they had been similarly draped for the funeral of Lance's father.

Gervase drove without speaking, his eyes trained on the road, and I allowed my thoughts to wander to those days I had served in the draper's shop with Alec Devlin's eyes trained on me from across the road.

We passed the village hall where he had taken me to my first dance, and the old crooked stile that Lance and I had climbed on our way to the Priory. The gates to the Priory were open and ahead of us stretched the long drive with the house in the distance.

I couldn't know Gervase's thoughts at that moment. In his childhood he had come here as a visitor, the son of a man his grandmother had disapproved of, an independent headstrong child who was aware of the resentment surrounding him, a strangely angry boy, jealous of an older cousin he deemed to have everything, even then. In the darkness of the car I stole a look at his dark handsome face. As if suddenly aware of my regard he looked at me and my heart began to hammer strangely and my thoughts were suddenly confused.

'Do you realize we're home, Lisanne?' he said quietly.

'Oh Gervase, is that all Lance's death means to you, that suddenly all this is yours?'

'Ours, Lisanne. All this is ours. Lance is dead. It is sad,

but his death was not my fault, and I never wished him dead. For the first time in my life I have what I've always wanted. I can feel sorry about Lance, but don't begrudge me this moment of joy for what we have.'

I should have felt some fear on returning to the Priory that I would be recognized as an impostor, but it had never occurred to me. I had come a long way from the girl who had come to alter Lisanne's dresses. I had become a woman of the world, beautiful and assured, and I was relying on my resemblance to Lisanne.

Geraldine showed no astonishment when I embraced her, and the servants who had been lined up in the hall to meet us merely bowed their heads in acknowledgement as we passed before them.

I saw no look of recognition on Cook's face, or the butler's. I was simply the new Lady de Bellefort wearing mourning for the loss of my cousin, and after the simple ceremony of greeting was over we passed into the drawing room.

Geraldine was pale and composed as she told us about the accident that had ended Lance's life.

'It is strange,' she said quietly, 'but I had a premonition that morning that something would go wrong. I didn't want Lance to turn out with the hunt, I begged him to refuse. His own horse had gone lame and was having treatment from the vet so he borrowed a horse from Major Acton over at Hawes. The horse was young, untried, and Lance had never ridden him before. The Major was confident he would be an excellent mount for Lance, but the horse was headstrong. I have been told that right from the very outset he was fighting Lance, who was having great difficulty in controlling him.'

'Are your children in the house?' I asked her thoughtfully.

'Only the eldest, Catherine. The two younger ones are with my mother and I agree with her that funerals are not for children. They are not coming up for Lance's funeral, it is a long way. But Catherine will be here.'

My occasion to meet Catherine came later over dinner. She was tall and slender, in time she would be pretty, but at the moment there were braces on her teeth and she resembled Geraldine far more than Lance.

Dinner was a silent meal. Occasionally I questioned Catherine on her schooling but she seemed remote and withdrawn, which I put down to the sudden loss of her father.

The servants at Langstone had always been well trained, now they ministered to us silently and deferentialy. Gervase sat at the head of the table wearing his dinner jacket and Geraldine and I wore black. Catherine's grey dress seemed far too old for her, and her pale little face seemed pinched and scared, while occasionally her eyes moved from one to the other of us. She picked at her food, and once I saw her eyes slide fearfully towards the library door.

Lance is in there, I thought to myself, lying alone in the library where once we had clung passionately in an ecstasy of love.

Later that evening we trooped in a solemn procession of family and servants to take our last look at him. It wasn't the Lance I had known, warm and vibrant with life, not this cold pale Lance with his dark hair greying and the harsh look of care which death had not eradicated from his face.

The women servants were dabbing their eyes as they moved around the coffin but Geraldine maintained a reserved calmness. At that moment I admired her, but later when I said as much to Gervase he merely answered, 'Neither of us know how much they cared for each other. If the caring doesn't go too deep it is easier to remain serene.'

'But he was her husband,' I cried angrily, 'the father of her children.'

'Of course. Have you forgotten, Lisanne, that you have just recently asked me for a divorce? How do we know what went on between Lance and his wife?'

'I don't suppose they were like us at all. Lance was kind, he would make their marriage work, I just know it.'

'You mean I am anything but kind, that I have never tried to make our marriage work?'

'I didn't say that, you're always so cynical and sarcastic.

You formed an opinion of Lisanne as a girl and never forgot it.'

'You mean you've changed?'

'I've grown up.'

He came and stood looking down into my face with a tantalizing half smile on his lips.

'Are you prepared to grow up a little more, I wonder? Are you prepared to play your part as my grandmother played hers? Are you prepared to forget the foolish notion that I shall let you go to marry this man you only think you're in love with?'

'I am in love with him,' I cried angrily.

'Shall I put you to the test, Lisanne, shall I make you see that he doesn't exist? He's a dream you've made up in your heart because you want more from me than I'm prepared to give.'

I backed away from him with flashing eyes. 'You're conceited, you're arrogant and impossible. He does exist, I do love him.'

He followed me and the look in his eyes was devilish, then suddenly his arms were round me and his mouth was bruising mine with the savagery of his kisses. I felt him lift me up bodily in his arms while all the time I struggled helplessly, then he threw me on the bed and my arms and legs were flaying underneath the weight of his body.

'Lie still, you little fool,' he hissed savagely. 'You're my wife, you have a duty which has been sorely neglected over the last few months.'

I could feel his hands tearing at the flimsy material of my nightgown and my struggles were becoming feebler. I was no match for his strength, no match for the relentless passion that consumed him, and he paid no heed to my cries of pain. Some devil within him was intent on making me suffer, extracting from me the full measure of our marriage contract, and then suddenly I came alive under his hands and I found my own passion answering his, every bit as wild, with all his eagerness until at last we lay sated and spent in the hours before the dawn.

They came from all over the county and further afield for Lance's funeral, and the villagers lined the lanes leading to the stone church on the hillside. Gervase walked with Geraldine and Catherine and I was glad that on this morning at least there need be little contact between us.

I was glad of the dark veil over my face. I had begun to recognize people in the crowded churchyard: Alec Devlin with his mother, several acquaintances of Aunt Liza, and some of the girls I had met at the village hall. Many of them clutched the hands of small children, but none of them could clearly see my face behind the veil. It was my guilty conscience that was making me afraid, there was never any danger that the figure of Lady de Bellefort would raise doubts in the eyes of the villagers.

I walked between two elderly men, Lance's solicitor and family friend, and an old man who Geraldine had said was the last relative from her grandmother's generation.

We stood at last before the huge stone mausoleum. The villagers stood back and now we were merely family and close friends, and under cover of my veil I stole a look at them. Lisanne would have recognized many of them but I felt strangely alone and detached in their company. Geraldine had shed no tears. She stood tall and slender like a statue carved out of marble, her face pale, and I was surprised to see that she had removed her veil so that everyone could see her face clearly. Beside her stood Catherine, clutching her mother's hand, her child's face achingly sad, and I felt such an overwhelming sense of pity for her I moved forward and took hold of her other hand.

It was over at last. People were milling round looking at the wreaths and Gervase was in earnest conversation with a group of people who had driven in that morning from York.

Sadly I turned away and began to walk back with some of the others towards the gates, it was then I felt my arm taken and a man's voice said gently, 'I'm sorry to meet you again on such a sad occasion, Lisanne.'

I looked up startled into Mark's sombre eyes.

'Mark, when did you arrive here?'

'Yesterday evening. I'm staying at the inn. As soon as I read about Lance's death I knew I had to come, we were friends a long time ago. And I wanted to see you. Perhaps that was foolish of me.'

'It's all so terrible, Mark. I can't even think straight. There are those three little girls without a father and Geraldine seems so distant and remote, she isn't helping her daughter at all.'

'Grief affects people in different ways, Lisanne. Your own life is going to be very different now. I expect you will come to live here at the Priory?'

'I don't know. It's all been so very sudden, we haven't discussed the future. Are you returning home today?'

'Tomorrow. My only sister is getting married on Thursday, I must be home for that occasion.'

'Of course. Oh Mark, I know so little about you. I don't know anything about your home or your family.'

'No. It was very unreal, our time together in London. We talked about all sorts of things but we never really talked about ourselves. Is there any chance that I might see you this evening, just for a few moments? I have something I very much want to give to you.'

'Oh Mark, I don't want anything from you. I shall remember how happy you made me, I don't want presents to remind me.'

'All the same, my dear, I think you will want this one. Can you possible meet me, just for a few minutes? I know it might be difficult on such a day but you can telephone me at the inn stating a place and a time.'

'I'll try, Mark.'

We could say nothing more. Gervase had left the other guests and was walking towards us. I watched as he held out his hand to Mark, saying, 'Good morning, Mark, it was good of you to come. You should have come up to the house.'

We left the two men talking together and after a few minutes Gervase joined us alone. I stood on one side holding Catherine's hand. I didn't want to talk to Gervase about

Mark, I was too afraid that I might betray feelings I wanted to keep to myself.

Luncheon was a banquet. Speeches were made, reminiscences were exchanged between friends who only met at weddings and funerals, and it was more than two before I could telephone Mark at the inn. I arranged to meet him at the stile beside the river in half an hour's time, so I promptly removed my funeral attire and donned a tweed skirt and jumper. Wearing a trenchcoat and with a silk scarf covering my hair I walked quickly along the corridor and down the back stairs.

I made my way through the kitchen and Cook looked at me, surprised, so that I felt I owed her some explanation.

'I need some fresh air, Cook, I don't want to interfere with the rest of the proceedings. I'm going for a quick walk in the park.'

'I knows just how you feels, Milady. It's a sad day for us all, but the funeral service was beautiful. And all them people, it just goes to show what a popular man the master was.'

'The meal was excellent, Cook. I think the servants should be congratulated, looking after all these people isn't easy. I feel sure Sir Gervase will be speaking to them later.'

She beamed her gratification and I let myself out of the side door and hurried along the drive. It was a fair walk across the park to the river but I was glad of the keen wind, and by the time I reached the path leading to the stile my cheeks were smarting in the wind and I felt warm and very alive. I had forgotten how beautiful it was with the willows dipping their feathery branches into the water.

Mark was waiting for me, holding a brown paper parcel in his hands. From its shape I knew immediately what it was.

'I can't take the painting, Mark,' I protested. 'I know how much you wanted it and I was too late. Please keep it for yourself.'

'I want you to have it, Lisanne. You knew the girl and I got the impression that at one time she was important to you. For me it was just a striking picture of an unknown woman. Please take it, I shall be bitterly disappointed if you don't.'

'Shall I ever see you again, Mark?'

'I don't know, Lisanne.'

For a few moments only he stood holding me close and I was filled with utter desolation, so acute that I could not have spoken, so agonizing that I could only smile at him tremulously before I tore myself from his arms and ran heedlessly back to the house. Tears filled my eyes and rolled down my cheeks and I saw the park and countryside through a blur.

People were leaving, cars stood in the driveway, and I hung back among the stout oaks that lined the drive, waiting until it was clear before I could enter the house and find the privacy of my room. Would they never go, I thought wildly, hadn't they talked enough over luncheon, hadn't they exhausted every topic, every memory? But still they lingered, and I was forced to wait helplessly out of sight, aware that Gervase would be furious with my absence.

He made his displeasure very evident that evening as we waited for Geraldine in the drawing room before dinner.

'Our guests travelled from the other end of the county and my wife couldn't even find time to be polite and wish them good afternoon,' he said coldly.

'I'm sorry, Gervase, I felt sick and I had a headache, I had to get some fresh air before I fainted after that huge lunch. I didn't think they would be going so soon.'

'Well you can be sure your absence will be talked about. We shall be living in this part of the world and will probably need all the friends we can get. It was stupid to antagonize them before we even had the opportunity to get to know them.'

'I've said I'm sorry, Gervase, I can do no more. You were here and so was Geraldine. It was after all *her* husband's funeral.'

'I'd hope you'd behave better after mine.'

'Now you're being silly.'

'Where did you go in your search for fresh air?'

'As far as the river and back.'

He was watching me narrowly and I forced myself to meet his gaze unflinchingly. All the same I was glad when Geraldine arrived.

That night we talked about her future and marvelled at the provision Lance had made for his family in the event of his death.

Geraldine and her children were to move into a small manor house Lance had bought near Harrogate. She had never liked his father's large property, and we learned that Lance had sold this only recently and it was now an agricultural college.

'What will you do with Glenmoor?' she asked curiously. 'Perhaps you would prefer to live there than here.'

'I haven't decided,' Gervase told her. 'Lisanne's spent a fortune on the house and I have friends in Ireland. I enjoy the hunting and the fishing, so perhaps I won't do anything about it for the time being.'

'Oh well,' she said evenly, 'you have one son who in time will inherit this place, if you have another he could be given Glenmoor just as your own father was. You're a wealthy couple, you could afford to keep on both houses and in time you might be glad you'd done so.'

When Gervase didn't speak she turned to me, saying, 'Have you no thoughts about Glenmoor, Lisanne?'

'No. It's true the house is beautiful now, but Gervase has always loved this house. I'm wondering just how much time we shall spend at Glenmoor.'

I listened to their voices making polite conversation about Geraldine's future. Catherine had pleaded a headache and had not come down to dinner, and I wished fervently that Geraldine would talk about Lance. It seemed incredible to me that in all this talk about her future not once had she showed any hint of real sorrow for the loss of Lance, only a commendable dignity and a remoteness that had created barriers through which there was no entry.

Gervase too was finding the conversation heavy going, and to change the subject he said, 'It was good of Mark Allenby to come to the funeral. I saw you talking to him,

Lisanne. No doubt you met him many times when you were here living with our grandmother.'

'I probably did meet him, one met so many people. I was supposed to know most of the people who came to the funeral.'

'He was friendly with Lance, he told me he remembered you.'

'Really. Did you ever meet him, Geraldine?'

'Of course, he came to our wedding, actually he was one of the groomsmen. I don't believe he ever married.'

The conversation went on about Mark and I learned more from them than he had ever told me himself. They talked about the house in Leicestershire which he called home; his father who had been a general in the Blues and his mother who was the youngest daughter of a Marquis; his career in the diplomatic service – until in the end I felt I would scream if they didn't change the subject.

I only knew I could never tell either Mark or Gervase that I was not Lisanne. I did not have the courage to face either of them and see the contempt in their eyes. Neither could love an impostor such as I, it was clear my secret would have to go with me to the grave.

How I wished I could find an excuse not to sit with them in the drawing room where Geraldine worked on her tapestry and Gervase sat immersed in the field magazines that were prominent on every table.

Promptly at eleven o'clock I rose to me feet, feigning tiredness, and Geraldine said quickly, 'Yes, of course, Lisanne, it has been a long wearisome day. I think I shall go to bed too. You don't mind, Gervase?'

'Not at all. Goodnight, ladies.'

As we walked up the shallow curved staircase together Geraldine said, 'You know this house as well as I, probably better, but there are things you should know about the position you will now occupy. Perhaps you'll come to my room in the morning and we can discuss them.'

'Yes of course, after breakfast do you mean?'

'Mid morning I think. I gave you and Gervase the Normandy Room but when I've gone you will no doubt wish to move into the room at the front of the house. Traditionally they have always been occupied by the head of the family.'

'This is all quite dreadful for you, Geraldine, I wish I could do more to help.'

'Everything that needed to be done has been done. The children and I all like the house we are moving into, we shall soon settle down.'

'I hope you'll visit us often and that we shall be friends. After all, it isn't very far away.'

'That's true, but once I leave the Priory I doubt if I shall be anxious to return. There are a lot of memories connected with this house, some of them happy, many of them sad. It was never really my house when Grandmother was alive, and since she died somehow or other I feel she's still here. Oh I'm being fanciful, I know, but she was a very dominant person. We never really had much in common.'

'I see.'

'You spent a lot of time here when your mother was abroad. Were you happy here?'

'I think so, but with Grandmother it wasn't always easy.'

'I'll say goodnight then, Lisanne. You'll come to my room about ten thirty?'

'Yes. Goodnight, Geraldine.'

I was glad that a fire had been lit in the bedroom and for the first time I looked around me with interest. Geraldine had called it the Normandy Room and now I recognized the French air, from the murals on the walls to the patterned damask at the windows. It had the feeling of a chateau with its high domed ceiling and wrought-iron balcony which overlooked the lily pond and formal gardens. If the de Belleforts had arrived in England with the Normans, they had brought much of Normandy with them as well as their name.

Before I climbed into the huge bed I took Kitty's picture out of the wardrobe and unwrapped it quickly. Her startling green eyes looked out at me, tantalizing and assured, and I could see again the cigarette smoke curling upwards in the dimmed nightclub, hear her voice, strong and low pitched, singing the haunting songs of France.

Suddenly I felt the picture being taken out of my hands and Gervase was beside me staring down at it. He had come into the room so softly I hadn't heard him, now I trembled unhappily as I waited for the questions which I was sure would come.

'Where did you find this?' he asked sharply.

'I found it in London. I went to an exhibition of the artist's work, and thought this was his best.'

'The house is filled with all sorts of valuable paintings and you have to buy this work by an unknown artist?'

'The artists who painted the pictures that fill this house were all unknown at one stage, most of them only became famous after their deaths. At least we are beginning to recognize contemporary artists during their lifetime. Don't you like the picture?'

'I suppose it has something. It's bold, the colours are good and the woman has a sort of earthy appeal. God knows where you're going to hang it.'

'I'll find somewhere.'

'I should put it in your sitting room, that's where Grandmother put most of the things she didn't want in the rest of the house.'

I remembered the sitting room where I had received my instructions on the rest of my life, now he was talking about it as being mine. I stared after him as he crossed the room to go into the dressing room and after a few minutes he came out carrying a briefcase.

'I have letters to write,' he said. 'I shall be returning to Ireland at the end of the week. You need not come with me, in fact I prefer you to remain here to familiarize yourself with your new role.'

'When will you be coming back?' I said sharply. 'Or are you intending to reside permanently at Glenmoor, appearing here at brief intervals?'

He came to stand beside me, looking down from his superior height with lofty amusement so that I bitterly regretted having removed my shoes with their high heels.

'You would like that, wouldn't you, Lisanne? For me to live at Glenmoor and you to be free to have your lover here.

Well, it isn't to be. I shall be visiting Ireland less and less. Harvey will see to the house and the estate, and from time to time I shall expect you to visit Glenmoor with me simply to see that the place is being cared for – our second son will have no cause for complaint when the time comes for him to inherit.'

'Our second son!' I gasped.

'Yes, of course. You needn't look so scandalized. I have forgiven your indiscretions, divorce is quite out of the question and I rather think we can both look forward to, if not a happy marriage, certainly one which will not lack for passionate involvement.'

I stared after him with burning cheeks, trembling with anger at his devilish amusement, his high-handed dismissal. I lay against the pillows still smarting with resentment, then I saw Kitty's portrait propped up against the chair where I had left it and she seemed to be smiling at me with quiet amusement. In some exasperation I sprang out of bed and after wrapping the picture in its brown paper I thrust it impatiently to the back of the wardrobe.

CHAPTER 41

I went to Geraldine's room promptly at ten thirty the following morning after breakfasting alone. Gervase presumably slept in his dressing room and he had gone out with the estate agent. This, I thought angrily, was going to be the pattern of married life, but it was probably all I deserved.

Geraldine was emptying her wardrobe, piling clothes on to the bed, and she looked up with a smile when I entered.

'I always hated packing,' she said irritably. 'I hated packing for school holidays and I hate it now. This seems to be the sum total of my life here, ball gowns and cocktail gowns, garden party dresses and dresses for Ascot and other race meetings. You'll find out, Lisanne. I hope you've got an extensive wardrobe.'

'Not like that I haven't.'

'Well, you will have. Lance liked to entertain. He filled the house with guests for the racing at York and Ripon, then there was the start of the shooting season and the musical season in Harrogate. It seemed we always had a houseful of people, that we were hardly ever alone as a family. Granny and Lance revelled in it.'

'Were you and Lance very happy, Geraldine?'

'If you mean were we ever in love the answer is no. I could have loved him once. He was a nice man, a good kind man. But he never loved me and I received no incentive to love him.'

'Oh Geraldine, I'm sure you're wrong. He was very anxious about you when your first baby was born, I know. I was in hospital in Plymouth and he wrote to say how worried he was about you.'

'He liked me. He had regard for me, I was his wife, his cousin, and I was a de Bellefort. He didn't make any effort to visit you in the hospital Lisanne. He sent you letters and flowers, but if you'd been Ellen Adair he'd have made the effort to see you in person.'

I gasped with amazement. 'Why do you say that?' I cried.

'I saw his face when he heard the news about the wreck. He was sorry for you, for the loss of your mother, but the loss of Ellen twisted his heart.'

'Oh, but you're wrong, you have to be.'

'I knew that first night, when Grandmother told me it was I who would marry Lance, that it was Ellen he was in love with. I couldn't sleep that night, I was far too excited. I hadn't met him since we were children and there he was, that tall handsome nice man I was soon to marry. I was half in love with him already. I went down to the library to look for a magazine or something, the door was ajar and through it I saw Lance with his arms round that girl. I stood watching while he picked her up and carried her over to the settee in front of the fire, then I took to my heels and ran for dear life up the stairs and back to my room.

'I never forgot that scene in the library, Lisanne, not even when I was his wife and he made love to me. I wished I was Ellen Adair and he loved me as he had loved her. Then when I heard she had lost her life in that shipwreck I was glad, until I saw his face and realized that though she was dead it was too late for him to love me.'

'Geraldine, I'm sorry. It was a pity you saw them in the library, but don't you think if he'd have loved her enough he'd have married her and not you? He watched her walk out of his life. Does a man do that if he truly loves a woman?'

'He does if he's a de Bellefort. Both my parents did it, my grandfather did it – leaving that girl to change my life.'

I stayed silent, hating myself miserably for having hurt Geraldine so deeply, but she was staring at me across the room. 'I thought on that first evening I met her how alike you were, now I'm not so sure.'

'What do you mean?'

'I don't really know. I haven't seen you for years, now I'm not even sure which one I remember, you or Ellen. I suppose she was a de Belleforts too.'

'Do you want any help with that packing?'

'No, Catherine will help me later. I should be telling you how you will be expected to spend your day. In the morning I see the housekeeper about the meals for the day, and we make arrangements if there are to be guests in the house.

'I sit on the committees of various charities. There's also the Musical Circle, the drama school over at Harrogate, and I'm constantly being called upon to judge flower shows, dog shows and craft exhibitions. I'm on the bench, and I know it's the Magistrate's Clerk's intention to nominate you – that can be very tying, with probation work and visits to prisons. Then there's work on the hospital board. You'll find yourself leading a very full life, Lisanne.'

'It sounds like it. What will they expect from Gervase? He's not at all like Lance, you know.'

'I've realized that, but though he's more remote he'll play his part – he's wanted this role most of his life. Grandmother said there was always resentment between the two boys.'

'Yes, I'm afraid that's true. How did you get on with Lady de Bellefort?'

'With Grandmother? Reasonably well. I was always aware that she was in charge, Lance deferred to her and so did I. In the early days of our marriage I couldn't forget Ellen Adair, and I blamed my grandmother for bringing her into the house. She was well aware of the resentment I felt towards her. I couldn't think what devious whim had made her do it, and once I asked her.'

'What did she say?' I murmured.

'Only that she had liked the girl and felt she owed her something. I never found Grandmother easy to talk to, she was always a little like my headmistress.'

'Perhaps we should go down to the study, that is where I interview the housekeeper and listen to any complaints.'

'Do you still use Grandmother's sitting room?'

'That is now your sitting room. I haven't disturbed anything, it's all exactly as she wanted it. I haven't even looked in her desk or in the bookcase. Perhaps you will do that?'

'I shall feel as if I'm prying into things which don't concern me.'

'That's what I thought, but someday someone must do it. She kept her diary every day until she couldn't see. I couldn't bring myself to look at it – I didn't want to read about Ellen, I only wanted to forget about her.'

In the study she showed me the account books and the engagement book. I sat beside her while she interviewed the housekeeper about the evening meal and after that we went into the small sitting room.

It was exactly as I remembered it, the beautiful Chinese carpet, the delicate pastel colours, the beauty of the watercolours and porcelain Lady de Bellefort had loved. From the windows I could look at the most beautiful view of all, the swans sailing majestically across the mere and the distant hazy fells.

The top of the small period walnut desk was tidy apart from the thick leather-bound diary bearing the de Bellefort crest in gold letters. Beside it lay a finely wrought gold pen tray and a long gold letter opener in the form of a goose feather.

'You can see, Lisanne, it is all exactly as she left it. I never sit at the desk, although sometimes I come in here to sew. I sit where I can see the swans and the mere, but I never feel that I am alone here: I can see her there at the desk, writing in that eternal diary every small thing that came to disturb her day.'

'I wonder if I shall ever feel comfortable sitting here?' I mused. In my heart I did not think I would. I would feel the old lady's eyes boring into my back, filled with accusation, willing me to tell the truth, daring me to be honest, telling me I had no right to be there.

Geraldine was saying, 'The butler visits the shops in the village for groceries, we like to patronize the local people. We get most of our bread and confectionary from the baker's shop in the village, except when there are house guests, then we get some of it from the caterers in Harrogate.

'There's quite a good draper's shop in the village now.

Apparently there used to be one years ago but that's now a cafe run by the Devlins. The new draper's shop is across the road, next to the baker's. If you want wool or embroidery silk she will get them for you.'

'Did you say it was a new shop?'

'Yes. Two elderly sisters have opened up there. The old draper's shop was very much missed, and they tell me this one is a small gold mine.'

'Is the cafe popular?'

'Popular enough. They go there for coffee and scandal, village gossip and any local news they can pick up. Mrs Devlin runs that with the help of her daughter-in-law.'

'I see.'

'I expect you remember the village quite well.'

'Is the doctor still at the same place?'

'Well, we have a new young man now. The old doctor retired just after the war. He said he'd had enough, and he and his wife are now living near the coast at Whitby. We've missed him, although Doctor Law is very capable and dependable.'

I would have liked to see Doctor Jarvis, but perhaps it was just as well he had moved away. I remembered his astuteness – he was probably the one person in the village who would have recognized me.

'Some of our stuff will need to be sent on, Lisanne,' Geraldine said. 'Catherine and I will leave around three o'clock, taking our personal luggage. You'll see to the rest for me, I hope.'

'Yes, of course.'

'It's mostly momentoes. Pieces of china, pictures, presents Lance gave me throughout our married life, and things the children want to keep. I think we should now take a look in the safe, you will no doubt want to see your jewellery.'

'*My* jewellery!'

'Well, yes. You will have your own personal jewellery just as I have, but these are de Bellefort pieces which are handed down from one generation to the next. The safe is in the library.'

I had not been into the library since the night we trooped

round Lance's coffin. This morning however a fire burned in the grate and my heart ached for that other night when I had found myself swept into his arms, the night Geraldine had watched from the door with bitter resentment in her heart.

I watched her open the safe and take out jewel case after jewel case which she placed on the table below the safe. Then she opened the cases, handing each one to me in turn.

I stared at them wide-eyed while the jewels flashed and dazzled against sombre velvet. Necklaces in diamonds and rubies, sapphires and emeralds, rings and bracelets, tiaras in diamonds and pearls. Geraldine was saying quietly, 'Gervase will no doubt give you jewels over the years just as Lance gave them to me, and they will be your own. But one day all this will belong to your son's wife.'

'But you have children too, Geraldine,' I cried unhappily.

'They are girl children. The de Bellefort jewels are for the wives of the heirs to the title. Lance was generous with our daughters, he laid money aside for their education, their wellbeing and for the good things of life he thought they were entitled to. These are for you, Lisanne. You need not look so unhappy about them. I've worn them all at some occasion or other, but never expected to keep them. Wear them and enjoy wearing them.'

She left them for me to replace in the safe, then with a small smile she said, 'I think I should see if Catherine's finished the rest of her packing and done something with mine. We'll meet at lunch, Lisanne.'

After she had left me I couldn't help thinking how remote she seemed. She had shown hardly any curiosity about my life at all, and even the invitation to visit her now seemed to have been given reluctantly and with the express adjuration to telephone first to see if it was convenient.

I doubted very much if Geraldine and I would ever be close friends, although no doubt we would maintain a family front for the rest of the world.

I accompanied them to their car after lunch while the servants lined up on the drive to say their farewells. I saw that one or two of them cried a little, and Geraldine was gracious. It was little Catherine who brought tears to their eyes as she followed her mother, clutching a small kitten in her arms, and as she entered the car she looked back towards the house, her small tight-lipped face pale and strangely old.

'If you need to know anything about the house you can telephone me,' Geraldine said calmly. 'Just as soon as we've got the house to rights I intend to spend a little time with Mother, she'll be glad of the company.'

'Yes, of course. I've been wondering why she didn't stay on here with you for a while.'

'She's living in Bournemouth. She has a ghastly new flat with modern furniture. Grandmother would have gone mad if she'd known about her selling the old place just as it was to some Americans she met in London and invited down for the weekend.'

'And yet you're wanting to spend some time in her modern flat?'

'Mother will be good for me, she's always loved life, had lots of friends, and it will be a life totally different from any I've known married to Lance and living with Grandmother.'

'Do let us know when you arrive back home, I'll be very happy to have you visit, Geraldine.'

She smiled politely. Then tapping the glass which separated them from the chauffeur she sat back in her seat and the long black car moved slowly down the drive and out of the gates. I watched until it had disappeared, in spite of the chill wind that ruffled my hair and brought the warm colour to my cheeks, then I turned and followed the servants into the house.

As the butler closed the door behind me he shook his head sadly. 'I can't think Lady Geraldine'll be paying many visits to the Priory, Milady,' he said gently. 'I never thought she was over-fond of the place.'

'No, perhaps not.'

'But the master was. The Priory was his life. He loved every stick and stone of the house, every blade of grass in the park there, every ripple on the mere. Will Sir Gervase love it like that, Milady, do you think?'

I stared at him, remembering the old man's amusement at the young Ellen Adair poring over the books in the library, his pride in the house, his joy that she was finding its history compelling, and gently I said, 'I'm sure Sir Gervase will love it just as I do. I'm not sure what changes he will make because no two people think alike or act alike, but whatever my husband does will be for the best, the best for the Priory I feel sure.'

'Of course, Milady. His father before him loved this place. I don't expect the master ever thought this place'd be his in a million years, and when you were a young girl stayin' here with your grandmother, you never thought so either, did you, Milady?'

'No, Carstairs, never in a million years did I ever think that one day I would be Lady de Bellefort.'

Gervase left the house at mid morning the next day and I was alone to eat my solitary meals in the dining room, staring down the long expanse of polished mahogany while soft-footed servants ministered to my needs.

'I think perhaps I'll eat in the morning room until Sir Gervase returns,' I said to the butler, whereupon he raised his eyes disapprovingly, saying, 'Her ladyship always ate in the dining room, Milady, whether she was alone or not.'

'When you say her ladyship I take it you are referring to my grandmother?' I said stonily.

'Well yes, Milady. Why I remember when you stayed here with her when you were quite small, you at one end of the dining table and her ladyship at the other, a great stickler for tradition she was.'

'Very well, Carstairs, I will continue to eat in the dining room. There are times when I think my grandmother is dictating policy from beyond the grave.'

He chuckled. 'She'd have liked that, Milady, she'd have liked that very much.'

The conversation decided me that I must take my courage in both hands and face her uneasy ghost in the comfort of her sitting room. It was a morning when rain lashed against the windows and the swans sat huddled on the banks on the mere.

I was glad of the glowing fire in the grate. A bowl of white and yellow dahlias had been placed on a table near the window and apart from those the room stared back at me impersonally, too tidy, too lonely. I was trying to remember how she had looked that last morning I had seen her sitting at her desk, erect and slender, her silver hair beautifully dressed, her rows of lustrous pearls shining against the black velvet of her gown, her knuckles white as her long slender hand rested on her ivory-topped cane.

In my imagination I could smell her perfume – floral, light and expensive – and instinctively I reached out my hand and opened the top drawer in her desk.

It was scrupulously tidy, the only thing in it being a handkerchief satchel which I opened to find a pile of beautifully embroidered linen handkerchieves, together with several in silk. The smell of perfume became stronger and I picked one of them up and held it against my face. For a few moments I felt faintly dizzy and I had to sit down because my legs were trembling.

The other two drawers held stationery, pale parchment envelopes and writing paper, all embossed with the de Bellefort crest, and there was a selection of pens and inks. Feeling like an interloper I closed the drawers and pulled my chair up close to the desk.

My fingers were trembling as I lifted the catch on the large diary resting on top of the blotter, then I started to read.

Every page was dated and numbered, and at the beginning her words meant nothing to me. Every day she had made a chronicle of what she had done from rising until she went to her bed, but in those early years I only recognized a few names. Letters she had received from her grandchildren from their various schools, visits from relatives and friends, tenants and dignitaries. Visits she had paid to local functions and others further afield. It was the diary of a busy woman who had taken pride in her position in the community, and impatiently I turned the pages until I found what I was looking for, then my heart skipped a beat as I read: 'Today I saw the girl in the draper's shop in the village and it is true her likeness to Lisanne is uncanny. I bought embroidery from her and learned she is Miss Ashington's niece who has come to live with her. I hope to speak with the girl again when her aunt is not in evidence.'

I turned the pages more slowly now, but for whole days there was no more mention of the girl in the draper's shop.

Then I read: 'I have discovered that the girl at the draper's shop is called Ellen Adair. The name means nothing to me but I am haunted by her face. She has been up to the Priory to sew for Lisanne, and I watched them walking in the garden together, so alike they could easily have been sisters. It cannot be coincidence, and I have to know. One of these days I must find an excuse to talk to the girl and find out something of her background.'

Then came a whole page: 'Miss Ashington has died very suddenly and the girl is alone in the shop in the village. I intend to send for her, I do not know what is to become of her and I cannot allow her to leave the village without satisfying my curiosity.'

It would appear that on that day nothing occupied her mind beyond the desire to talk to me. Then two days later: 'I have spoken to Ellen and have learned that her grandmother was Sarah Saxton. When she was sent away from the Priory I did not know that she was expecting William's child, now the pattern has fallen into place. Poor Ellen has not had a happy life. She ran away from home because she hated and was terrified of her father, her grandmother is dead and her mother sounds like a poor frightened creature, completely dominated by her husband. I liked the girl. She is like Lisanne but without her assured independence. This is understandable when one considers the sort of life she has led. She has clear blue eyes which meet one's own without guile, straight and honest, and she has great courage. She has needed plenty of that, and there has been precious little happiness living with her aunt in the village.

'The shop is to be sold and she has no employment to go to. Speaking to Ellen I constantly told myself: 'This is

William's granddaughter, she might have been yours and she is alone in the world and without means.' It seems to me that I owe Sarah Saxton something, I have thought about her so seldom across the years but now I feel I must make some retribution. Fate has brought this girl into the village, and I believe the time has come for me to make amends.

'I have offered Ellen Adair a home and employment as companion to Lisanne. I could not bring myself to ask her to act as lady's maid, they do after all share the same grandfather and it could be that Ellen will bring a stability into Lisanne's life which she sorely lacks. I pray to God that I have done the right thing.'

For some time in the diary Ellen was mentioned only in passing, to say that it would seem things were working out reasonably well. Then once more I came across several pages closely written, pages which made me relive painful memories.

'I have invited the family here. I have not seen Geraldine for some time but already I have decided that she should marry Lance. She is pretty, intelligent and amenable, she will make a fitting wife for him although I am aware that he is fond of Lisanne. Lisanne is too flighty, too much like her mother but without her mother's character, and she will be better with Gervase. They are two of a kind, they will spend their money like water, live their own lives and hopefully in time accept what they cannot change.

'I should have made an effort with Gervase but he refused to meet me halfway and I am after all his grandmother. I saw him as a handsome wilful and remote boy who showed quite plainly that he didn't like me or the things I stood for, and in all that long summer when he tramped alone across the fells I came no nearer to understanding him, his resentment was too strong.'

Again I turned the pages before I sat back stunned.

'Lance is in love with Ellen and she with him. I have watched them at the dining table, walking in the park, dancing together. I have seen the way he looks at her, the anguish in their eyes, and I am troubled by it. I would never have taken Ellen into the house if I had thought this would happen. It is too cruel: now he will go unhappy to his marriage with Geraldine, and Ellen will stand between them like a dark shadow.

'I shall pray that Lance will forget her just as William was asked to forget her grandmother, and I am glad that Delia is taking Lisanne to Europe. For the first time in my life I am grateful for the restlessness that has always spurred Delia on from one place to the next.'

After that there were whole pages filled with her disquiet about the war news and a brief paragraph saying: 'Delia and the two girls are in Antibes. It was foolish to go to the south of France instead of returning to England, but no doubt after that dreadful scandal in Paris they had to get away quickly. How could Delia let such a thing happen? Now I dare not think what will happen to them when war comes, for I think war must be inevitable.

'I wish I understood Geraldine more. She is always so polite, so restrained, and I fear she is destined to produce daughters. I dare not ask myself if she and Lance are happy, they play their part but there are times when I long for the old Lance who made me laugh. He has grown so sedate and correct.

'I have been thinking a lot recently about Ellen and wishing she had been my granddaughter and not Sarah Saxton's. How much happier Lance would have been married to Ellen, perhaps she was the best de Bellefort of them all. It seems that all my life I have schemed and plotted in an effort to do my duty as I saw it, and now that I am old and very tired I have come to realize that fate does not always place the right people in the right places.'

After that there were dozens of blank pages and then some brief notes in handwriting that wavered and scrawled across the page, and I was unable to read any of it. I imagined that already her sight and her interest in life were fading.

Sadly I closed the diary and sat for a few moments with it in my hands while I stared unseeing through the rain-splashed windows. I felt no anger or hatred in that gentle firelit room, no burden of resentment against the role I had usurped, only an atmosphere of peace as ethereal as the haunting perfume that still lingered.

A new and powerful resolution was born in me in that room. There was no going back, I could only go forward, and I knew I could not live my life as Gervase's wife in an atmosphere of indifference and destructive separateness.

I knew now that what I had felt for Mark was not love. He had been a charming interlude, someone who had shown me love and gentleness, tenderness and understanding, all the values denied to me in my lonely childhood and the years that came after. It was the sort of love I wanted from Gervase. I could not live in an atmosphere of resentment interspersed by rare nights of passionate abandonment which somehow left us further apart than ever.

I understood him. I understood his bitterness and jealousy. That remote moody boy had grown into a man writhing with resentment that he was destined to be second best, even to the wife who had not been thought suitable for Lance to marry, pretty frivolous flighty Lisanne who he believed was hating him for the very same reasons he was hating her.

I ached to tell him the truth but it was impossible. He would hate Ellen Adair far more fervently, for deceiving him, for not being Lisanne.

We had to talk. I had to make him see that I was not his enemy. I needed to be his wife, the mother of his children, and if I couldn't make him see that, there was no future for either of us.

It was several days later when I heard a car approaching the house and I ran to the window to see who my visitor was. It was Gervase's long black tourer, and with my heart thumping I watched while he climbed out and stood for a while looking back along the drive.

I knew what he was thinking, what Lance had thought years before when we had stood together in the snow: Mine, all mine, the park and the trees, the mere and the fells as far as the eye could see. The farms nestling on the hillside, the stone villages and tiny hamlets with their ancient churches and comfortable inns, surrounded by rolling hills and stark crags, all of them reaching far back into a history created in days when armoured knights fought each other for tracts of land where they could build their castles and great houses. There they had lorded it over other men and made stern laws to ensure that they could hold what they had, until those laws became as much a part of this land as the falcons sailing majestically on the north wind.

With a strange kind of urgency I left the room and ran out into the hall. I flung open the stout oak door and stood for a moment looking down on to the terrace where Gervase was still contemplating his domain, and trembling with nervousness I waited for him to turn his head. In that first moment I was aware of the reserve that clouded his eyes, the remoteness I had come to dread which came over his face like a shutter excluding the light, then with a little cry I ran down the steps and throwing my arms round him I cried, 'Oh Gervase, you're home, I'm so glad you're home.

For a moment he held me away from him, staring silent and brooding into my eyes until once again I felt afraid and uncertain, then suddenly he gathered me close with a new and desperate longing, a tenderness I had never known from him, and a new and sudden joy flooded my being.

As we walked into the house he said dryly, 'You take my breath away, Lisanne, I hadn't expected such a greeting. Have you been very bored?'

'Gervase, we have to talk,' I replied urgently.

'About what? Has something momentous happened while I've been away?'

'I realized how much I was missing you.'

'Despite the fact that you have recently asked me for a divorce.'

'Can't we talk just once without your cynicism clouding everything?'

'We can try. But not now Lisanne, I have things to do. Tonight perhaps, after dinner.'

'Why can't we talk now, what is more important than our marriage?'

He raised his eyebrows in that maddening surprise that made me want to hit out at him, instead my eyes filled with tears and apologetically he said, 'I really do have things to do right now, Lisanne. We'll talk later.'

Miserably I was about to turn away when he caught hold of my hand. 'My poor Lisanne,' he said gently. 'When you were a little girl you only had to ask for something and it was there immediately, even now you can't understand that it isn't always possible to have everything your way.'

Bewildered I cried, 'Will you always hate me, Gervase?'

'My dear girl, I don't hate you.'

'You don't love me either.'

Cynically he said, 'Is that what you want, Lisanne, all this and love too? We would indeed be fortunate.'

With a brief smile he left me standing in the hall staring after him while he ran lightly up the stairs.

How could I ever have thought that it would be easy, how could I ever have expected him to overcome the resentment of years? I heard him go out while I stood at a window staring out towards the mere. The late afternoon sunlight gilded the beeches and already the leaves were turning. Soon now the chill autumn winds would sweep from the North Sea across the fells and the wild geese would be flying inland – a prospect as chill and unwelcome as the next encounter I was expecting with my husband.

Dinner was a silent meal. Gervase seemed preoccupied with his own thoughts while I was rehearsing how I could begin as soon as the meal was over.

For what seemed like hours I sat in the drawing room alone while he talked on the telephone from the library. He came at last, apologizing for his tardiness, helping himself to sherry and placing a glass on the table by my chair.

He stood near the fireplace staring down into the flames and I thought how handsome he was with his raven hair shining blue under the lamplight, his dark perfect profile haughty and brooding before he looked up suddenly and I was achingly aware of his steely blue eyes looking coolly into mine.

'You wanted to talk, Lisanne,' he said evenly. 'I take it

you are no longer interested in a divorce, there is a new game you wish to play, and a new role you are anxious to adopt. The perfect Lady de Bellefort, dutiful wife, perfect hostess, caring mother, isn't that so?'

'I don't want to be less than your grandmother, less than Geraldine. I want people to see that we're worthy of this house and all that goes with it. I wouldn't be able to bear it if people looked on us as interlopers because we merely covered our hopeless marriage with a façade of respectability.'

'You think people might be prepared to see us as a devoted family?'

'Yes, if we try, for our son's sake. We owe it to him.'

'I understood the old Lisanne better than the Lisanne you are trying to show me now.'

'I don't know what you mean.'

'The old Lisanne was greedy for life. I saw myself in her, grasping and selfish and not a little ruthless. Leopards don't change their spots, Lisanne, although I must admit there are times when you puzzle me, when I think that perhaps life has moulded you into a person I could love. Then I start remembering things I would prefer to forget.'

'What sort of things?'

'That our respected grandmother thought we were two of a kind, that we deserved each other. You hadn't changed when you went to Paris, your escapades there made headlines, my dear.'

'You knew about Henri?'

'Like I said, it made headlines. Society beauty in shooting scandal. None of the hoary details were left out of the gossip columns.'

'There were no hoary details. All I was guilty of was foolishness.'

'Of course it reassured our respected grandmother that she had been wise in selecting Geraldine to marry Lance, while you and I were considered worthy of one another. I was never her favourite and now you too had forfeited any right to that honour.'

'And you're not prepared to see that I've changed, that

I've grown up. I don't want to be the old Lisanne who thought only of pleasure, who hurt people without thinking and wanted everything regardless of the cost. I want to be a good wife and mother, I want us to be respected. Can't you see I'm not blaming you for the way you grew up, why must you blame me?'

'Lisanne, I can't be bullied into loving you.'

'Does that mean that you can't love me, that for the rest of our married life you are going to make me aware that ours will always be a marriage of convenience?'

He didn't answer me. Instead his gaze reverted to the flames and I could feel the hot stinging tears filling my eyes before I scrambled to my feet and walked swiftly across the room and out through the door.

I needed to escape from the house whose walls seemed to be closing in on me. Snatching a scarf and coat from the cloakroom I flung open the front door and pulled it fast behind me, then I started to walk. I had no idea what time it was or where my footsteps would lead me but I walked quickly with my head bent against the wind, my hands thrust into the deep pockets of my tweed coat while the force of the wind brought the tears back into my eyes.

I came at last to the boathouse and sat forlornly on the wall near the slipway where once I had sat with Lance while I came to terms with the rest of my life, a life without him. Now once again there were decisions to be made, decisions that were far harder than those I had been asked to make before.

I had been a fool to ever think that I could live the rest of my life as Lisanne de Bellefort without robing myself in her personality. Lisanne would have met Gervase on his own ground. His moodiness and remoteness would not have disturbed for one moment the equilibrium of her life because she wouldn't have cared. I on the other hand cared too much.

I had been a fool to believe the things Kitty had said when she told me nothing was easier than to pretend to be Lisanne, to marry Gervase and live the rest of my life cocooned in wealth and privilege. Not so easily could I kill

Ellen. I did not have Kitty's ruthlessness. If I were to survive I would do it on my own terms. The risk was enormous, it was a risk that in the end would probably cost me my husband and child, but it was a risk I had to take if I were to preserve my integrity. I had to make Gervase see that the woman he thought of as Lisanne had changed, because she was not Lisanne, she was someone he had never known.

My resolution made, I jumped up and started back to the house. The lights in the drawing room had been extinguished but as I crossed the hall I could see a light shining under the library door. First of all I went into the study and picked up Lady de Bellefort's diary where it lay on the top of the desk. Her words more than mine were capable of describing Ellen Adair. They could not make him forgive the deception but they might in time help him to understand.

Only one light burned in the library, over the easy chair set in front of the fire. He sat with his eyes scanning a large leather-bound volume and I had almost reached his chair when he looked up in surprise.

'Where have you been?' he asked. 'I thought you'd gone up to bed. I seem to remember it was always a worthwhile tactic when you failed to get your own way.'

'I went for a walk. I needed to think.'

'I hadn't realized that walking in the dark was conducive to healthy thinking.'

His sarcasm was making it easier than I had thought, and trying desperately to keep the anxiety from my voice I said, 'I have something to tell you Gervase, and I'd rather you didn't say a word until I've finished.'

'Not more histrionics, I hope.'

'No, I'm going to tell you the truth and it's possible you will hate me more, much more than you ever hated your grandmother or Lisanne. I'm sorry. I should never have thought for one moment that it would work, now I know it was the most stupid, terrible thing I ever did, but I have to tell you the truth even if you kill me for it.'

He was staring at me fixedly and when he didn't speak I

went on, harnessing my words with a devastating clarity that surprised me.

'I'm not your cousin Lisanne, Gervase. Lisanne was drowned in the shipwreck. I'm Ellan Adair who you never knew existed, and it started innocently enough in the hospital where they took us after we were picked up. Lisanne and I were very much alike and I was clutching her brooch engraved with the letter L when they took me into hospital. I tried to tell them I wasn't Lisanne but they thought I was rambling and in the end I allowed them to go on thinking I was Lisanne. I hadn't any money, I had nowhere to go and no job. You have no idea how easily everything fell into place.

'I'm not proud of what I've done, I'm bitterly ashamed and I shan't blame you if you hate me for the rest of your life. This is your grandmother's diary which she kept meticulously. It will explain how Ellen Adair came here, what happened to her afterwards and why she came to be travelling back to England with Lisanne and her mother. Please read it. It won't make it any easier to forgive me but it might help you understand a little.'

Firmly I thrust the diary into his hands. His face was filled with astonishment, there had not been time for anger to take its place, and without another word I turned on my heel and left him alone. I had not told him anything about Kitty's part in my deception. I had not needed to listen to her, and in the end it was I who had to face the music.

Upstairs I started to pack a valise with my personal things, a small amount of underwear and a sweater. I took no jewellery except my wedding ring and my wristwatch, but from the table near the window I picked up a photograph of my son, the last that had been taken before he went off to school. He smiled back at me from the photograph, and I realized how achingly like Gervase he had become with his dark hair and steely blue eyes.

With tears in my eyes I laid it in my case. There would be last-minute things to pack in the morning, but for now all I could do was bathe and go to bed. It was too late to leave the house but I took the precaution of locking the doors leading to the hall and dressing room. I wanted no more scenes with Gervase that night, morning would be soon enough. But I had no hopes of sleeping.

The night seemed endless as I lay staring into the darkness. The wind had become a crescendo round the house and occasionally flashes of lightning lit up the room. I strained my ears to hear if Gervase had come into the dressing room but inside the house there was only a stillness except for the musical chiming of a clock. I listened for the closing of doors, for the creaking of some board in the corridor outside the room, but there was nothing. I could picture Gervase sitting in the library staring into the dying embers, tortured by the knowledge that he had been deceived by an unknown woman, far more treacherously than he could ever have been decieved by the cousin he believed he hated.

The first faint light of a new day found me still sleepless, but dawn came relentlessly, and now I was able to distinguish the outline of furniture in the room. The wind had died and the rain had stopped, that much I was aware of before I pulled the heavy drapes back from the window to face a morning sky streaked with gold and the promise of a lovely day.

I dressed quickly in a charcoal-grey skirt and white silk blouse but it seemed incongruous to brush my hair and apply make-up as though this was just an ordinary day, when it was probably a day I would remember for the rest of my life. It was a day when I must face my husband's anger and the desolation of all that came after. The loss of my home, my son, all the normal everyday things I had begun to accept as mine. But I forced myself to go on with my tasks. To collect my toilet things and arrange them neatly in my case. To choose the plain black kid court shoes I would wear and finally, when I was satisfied there was nothing else I needed, to snap the case shut.

It was just after seven o'clock and very soon now the house would be coming to life. The tweed coat and scarf I had worn in the park the night before lay across the back of a chair and I decided that these would be my travelling clothes. In my purse was a small sum of money, about sixteen pounds, but there w s a large sum of money in the bank.

If Ellen Adair had been more sensible about her money she would probably have returned from France to find the sum of two hundred pounds in her bank account. This much I decided to take out of the de Bellefort account, the rest was for Gervase to do with as he thought fit. Now, all that remained was for me to listen to his scorn – but with the fervent hope that from time to time he would allow me to see Lance.

I couldn't think that Gervase would wish to make my deception public, he had too much pride. Idly I wondered what he would tell our neighbours and the rest of the family.

I sat in a chair in front of the window watching the pale sun gilding the lawns while along the drive from the direction of the gate two men walked towards the house with their dogs, two of the gamekeepers starting their day's work. I started nervously at the sound of the dressing room door being opened from the corridor, then the sound of the shower in the bathroom. It was evident Gervase had not slept in the dressing room and I thought about him spending the night in his chair in the library with his grandmother's diary lying idle in his hands, sleeping fitfully, and in his moments of wakefulness seething with anger and frustration at the betrayal which tortured his soul.

I was trembling as I waited for him to show some sign that he wished to speak to me, listening anxiously to the sounds from the room next door, the opening and closing of drawers, the sharp click of the wardrobe door. I jumped nervously at the curt tap on the dressing room door and, squaring my shoulders, went forward to open it.

In those first few seconds we stared at each other without speaking, then his eyes fell on the valise and the tweed coat.

'You intend to leave then, Lisanne?' he said distantly, then more helplessly, 'My God, what do I call you?'

Willing my voice not to tremble, I said, 'I've packed what I shall need for the next few days. You will find the rest of my clothes in the wardrobes and the drawers and I am not taking any jewellery apart from my wedding ring.

'I intend to withdraw two hundred pounds from my account, I think that roughly represents the sum I might have expected to find waiting for me in England before I decided to remove it – most foolishly, as it turned out.'

He was staring down at me enigmatically, his face haughty, distant, and suddenly my voice was trembling and the treacherous tears were filling my eyes and rolling dismally down my cheeks.

'I shall need to see Lance from time to time, Gervase, I love him very dearly. I am not asking for him to live with me permanently, he is your son too and you will be able to do far more for him than I could.'

His eyes were dark blue and coldly angry. Suddenly he snapped, 'I suppose you're going to this man you met in London?'

My eyes opened wide. 'Well of course not, how can you even think it? I'm not going to anybody, I'm on my own. I'm Ellen Adair again and I shall find work, there must be something I can do. I was going to look for a job when I came back to England after the war, I shall do it now.'

'My grandmother thought you were in love with Lance. Was that true?'

'Yes, I loved him. He was the first man I ever loved. I'd never met anybody like him, educated, polished, caring and kind. I was ready for love, nobody had ever loved me before. And Lance didn't love me enough.'

'Did you love him when you married me?'

'Oh Gervase, of course not. I hadn't loved Lance for a very long time. He was married to Geraldine and I was living a strange sort of life in occupied France. For me to go on loving Lance in situations like that I would have had to be very sure that he loved me in return, and there was no such certainty.

'Gervase, I'm sorry for what I've done, sorry and bitterly ashamed. I couldn't blame you for anything you did to me.'

'I should take you by your pretty neck and squeeze the life out of you. I should haul you up before the world as an impostor, a woman who cheated me by pretending to be a de Bellefort, a woman who even went as far as marrying me in another woman's name.'

At that moment anger came to my rescue and with flashing eyes and deep resentment in my heart I raged, 'I am a de Bellefort. I'm a better one than Lisanne or Geraldine. If you read your grandmother's diary you'll know she thought so too. This family owes me something. They made a scapegoat out of me and didn't know or care how I survived. Well I'm sorry for what I did but there are other things I'm not sorry about. I tried to be a good friend to Lisanne, I really did try to make her the sort of girl her grandmother would have been proud of, and I tried to save her life.' I was sobbing now, scrambling in my bag for my handkerchief.

Calmly handing me his, he said, 'What other things are you sorry for?'

'I'm sorry I ever thought I could make you love me. I'm sorry I thought you had it in you to care more for me than this heap of old stones and your rambling acres. You de Belleforts are all the same. I was a fool to think you, of all people, would change.'

'Is it too much to ask where you think you are going?'

'I don't know. I'll think better when I'm out of this house, and I'll let you have my address as soon as I'm able. I'm quite sure you'll want to divorce me as quickly as possible.'

I pushed my arms into my tweed coat and picked up the valise while he stood impassively watching me with maddening composure. He doesn't care, I thought wildly, I'm walking out of his life and he is totally immune from any feeling of sorrow or loss.

I opened the door and started to walk firmly along the corridor and down the stairs, and to my chagrin he walked with me, companionably, as if we were embarked on a day's outing. Carstairs was crossing the hall as we got to it and if he was surprised to see us leaving the house at that time in the morning, like the well-bred servant he was he showed no sign of it.

Outside on the terrace I was surprised to see Gervase's

tourer and he went to it immediately and opened the passenger door for me, saying, 'It's too far to walk, I'll drive you.'

'There's no need,' I said firmly, 'I've walked it often enough in the past.'

'Nevertheless I don't expect you to walk this morning. Please get in the car.'

He took the valise out of my hand and put it in the car, then he walked round to the driver's door and got in the car. We drove in silence. I could read nothing from his calm austere profile and I sat beside him miserable and close to tears.

I had been married to Gervase for many years but he had never seemed more remote.

The village was coming to life, people were setting out their stalls for market day and already Alec Devlin was outside his father's shop sweeping the footpath. The homely smell of baking bread came through the open window of the car.

We left the village and headed for the station, and I found myself stupidly wondering if he would wait with me for the train or simply deposit me at the station before driving out of my life.

He ignored the station road and instead drove on towards the moor. I stared at him but his expression gave nothing away, and in some agitation I cried, 'You've missed the road. You can turn at the crossroads.'

He ignored me, driving past the crossroads and on to the long winding road that crossed the moor and climbed towards the crags that rose in isolated splendour against the misted hills. On any other morning I would have delighted in the sun striking the crags like molten gold and the heather in the distance shading blue and purple. But now my heart was hammering in my breast so loudly I felt sure he must hear it. Fearfully I began to believe that he was capable of killing me up there on those lonely fells with only the swooping curlews to see what he was about.

The long car climbed steadily and soon we were on a single track used only by weekend ramblers and climbers. My hands were clenched together to stop their trembling and I made up my mind that as soon as he stopped the car I would scramble out and start to run down the hillside. Then as soon as it was born I stifled the idea. Gervase would follow me mercilessly and I was wearing ridiculous high heels which were quite unsuitable for a headlong flight across the harsh moorland.

At last he could drive no further but contented himself by reversing the car into a narrow space where the crag towered above us and the track came to an untidy end. Without a word he got out of the car and came to open the passenger door.

'Come with me,' he commanded, 'I have something to show you.'

For several seconds I shrank back in my seat but his fingers closed round mine with steely strength, forcing me to obey him, then he was holding my arm and I was walking with him towards the spot where we could look down on the village of Langstone and the imposing pile of Langstone Priory which dominated the picture spread before us as surely as the crag behind us dominated the fell.

Had he brought me up here to show me how completely the Priory and its vast acres mattered? If so I had heard it all before, and at that moment anger came to my rescue and impatiently I struggled in his grasp, unprepared for the gentleness, the normality of his voice.

'When I was a boy I used to come up here, Ellen,' he said softly, and the sound of my name on his lips brought my struggles to an end. I waited anxious and breathless for what I now knew would be important for both of us.

'I used to tell myself that that was Lance's castle and this was mine. We were medieval knights fighting for land and the women we would marry, and my grandmother was some omnipotent medieval queen watching the tournament where one of us would die and the other would have everything.

'It was a dream, Ellen, the sad dream of a foolish resentful boy who in his heart was refusing to accept the role that fate had dictated. Now fate has relented and all the things that boy once longed for are mine. There will be no scandal to mar it, Ellen Adair, there will be no sniggers of contempt or pointing fingers, no sly innuendos that Gervase de Bellefort was deceived into marriage by some unknown girl society would condemn as nothing more or less than an adventuress. You are my wife, Ellen, and you will remain my wife. Do you understand?'

For what seemed an eternity I stared at him blankly, then suddenly an anger such as I had never known made me snatch my arm away from his grasp and with my eyes blazing I stormed, 'I won't stay married to you to keep up appearances, you'll have to kill me first. You only want me for a wife to satisfy your ego, to thwart your grandmother even now when she's dead. Every time you look at me you'll be congratulating yourself that you've stolen a march on all of them by marrying a nobody. It won't make you care for me, but God knows it will make you feel twice the man you are by watching me play a part I have no right to and feeling that between us we've defeated every de Bellefort who ever lived. I'm sorry, Gervase, I won't do it. I'm glad it's all over, that I can be myself again, that I don't have to deceive anybody ever again.'

'I thought you wanted me to love you,' he said stonily.

'You'll never love me,' I cried. 'You have too much pride, and so have I.'

I turned and walked away with my head head high.

He came after me, turning me round to face him with his hands on my shoulders. There was no anger in his face, only a whimsical sort of humour.

'Would you believe me if I said I did love you, Ellen, that I'd fought against loving you for a very long time? I didn't want to love you, I couldn't believe that I could possibly be falling in love with Lisanne. But now I can see that you were never Lisanne. Ellen, there is no way you are walking out of my life to ease your conscience. You'll stay and do you duty as a good wife and mother.'

'No, Gervase, I will not. In some strange perverse way you want me in your life as a constant reminder that you are paying back your grandmother for every slight, every mean and tortured thing you imagined she did to you.'

'I did hate her, Ellen, I openly admit it. But last night I

spent reading her diary, and bit by bit I began to understand her, and understanding her I began to love her, to wish I'd loved her when she was alive. I saw so much of myself in that indomitable old woman, the pride that was my pride, her fears that were my fears, and through her eyes I began to see the young Ellen Adair who was the best de Bellefort of us all. Ellen, if you walk out of my life now none of that you see down there will have any meaning, nothing will matter if you're not there to share it with me.'

I looked for mockery in his face, the old tantalizing remoteness I had struggled to break through, but his face was serious, his eyes beseeching me to believe him. And still the doubts persisted.

'Oh Gervase, I wish I could believe you, I wish I could be sure that you mean what you're saying.'

'Ellen, even when I made you most angry, when I hurt and tormented you, did you ever know me say a single word I didn't mean?'

'No, perhaps that's why I can't believe that so much resentment and anger can be replaced by so much caring.'

'Then come back with me. A whole new start, Ellen, a different world for both of us.'

'Gervase, you are asking me to be Lisanne all over again, to live at the Priory where everybody believes I am Lisanne. I do so desperately want to be myself.'

'You will be, Ellen. Neither of us can obliterate the past entirely. You created the lie and in some respects you will have to live with it, but between you and me there will be honesty from now on. To me you will be Ellen, I shall never call you Lisanne again.'

'You can't call me Ellen.'

'I know. I shall call you darling, it's what I've always wanted to call you anyway.'

His arms were about me, holding me close and with a tenderness I had never thought to find in him, then he was holding the car door open for me and he knew he had won.

For the first time as we drove through the village of Langstone I felt I was going home. In the months, even the years ahead of us we had much to discuss, much to explain.

He had to meet the young Ellen who had fled from her father's house in fear and anguish, and those others who had made up her story, and in my imagination they all came trooping back. My poor downtrodden mother and bombastic father. Aunt Liza with her sharp disapproving face and Aunt Mary with her brood of children and her feckless husband. More than any of the others, though, there was Peter who I had loved and agonized over. Now I would be able to seek him out and bring him back into my life. And Kitty, for no story of mine would ever be complete without her, and in my imagination I was seeing the old Kitty with her red curls and the freckles on her pert nose.

He reached out and covered my hand with his.

'So silent, darling,' he said quietly, 'I wish I knew what you were thinking at this moment.'

'You will, Gervase,' I assured him. 'There is so much I have to tell you, it will take forever.'

He smiled. 'Here we are, darling. Welcome home.'

We were passing through the huge iron gates and ahead of us the Priory basked in the morning sunlight. I stole a look at his face and somehow the old bitterness had gone and in its place were a serenity and a new maturity. He turned his head to look at me, then he smiled, and in his smile was the promise of great joy.